The Strange Treasures of Gramma Zulov

BOOK IV

The Elixir of St. Germaine

The Strange Treasures of Gramma Zulov

BOOK IV

The Elixir of St. Germaine

Alex Ross Carol

Blue
M
Blue M Publishing – Chicago

Library of Congress Cataloging-in-publication data
Names: Carol, Alex Ross
Title: *The Strange Treasures of Gramma Zulov. Book IV – The Elixir of St. Germaine.*
Description: First edition | Blue M Publishing, Chicago, IL [2023] | Series: Book four of monographic series | Contents: The Elixir of St. Germaine | Summary: Now a young man, Will discovers another relic that propels his family and friends into one more turbulent adventure to try to save the world | Audience Note: Recommended for readers thirteen and older | Language Note: Infrequent offensive language.
Identifiers: ISBN 978-1-945385-33-9
Subjects: LCSH: sh85047117 Fantasy fiction, American | BISAC: FIC061000 FICTION / Magical Realism | FICTION / Fantasy Contemporary | GSAFD: 00000cz a2200037n 45 0 155 Fantasy fiction | 455 Fantastic fiction | Genre/Form terms: gf2014026333 Fantasy fiction/Heroic fantasy fiction.
Classification: LCC PS370-380 | DDC 813/--dc23

Carol, Alex Ross
The Strange Treasures of Gramma Zulov. Book IV – The Elixir of St. Germaine.

ISBN 978-1-945385-33-9

Printed in the United States of America
www.blueMpublishing.com
Book Cover Design by Allendorf-Vigenere

Blue M Publishing
Chicago, IL 60525

Rating: PG-13* for use of moderately harsh language and some images of violence or threats of violence. No drug and alcohol use are described. There are no scenes with explicit or implicit sexual activity.

*Rating is provided by the author as a parental guide and is not based on any established rating systems. PG – Parental Guidance suggested. Suitable for readers 13 and older.

The Strange Treasures of Gramma Zulov
The Elixir of St. Germaine – Book IV

Book Summary

Will uncovers two bottles of mysterious elixirs within his Gramma's trunk of relics. The bottles come from a source in South America--one originally discovered by St. Germaine, a legendary French aristocrat. Germaine is a name wrapped in mystery as it has surfaced and resurfaced often throughout the ages—from the seventeenth through the nineteenth centuries. All sightings of the man have been associated with the Fountain of Youth and eternal life.

But when an outbreak of a virulent contagion spreads across the globe, a link is made between the plague and what is contained within the two bottles of Gramma Zulov. Could they be the source of the plague or the cure?

Will's family and friends are again placed in a maelstrom of confusion and danger as powers far greater than they are threatened. At risk of being connected to the growing global scandal, these powers will not sit idle and watch decades of planning go down in flames. They will strike back.

*****

Contents

The Strange Treasures of Gramma Zulov: The Elixir of St. Germaine

Book IV

Part I

CH 1 – Pyramid of Dreams

Washington, D.C., 2038

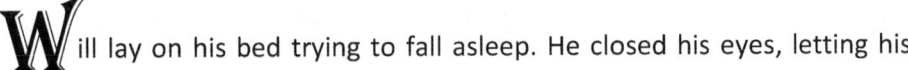

Will lay on his bed trying to fall asleep. He closed his eyes, letting his mind wander, floating from this to that and then on to something else. He was unsettled and anxious, but about what he didn't seem to know.

Finally, his thoughts landed on a vast sea of green. He hovered—his body suspended above the verdant landscape that expanded in all directions as far as he could see. It was a dense rainforest—one so packed with tall, strapping trees that it was hard to distinguish one from another. He felt the light breeze blow gently across his face as his body drifted down through the lush jungle canopy before eventually landing softly and quietly on an emerald carpet of fresh banana leaves.

Yet, as soon as he was back on *terra firma,* the scene changed, and he found himself lying in the middle of an ancient town square with scrub bushes and trees growing randomly as if they were the sole descendants of the wild inhabitants that once lived there. To Will, it appeared to be the ruins of some ancient civilization that had long ago ceased to exist. Only the lifeless husks of stone edifices remained, lining both sides of a once bustling street. The smooth, square-cut stones that defined the buildings were huge – some a yard high and two or three yards long—and were all stacked precisely one on top of the other.

Will's body glided effortlessly down one` of the broad, abandoned boulevards, moving slowly to the end where the buildings were taller and grander. Each seemed bigger than the one before it, until, by the time he reached the end of the street, he gazed in wonder upon a gargantuan pyramid. There were hundreds of steps that led to the top—a staircase repeated on each of its four sides. But instead of laboring up the steep ascent, Will floated as if cast under a spell, reaching the summit without breaking a sweat. At the peak, the view of the city vanished, and in its place was an aerial view of a rich and vibrant jungle all around him with a backdrop of towering steel-blue mountains—their snowcapped tops unwilling to give up what they'd captured during the previous winter.

As he looked out from atop the pyramid, a strange, dark-skinned man dressed as an ancient, Indian warrior suddenly appeared beside him. He was young and bedazzled in gold with necklaces and bracelets thick with the precious metal. His coffee bean skin was painted with vibrant colors, streaks of azure blue, tiger orange, neon yellow and carmen red, all radiating their own brilliance. Each band of color sparkled, even glittered, as if powered by its own energy source. Whirling around the man's head were gold stars and flickers of white light, all orbiting within a cloud of silver mist like a spiral galaxy in the heavens.

The man held a crude, wooden spear that was twice his height as he stood with Will on the pyramid's narrow, flat top. Oddly, however, the tip of the spear held no arrowhead or sharp point. Instead, there was a small jet of water bubbling from it and flowing down the staff to the stones beneath their feet before vanishing into nothingness.

Behind them, two massive black doors appeared out of nowhere and as they opened, they cried out in anguish like a small animal in pain. The two men turned to look as a tidal wave of water gushed forth from inside, nearly knocking them over. Instead, it surged past them and rushed, unbridled, down the long steep stairs like a gushing Alpine stream. When the water reached the bottom of the pyramid, it disappeared—evaporating instantly.

Will watched as woman emerged from the black doors, unaffected by the force of the water flowing around her. Like the other warrior, she wore a headdress, but hers was grander—of more gold and with different-sized rings. These ranged in size from the smallest one on her forehead to the largest one on her crown. The rings were all held within a bigger and thicker crescent ring that wrapped from one ear to the other.

She must be the high priestess, Will thought, astonished at her beauty.

The priestess noticed Will and smiled at him. She raised her hands and gave him two strange and ancient bottles. One was ebony and had the face of a warrior on one side – the same face as the warrior standing next to Will. On the other side of the jug was the same face but much older and with its eyes closed—perhaps near death. Will then looked at the ivory jug. It too had the youthful face of the warrior on one side. Yet on the other side, the old warrior's face had eyes that were vibrant and alive.

Will looked back at the young warrior who had been standing beside him and gasped. No longer was he young and vital. Now, he was old and feeble, and his spear had turned into a long crutch which he used to keep himself steady as his hands trembled from an unknown affliction.

"What are these jugs?" Will asked the priestess. "Why have you given them to me?"

The priestess smiled. "You will know when it is time."

"I don't understand."

"Trust," she said, pointing to one of the jugs, "it will help you if you have faith."

Will looked down at the jug and up again at the priestess, but she was gone. Gone too were the black doors, the old warrior, and the stairs. In fact, now Will found himself sitting back on the ground in the heart of the jungle. There were no buildings around him or any other evidence of a town square. The only thing he had were the strange jugs which he held in his hands.

"What?" Will woke up. He remembered every detail of his vivid, yet bizarre dream.

Rubbing his head, he suddenly felt lightheaded. "*Whoa*," he mumbled, sitting back on the edge of his bed. Then, he got another sensation—like someone was watching him. It was the same feeling he used to have when his brother Daniel was about ready to play a trick on him.

Will hurried down the hall to Daniel's room, hoping to see his brother's or his Gramma's spirit.

"Danny?" he said excitedly as he opened the door to the room. "Are you in here?"

His brother had died tragically a few years earlier, and to Will's disappointment, there was no sign that he had returned to him as his Gramma had so many times before. Dejected, he started to leave but then thought he heard something; it was a whisper, a voice—his brother's voice.

"Will. It's under the bed. Look under my bed."

Will lifted the striped bed cover and looked under the bed. There sat his Gramma's trunk, but, oddly, the lid was ajar. Will knew he had locked that trunk when he'd slipped it under the bed after the last harrowing trip on which his Gramma had sent him. Excitedly, he pulled the trunk from under the bed and pushed open the lid. He had been through that trunk so many times, he knew every item in it—or so he thought.

What? he thought. *It can't be.*

On top of everything inside were two things he'd never seen before: two jugs—one ebony and one ivory.

Will shut his eyes and opened them again, thinking he was just seeing things. However, it wasn't a hallucination. The jugs were there; they were real.

Will thought he heard a strong gust of wind strike the side of the house outside, and he glanced across the room at his brother's bedroom window, expecting it to suddenly blow open and make the curtains billow. It would be just like his brother to stage such a grand entrance before making an appearance. Yet Will waited … and waited … but when nothing happened, he could only sigh.

"Why are you doing this?" Will said aloud. "Stop taunting me!"

He looked down at the jugs, expecting them to do something strange or magical like levitate or fly across the room and begin pouring out their contents on the floor. Then, when they too did nothing, he called out, "All right, Gramma. You've had your fun. Now, tell me what's going on."

In the past, his Gramma had often appeared in a whirl of white, swirling mist. She would come in a mysterious cloud and talk to him, telling him bits and pieces of what he must do, places where he must go, or people whom he must meet. But this time, there was none of that. There was no such mist, no apparition, no talk and no vanishing trick. There was no Gramma and no Daniel. It was just him and the strange jugs.

What lay ahead for him and the jugs, he had no clue.

*****

CH 2 - Update

It had been two years since the Wheel of the Han and the dramatic scenes in Shanghai, China. Much had happened.

With a small group of family and friends looking on, Raya and Jack were married in a church in Middleburg, Virginia, just outside of Washington, D.C. Raya was working as a professor at The American University, and Jack was still doing intelligence work for the State Department. Will was finishing his coursework at Georgetown University—the same college from which his late brother had graduated—and while he still had one more year before his graduation, he couldn't wait to move on.

Will had been asked many times about what he was going to do after college, but going into his senior year he still didn't know or, at least, wouldn't say. It was when his mother finally cornered him in the kitchen one day as he waited for his bagel to pop from the toaster that he was forced to share.

"So, Will, you start school next week. It's your big senior year. Yet, I still don't know what you're planning to do when you graduate," Raya said, taking a sip from her white Snoopy coffee mug. "I've been pushing you for an answer for months now, and you still haven't given me one. Have you decided?"

"I'm not sure," Will answered, being intentionally vague.

"You'll need to finish all the courses for your major this year, 'cause I'm not funding you after May comes around. You'll need to graduate with something. I'm assuming you're going to law school like your brother. Are you?"

"Mom, I'm still thinking about it."

"You have to do more than think about it, Will. You only have two semesters left for God's sake. It's too late to change your major. You're still Poly Sci, right?"

"Yeah."

"All right, then I guess you're going to law school."

"Mom."

"What?"

"I *have* decided, but I didn't want to tell you. It'll just make you mad."

Raya stared at her son. Her displeasure was only growing.

"All right. If I'm going to be angry, then let me be angry right now," she answered, putting down her mug. "I'm not spending all this money on your education to learn that you're going to be a free-lance, nuevo arts dancer or something."

Will's face brightened. "Well, at least it's not that," he remarked cheerfully.

However, Raya looked at him sternly—she was not amused. Her face was pensive, bracing for what was coming next.

"All right, then." He took a deep breath and spit out the words he knew she didn't want to hear. "I want to be an agent."

"An insurance agent?"

"No, Mom! CIA."

"*Crap!*" said Raya, turning away from him. "I *knew* you were going to say that."

"It's what I want to do, Mom."

"Of all the things you could do, and you want to do *that*!"

"Yes. That's really what I want to do."

"You want to be like your dad and work at one of the agencies."

"Yes."

All Raya could do was shake her head and sigh. "Well, I guess you'll make someone else happy too," she moaned.

"Who's that?"

"Your stepfather, Jack."

"Mom, I'm not doing it for him or for Dad," Will answered. "I'm doing it for me. I've known this ever since I was thirteen. I've always known. With all these weird experiences I've had and traveling all over the world, I thought maybe I should go into something like paranormal studies. But there aren't many jobs in that. And since I'll have a minor in criminal justice, I'm going that route—CIA or maybe FBI."

"It got your father killed, Will. You know that."

Will's father, Benjamin Curtis, had covertly worked for the CIA for most of his adult life. He hadn't started at the agency, but he'd been sucked into it as if it had been his calling too.

After Raya and Ben had married, he had been approached at his software engineering company by two men in dark suits. It was a small shop of only a half dozen engineers, but they developed some of the highest-level spy software in the country. And while Ben was a skilled technical engineer, he had many other skills—instinctive, social ones. This made him a valuable resource to deploy to infiltrate foreign digital operations and obtain critical, national "trade secrets," as they were called. Someone like Ben would know what was valuable and what wasn't just by looking at it.

However, his work at the CIA had come with a heavy price. He hadn't been home much while his young boys were growing up. Raya knew the nature of his clandestine work, of course, but she too kept it secret from their sons. It was only when Ben died tragically in Europe that her older son, Daniel, dug deeper into his dad's occupation.

Both children—Daniel and Willie—had been extremely smart, and Daniel had doggedly pursued the truth after his father's death even though he had only been nine at the time. Raya had always told the two that their father worked in the fashion industry and ran a clothing factory overseas. She had claimed it was the reason why he was gone so much of the time. But when Daniel had pressed his mother on where the plant was, what they made, how they got the clothing sent to the states, etc., it had become more difficult to hide the truth. Three years later, when Daniel had finally confronted his mother with his suspicion about his father being a spy, she had laughed and brushed it aside as ludicrous.

"Danny," she had said, "why on earth would you ever believe something like that? You've been watching too many James Bond movies, I think." However, when Daniel didn't back down, she finally relented. "Danny, you're a smart boy. I can't keep telling you these stories about your father as it's clear you're not believing them anymore."

"No, Mom. You're not telling me the truth. I can tell."

"No, I haven't. But there's a reason. What he does is top secret. If anyone finds out, your dad's life will be in danger, and we can't have that. And for sure, you *can't* tell your brother, Willie. Your father's work overseas has been hard on all of us. He knows that too. Yet, it's for the good of all of us that he does what he does. He's a patriot. He's a hero, Danny."

"Yeah, Mom. I figured he had to work for the CIA or FBI. It only made sense."

Raya had smiled, proud of the boy she had raised. "Well, your brother is too young to understand things now. Perhaps later when he's older we can tell him."

Yet, like his older brother, Willie had begun to ask more questions about their father. When Willie was still only ten, he asked Daniel what their dad did at work. It had been part of a homework assignment. Willie had said he didn't understand what business really was and what their father did when he traveled so much.

"Willie," Daniel had said, "Dad's company makes clothes for people. He makes stuff like shirts, pants and things. But he makes most of those in other countries, not here in the U.S."

"Then why doesn't he make new stuff for us, Daniel? Why does Mom always have to go to the store and buy stuff we don't like? And why do I have to wear the old, junky stuff you had?"

Daniel didn't like to lie. In fact, their father had always been strict with the boys, insisting they always tell the truth—no matter what.

"Willie," Daniel had finally said, "Dad doesn't make clothes for people. That's not what he does."

Willie had looked puzzled. "What? But you just said ..."

Daniel put his arm around his younger brother and pulled him close. "Dad works for the government."

"What do you mean?"

"Willie, Dad is a spy."

"For real!" Will had said, his eyes on fire with excitement. "A real spy? Dad is a spy?"

"Yeah, but you can't tell *anyone!* In fact, you can't tell Mom either."

"She doesn't know?" Willie had asked.

Daniel had laughed. "Oh, she knows, bro'. But I wasn't supposed to tell ya'. She'd be really mad if she found out I told you. So, don't say anything, okay?"

Willie had nodded and made a motion with his hand that he was zipping his mouth shut. Like his brother, Willie didn't tell anyone—not even his mother. He was good like that. It wasn't until much later—years, in fact—when Raya learned that Willie had also known the secret of their father's occupation.

However, what they didn't know—none of them—was how and why Ben had been killed.

*****

CH 3 – Caged Animals

1962

Luka and Tulia decided to scrap their plans to fly to Paris from Quito, Ecuador, when Tulia had become ill. They had been in South America in search of more treasures when she had become sick. But instead of flying to Paris to expand their search for answers regarding the strange bottle of elixir they'd received in Ecuador, they returned to New York. And when Tulia didn't improve, they visited the doctor.

"So, what's wrong with her?" asked Luka, sitting beside his wife.

"She's got a very common affliction that strikes women who have become married," said the doctor, who was oddly smiling.

"What?"

"Your wife is pregnant," he said laughing.

"Really!" exclaimed Luka, thrilled at the news.

"Yep! I'd say so."

Luka turned to Tulia, who sat in surprised shock. "I guess this means we'll have to bench you for a while," he said. "You can't travel with me on these odysseys around the world anymore."

"That's not funny, Luka. Not one bit," she said to him.

Although Tulia had wanted a family at some point, she wasn't sure she wanted one that early in her life. As Luka had told her many times during their marriage, "There is more of the world to see, and so many more relics to discover."

When Tulia began to show, she took more naps and grew crabbier with her morning sickness extending well into the afternoon and sometimes the early evening. Luka tried to be supportive and got her whatever she needed to make her feel better. But it was a new experience for both of them, and they struggled to adjust. Neither had any family in the big city to help them, having to rely on themselves to make things work.

Luckily for Tulia, the principal at the school where she taught had been more tolerant than most. He liked her and thought she did a great job. So did her students. Reluctant to fire her, the principal kept her on—being lenient with her growing tally of sick days.

Soon the day came when Tulia went into labor. At the hospital, Luka paced anxiously around the dingy, green waiting room, hoping for news about his new son or daughter. He later remarked that he had been more nervous in the hospital than at any time during one of his KGB missions—even when a gun had been pointed at his head.

However, eventually a white-coated doctor emerged through the swinging double doors, taking off his powder-blue hospital mask. He walked to Luka in the waiting room and smiled. "It's a girl," he said. "Congratulations. You can follow me back to see your wife. She's awake, and both she and your daughter are doing fine."

They named their daughter Natalia, and within a year Tulia had birthed another child—a son they named Leonid. Things changed after they had their second child. Tulia decided not to return to the school but to stay at home and raise her family. It took her some time to acclimate to motherhood and being a homemaker, and while she had enjoyed her teaching job immensely, she found the work at home to be just as, if not more, important. For her, the problem was that it was mundane, especially after the excitement of life combing exotic markets and bazaars around the world with Luka by her side.

As it always had, the world still beckoned her. She had an itch that needed to be scratched, and she found the stifling nature of being confined at home or to the neighborhood playground growing every day. After Leonid's birth, the feeling of captivity only got stronger. While she loved her children, she felt she needed more.

"You know, Tulia, I was thinking about that black jug you found in Ecuador. It's been almost three years ago now." Luka pointed to the urn that was now resting on the fireplace mantel. "Do you remember that?"

"Of course. How could I forget any of those trips, especially that one," she said, holding baby Leonid in her arms and trying to rock him to sleep. "If I recall, we were going to go to Paris, but you never took me there."

"No, because you came down with … well, you know what."

"Don't act like you had nothing to do with it," she answered him.

"What I was trying to say," Luka continued, ignoring her comment, "is that we never did look into that connection."

"You mean the one with that Frenchman … I believe his name was Condamine."

"Yes, Charles Marie de la Condamine," said Luka, rattling off the name in his worst French. "I found my notes on him. He explored the Amazon in South America, and allegedly the Incas told him where he could find the Fountain of Youth."

"You don't believe that. Do you?"

"I don't know anymore, Tulia. We've seen some pretty bizarre things in our lives, haven't we?"

"Yes, but the Fountain of Youth?" Tulia looked at the black urn as if it contained the ashen remains of a family relative. "I don't think so."

"So, what do you want to do?" Luka asked, going to the mantel and holding it up for examination.

"Well, with two children, I can't do much of anything."

"I mean, with this bottle," said Luka. "Do you want me to look into it?"

"You can throw it out," she answered him, frustrated by Leonid's squirming. "I don't think it's worth anything, anyway."

Luka continued looking at it, noting the haunting figures and cryptic etchings on the sides.

"I don't know, Tulia. I think we should keep it. Something tells me it's worth something—maybe a great deal."

"Fine," she answered, "but don't accuse me of being a hoarder. I hate keeping things around we aren't going to use."

"Then what about the Sri Lankan trunk we have that's packed *full* of stuff we don't use?"

"That's different! Those *are* relics—I know *they're* worth something."

"So those are relics, but this urn—which could date back over a few thousand years—isn't. Really?"

"I don't know, Luka. A lot has changed. We're parents now. We have kids to think about. We can't just run off anymore, searching for the next Dead Sea Scroll."

"I suppose our days of scouring third-world markets searching for ancient artifacts are over, then," said Luka with a touch of melancholy in his voice.

"Yes, I guess so."

"So, it sounds like you're not interested—not in one last trip?

"Just because I see nothing of value in that jug doesn't mean I don't think there are other things out there for us to do or discover," she finally answered, taking his bait.

Luka shot back a smile. "Does that mean …?"

"Perhaps," she answered, still wrestling with her feelings. "I'm like a caged animal right now, Luka. I think we're both feeling the same way. We have to find some way to balance raising our family with our need to explore the world."

"You're right. So, how do we do that?"

"I don't know, but I'm sure *you'll* think of something," she answered with a glare and a smile.

*****

CH 4 – Re-appearance

It seemed like an ordinary day as Will sat through all his classes taking notes on his computer tablet and highlighting things he thought might appear on the next exam. After his last lecture at one o'clock, he spent the rest of the day at the Lauinger Library preparing for a chemistry exam he had to take later in the week. Coming home late in the afternoon, he found the place empty and quiet as it usually was at that time of the day. His mother was at the university, and his stepfather was downtown at some undisclosed location, likely at some important meeting or getting a briefing on something at the State Department.

Will took a diet soda from the frig and popped it open. He then tossed his backpack over his shoulder and trekked upstairs to study some more in his bedroom. It was only about half past five when he heard a rumbling in the room next to his—Daniel's room. Trying to ignore it, he pressed on with his reading until the distraction became too much.

"All right, all right!" he muttered as he rolled grudgingly off his bed. He hurried down the hall and threw open the door.

He knew he was being summoned, and his mind raced with a flurry of crazy ideas of what his Gramma might have planned for him. It had been a week since he had been in the room and opened the trunk. Nothing had happened after that, and he had hoped nothing more would come of it. Even looking at the trunk under Daniel's bed gave him anxiety, and this time, coming into the room, he only hoped the disturbance had all been inside his head.

But it hadn't.

"Will?"

"Sh*t," he muttered, hearing the voice. It sounded a bit garbled—like the room was filled with water.

"You know what you need to do," said the voice.

Will crouched under the bed and pulled the trunk out. However, unlike anything that had happened before, the trunk began rising off the floor on its own.

It's possessed! thought Will, backing away.

"Take it, Will. Grab onto it."

He tried to grab the worn leather handle of the trunk but found the troublesome locker fighting back. The harder he pulled on it, the more it resisted.

"Well, do you want me to open you or not?" Will called out, still struggling with it.

"Will ..."

This time the voice was clear and distinct.

"Gramma?"

"Yes, Will, it's me."

Will released the trunk and backed up.

"It's been a while, Gramma. Why have you waited so long to contact me?"

"I've had other things here that keep me busy, child," she answered. "You don't think you're the only project I'm working on, do you?"

"You do things in heaven?" Will asked.

"Of course. We don't just sit around the garden and play the harp, you know."

Will laughed, but at the same time he didn't know what they did on the other side.

"Seriously, Will. We have much work to do."

"*Oh*, no. Not again, Gramma. Mom said that we weren't going to do anything for you anymore. She thinks you're a demon, and you're out to destroy our family. She says you're up to no good, and that I should ignore you if you come calling again."

"Up to no good, *eh*?" quipped his great grandmother. "Well, you've only managed to save the world a few times since I came to you in my attic all those years ago. Doesn't she realize that?"

"Yes, but it cost her and me dearly. You know that."

"Daniel," she answered.

"Yes."

Daniel was killed when a car driven by two thieves who were trying to steal one of Gramma's relics—the Wheel of the Han—struck him in a parking garage. Neither Will nor Raya had ever really recovered from the tragedy, and Raya had always blamed her grandmother for causing it.

"Ah, yes, your brother. Well, he's here with me, Will. Would you like to talk to him?"

"Can I?"

"Sure."

It was a moment before a familiar misty fog sprang up in the center of the room. Unlike other times, this fog did not swirl but rather drifted about as an amorphous blob—expanding and contracting at will. Then, suddenly, a hazy image of Will's older brother appeared, and his voice cut through the gray veil hanging in the room.

"Will, this is your brother. I've been watching over you, you know. I haven't abandoned you or our mom. Believe me, I would never do that."

"Danny!" Will shouted. "Is it really you?"

Wills eyes began to water. He sensed a longing, a sadness, that he hadn't felt since his brother died.

"Yes, Will. But I can only be with you for a moment."

"Danny! Are you alright?"

"Yes, of course. Everything here is fine. There is a lot to do, you know, watching out for you and Mom is a full-time job! And from what Gramma tells me, you're going to be very busy again. You have some very important work to do—probably the most important yet!"

"Oh, Danny, I miss you."

"Will, don't worry. We'll all be together again eventually. However, for you and Mom, there is more time until then. You must know that everything will be fine. Now, listen to your great grandmother. She has some very important things for you to work on. Take care, Will. We will talk again soon. I love you."

"Wait, Danny!"

But the image faded, and the voice stopped, both replaced by those of his great grandmother. "Will, I need you to open the trunk."

Will did as he was told. This time when he went to pull the pesky trunk down to the floor, it obeyed. There, he grabbed the lid and pried it open. But things weren't the same. Those things were now missing.

"Where are those two weird bottles that were in here before?" Will asked.

"The white and black ones."

"Yeah. Where are they? They aren't in here," said Will. "I put them on top last week. Where did they go?"

"Keep looking, Will," instructed Gramma.

Will continued to move things around within the trunk until he found a thick, tightly packed bundle of brown paper. He unwrapped it. Inside was a jug but only a white one.

"Gramma? Where is the black one?"

"Keep looking," she said.

Beneath the bundle was another, and Will carefully unwrapped that one too. This time, he found the black urn.

"Okay, there're here. It's the same urn. One's black, and one's white," said Will.

"Not quite," said Gramma. "Look more carefully. You have to master greater attention to detail if you're going to be a CIA agent, you know."

The two jugs had slender tops descending into potbelly bottoms. On each were two small, tight rings on opposing sides, barely large enough to put a finger through. Also on opposite sides were geometric shapes arranged around two crude, but mysterious, images of a tribal warrior. Through the warrior's nose were many white rings—each possibly signifying a battle in which he had fought. Above his head were an array of more rings of different sizes spread out from his forehead to his crown. Most striking, however, was the fact that they were two figures of the same warrior—one was young, and one was old. They were images Will sensed he had seen before.

"I don't see any difference in them," said Will, glancing from one urn to the other. "They both have the same warrior and same markings."

"How do the figures appear on the white bottle?" his Gramma asked.

"One side has a young warrior while the other side has an old, decrepit one. They're the same on the black urn."

"Are they? Look closely at the faces."

Will then remembered his dream. He looked again at the white urn and found the old warrior had both eyes open while those on the black bottle had both closed. Everything else appeared the same.

"It's the eyes, then?" Will asked.

"You tell me," said his Gramma.

Will looked again at the symbols. He had to look twice.

"Wait a minute," he said. "They've changed."

"What do you see now?"

"The symbols on the white urn are …"

"Yes," said his Gramma, cutting him off. "Good, Will. You are catching on." His great grandmother's image began fading in and out. "It is becoming more difficult for me to come to you in your world, Will. There are forces—evil forces—that are fighting against me. Our Creator is giving me strength, but it is hard. So, I don't know how many more times, I'll be able to show you the way of the treasures in my trunk. However, this time, I will tell you what you need to know. You need to use the Number Wheel of Xerces very carefully for it is …"

"Gramma, I don't have a number wheel …" Will said looking through the trunk. "You already had me dig out the Wheel of the Han the last time. Remember?"

"What about the Wand of Merlin?"

"I don't see any wands in here," said Will, rummaging through the trunk. "Gramma, you told me to find the urns."

"Oh, you're right. It wasn't the wand; it was the elixir of St. Germ... Do you have that?"

"An elixir of what?" Will asked, now only getting staccato bursts of what she was saying.

"My boy, I said the elixir of … Ecuador … Do you …"

"What? Come again? You're breaking up, Gramma. What was that?"

"I … said …" The voice began coming through in unintelligible bits and pieces. "You should destroy the …"

"The what?"

"… urns are two sides of … curse … cure, Will."

Will's head was spinning. "Gramma, say again?"

Will watched as the misty fog evaporated. The energy was gone. The room was empty. He was, once again, alone.

Crap! he thought. *How the hell am I supposed to figure this out when I can't understand what she's saying!*

27

"Gramma!" he shouted. But there was no answer.

*****

CH 5 - Go Ask Jack

Will knew better than to tell his mother about his great-grandmother's spectral visit. He had done it many times before, and each time things hadn't worked out very well. It wasn't that she didn't believe in the supernatural; rather, she was afraid that her son was getting too deeply involved in it. She feared the crazy schemes coming from beyond were, indeed, demonic or, at the very least, intentionally harmful to Will and their family. To her, there was already ample proof of that. A previous encounter had resulted in the death of her elder son, Daniel, and Raya did not want the same to happen to her only remaining one.

So, even though he loved his mother dearly, Will turned to his new stepfather, Jack, for advice. Jack had helped him in China during the last mission with which he had been charged by Gramma. Thankfully, Jack was very open to new ideas and possibilities, and it was always easy to talk to him.

At the same time, Will knew Jack's character was unassailable. He was certain that his stepfather would steer him toward the right path and away from anything he felt could be nefarious or deleterious to the family. And although Jack wouldn't do anything behind Raya's back, he was sympathetic to Will's fierce, youthful desire for independence and adventure.

"So, what should I do?" Will asked his stepfather.

Raya was still on campus, and Will and Jack had just finished some Chinese carry-out, complete with soy sauce and hot wasabi.

Tying up the white garbage bag to ready it for the outside trashcan, Jack replied, "Why don't you show me the things your great grandmother led you to—what was in the trunk that was so important this time."

Will retrieved the jugs and placed them on the kitchen table in front of them.

"This is what I have," he said, pointing to the nearly identical vases. "This is what she showed me."

Jack picked up the jugs and looked at each. Skeptical, he turned them over and looked carefully at the images and symbols. "Have you opened these?" he asked.

"No. I didn't think it was a good idea. I don't know what might be inside. Knowing Gramma, it could be anything from a magic potion to chocolate syrup."

"Or maybe something completely different," said Jack. "You just never know."

Jack took the black urn and started to ease out the old, battered cork. It was stubborn, and he was afraid he might break it off in the neck, leaving the remains trapped inside and harder to get out.

"Are you sure this is a good idea?" Will asked.

"Nope," said Jack, "but if the urns are empty then there isn't much to worry about, is there?"

With one last tug, the cork popped out, and Will closed his eyes, afraid of what might happen next. When he heard no screaming or gnashing of teeth from his stepfather, he re-opened them only to find Jack sniffing the top of the jug.

"Do you want to get yourself killed!" said Will urgently.

"It has a strange odor to it," said Jack. "It could be something like absinthe. That was the toxic liquor that was drunk during the nineteenth and early twentieth centuries by celebrities and the rich. Edgar Allan Poe, Hemmingway, James Joyce, Van Gogh and others drank it." Jack put the jug down and pushed the cork back into place. "*Nah*, I don't think it's that either. This has a peculiar smell—almost citrusy."

"Let me smell," said Will.

Jack uncorked the bottle once more and let Will take a sniff too, but his stepson drew back. "*Ew!* It smells like … I don't know, but it's awful."

"What else did your Gramma say?" Jack asked, resealing the cork.

"She began to tell me what I was supposed to do with them, but her image faded before she could finish. She said something about Ecuador and an elixir of something or someone."

"You didn't catch a name?"

"It was some saint. St. Germ, I think."

"I don't think there was a St. Germ. Did she mean someone from Germany, maybe?"

"Maybe," Will said, shrugging. "It's hard to tell with her." But as his stepfather was looking more carefully at the white urn, Will added, "Gramma told me something else too."

"What was that?"

"To destroy it."

"Destroy what? The urns?" Jack asked.

"I think so. She said something about a curse or a cure too. It seemed like it's all connected somehow."

That comment caught Jack's attention. "That's what she said: 'curse'?"

"I think so."

"Has she ever used that word before?"

"No. This is the first time."

Jack looked back at the vases, now as if they were just that … cursed.

"Well, your great grandmother has been right about a lot of things since her passing. I think you should heed her admonition."

"So, I *should* destroy them, like she said?"

"I would, Will. Yes."

"Then, how do we do it? Should I just throw them away? Dump them out? What?"

"If you just throw them out, they won't be destroyed. So, I think our best option is to burn them."

"Burn pottery?"

"Well, at least whatever is inside them will burn. You'll be rid of that," said Jack.

Will found a spare metal trash can in the garage and the used that to contain the fire. Then, they took a red gas can and poured gasoline over both urns before dropping in a lighted match. There was a brief explosion as the fire caught hold, and the flames lapped up the sides of the silvery metallic coating inside, blackening them as dark smoke roiled off the top.

Will stood next to Jack while the fire blazed before quickly burning down and going out. Even without the fire, the smoke continued to billow from the trashcan, making Will worry about his neighbors calling the fire department.

Even though the smoke continued, Jack grew tired of waiting and took the garbage lid to seal the can. Then, they went back into the house.

"I think that should do it," said Jack, closing the back door. "At least you can cross that off your list for your Gramma."

"What do we do now?"

"I guess you need to wait for something to happen. Your Gramma didn't say for you to do anything else, did she?"

"No, not that I ..."

"Okay then. There's nothing more for you to do, Will. Don't let this trouble you anymore. It's behind you. Focus your energies on school and that girlfriend of yours."

"She's not my girlfriend," said Will. "She's just a friend."

"Sure," said Jack with a grin, "whatever you say."

"But what if something *does* happen?" Will asked nervously.

"We'll cross that bridge when we come to it."

Will went back to Daniel's room and stuffed the trunk farther beneath the bed, pushing it against the wall. He thought he would feel relief, but instead he only felt greater anxiety.

That night gave him a fitful sleep, and the next morning he came downstairs to grab a quick coffee before jumping on a city bus to get to school. Max, their aging, wrinkly pug which Raya had found at the dog shelter, was lying on his side, sleeping beside his watering bowl. He had been a lifesaver for both Raya and Will—filling a hole left behind after Daniel had died.

"Will?" asked Raya.

"Yeah, Mom?"

"What's this?"

His mom sat down next to him and put two things on the table. "Do you know what these are?"

Will was stunned. "Where did you get those?"

In her hand were the urns. They were pristine, showing no signs of having been burned or scorched in any way.

"They were sitting on the kitchen table this morning when I came down to get my breakfast. Are these yours?"

"*Uh*, yes, Mom. I'm sorry. I must have left them there after I came home from school yesterday."

"Why would you have bottles like this?" she asked. "These look more like what your Gramma would have had. Are they?"

"*Uh*, they're just something I found at a garage sale in the neighborhood. I thought they looked pretty cool."

"Will?"

Without waiting for his mom's reaction, Will grabbed the vases and took them back to his room, opening the trunk and burying them at the bottom before slamming it closed and securing a lock. *There,* he thought, *that should keep you away from us.*

Coming downstairs, Will hustled out the door to catch the bus, calling back to his mom, "I have to get going. I don't want to miss the bus. I'll see you tonight. Bye!"

As he ran to the bus stop, he could only think about the urns and how they had gotten into the kitchen. More than that, he wondered how they could have been there without black marks or any indication of having been burned in a fire.

Later in the day, Will got a call from Jack.

"Hey, Will. What's going on with your gramma's stuff? Your mom told me she found something in the kitchen this morning. Were those the urns—the same ones we burned in the trashcan? Call me."

Will returned his call. "Jack, I got your message. I don't know. Yeah, it's the same urns. It doesn't make sense. We both watched those bottles bake in that garbage can. They were black, right? I thought they'd be melted as hot as we had that going."

"Did you check the can?"

"No, I'll do that when I get home."

"Let me know," said Jack.

Will got home and headed straight for the trashcan in the back where they had burned the bottles. Jack had told him to take the can to the landfill after they had scorched it, but now he was hesitant. Opening the lid, Will peered inside.

"Nothing?" Indeed, it was blackened, but there was nothing inside. There was no sign of the urns.

Will immediately called his stepfather.

"Jack, they weren't in there—not in the trash can where we left them. I didn't expect to see them since they were inside this morning, but I'm shocked. I can't explain it."

"That's not possible," Jack answered. "We watched them burn! And you didn't go out and get them from the trash can afterwards?"

"No, I swear," said Will.

"Where are they now?"

"I put them back in the trunk—buried in the bottom. I didn't know what else to do."

There was quiet on the line. "You're sure you didn't …"

"Jack, I swear. You were there. You saw it too."

"Yes, Will, but how do you explain it?"

"I can't. But they're locked away now. They can't get out by themselves. At least, I don't think they can."

Three days later, Raya found the urns out again on the kitchen table.

"Will, I thought you were going to keep these in your room? Can you please put your stuff away?"

"Yes, Mom," Will answered, again taking the bottles with him. His hands were shaking. He could feel there was something not right about them—something sinister and dark. He stared at them for a moment. Then, it suddenly came to him. He knew what he needed to do next.

*****

CH 6 – Medical Emergency

Raya had gotten their dog Max when he was already eleven years old. It had been shortly after Daniel's death when she and Will had gone down to the Humane Society to see if there were any lovable, four-legged companions looking for a permanent place to stay. As soon as Raya walked into the noisy lobby that was filled with the cacophonic barking of its residents, her eyes fell on a poor, lonely gray and black dog who lay quietly on the floor of his cage. He seemed sad, even forlorn, as if resigned to never finding a loving home again. Thirty minutes later, his tail was wagging furiously as he and his new owners left the shelter, all with a vibrant spring in their step and a new lease on life.

Although pugs were never known for their energy and spunk, Max was, by now, beginning to show his age—now rarely moving far from his blue, furry bed that lay beside the matching sofa in the corner of the TV room.

"I'm afraid he's just getting older," Dr. Turnbull, the veterinarian, had said—words Raya had not wanted to hear. Max had quicky become part of their family and to Raya a surrogate child of sorts. He was a new son for which she could care and, sometimes, even spoil.

"How long do most pugs live?" Raya had asked the vet.

"Pugs will live between twelve and fifteen years. Max is, what, eleven ... almost twelve?"

"Yes."

Dr. Turnbull had shaken her head. "I think you should savor the time with him and take care of him until ... you know ... the end. Enjoy him while you have him."

This had hurt Raya, opening fresh wounds as her thoughts were once again forced to the inevitability of losing another member of the family.

This day was another normal one for Will, and he came home to get a snack and take Max out for a short walk before he began studying. The walks usually lasted between twenty and thirty minutes—sometimes more, depending on the weather—and ended with a milk bone treat which Max always looked forward to. Yet, recently, it had been difficult to get Max to finish even two neighborhood blocks before stopping to rest. As the arthritis in his joints was making it more painful to move, Max often preferred to sleep most of the time instead of jumping at the chance to go outside with his best friend, Will.

Then, one day after school Will came home but couldn't find his dog.

"Max? Oh, Max? Where are you? It's time for our walk," he said, scouring the house for his pet.

Eventually, he heard a muffled bark coming from inside his room. Pulling up the bed skirt, Will found his best friend with his collar caught on something under the bed. But there was something more.

"Max? What have you done?"

To Will's astonishment, Max had somehow gotten into Gramma's trunk which he knew he had locked more than once. When he pulled the trunk from beneath his bed, he saw that both jugs were sitting upright inside, but this time, their corks were open.

"Max! Bad dog!" said Will harshly, unhooking Max from a spring and pulling him away. Yet, as he disentangled his canine, he noticed a black, syrupy elixir around Max's snout and mouth. "Did you get into those vases? You shouldn't have done that, Max. That was bad!"

Freeing his pet, Will found the corks and slid them back into the thin necks of the jugs, repositioning them once again inside the trunk. Frustrated with the stubbornness of Gramma's trunk, he kicked it before ramming it back under the bed. But when he turned around, he saw Max scampering around the room like his tail was on fire. As if he were a two-month-old puppy again, Max seemed to have boundless energy.

"What's gotten into you?" Will asked sternly, but surprised at what he was seeing.

With his tail whipping madly back and forth, Max began jumping up on Will wanting to play, just like the good-ole' days. At first, it was comical, but when Max didn't settle himself, Will became worried. Again, he didn't want to call his Mom for fear she would be angered by his "irresponsibility" of not properly locking Gramma's trunk, nor did he want to worry her over Max's health, coming after eating some of the black elixir. So, Will did as he had before and dialed his stepfather. But then, just as quickly, he cancelled the call. *Jack will be angry too,* he thought. *He won't be happy with me either, even though I did lock the trunk.* It took him a moment, but he came up with another option. He looked at his Friend's List in his Contacts and pressed one of the speed-dial numbers.

"Shannon, you have to come over right away. It's a long story, but you have to help me with Max."

Shannon Evans was his high school sweetheart--someone with whom he'd shared many ups and downs during the years. Indeed, her family had been entwined with Will's ever since discovering the Map of Ptah in Gramma's notorious trunk of treasures. They had all suffered as Shannon nearly lost both of her parents in Egypt after they came searching for her. Will's mother and brother fell down a long, dark shaft near the pyramids, winding up in an alien world from which they narrowly escaped.

Shannon pulled up to the low, round curb at Will's house, slamming on the breaks before laying on the horn to let him know she had arrived. Will opened the white front door and came out with his dog on a leash, both of them sprinting across the lawn as Max wagged both his tongue and his tail furiously. Will put Max in the backseat before climbing into the front and catching his breath.

"Where's your vet?" Shannon asked, putting the car in Drive.

"Just take Wisconsin here," said Will, pointing. "I'll get you there."

On the way, Shannon began asking questions to find out what had happened. Will filled her in, but only on what had happened that day—intentionally leaving out the backstory of the strange urns.

"But how could Max get the corks out of the jugs?" she asked. "That's what you said, right?"

"Yeah, or how he picked the trunk lock in the first place," said Will. "I *know* I locked that trunk, Shannon. I know it."

"Why didn't you bring the jugs with us? Shouldn't you show the vet what Max might have eaten?"

Will extracted a slim, glass test tube from his pocket and held it up. "I took this sample," he answered her, "but I didn't want to raise any suspicions by bringing the ancient-looking urns. She might ask me a million questions about them which I don't want to have to answer."

"If you're not going to answer them for her, then answer them for me," said Shannon.

"What's that supposed to mean?"

"What are these urns you're talking about? You said they were in your Gramma's trunk? That doesn't sound good to me."

Will sighed. He had hoped to avoid this entire line of questioning, but knowing Shannon, he realized it was inevitable.

"It's a long story," he said.

"I have time," she answered.

Will proceeded to tell Shannon about the visit from his Gramma and the cryptic message from her that he hadn't been able to decipher.

"Do you even know what's in the jugs?" she asked. "Do both jugs have the same thing in them? Are the liquids both black?"

"Yeah, they're both black-ish. I really didn't notice they were that different."

"What if you have stuff from the wrong jug?" she asked, continuing to press. "What if Max ate from the other jug? If the vet treats him for the stuff in the wrong one, it could make things worse, not better!"

Will knew she was right, but he didn't want to go back to the house to figure it out as his mom would be coming home soon. He had left her a note, telling her he was out on a walk with Max in case she arrived while they were gone.

"I'm sure it's all the same stuff," said Will, trying to reassure himself. "They looked pretty much the same when Jack and I took off the corks and smelled them."

"Will! I don't understand you!"

"What?"

"You make me crazy sometimes. You know that! Don't you think?"

"What do you want me to do now, Shannon? We can't go back to the house right now."

"Ugh!" she grunted but continued to drive.

Shannon sped ahead, even running a few traffic lights to get to Dr. Turnbull's office more quickly. And as for Max, he didn't seem to mind the frantic trip at all, making himself comfortable in the backseat with his mouth open and jovially panting as the car maneuvered along the busy streets. Once they left the main road, Max sat up and pressed his cold nose against the window, watching as other cars streamed by heading in the opposite direction.

When they finally arrived at the animal hospital parking lot, there were no other cars there except for Dr. Turnbull's and that of Marjorie, her tech assistant. Shannon stopped in front of the entrance letting Will and Max hop out while she parked. Once inside, Will approached the counter.

"Hello," said Will, with some urgency, "I think my dog's been poisoned, and I need to get him looked at right away."

The young woman behind the counter wore a white tech uniform with a nametag that read: *Marjorie*. With her blonde hair pulled back into a tight bun, Marjorie had a warm, friendly face which gave a glow of compassion and endearing empathy. Her broad white smile and soft green eyes made Will feel instantly at ease.

"Oh, I'm sorry to hear that," she said, her pitch dropping to show concern. "Do you know what he ate?"

"Uh, I think he had some of this," Will answered awkwardly, holding up the test tube. The liquid was thick and viscous like he'd merely poured motor oil in the tube.

Marjorie took the vial and tried to swirl what was inside, but the black substance was so syrupy that it resisted any attempts to make it move.

"It looks like used crankcase oil. Is it motor oil?" Marjorie asked.

"No, I don't think so," answered Will. "Max wouldn't eat motor oil anyway. No, I think it came from an old bottle he found in the basement," Will added, stretching the truth.

"Was it a black liqueur, then?" asked the tech, still perplexed by the tube's contents. Will only shrugged. "Well, we'll figure it out. We have ways to analyze things like this. It happens all the time. Most of the time it isn't anything to worry about, but I'll let Dr. Turnbull decide. Let me take him back and have the doctor look at him."

Will took a seat in the lobby as Shannon entered, stuffing her keys into her fashionable, oversized shoulder purse. She was covered with wet spots that dotted her pink and yellow top like a Seurat painting.

"It must be raining," said Will, as she took a seat next to him.

"Yeah, it just started," she answered, brushing herself off. "What did the doctor say?"

"They just took him back. They'll have to analyze that black elixir to see what it is."

"They'll do that here?"

"Yeah, I guess they can. That's what she said."

"How long before they know something?" Shannon asked.

"The lady at the counter didn't say. She said she'd let the doctor take a look at him first and see."

An hour went by before Dr. Turnbull finally came out to talk to them. She was an experienced veterinarian. In her early fifties, she was used to treating all kinds of animals for all kinds of things. While not a large-animal vet who would treat farm animals like cows, pigs, horses, and such, she had seen some unique pets during her career—pets like iguanas, tortoises, boa constrictors, pet pigs, and even monkeys.

"Do you know what was in the tube you brought in?" the doctor asked, looking over the tops of her black, half-framed reading glasses.

Dr. Turnbull was kind and soft-spoken—more of a motherly figure than an authoritative, doctorly one. A little over five feet tall, she was heavy-set with short, graying hair cut just below the ears. Her eyebrows were meticulously manicured, and her makeup was light and unpretentious. Framed by her glasses were a pair of rich, caramel brown eyes, which now looked intently upon the young man sitting in front of her.

"No, I don't," said Will, now worried it may have been something illegal.

"I ran some preliminary tests and, honestly, it has me stumped. I can't figure it out. It's a mixture of amino acids and proteins, but it's a configuration I haven't seen before."

"What about Max?" asked Shannon. "Will he be okay?"

"Your dog seems fine. I pumped his stomach just in case what he had was harmful or he ate something else too. You can take him home, but I'd advise that you watch him. If he starts to have a problem, bring him back, and we'll run more tests on him. In the meantime, I'll send off some of this sample to the Global Substance Database, the GSD, to see if I get a hit on what it is. It should match some chemical signature on file there—everything is in that database."

Marjorie brought Max out from the back of the clinic; his tail was still wagging joyously. Once they got him packed up in the car, they drove back to Will's place.

"Thanks for going with me," Will said to Shannon. "I wasn't sure what to do."

Shannon looked at Will and put her hand on his. "Of course. You know that you … and Max … mean a lot to me," she answered, smiling. "I'm here for you anytime."

Then, Will's phone rang. "Yes?"

"Will, this is Jack. Did you just use the credit card I gave you? It was supposed to be for emergencies?"

"Yes, Jack, I ..."

"Is everything okay? I got a call from the credit card company telling me the card was used at a veterinary clinic. Is there something wrong with Max?"

"What did you tell them?" asked Will.

"I told them I'd have to find out and call them back. Do you have the card with you?"

"Yes, Jack. Everything is fine ... at least I hope it will be. Max got into something he shouldn't have, that's all. I took him to the vet's just to be sure."

"Is Raya with you?"

"No, Mom's not here. She ... she doesn't know, yet."

"Well, you'd better call her and fill her in. She'll be worried."

"Jack ..."

"What?"

"Let's not say anything to her about this, okay? Max got into one of those jugs in the trunk. I was afraid it might have poisoned him."

"How could he get into that? I thought you locked it?"

"I did ... I know I did. Listen, Jack, none of this makes any sense. But I don't want to alarm Mom. Do you understand?"

"What did the vet say?"

"She said to watch him. If there's a problem, we're to bring him back to get re-examined. She didn't know what to make of the black liquid."

"You have to tell your mom, Will."

Those were the words Will was expecting, but he really didn't want to hear. He knew what Jack was saying was the right thing to do. He also knew that he couldn't continue to ask his stepfather to cover for him.

Will groaned. "All right," he answered reluctantly.

Will called his mom and explained things to her—at least some things. However, he conveniently forgot to mention that Shannon had helped him get Max to the vet, that Max had eaten some black elixir, and that it had come from a strange jug found inside Gramma's trunk.

"Well, we'll just have to watch him like the vet told you to do," she said, still at work at the university. "He wasn't doing well before this happened. I'm afraid of what this might do to him."

However, during the days following the incident, Max continued to improve. In fact, he was better than he had been in years. Yet, even this concerned Raya, and she called Dr. Trumbull to get the scoop directly from the vet herself.

"I don't understand," Raya said. "Max seems to be better than ever. Did whatever he ate help him or could something else happen to him to make things worse?"

"I don't understand it either," Dr. Turnbull answered. "The results from the blood and enzyme tests came back from the lab. He doesn't have arthritis anymore, and his vitals are those of a dog half his age. Whatever it was or whatever else you've done for him has helped. I still wouldn't let him nip on any more of those liquor bottles you have in the basement. Liquor isn't good for dogs."

"Liquor?"

"Yes, Will mentioned that Max had gotten into a bottle in the basement— some old bottle with a thick, syrupy liquid in it—like what he brought into the clinic. We assumed it was some liqueur, but the tests haven't been able to verify that."

Raya didn't dispute what Will had told the vet. She hadn't been aware of any liquor in the basement—at least none that Will had told her about. But rather than raise the issue, Raya let it go. There was enough going on in the Curtis family with Will's studies and upcoming graduation and some new mission for Jack she had only recently learned about. Those were enough to keep her mind from being idle.

*****

CH 7 – Smithsonian Discovery

Will couldn't help but think about the black liquid. He went back to the trunk and dug out the two jugs to see what was inside each. Indeed—and not surprisingly—Shannon had been right. A blacker liquid came from the black jug, while a lighter black, almost grayish, elixir swirled reluctantly within the white one. To Will, he couldn't smell any difference between the two; to him, they both smelled putrid.

However, having learned from his experience with Gramma's other treasures, Will understood that each should be treated with utmost care and respect. It would be improvident to do otherwise. Even as he obsessed now about *double*-locking the trunk—or even *triple*-locking it—deep down he knew it wouldn't make any difference. Gramma's things always had a manner and means of getting their way. Little, if anything, seemed able to stop them.

As Max continued to enjoy his rejuvenation—one free from arthritis and the other aches and pains of old age—Will took the time to do some exploring on his own. Still curious about the liquids and not having anything definitive from the vet's labs, he went online and began researching. But his investigation didn't stop with just the liquids. He also dove deeply into the origin of the urns and the nature and history of South American pottery— particularly those from Ecuador. He spent hours combing websites on the ancient Incan civilization and their rituals and customs. There were hundreds of pictures of pottery pieces that had been excavated at various archeological digs in Peru, Ecuador, Columbia and northern Chile. Yet, none matched the two vessels Gramma had collected while Luka and she had been down there.

Then, one day after his last class, Will took the 33 Bus to the Archives metro station where he got off carrying his backpack and reference materials. The Smithsonian Museum complex was not far away—right on the National Mall—and he headed for the Museum of Native American Indians. However, when he arrived, he found very little on display—mostly a theater, a few temporary exhibitions, and a gift shop. As he was about to leave, he found the central office and stopped in.

"Hello?" he asked, looking around. "Is there anyone here? Hello?"

"Yes, may I help you?" came a voice from the back.

Hidden behind a computer monitor was a young man not much older than Will who was working on something and taking notes as he clicked through different screens. He wasn't Native American but rather a black man who wore stylish, red-framed glasses and an orange-striped dress shirt.

"Yes, hello," said Will. "I'm looking for the Smithsonian Museum that has ancient Native American pottery—you know, someplace that might have an exhibit of some ancient Incan pottery? I didn't see anything like that here."

"Incan pottery? No, we focus on *American* Native Indians," said the man, "not Incan pieces."

"Do you know anyone at the Smithsonian who could help me with South American pottery?"

"No, 'fraid not, sorry," and with that the man turned back to his monitor.

Just as Will was about to leave, an attractive middle-aged woman came out from the back offices. She wasn't Native American either. "Did I hear someone ask about Incan pottery?" The woman was African American and likely in her early-to-mid fifties. Her demeanor seemed both calm and matronly.

"That guy there," said the other employee, gesturing toward Will.

"Yeah, I'm looking for someone who …" Will began.

"I majored in Incan pottery," said the woman, "but that was a long time ago. I never thought I'd get to use that again."

"You majored in it?" Will asked, excitedly.

"Sure did. I minored in Native American culture, but I always had a fondness for the ceramics and pottery of South America. What can I help you with?"

Will spent the next three hours with her.

Her name was Alicia Collins, the assistant director at the Native American Smithsonian Museum. He was struck by her passion for what she did and her delight at being able to share it with him.

"You see, Will," Alicia began, "the most common of Incan vessels like what you're talking about was a vase with two handles on either side and a pointed bottom. Usually, they were between two and two-and-a-half feet in height and able to hold six or seven gallons of chicha, which was a beer made from corn. The vase, or jug, as you call it, had two band-shaped handles attached vertically to the lower body, and above that rose a very long, thin neck. Each jar had two pierced, nubs that were attached to its rim."

"What were those for?" asked Will.

"The Incans believed in demons, especially those who might cause mischief."

"What kind of mischief?"

"Oh, like making someone fall off a canoe or trip while walking back to their village and break a vase, spilling chicha onto the ground. To prevent that, women would tie something to cover the opening of the bottle and secure it with the nubs. But they would also strap a rope around the nubs so they could carry the vessel more easily on their backs. Almost everything the Incans did was for a practical or religious purpose."

"What did they call these vessels?"

"They were called *aribalo*, if I remember," said Alicia. "They were used for the chicha and in important religious ceremonies. Some archeologists think they were also used for blood rituals, but that has never been validated."

"Blood rituals?"

"Yes, but I don't believe that. The Incans weren't quite as bad as the Aztecs when it came to blood sacrifice."

"Then what about these?"

Will pulled out his cell phone and scrolled through his photo library. Finally, he came to the pictures he'd taken of the black and the white urns. Turning his phone around, he showed them to her.

"Interesting," she said, her forehead collapsing into furrows of perplexity. "They look ceremonial, but most of that kind of pottery had designs that included animals—you know, felines, snakes, birds, jaguars, alpacas, llamas, bees, butterflies, etc. There were some with geometric designs like these have, but only rarely did they show human forms unless they were mythological beings."

"But this doesn't look like an *aribalo*; it doesn't have a pointed base," said Will.

"No, the pointed base was formed so they could plant the vessel into a pre-made hole in the ground—usually ones they had made where they cooked and ate. The design also made it easier to tilt or pour out the vessel's contents and prevented it from being damaged when returning it to its original position. These got really heavy when they were full of beer."

"Aw! Just like kegs on campus," said Will grinning.

"Ah, yes," said Alicia with a smile. "But the Incans—as were most of the Native Americans—very clever in their designs. It all took time—over many generations—to arrive at something that worked so well."

"But that doesn't explain these." Will pointed back at his pictures.

"You're right. It doesn't. We still haven't gotten to the bottom of what your jugs are or where they came from," said Alicia. She looked up at her bookshelf and scanned the titles. Then, she pulled one tome from the middle section and opened it. "There was a tribe in Ecuador that the Inca's conquered sometime during the early sixteenth century before Pizarro arrived. It was part of the Huayna Cápac. There, it is said, they had many strange customs and rituals—those far different than that of the rest of the Inca." She laughed and then added, "Some even claim that the gods put them in charge of protecting the Fountain of Youth."

"The Fountain of Youth?"

"Only the one of myth and legend," said Alicia. "However, the fountain is one that has illuminated our rich history of exploration, storytelling, art, and culture. It seems to be one of those tales which has no beginning and no end."

"My great grandmother once talked about it," said Will. "She said these vessels were connected in some way to that legend."

"The symbols and markings on your jugs suggest that they belonged to that tribe, though. See here ..." She pointed to a page with pictures of vessels very similar to the ones in Will's photo. They, too, had images of warriors—both young and old on opposite sides of the same jug. "There is also a story about a French nobleman who allegedly got some of the fountain's waters. He was said to have taken some of it back to France or somehow secured it from another explorer. The story goes that he used alchemy to perfect its properties, and he was reportedly seen on several occasions throughout the eighteenth and nineteenth centuries."

"Was his name St. Germ?"

"Germ?"

"It's just something else my great grandmother once said. She mentioned someone named St. Germ."

"I believe his name was St. Germaine, but you would need to look that up."

Will looked at his cell phone and saw it was getting late.

"Ms. Collins, thank you so much for taking the time to talk with me. This has been really helpful."

"The pleasure was all mine. I assure you," she answered with a broad smile.

*****

CH 8 – News from the Vet

Raya got the call from the vet.

"Raya, this is Dr. Turnbull. How are you and Max doing?"

"Oh, he's doing very well, doctor. I expected him to come out of this energy spurt, but he still hasn't. He's as active as he was a few weeks ago. I love him to death, but I really wasn't ready for another puppy. That's what he's acting like—a six-month-old puppy! I don't quite understand it."

"That's wonderful to hear. I was just calling because I was hoping to get another sample of that black liquid your son gave me a few weeks ago when he brought him in for a visit."

"You mean the liqueur?"

"Well, we're not sure what it is at this point. As I mentioned earlier, the blood results for him were inconclusive. As I mentioned earlier, I submitted your son's sample to the Global Substance Database to see if there is anything on file there. So far, they haven't been able to find a match either. They claim they need another sample to continue their research."

"I'll have to check with my son. I don't know what bottle he was talking about. I'm sure it's in the basement, and we can bring it by."

"That would be great," said the vet.

"I'll just leave it at the front desk with Marjorie when I come in," said Raya.

"Well, if you don't mind, just have Marjorie let me know when you arrive. I'd like to take it personally. Marjorie is good about things, but I want to be sure this gets sent off to the lab as soon as possible so we can get an answer for you."

"Of course. I understand. It won't be a problem. I'll talk with my son about it right away. We'll get you whatever he can find."

Raya hung up and went up to Will's room. The floorboards moaned as she stomped up the staircase.

"Will," she said, knocking on his door. "I need to talk to you."

"Yeah, come in," Will answered, sitting up in his bed. He had his computer in his lap, and he was intently watching something on the monitor.

Raya walked in and put her hands on her hips.

"I forgot to tell you that I talked to the vet a few days ago. I guess you forgot to tell me about a few things when you took Max to see her. What really happened?"

Will looked at her blankly. "What really happened? What do you mean?"

"Will. The vet said something about liquor in our basement?".

"It wasn't anything, Mom. I just saw Max had drunk something, and I …"

"Will Curtis! You'd better tell me the truth! What's this about some liquor in the basement? You never mentioned finding anything down there to me!"

Raya was angry, and Will wanted to crawl under his bed to escape. Instead, he groaned and closed his monitor. Jack had advised him to tell her the whole story, but he had not wanted to face her wrath. Now he had no choice.

"I … well … I found Max trapped under Daniel's bed. It wasn't liquor or any bottle in the basement. It was the two bottles you found in the kitchen. Remember?"

"Wait. You mean Max got into those bottles?"

"Yeah, well, at least one of them."

Raya steamed.

"And you found these bottles where? You said they were from a garage sale."

Will looked down at his computer.

"Will!"

"They were in Gramma's trunk. All right?"

"No, it's not all right. Why did you lie to me? Why did you lie to the vet?"

"I just told the vet that so she wouldn't get too curious about those ancient bottles of Gramma's. You know what happens when …"

"… yes! I know what happens when you get involved in Gramma's stuff. I'm painfully aware, Will, and so are you. Still, why did you lie to me?"

"Jack told me not to."

"Jack? Jack knew about this?"

Will was now only digging the hole deeper for both him and his stepfather.

"It's not like that!"

"So, this is about Gramma's trunk again?" said Raya. "Will, so help me God …"

"I know, I know. But I locked the trunk. I double-locked the trunk, and still somehow, the trunk was opened. I swear on a stack of Bibles, Mom. I locked that trunk so no one—especially not Max—could get inside it. But … what can I say … it was open."

"Will, I told you a thousand times to get rid of that thing! I didn't think we still had it in the house!"

"Yeah, well, I'm sorry. It was under Daniel's bed."

"So, you hid it from me."

"Uh, well, I …"

"Will! This has to stop!"

"I know, but I didn't do anything! When I pulled the trunk out, I saw there were two jugs on top with their corks opened. Max had a black liquid all over his face. When I got him freed, he began running around all over the place. I thought I'd poisoned him, so Shannon and I took him to the vet. That's it— that's all, I swear."

"Shannon? Shannon was involved?"

"Yeah, I called her to help me."

"Oh, God! Why? We've already caused those poor people so much pain. Why did you get them involved?"

"She's a friend," said Will. "She's my best friend."

Raya shook her head. "It just keeps getting better and better. Doesn't it?"

Will gave her a remorseful look because he was truly sorry for what he'd done.

"Why didn't you tell me everything the first time?" she asked him.

"Because I knew how mad you'd be that I had the trunk in the house. But I locked it up! There's no way Max could have gotten into it. I don't understand how he did."

"You're right! I told you to get rid of that trunk years ago—especially after what happened in China. What is wrong with you, Will?"

"But Mom …"

"No!" she screamed. "I want that trunk gone! Do you hear me? I want you to get rid of it right now. I never want to see it again—ever! I won't ask you another time. Do you understand me?"

Will huffed. "Yes, Mom. I'll get rid of it."

"Is there anything else you want to tell me?"

Solemnly, her son shook his head.

"All right. Then I want this to be the last discussion we have about that damned trunk!"

The next day, Will lugged the trunk from his brother's room, and Raya helped him take it downstairs and put it in the back of their car. Then, he headed to the city landfill which was several miles out of town. After only a few miles, however, he noticed a plume of gray smoke rising up in his rearview mirror. Will instantly thought his seats were on fire and hastily pulled over to the side of the road, jumping out fearing the car would explode.

Yet, there was no fire.

Looking into his backseat, he said, "Gramma?"

Will knew from experience what was coming and who was coming. Quickly, his great grandmother appeared, as clear and visible as he'd ever seen her. Rather than spinning in a foggy mist, she seemed as real as when she had walked the earth. This time, she was sitting in the middle of his bench seat in the back and dressed as if she were going to church. But instead of looking joyful and cheerful, she had a pouty frown on her face.

"Will," she said sharply, her arms crossed as if she were angry at him. She wore a simple white dress with small indigo and citrus violets covering it. They were tiny, delicate-looking flowers with black edges – a dress she would often wear to church on Sundays or occasionally to attend choir practice the evening before.

"What now, Gramma?" Will asked, preparing himself.

"What are you doing?" she asked, scolding him.

"I'm getting rid of your stupid trunk, Gramma! Mom wants it gone."

"Oh, Will. I know I've put you in a difficult position, but you can't do this. You can't!"

"Gramma, I *have* to. This time, I have no choice. Believe me, if I could ..."

"Will, can't you see all the good that has come from the little missions I've sent you on? Haven't they saved or benefited mankind? Haven't they been for a greater good? If you hadn't done what you did, would the world be a better or worse place right now?"

"I know what you're saying."

"How many people have been saved because of you and my trunk of stuff?"

"A lot."

"You saved this country once, you know."

"Yeah."

"And an entire civilization of beings that came to Earth before humans. They wouldn't be alive right now if it weren't for you," Gramma said, referring to the Atlantians he had saved in the subterranean world in Egypt.

"Gramma, I get it, but ..."

"And what about all those people in Shanghai who would have died had it not been for you?"

"Gramma, I can't. I can't do this anymore."

His Gramma was quiet for a moment and then said, "Well, I guess we have to let millions or perhaps billions, perish this time then."

"What?"

"Will, do you think this mission is any less important than the others?"

"Gramma, I don't know what this mission is, so how can I tell?"

"You didn't really know what the others were either before they started, did you?" she asked.

"No."

"All right. Then, do you trust me?"

Will didn't answer.

"Will? I asked, 'Do you trust me?'"

"Of course, I trust you, Gramma," he blurted out.

"Good. You should. Then, you need to turn around."

"But Mom doesn't, and she wants me to get rid of it."

"Then you need to do this. You need to call Shannon and ask her if she will take the trunk for a while," said Gramma.

"Why would I burden her with that? Like Mom said, we've already caused the Evans family enough pain. I care for Shannon. I ..."

"I know you do, Will."

"What do I say to her?"

"Just ask if she will take the trunk. She will say 'yes,'" said Gramma. "Then you need to finish your research on those vessels I gave you. You've already discovered a great deal, but you will find more if you dig. You will discover something important—very important. But ..." She stopped.

"But what?"

"You will need to be careful. Like the other missions, this one will be filled with treachery and evil. You must navigate through this to get to the other side. This is something that's important to the entire world—to the entire human species."

"Come on, Gramma! You're exaggerating."

This time his gramma didn't spin into the ether, and she didn't garble her speech to the point of incoherency. This time, her image merely vanished, fading out quickly only to leave behind an empty rear seat.

Will turned the car around and drove back to town. As he did, he called Shannon, and just as his great grandmother had predicted, she told him keeping the trunk at her place wouldn't be a problem.

"But what are you going to do now?" she asked, helping him take it upstairs to her room.

"I'm going to find out more about the jugs and the stuff in them. Gramma said I'm finding answers, but there is more I need to know."

"If I can help you, I will," she answered him. "And Will ..."

"Yeah?"

"... be careful this time. Okay?"

When Will returned home, his mother was working in her office, preparing for one of many class lectures she was supposed to give during the term.

"Did you get rid of the trunk like I told you?" she asked him, hardly looking up from her computer monitor.

"Yes, Mom," he answered.

"Good."

As he was leaving, she stopped him. "But I did forget one thing. Did you happen to save any of the stuff inside the jugs before you got rid of the trunk? The vet called and asked for more of it. I had forgotten that when I told you to get rid of it."

"No Mom."

Raya shrugged and turned back to her monitor. "That's fine. I'll just tell her we don't have it anymore—that you threw it out. We'll just be rid of it. We'll be rid of everything. That's the way it needs to be anyway."

Following the incident, things seemed to return to normal at home. Will's studies kept him busy as he tried to finish the courses needed to graduate on time. When he had time, he did more research on his jugs. Shannon too continued her work at school—George Mason University—also preparing to graduate but planning to attend law school there. And as for Max, he was still the same as before, still in good spirits and still full of high energy.

However, like one standing in the eye of a hurricane, this quietude would not last long.

*****

CH 9 - Bad Reaction

"Did you get it?"

"I'm trying," said Dr. Turnbull, nervously watching the agitated man in her office. "But my client called and said she doesn't have it anymore. She said she threw it out."

The man moved toward her menacingly. He was as large and thick as a redwood—so huge she suspected he'd once been a pro football player. Taking off his dark aviator glasses, he leaned over the veterinarian's desk and put his gnarly hands on either side of her computer monitor. His eyes were black, emotionless and empty.

"Didn't I tell you how important that vial of black liquid is?" he asked, not backing down.

"Yes, Rod, but I can't get something my client doesn't have. I don't know why you're so interested in it anyway. I sent it to YAF which employs you and your company. They were supposed to analyze it and figure out its composition. Why couldn't they do that with what I gave them? Now you want more?"

"There wasn't enough for us to analyze."

"You first told me that it was just some amino acids and proteins—nothing unusual. Your people didn't seem to think it was anything *that* was out of the ordinary. Now, things have changed, and you demand more of it. What's going on?"

"Are you going to get me the liquid or not?" he demanded.

"I can't. And at this point, I won't. I'm not going to badger my clients."

"That's unfortunate."

Rod pulled something from his coat. It was a tiny, amber bottle. He opened it and poured the contents into her coffee mug.

"What's that?" she asked.

"Drink it."

"No. I'm not drinking that," Turnbull protested. "Now, get out of my office!"

"Either you drink it on your own, or I will help you with it."

"It won't be either!" she answered him defiantly. "I'm calling the police!"

Rod smiled. "I see. Well, then I guess it will have to be my way."

Rod grabbed her by her throat and jaw and squeezed. Forcing her mouth open, he took the coffee and poured it down her throat. Even though she began to gag, he kept pouring, making her swallow it. When he'd finished, he slammed her back into her chair and screwed the cap back on his bottle, putting it away in his jacket.

"That should make you feel better, doctor. Have a nice day."

Turnbull coughed repeatedly having gotten some of the coffee in her lungs. Hacking, she stumbled out to where Marjorie was working at the front desk. She couldn't breathe, and she pointed to her throat with a look of panic on her face. Her throat was swelling quickly, sealing off the airway to her lungs.

"Dr. Turnbull, what's wrong?" Marjorie exclaimed, frightened.

When the doctor began to collapse, Marjorie tried giving her the Heimlich maneuver, believing she was choking on something. But when that didn't help, she called 911.

Waiting for an ambulance to arrive, Marjorie continued to try to resuscitate her boss, yet within a few minutes, the doctor's responses to her efforts grew feebler, and finally, they stopped all together. She lay, quiet and still on the floor—her eyes already fixed and dilating.

The medics came within ten minutes, but they found Dr. Turnbull unresponsive. She was dead. The coroner's report would show that she died of an allergic reaction to something – that her trachea had gone into spasms and closed off her windpipe. The case was closed, and no police report was filed. No toxicology tests were performed, nor was an autopsy. Strangely, her family—shaken by what had happened—seemed unwilling or unable to allow either to take place. Whatever was the cause, it was a secret Dr. Turnbull took with her to the grave.

Raya learned of it later when she was reading the local paper online. Listed in the obituaries was her veterinarian.

> *Dr. Susan Turnbull, veterinarian at Georgetown Veterinarian Clinic, died September 23 from an allergic reaction. She had worked at the clinic for ...*

"Jack, our veterinarian just died," said Raya. "I don't think she was that old, but she died of an allergic reaction to something."

"Those kinds of things can happen," said Jack, not paying much attention as he watched a cable documentary on the Pandemic of 2020.

"What's wrong?" asked Will, coming into the room and overhearing the last part of the conversation.

"Dr. Turnbull, our vet, died last week," said Raya.

"She died?"

"Yes. Apparently, she had an allergic reaction to something at the office. That's what the obit said. She was only fifty-two. So young."

"Young?" said Will.

"Yeah, that's young," said Jack, answering for Raya. "When you get to be our age, you consider anyone about your own age as 'young.'"

"When did she die?" Will asked.

"It says she died September twenty-third."

"That's the day after you made me get rid of the trunk."

"Yes, why?" asked Raya.

"Did you talk to her about not having the vial?"

"Yes. I told her. I called her about it."

"When did you do that?" asked Will.

"When you took the trunk, on the twenty-second."

"So, you told her the day before she died."

"Yes. So?" asked Raya.

Will looked over at Jack who was no longer watching his show. Now he was totally engaged in the conversation. Both Will and he were thinking the same thing, and it wasn't that the incident—the allergic reaction—had been merely an accident or a coincidence.

*****

CH 10 - Bhatti

Dr. Saloni Bhatti studied the reports she had just received from her lab. On one was a spectrograph giving her the decode on the chemicals comprising an unusual substance she had received for analysis. Infrared spectroscopy had been used for decades to excite molecules, first absorbing and then releasing a photon of energy, to reveal the chemical elements that comprised the sample of matter. By measuring the frequency of the energy given off, scientists were able to determine which chemical molecules or compounds made up the matter and, thus, link it to other substances known to contain that composition of elements. In essence, the process showed telltale fingerprints of elements such as carbon, oxygen, hydrogen, and others which would indicate the presence of complicated inorganic molecules such as ethanol, butane, etc., as well as organic ones. They would show any compounds that are ingestible by humans—biologic ones that comprise carbohydrates, proteins, lipids, and nucleic acids.

As she studied the graph, Bhatti's finger tracked the markings of the trace elements within the sample, revealing its composition. Carefully, she scribbled each on her notepad, adding valences and bonds to reconstruct what she was seeing.

"Dr. Ghadre, would you step into my office?" Bhatti asked, pushing a call button on her screen.

"I'll be there in a few minutes," answered the voice over her computer speaker.

"No, doctor. I want you now!"

A few minutes later, a man in his early seventies wearing an ill-fitting, white lab coat entered the office and stood behind one of two red armchairs that guarded Bhatti's mammoth desk.

"Yes, Dr. Bhatti. What is it?"

Dr. Hakim Ghadre had been the Director of Operations for YAF Labs for many years. He was Pakistani and grew up in a wealthy family in a town along the coast of the Arabian Sea near Karachi. When he was twelve, his family moved to New Delhi, India, for better opportunities for their six very-bright children. There he attended the prestigious Indian Institute of Technology, earning his doctorate in organic biochemistry, microbiology, and genetic perturbations. Without a doubt, he was one of the most brilliant scientists of his time; yet, amazingly, he had avoided notoriety, preferring instead to commit himself to his work in the laboratory at YAF.

"Sit!" barked Dr. Bhatti, who was Ghadre's boss and, more than that, was the CEO and part-owner of the enterprise.

Even though Bhatti had graduated from the Indian Institute of Science in Bangalore, her career had been much less stellar and noteworthy than that of Ghadre. It hadn't been her accomplishments that had garnered her the top job, but rather her family and its money. Her degree had been in biochemistry, but her father had largely paid the college to give her a degree. Coming from a lineage whose patriarch was a close friend of India's Prime Minister, Gatik Dara, Bhatti had been made the company's chief executive officer after the founder, her father, had retired from the business.

Far more ruthless than her father, Bhatti's approach to the business had replaced humanity and compassion, which he had been the cornerstone of the operation for over fifty years, with a plantation mentality—enslaving all beneath the iron fist of the plantation master—Saloni Bhatti. Instead, her unpublished mission statement could have been summarized quite simply:

> *Crush your competitors to make money. Crush everyone else to wield power.*

"What do you know about this sample our lab in the United States got last week?" she asked, gesturing toward her monitor.

Ghadre shook his head. "Which one are you referring to?"

"The Curtis sample – you know, the one from DC."

"That one was most unusual. We're still running tests on it."

"I've looked at the spectrographs. Have you seen anything like this before?"

"No. It is very unusual."

Bhatti was young—still in her early thirties. She had shoulder-length black hair which flowed around her narrow face. Her eyes were large, dark and deep set, and her mouth and lips were full and, especially for a scientist, very seductive. Although short and a bit overweight, she was a beautiful woman on the outside. Yet, what was on the inside was something very different.

Dr. Ghadre, on the other hand, was thin, very thin—almost to the point of emaciation. His brown eyes were sunken, and his face sallow, revealing a boniness that was common within his extended family. His arms, wrists, and fingers were small, and, taken as a whole, he looked like a walking corpse.

People in the company often wondered if he ever ate anything; however, at seventy-three, he was still active and vigorous, putting in the long hours demanded by Bhatti and the others she had hired to fill the upper ranks at the company. Ghadre was one of the few holdovers from her father's executive staff and a broader regime that was more dedicated to its written mission of serving humanity.

"I need to know what that substance is!" demanded Bhatti, "and I want that answer within the week. Do you understand?"

"Why the urgency?" Ghadre asked as he moved toward the door to leave. "You know the backlog I have in the lab."

"That's for me to know. Just get me the answers."

After Ghadre left, Bhatti reached for the com button on her monitor once again. "Get me Chip. I need to talk to him right away."

Chip, a nickname for his surname, Cipriani, was her security chief who worked out of their New Delhi office but ran the company's protective services globally, ensuring all the plants were equipped with cameras, fencing, and, if necessary, barbed wire and guard houses. From a technology standpoint, he had established a series of sophisticated firewalls for their computer network that were nearly impregnable and was in the process of installing the next generation of network defenses.

For a resumé, Chip grew up in a military family and had risen through the ranks of the Special Frontier Force, one setup specially to deal with India's border issues with Tibet. Reaching the rank of major, Chip received an honorable discharge to pursue other interests—notably computer security and forensic science.

But in the business world, Cipriani adapted quickly and became a corporate survivor. He enjoyed doing things that were outside the main focus of his job. Often, these requests were less than legal and involved mitigating more than just computer viruses or hacking threats. Sometimes, they involved mitigating human threats as well.

"Yes, doctor?" It was Chip's round, bearded face that popped up on the screen.

"I need a better result on this next assignment than you gave me on the last one. Do you understand?"

"Yes, ma'am."

"When I tell you to get something for me, I mean *to get it* – *not* screw things up. We can't be forced to kill everyone who doesn't cooperate with us. It creates too many loose ends, and we can't risk getting tied back to that. We need to be more *persuasive*. You do understand."

"Yes, ma'am. It was an unfortunate incident. My guy in Washington didn't follow my instructions. He has been terminated."

"I don't care how 'terminated' he is. We can't let that happen again. Everybody we leave behind is evidence. We can't leave evidence."

"Yes, ma'am."

"I'm glad we understand each other. Especially for you and your wife. It's a good that you have no children, but not so good that your parents are still living."

"Yes ma'am," he answered stiffly, trying not to show discomfort or fear.

"Good. Then this next little matter will be taken care of without an incident, I trust. I want it handled within the next three days."

"I'll take care of it. There won't be any issues this time, doctor. I assure you of that."

*****

CH 11 – Finally, It Arrives

1964

A lot had happened during the previous two years. Although intent upon re-engaging in their global search for relics, Luka and Tulia found going back to their former lifestyle more difficult than they had imagined, and plans to globe trot in search of ancient relics continued to get pushed.

After the birth of their daughter, Natalie, and later, their son, Leonid, Tulia and Luka decided their next big adventure would be something less exotic. Both felt it would be best if they left the big city in New York and moved to the Midwest. Bound for Chicago where Tulia had extended family and where they thought they could easily find jobs, the two packed up the family and took a Greyhound bus seven hundred miles to their first stop: Indianapolis. From there they would hop on another bus that would take them four hours north to the Windy City.

However, while at the Indianapolis bus station, Luka noticed a huge bulletin board filled with job postings. He didn't know much about the small town, but then again, he didn't know much about Chicago either, other than it was yet another big city. However, Indianapolis—or Indy as it was known—was a fraction of the size of the other two behemoths with a tenth or less of their populations and seemed to offer them the opportunities for which they were looking.

"Tulia," Luka said while still perusing the Indy jobs board, "it looks like there is a lot of work here in this town., and it's much smaller than either New York or Chicago. What do you think about just planting ourselves here?"

Tulia was tired and in no mood to argue. The two kids were inconsolable, crying and squirming, and it was all she could do not to lash out at her husband. "But my relatives live in Chicago?"

"It's only four hours north of here. It's not hard to get there. We can see them anytime."

Not wishing to fight, she sighed. "Fine. I don't feel like sitting in a bus for another four hours. Indy it is."

So that's how the decision was made. Indianapolis would be their new home—a place they would live for the rest of their lives.

***

When Luka got home from a long day of physical labor at the plant, he opened their second-floor apartment door and threw his keys down on the entryway table.

"I'm home," he announced, exhausted and ready for a good, home-cooked meal.

Little Natalia came running to meet her father while Tulia came out of the nursery carrying Leonid who was swaddled in a canary-yellow, wool blanket, looking like an overripe banana. Tulia had made the blanket for Natasha and had started to knit a blue one for Leonid, but she hadn't quite finished it by the time she'd given birth to him.

Luka picked Natalia up off the floor and swung her around, giving her a dry peck on the cheek.

"Be careful with her!" Tulia scolded, rocking Leonid back and forth in her arms. "You're going to hurt her doing that!"

"*Niet!*" said Luka, not taking his eyes off his daughter. "This Natalie," he said using his daughter's Americanized name, "she's a strong kid. We don't have to worry about her, Tulia. We don't have to worry about either of them. They are strong like their papa!" He grinned again and whipped Natalia once more around his big, muscular frame like she was riding on a merry-go-round. Much to her mother's dismay, Natalia merely squealed with delight and asked him for more.

Rolling her eyes, Tulia started to the nursery to put Leonid back in his crib. It was then that Luka called out at an inopportune moment, "Tulia? What's for dinner? I'm starving."

Holding her anger, she answered with mocking sweetness, "Dearest husband, I didn't have time to start anything, and if you ask me again, you're a dead man."

"What?" he asked, apparently not hearing her.

"I said, go find something in the refrigerator yourself!"

Luka grunted his disappointment but headed for the refrigerator anyway. "But what's Natalie going to eat?"

"Listen, Luka! You try staying home all day with them! It's tiring. I have no one to talk to; I have no one to help me; I have to chase Leonid around the place to make sure he doesn't hurt himself. It's hard!"

Luka nodded and backed off. "I'm sorry. You're right. I'll just go out and get something for us. Okay?" After years of marriage, he knew when to stop pushing, and now was the time. "What do you want? I go get it."

Tulia re-emerged. "I'm not hungry, and I've already fed the kids. Get whatever you want."

Luka sighed. Instead of going out again, he relented, opening the refrigerator and pulling out a brown bottle of Budweiser. After prying off the cap with an opener, he took two gulps before sighing again—this time grabbing the newspaper, plopping down on the sofa, and putting his feet up on the coffee table.

"Oh, Luka," Tulia said from the other room, "we got a message on our mailbox downstairs today. There is a large crate at the post office, and they told us to come pick it up."

"A crate?" he asked. "Who would send us a crate?"

"I don't know, but you'd better go there tomorrow and see," Tulia said. "They don't keep things like that around forever. You know, someone is likely to take it if it sits there too long."

Luka took two more swigs from the bottle and folded his paper. Then he went into the only room that had a radio. Turning it on and rolling a dial to one of the AM stations, he took a seat to listen to the evening news. They didn't have the money for one of the big, fancy cabinets that held a black-and-white television set. But they did have an old Motorola radio, and that was all he needed.

Luka closed his eyes just as Steve Rowan of CBS Radio News began his broadcast, but within minutes he was asleep, snoring soundly on the second-hand recliner they'd picked up at a flea market just after they'd gotten their apartment.

***

The next day Luka stopped by the post office, expecting the crate to be something he could toss into the back of his 1957 Chevy sedan and drive home. Instead, he found a full-sized, wooden pallet with a crate—a three-by-four-foot pine carton—stacked on it.

"Sign here," said the pudgy, middle-aged post office clerk, bored with his job as he unenthusiastically shoved the clipboard out for Luka to pen his name.

"How am I supposed to get this thing out of here?" asked Luka, staring at the large size of the package.

"That's your problem," said the clerk walking away, not caring one way or the other. Then, he added, "But you gotta get it outta here within the next twenty-four hours or I'll have it taken to the city dump!"

"Fine," Luka muttered. "I'll be back."

He returned an hour later with a few of his buddies from the factory, and together they loaded the crate onto the back of his buddy's well-worn '58 Ford truck.

"Tulia, I'm home," Luka said, staggering inside the apartment.

Tulia emerged as she had the day before, cradling Leonid in her arms. "We have a guest, Luka."

Luka glanced over at the faded, lumpy sofa. Smiling back at him was a familiar face, but one that had many more wrinkles and gray hair than it had the last time he'd seen it.

"Brandon!"

Luka hurried to greet him, and as he put his arms around him, he gave his friend a peck on each cheek as was the European custom.

"Good to see you Luka," said Brandon, his British accent strong and distinct. "It seems like each of us has been through quite a bit since the last time we saw each other. Your lovely wife has been filling me in."

"I'll say," said Luka. "I didn't know you were coming."

"Did you get the package?" said Brandon.

Luca smiled. "You know, Brandon, you couldn't have timed your visit any better. Here, give me a hand with this crate you sent. I have some guys from work downstairs to help. There is no way I can get it up here into this small apartment without them—or you. Follow me."

Even with five husky men, they struggled to move the heavy crate up the narrow staircase to the second floor. Once inside the apartment, Brandon helped Luka pull off the pine boards to reveal what was inside. It only took the removal of a few boards before Luka stood back and smiled.

"The stone trunk," said Luka, nodding. "You really did send it!"

"It comes with a set too," said Brandon.

"A set of what?" asked Tulia.

"A set of Sibylline Books, of course."

"The Sibylline Books?" said Tulia, her voice trembling as if she had suddenly seen an apparition. "I never thought I would hear those words again." She glanced at Luka and saw his angst. It was a *déjà vu* moment, one that had teleported both of them backward in time and one both preferred to forget. "Luka, I don't think ..."

"It will be fine, Tulia. They're only books after all," said Brandon.

Luka smiled and began tearing apart the crate, extracting rusty nail after rusty nail until he could see deeper inside. Buried under yellow straw was the ancient, stone trunk carved with all the strange figures Luka had seen back in Moscow. Brandon ran his hand over the top of it trying to find where the seam of the lid divided the trunk from its cover. After some searching, he moved two corner pieces that blended so well with the surrounding pattern of the lid that they were virtually invisible. Pushing them outward toward their respective corners, he felt the top release its hold and pop up a fraction of an inch above the trunk base.

"Help me with this, will you Luka?"

Together they lifted the heavy, stone lid and placed it on the carpet next to the trunk.

"Well, I guess the Oracle has returned," Luka said.

"Yes," said Brandon, taking a sip of his wine, "but not all the volumes are in there, you know."

Tulia glanced into the hold of the trunk and mouthed the numbers as she counted each volume. "One, two, three, four, five, six," she murmured. Then, looking up at Brandon, she contorted her face into a curious grimace. "But I don't understand," she continued. "Where are the others?"

There had been ten volumes of the Sibylline books when they had initially been brokered in Moscow. However, only numbers seven through ten still held prophesies that were yet unfulfilled. The others were now mere history books, having recorded those that had come and gone, already entered into the records as events that had, indeed, come to pass as foretold.

"Yes, well, let me explain," said Brandon.

Brandon told them of the problems at U.S. Customs in New York and how they had confiscated the other trunk with volumes seven through ten.

"Where are those books now?" asked Tulia. "Does the government have them? As you know, those were the most valuable."

"Yes. The government has them, but we don't know what they did with them. They won't tell me. They only said they were considered contraband, and that if I pressed the matter, I would be arrested in London and thrown in prison there. I'm not sure how they could do that, but I was in MI6 long enough to know that if there is something the government wants to hide, it will and it will make sure it stays that way."

"Those books are dangerous," said Tulia. "You know that, right?"

"Yes, but that's all I know," Brandon answered. "You're the scholar on those books, not me. I was merely an innocent bystander—someone who got caught in the crossfire." He laughed.

"Yeah, I regret that," said Luka. "It's terrible what happened to you."

"Hey, it was all part of the job. And anyway, what are friends for?" Brandon said, smiling.

Tulia treated them to a nice dinner even though Leonid cried through much of it. And when Tulia took the children back to their room to put them to bed, Brandon pushed his empty plate forward and slid his mug of ale to within easy reach.

"Tell me, Luka, how do you like it here in America?" Brandon asked.

Luka smiled broadly. "We do. We really do. It's the first time Tulia has felt safe. It's the first time I haven't been looking over my shoulder worrying about whether a KGB agent was trailing me, ready to put a bullet in the back of my head."

Brandon nodded and took another sip of his beverage. "I thought you'd say that. I haven't been here that long, and I'm feeling the same way."

"Where are you now, Brandon? Are you living in London?"

"Yes, I'm in London, in Croydon, but I only have a flat there. There is nothing there tying me down."

"So, you're thinking about America?"

"Maybe. But I certainly couldn't live this far out … in the Midwest, that is. If I came to the U.S., it would likely be Washington, D.C. That feels more like where I would want to live. It's got much more of a cosmopolitan flavor than most other American cities."

"Well, Indy does take a little getting used to. But they do have Weir Cook Airport, so we can still get out of here when and if we want to. We've already got our next trip planned," said Luka.

"Really? Where are you going? With your growing family, I would have thought you'd have your hands full right here." Brandon nodded toward the children's bedroom. "

"Actually, we're thinking of traveling to Asia," said Luka. "Tulia feels trapped here with the kids and wants to get away. She has family in Chicago that could take care of Natalia and Leonid while we're away.'

Brandon pushed his chair away from the table. "You are joking! Where in Asia?"

"China," Luka clarified. "We hope to be there in about a month."

"And you think the children will be fine while you're gone that long?"

"Why wouldn't they be?" asked Luka, answering as his father would have in the old country, the Soviet Union.

"Are you looking for something in particular or just going to see what you might find while you're there?"

"There are some ancient relics Tulia is searching for. They're called bi cong discs. Have you heard of them?"

"No, what are those?"

"They're ancient stone discs," said Tulia. "They were usually made of jade and put in the tombs of emperors for the afterlife. The 'bi' represents the sky and the 'cong' represents the earth. They were religious artifacts that date back a few thousand years."

"Where are you going in China where they have those, then?" Brandon asked.

"It's a place called Luoyang?" Luka asked.

"I haven't heard of that. Where is it?"

"Central China. It's not easy to reach. You have to fly into Peking, or I guess they call it Beijing. Then you must travel several days over rough, dirty roads to reach Luoyang. Tulia has been writing to a man there who says he has several and is willing to sell them."

"Fascinating," said Brandon. "I guess you two really enjoy that kind of thing. Why not just go to Miami and spend time on a beach instead?"

Luka laughed. "What's the adventure in that?"

"I'd really like to go with you to the ends of the earth in China," said Brandon, "but I have to get back to London. My sister says our father is not doing well."

"I'm sorry," said Tulia.

"Yes, but he's in his eighties and has had a good life. Thank goodness he didn't know what I did for a living, or he wouldn't have made it this long. He's always had a bad heart."

"Well, if we find anything that can cure old age, we'll bring it back for you," said Luka.

Brandon laughed. "You do that. Perhaps each of us can take a swig of that too—just as a prophylactic, of course."

"You really want to live that long?" Luka asked, as Leonid began shrieking in the back bedroom. "I'm not sure that's for me."

"I guess I'll have to let you know after I have a family," said Brandon smiling. "It sounds like my answer may change by then."

*****

CH 12 - YAF

YAF was a company formed by the Bhatti family back at the turn of the twenty-first century. It had grown in power and size, mainly through the efforts of Dr. Sing Bhatti, the father of the current CEO, Saloni Bhatti. However, while he had strived to do things right and stay true to the path of moral and ethical business practices, his daughter had strayed.

But early in the 2000s, Sing's company was struggling; he was running out of money. A Brahman, Sing Bhatti lived well, inside a high-walled and guarded compound in New Delhi—a place that was complete with servants, maids, drivers, butlers and assistants of every kind. However, when his lab failed to get approval for its first drug, the money began to run out fast. So, he turned to friends of his father who had cultivated strong connections with those in powerful positions within the Indian government. In return for big stakes in Sing's company, government officials cut him a break on taxes and offered him huge grants to begin research on several other promising drugs.

One such drug was *Illexovere*, which was used to cure Hepatitis C. Another drug was *Yesoklovin*, which was created to combat the effects of a deadly strain of SARS virus known as Meningitis-25. The company had made trillions of rupees—equivalent to about fifteen billion US dollars—from these two products alone. However, although the family did well, government officials took the majority of the profits as anonymous shareholders able to benefit from their own government largesse and at the expense of Indian taxpayers. But it was not enough; it was never enough. There was always more to be taken.

In 2033, the silent shareholders forced Sing Bhatti to retire, and they handed the reins to his daughter, who had shown a ruthless ability to grow the company and crush her competition. She had undermined her father and convinced Indian authorities that he was no longer competent to run the operation. Shortly after his retirement, Sing had suffered a stroke and was under constant care, imprisoned within the four walls of his compound. This convenient incident had ensured that he would never again walk through the front doors of YAF.

However, then rumors began circulating about the cause of the founder's stroke and who might have been involved. An investigation was conducted and, eventually, a potential link was made to a drug YAF was working on at the time—one that may have resulted in the stroke. An anonymous article suggested that Saloni had used large doses of the drug to trigger the hemorrhage in her father that ultimately killed him.

After the takeover, she sold more shares of the company to third-party outsiders who were later found to be government officials. Yet, it was when a second article was published suggesting that Saloni was plotting to kill her mother too, fearing she was trying to uncover the truth about her husband, that action by federal authorities was taken to shut it down. No one ever found out whether the allegation of Saloni's involvement in her father's death were true, nor what happened to the person who initially leaked the story. The matter simply disappeared.

Yet, having made a Faustian bargain with India's political elites, Saloni was now a puppet on their strings—one who danced only when and how they commanded. So, she found an apartment in New Delhi, close to the seat of government, and went to work asking for funding for the next great drug to cure cancer.

"I'm only asking for eight thousand crore," said Saloni Bhatti, talking to Ansh Aiyar, one of the Members of Parliament from the Council of States, also known as the Rajya Sabha. One crore was ten million rupees. Eight thousand crore was large, amounting to about one billion US dollars. Still, in the larger scheme of the nation's budget, it was a mere pittance.

Aiyar had been an MP for over twenty-four years, serving four terms, and was expected to be re-elected to a fifth. He was the leader of the Dravida party and had an iron grip on all that happened in the Upper Chamber of Parliament.

Aiyar laughed at Bhatti's request. "Ha!" he exhorted. "You mean eight thousand *lakh!*" The difference between a crore and a lakh was huge. A lakh of rupees was one percent of a crore or only 100 thousand rupees. So, rather than a request totaling one *billion* US dollars, Aiyar suggested an amount of only ten *million*.

"No, Mr. Aiyar, I am asking for eight thousand *crore*," Bhatti insisted.

Aiyar smiled and leaned back in his rare, 17th century French Baroque armchair. He was balding, and what hair he had left was gray. In his early seventies, the senior member of parliament had seen all sorts of bold, young entrepreneurs come into his office demanding outrageous things, but this ranked high on the list. Pushing his silver-framed glasses higher on his nose, he took a moment to collect his thoughts.

"You realize you're asking for eighty *billion* rupees—that would be over 900 million US dollars."

"Yes," she answered flatly. "Actually, closer to a billion."

"I'm afraid that is out of the question. It is an outrageous sum to request and not within the scope of this, or any, government to grant."

"What if it led to a cure for cancer?"

"Drugs to cure cancer? Really?"

"Yes, I believe my lab can do that."

Aiyar crossed his arms and smiled. "You are naïve, doctor. Drugs have been in existence for decades that can cure cancer, but there was too much money involved in cancer cure research to permit their release for public use. Those cures are buried, just as yours would be. I'm not wasting any more money on cancer cures."

Bhatti was shocked. Even she had no idea that what he said was true. And in a rare moment, she sat speechless.

"But you are a Bhatti, and I had great respect for your father," said Aiyar. "Let me make a call."

He reached for one of two hardline phones on his desk, and the one he picked up was connected to a most obscure but powerful source. After dialing only three numbers, he reached someone on the other end.

"This is Aiyar. I have someone in my office who may be able to help us with the scheduled project this year … Yes, she can be trusted, she's Dr. Sing Bhatti's daughter … Yes, YAF … We do have leverage with her—financial leverage … May I engage her in our plans?"

Aiyar listened to what the person on the other end of the line told him and after several minutes said, "Yes, I agree. We will get the papers drafted and take additional steps that are necessary to secure our position in the matter."

Aiyar hung up and turned back to Saloni.

"We do have a need," he began.

"And what is that?" she asked.

"I can't tell you now, but I will be in contact with you about it. If things work out, this will be an opportunity of a lifetime."

"What's that supposed to mean?" she asked.

"It means a very big number for your top line of revenue."

"Millions?"

"Billions," Aiyar answered.

*****

CH 13 – Hobson's Choice

After the tragic death of Dr. Turnbull, Jack asked Will to be vigilant. Perhaps it was his years working undercover or just an innate sixth sense, but Jack didn't want anyone in his family to become the next victim. The vet's death had been unexpected, but when nothing else happened, it seemed that the incident had been strange and isolated but nothing more. So, each went back to his or her normal life routines—even Max, who still found chasing frisky, bushy-tailed squirrels in the backyard entertaining.

As for Jack, things had changed dramatically since the recent election in 2036. The State Department was no longer being run by Marilyn Stone, someone with whom he had developed a trusting, professional relationship. Under the Twenty-second Amendment of the *Constitution*, President Ross could not run for a third term, and a new president, Clarice Carpenter who was from the other party, had taken the reins of power. The new Secretary of State superseding Stone was Ernest Perez, who had brought in his own team to run the department.

Jack's service to the State Department was suspended immediately after Perez was sworn in as secretary. However, within a few months, that decision was reviewed and, surprisingly, reversed. No reason was given for the change of heart, but Jack suspected they had an urgent need and had not yet found a suitable replacement for him. Given how slowly the bureaucracy operated, he understood it could be many months, if not a year, before someone might be found.

As a result, Jack had agreed to help the department during the interim, and the first meeting with his new boss, Deputy Secretary Elisa Katz, was scheduled for the very next week.

"Jack, please have a seat," said the deputy secretary with little warmth in her voice.

Katz had been a long-time party hack with no real-life experience in the matters of the State Department. As with most senior appointments, she merely had to ensure the orders of the higher-ups were followed and not questioned. Hers was an enforcement role—nothing more. Additionally, identifying anyone thought to be a malcontent or outright saboteur of the department's often-times illegal or nefarious programs was also a key part of her job description.

"We have an assignment for you," said Katz, "one that will take you out of the country for a while." It was clear from the start that Katz disliked him, but since he was needed, she was forced to tolerate him.

Jack groaned quietly at the new assignment. Going out of town for long periods was something in which he had little interest, especially on such short notice.

"You will be working with CIA and Interpol on this one,"

"Interpol? Do I have to work with them?"

Interpol was the International Criminal Police Organization headquartered in Lyon, France, whose responsibility was to track down international criminals—both civil and criminal. Tied directly to the United Nations, Interpol was intended to be the investigative arm of the world. Unfortunately, the group had become corrupted like many other international bodies, including the UN, WHO, IMF, and others. The huge Interpol staff relied almost exclusively on locals who did their work for them. Jack had run into this problem during a mission he had in the Democratic Republic of the Congo three years earlier. There, Interpol used Jack and locals in Lubumbashi, near Zambia, to apprehend a tribal warlord accused of mass genocide. When corrupt Zambian police interceded, Interpol agents denied any relationship with Jack, going so far as to implicate him in the affair. Jack was rescued only because then President Ross ordered the CIA to send in a force via a UH-62 Blackhawk to extricate him.

"Yes, Jack," Katz said, rejecting his complaint. "Interpol is critical to us in our fight against terrorism. They do an excellent job of helping the CIA and this department root out corruption and organized crime throughout the world."

"With all due respect, you're not serious. You know as well as I do that they are neck deep in the corruption!" said Jack. "Why would we trust them with our intel?"

"Jack, come on!" said Katz. "This is a new day and a new administration. We are more open than the last one. We embrace everyone. We don't exclude. We will only succeed if we *all* succeed. These are global problems that require global solutions. We must all work together for the greater good."

"Right. If only we all had the same objectives, that would be true. But Interpol and the UN don't. So, I'm afraid, you'll need to speed up your search for my replacement."

Jack began to get up from his chair.

"Jack, sit down!" Katz said harshly. "I don't want to have to do this, so let's just say that I'm going to ask you nicely one more time to work on this project."

"Or?"

"We don't want to go there, Jack. It would be terrible for you and your family."

"Are you threatening me and them?"

"Let's just avoid all the unpleasantries and just cooperate. Okay?"

Jack could read between the lines. He knew it was a fine line between government control and tyranny. They had been on the edge before and narrowly escaped after Will had found the Sibylline Books. It had only been the overthrow of the president by the people and the fair election and installation of President Ross that had pulled them back from the brink. She dismantled the illegitimate election mechanisms—hardware, software, and mail-in voting—and ousted several top judicial appointees to enable those changes and the restoration of the Republic. Yet, Jack had seen the head of the beast begin to rise again—and more quickly than ever before. He knew "accidents" involving agents and department employees happened all the time, and since their work was often clandestine and off the radar, their mishap could easily go undetected.

Jack could read it in Katz's face. He didn't know her, but he had known many like her. *When sitting bound and gagged in the corner of a hungry lion's cage, one doesn't provoke one's captor,* he thought.

"I understand," Jack said, unhappily. "What's the mission?"

"Good. I thought you'd come around." Katz pulled up a file marked *Top Secret-Compartmentalized* on her computer, clicking it to open. "This is Al Kierney, also known as 'Sawmill.' He is involved in a global mafia ring that is trying to undermine the West and promote worldwide anarchy. We believe he is funded by major drug cartels that are thriving off their weak national governments. This is especially true in Columbia, Ecuador, Mexico and other Central and South American countries."

"Is he American?"

"Yes, but his background is murky at best. What information we have is that he first appeared on Indian police reports about five years ago. His name was linked to several high-visibility events, like the terrorist bombing of the airport in Mumbai and the fire that was set at the Circular House of

Parliament in New Delhi. If you recall, that blaze almost totally destroyed the entire complex."

"Yes, it was awful from what I remember," said Jack.

"Now we believe he's trying to destroy key laboratories in that country—ones trying to develop vaccines and cures against potential epidemics—both natural and those being concocted by China and Russia."

"Like China did in 2020—the one that led to the jab hoax," said Jack. "People lost their livelihoods and their lives because of it."

"You're misinformed," Katz answered sharply. "The WHO and CDC *saved* America and the world from a catastrophic death toll with those vaccines. It would have been much worse had they not stepped in to require vaccinations."

"You still believe that crap?"

Katz glared at him. "It's not crap! It's a fact! It was all based on the science!"

"Yeah, with nearly four hundred million fewer people thanks to your kill shots. All those people who died from vax complications—that was fact!"

Katz ignored him. "What's important *now* is that Kierney be stopped." She pushed a hardcover file across her desk, also marked *Top Secret*. Jack immediately flipped it open. Inside was a picture of a man in his early sixties, bald with a cold stare. He had keen blue eyes and a taut-lipped mouth that suggested a no-nonsense approach to life.

"How is he a threat?" asked Jack. "He's like seventy?"

"Sixty-seven, and in addition to being an anarchist, Kierney is an anti-vaxxer, which is worse. He's been involved in mafia-styled hits on top scientists at bio labs in India and has been connected to several where fire-bombings led to many deaths. The Indian government is trying to deal with the problem, but they claim he is an American, and they want our help in finding him and eliminating their problem."

"You mean, eliminating *him*."

Katz again ignored his comment and continued. "Kierney moves around a lot within India but seems to have quite a few connections high up in the Indian Parliament. We aren't sure who these connections are but assume they all tie back to the cartels in Central and South America. Money could only be funneled to him and his base in India through bureaucratic channels greased with drug money."

"Sounds easy enough," said Jack, closing the file.

"Here are some others you need to meet."

For this segment, Katz turned on a projector installed in the back of her office. Images quickly filled a white screen mounted on a side wall.

"First is James Herron, our Chief of Missions in India," she said. "He's the number two behind our Ambassador, Francis Marshal. Herron has been working with Indian police to track down Sawmill, so he will have up-to-date information for you. In addition, we have an asset there who goes by the name Uri Biendar. He will contact you at your hotel once you arrive in New Delhi." From across the desk, she pushed to him two pictures—one of Herron and one of Biendar. "Finally, I have a download of other information you'll need. It's encrypted, of course, so you'll have to decrypt to view it. Make sure all your firewalls and encryptions are up to date. We wouldn't want any of this to fall into the wrong hands."

"Do you have any idea where this Kierney might be in India?" Jack pleaded, trying to make his task a little easier.

"Our intel suggests he's currently in New Delhi. Where, we don't know. He moves frequently and has many safe houses. Again, Herron and or Biendar will have more information for you."

"New Delhi is a big place. It's got, like, twenty million people there," said Jack. "It's not going to be easy to find him."

"Try over forty-five million," said Katz, "and yes, it won't be easy. But then again, we have you, right?" She was being sarcastic, but Jack only smiled.

"You're right," he answered confidently. "You do."

Jack got up to leave but his boss called out to him. "Oh, and Jack?"

"Yeah?"

"Don't let us down. There's a lot at stake—for your country, but also for you and your family. Understand?"

Jack nodded and closed the door behind him.

*****

CH 14 - Where is Max?

"Max? Max?"

Will called for their dog but couldn't find him anywhere. Their house wasn't that big, and usually Max was resting on the well-worn sofa in the family room, making sure it didn't move to any other part of the house during the day. This time, he wasn't on his canine throne.

"Mom? Have you seen Max?"

"Yeah, I just let him out a few minutes ago to go to the bathroom. He's out there someplace," Raya answered, in the middle of folding laundry.

But when Will went to find Max in the backyard, he wasn't there either.

"Max?" he called out. "Max? Come here, boy!"

There were many trees and bushes but few places to hide. Largely unlandscaped, the grounds were occasionally mowed when Will got around to it, and the three flower beds occasionally watered—again, based on when Will was reminded by his mother. Yet, after thorough searches behind the garage, near the shed, and in the neighbors' backyards, Will found nothing.

"Are you sure you didn't let him back in?" Will asked his mother, after he came inside.

"No. He isn't back there?" asked Raya, now more concerned.

"Nope. I looked everywhere."

"Maybe he slipped through the fence. Did you check for an opening or loose board?"

"No, but I looked in the neighbors' yards and called for him. He isn't there either."

Raya went out with her son to recheck the yard. But soon she spotted something on the side door of the garage that caught her eye—a small, white note card that was tacked to it. Going to the door, she ripped it down to read it.

> **WE HAVE YOUR DOG. IF YOU WANT HIM BACK, YOU WILL GIVE US THE BLACK LIQUID YOU BROUGHT TO THE VET. WE WILL CALL WITH INSTRUCTIONS.**

"Will! Come here! I found something!" cried Raya.

Will ran to the garage and read the note over his mother's shoulder.

"Who would kidnap Max?" she asked.

"I ... I don't know. But they want that black elixir that Max ate—the stuff the vet wanted more of too."

"*Crap!*" Raya muttered, re-reading the note. "I'm scared for Max," she said.

"Yeah, 'cause I don't have it anymore. But there's something else, Mom."

"What?"

Will looked scared—more than his mother had ever seen him.

"I'm think whoever wrote this note is the same person who killed Dr. Turnbull."

"No, it can't be, Will. Dr. Turnbull's death was an accident. She had an allergic reaction."

"Was it that?"

"Yes. That's what the obit said."

"Mom, I talked to Marjorie at the vet's office. She's in bad shape. She told me there was a strange man in the office just before Dr. Turnbull died. She said the doctor wasn't allergic to anything that she knew. Marjorie said she's been afraid for her life ever since Dr. Turnbull died."

"She think's Dr. Turnbull was killed?"

"Yeah, she does. And so does Jack."

"Why didn't you say something earlier? We should take this to the police!"

"Take what to the police? This dog ransom note?"

"No, about our vet being murdered!"

"There's no evidence. Marjorie said they've already closed the case. There's nothing more they're going to do. Jack even said so."

"Well, we have to do something! And now with Max gone!" exclaimed Raya, now more visibly shaken.

"All we can do is try to get Max back," said Will.

"Where's the serum, then ..." Raya asked, still clutching the note, "... the stuff Max ate?"

"I got rid of it, just like you told me."

"*Crap!*" she said with greater exasperation. "Where is it then? We have to get it back to we can free Max. Do you remember where in the landfill you put it?"

"It's ... it's at Shannon's," Will said reluctantly, waiting for his mother's reaction.

"What! Why on God's Earth would you do that? I specifically told you not to involve the Evans!"

"I'm sorry. But isn't it better that she has it than for it to be out in the dump? It could have gotten smashed and lost forever by now out there. Isn't that a good thing?"

Raya knew he was right, but she didn't want to admit it. Instead, she just said, "At this point, I don't care as long as we get that elixir and get my Max back. We have to get him back, Will! We have to!"

"I know, Mom."

"Go to Shannon's right now and get those bottles. We don't have any time to lose. They could call any minute!"

Will nodded, but he worried now that it was too late for Max, even as they were speaking. It would be nothing for someone who could murder a veterinarian to snuff out a poor, defenseless dog. Now, they had no choice but to face that possibility. *If we just give them the stupid elixir, maybe they'll leave us alone,* he thought. He was hopeful, but hope was all he had left.

***

Five days passed, and there were no calls, emails, posts or other communication from the dognapers. Meanwhile, even reaching Shannon had been a challenge. Will had left a number of messages but had heard nothing back from her either. It was unlike her, and he began to worry about her as well.

Finally, she called. "Will, I see that you tried to reach me. What's going on?"

It sounded like her, but the voice seemed robotic and staid—not the usual upbeat and carefree self Will had grown to love.

"Shannon? Is everything alright?" Will asked.

"Of course. Why wouldn't it be?"

"I can hear a strain in your voice. That's all," said Will.

"There is no strain Will. What do you want?" Her words were now sharper, more cutting.

"Uh, well, I was just wondering how you are."

"Fine."

Will immediately thought she was trying to get rid of him. *Perhaps she has a serious boyfriend? Perhaps he had done something or hadn't done something that had pissed her off? Or perhaps she too had been threatened.* All those thoughts raced through his mind.

"Okay, well, I wanted to let you know that Max has gone missing."

"Max?"

"Yeah, Max. We found a note from the dognapers. I need the jugs back that were in the trunk I gave you. They're demanding the elixir in exchange for him."

"Mom found the trunk in my closet," Shannon blurted out.

"What?"

"Yeah, she's pissed. She doesn't want me to have anything to do with it, with you or with your Gramma. She told me never to see you again."

Will was quiet. "I'm sorry."

"Yeah, so am I. And I'm sorry about your dog." Her demeanor changed back to her usual self after realizing she was being unduly harsh with him. "And Will?"

"Yeah?"

"You need to come by today and get the trunk. Can you pick it up this afternoon?"

"Yeah. I'll be by, and Shannon ..."

"Yeah?"

"I'm really sorry."

He hung up. He was devastated and heartbroken.

"Well?" asked Raya, standing beside her son as he made the call.

"I'm going to Shannon's to pick up the trunk this afternoon."

"Good. We'll get the bottles from it and then take it to the dump where it belongs!"

"Yes, Mom."

Will didn't bother to tell his mother about being de-friended by Shannon. It had hurt him deeply, but he held out hope that it wasn't really the end. He couldn't bear the thought of that. Losing Max was bad enough—losing Shannon would be a blow from which he wasn't sure he could ever recover.

*****

CH 15 - Benjamin Curtis

Washington, D.C. 2018

Benjamin had been married to Raya for over ten years. They had two sons, Daniel and Will, ages seven and three, respectively. Daniel had been the easy birth, coming out at seven pounds, six ounces, screaming and thrashing about as a normal newborn. Will, on the other hand, had been a breach baby, and the doctors had decided to take him—also kicking and screaming—via Caesarean section.

Although the all-nighters—getting up to console their boys when they had bump-in-the-night nightmares—were getting fewer and farther between for the couple, the nights were becoming lonelier for Raya as her husband was increasingly being sent on assignments overseas.

Before he would leave, Ben would kiss his sons goodnight, telling them he would see them in a few weeks. With sadness in her face, Raya would say goodbye to him at two in the morning when a dark government sedan would arrive to pick him up and take him to the airport. She wouldn't be able to sleep soundly again until he returned, safe and sound.

But when Ben was in town, he made every effort to spend time at home. Often, he would take the boys to Rock Creek Park or down to the National Mall to the Air and Space Museum. The nation's capital was always glorious during the spring and summer seasons as the brilliance of the foliage and beauty of the flowers lit up the dull, gray Indiana limestone that constituted most of the federal buildings. With the efficiency of the DC Metro trains, it was easy to get from one side of town to the other in just a few minutes.

Yet, this day Ben couldn't take off. He had an important meeting at CIA headquarters in Langley, Virginia. Ben knew where the deputy director's office was at the Langley Center, a large complex tucked away in the dense woods just off the historic Potomac River, and after passing through the multiple checkpoints and parking his car, he hurried to his scheduled meeting at 3:30. He was there to see Dwight Eichenberg, the newly appointed Deputy Director of Intelligence and Foreign Affairs. However, as was usual at the CIA, the director was running late, and finally at 4:25, Ben was allowed into his office.

"Ben, good to finally meet you," said Eichenberg, reaching across his desk to shake Ben's hand. "I've been spending a great deal of time lately talking to my department chiefs and finding out about our field staff. Your name comes up quite often, I'm pleased to say."

"Thank you, sir," said Ben. "I've enjoyed working for the agency."

"Good to hear. Please …," said Eichenberg, motioning toward a gold and burgundy upholstered, armchair that matched the style of his colonial desk. "Ben, we have some news coming out of Eastern Europe that is disconcerting, and we need someone who can control the situation."

"Yes, sir. What's going on?"

Eichenberg pushed a button on his console, and the large flat screen on the wall behind him illuminated. Immediately, there were three pictures that came into view. On the top left was a military man wearing an army colonel's uniform with eight rows of ribbons above his left breast pocket and gold eagle pins on each of his epaulets. He looked hard and rigid with a taut, square jaw, piercing blue eyes, and a harsh demeanor—one he clearly didn't try to hide. If he had wanted to look intimidating, he had succeeded.

Then, there were the other two pictures. Like the one above it, this gentleman wore a uniform, albeit one of a general, but not of the United States. He had a round face, suggesting his girth was much bigger than when he had first joined his country's armed forces. He had a thick, black beard, and steely dark eyes that made Ben uncomfortable. The other photo was that of a younger man, one near Ben's age. He had a military grade hair cut but was dressed in a dark suit, white shirt and plain, solid-red tie. Juxtaposed against the other photos, this one showed a man without a military demeanor. In it, he was smiling, although perhaps disingenuously, as if he had just told his wife he was 'thrilled' that her mother was coming to stay with them.

"You won't recognize these faces," said Eichenberg, "so let me put them in perspective. There are several valuable biolabs in the country of Ukraine— all doing important research that will benefit mankind. The United States is in partnership with the World Health Organization—the WHO--which has begun funding labs like these to further the development of cures and vaccines for virulent diseases around the globe. This is important work, and this Administration believes fervently that it must proceed without interruption."

"Of course," said Ben.

"But there are some who want to stop this research."

"Why would they do that?" Ben asked.

"Good question. You'd think no one would. Yet, as you know, the West has many enemies, and they don't want us to have the means to defend ourselves against such pathogens. As a result, they have found willing accomplices who are more than happy to exchange morality for money. We believe they have been compromised—blackmailed or paid off to destroy the work at these labs."

"Who runs these labs? Is it the WHO?"

"No. Not directly. They are run by various NGOs—non-government organizations—that want nothing more than to help humanity. Ben, it's terrible that people would put money and influence before what's right in the world, but it happens all the time."

"What are the labs working on now?"

"From what we know, they are researching vaccines for new contagious diseases in the event there is a major outbreak in the world. Our enemies like China, Russia, North Korea, and others, are known to be developing viruses they can use as bioweapons against us and our allies. We fear they may release something that could devastate the US and Europe, leaving us crippled and vulnerable to a military attack."

"You mean, like the Ebola outbreak in Africa several years ago."

"Yes, but that was very localized. No, we're talking about the wide-spread distribution of a lethal virus, like the one we dealt with in 2003-SARS. We think they may release it to create a *global* pandemic."

"But the SARS thing didn't really amount to anything back then. Why would it now?"

"We have intel that they are working to re-create it in another, more lethal, form. If we don't find a vaccine for it, we could find ourselves in a pandemic worse than the Black Death. It's a national security threat, Ben, and we need someone to stop those trying to sabotage the good works going on in those labs over there."

"Who are these people, then?" Ben asked, pointing to the images on the screen.

"On the upper left, you have Colonel AK Williams, commanding officer of our forces stationed in Wiesbaden, Germany. That is the division that oversees our covert operations in Ukraine. Bottom left, you have General Matviy Pipenko, who heads that country's Ministry of Security. He and his family also have significant investments in the pharmaceutical sector and have amassed great wealth within the last twenty years. He had connections with the previous President Poroshenko but suddenly severed those in 2014 when the current president came to power. Bottom right is one of our assets in Ukraine. His name is Uri Biendar. He will be a key source of information for you. You will be contacting him when you reach Kiev. We believe that Col. Williams has been compromised and is involved in trying to sabotage the bio labs rather than defend them. We think he's being manipulated by Chinese intelligence and, perhaps, is a double agent. The latest data we have is that he is working with the Chinese to try to destroy the labs."

"That will never fly," said Ben.

"You'd be surprised. They want to destroy them so the West will have no defenses against the virus they're planning to release," said Eichenberg.

"We know for certain they're going to release a virus?"

"We don't know for sure, but we have information to that effect."

"Yeah, that would be bad."

"That's why we need to protect those labs," said Eichenberg. "The Chinese have developed very sophisticated ways to alter a virus to make it more transmissible and more lethal. We think that's their plan to destroy us."

"So, what do you want from me?" Ben asked.

"We want you to stop Williams."

"Don't we have those kinds of assets over there already? I mean, I'm not really in that line of work."

"You've been vetted and cleared for this mission."

"By whom?"

"That information is not available."

"I see."

"Good. I thought you'd understand," said Eichenberg. "Now, you fly out in two days, meet Biendar in Kiev, and take it from there. The Chinese have spies everywhere in Kiev, and so do the Russians. They may be working together on this, so be careful. You need to gather evidence against the colonel that I can present to my superiors who will grant approval for the final execution of your orders. Biendar should be able to help you with this."

"Final execution?"

"Yes. *Final* execution," said Eichenberg coolly. "We need Williams stopped. Here are the case files to review. You know the protocols. I will answer any questions you have before you leave. We will have limited contact after that. Good luck."

*****

CH 16 – Opportunity Knocks

YAF, Ltd. was getting to be a large company—doing work for both the Indian military as well as for civilian agencies. With so many government contracts, Bhatti's top line revenue and bottom-line profits had exploded. However, she was struggling on two fronts. Her latest project wasn't doing well—finding a vaccine or cure for the Hepatitis C. And the second, a long-awaited therapy for Parkinson's disease, wasn't faring much better. Bhatti had made the mistake of prematurely announcing a breakthrough in the Hep C cure a year earlier; however, it had been a miscue, and the real solution was still nowhere in sight. Pressures were increasing, and powerful investors were looking for either a substantial profit or a pound of flesh.

She continued working on the Hep C and Parkinson projects even though she knew her ultimate fate lay with the new project she hoped she would get based on her conversation with Parliament member Ansh Aiyar. It was a call she anxiously awaited and one that finally came.

"Dr. Bhatti, it's good to talk to you again," said Aiyar, connecting with her over the phone.

"Yes, Mr. Aiyar. And what is it that I can do for you?"

"I'll keep this simple," he began. "I'm sure you are aware that your father and I had several joint ventures together—work on the side that yielded significant profits. These were the profits that ultimately funded the startup of YAF and the growth you currently enjoy."

Bhatti knew that some monies used in the company's startup had come from "outside" sources, but she was also well aware that most of the company's funding came from parliament members and other high-worth investors.

"Yes, yes. And what about the project that you thought would be mutually beneficial to us?" she asked.

"Well, you see, your father and I had a mutual friend. Let's call him Mr. B. Well, I spoke with Mr. B about a massive project he is working on, knowing he may need a local lab. Indeed, he is. So, I floated the idea of his using YAF as his source. Although it took some convincing, he now believes that you could be a valuable asset to his cause."

"A billion-dollar asset?"

"Perhaps, yes. Your company would indirectly partner with another company—his company—to provide a cure or therapy for a contagion that company is developing."

"I don't understand."

"Let me be frank. He is working on a disease—a pathogen—and he wants you to work on the cure. That way, you both make money."

"So, he's creating a pathogen? What is he going to do with it?"

"That information isn't necessary right now. Right now, he needs to know if you're interested. We'll get into the details once all the papers are signed."

"What's the name of his company?"

"Labac, LTD."

"Will this generate lots of money for YAF?"

"When all is said and done, you and he … and I … should stand to make millions, or more likely billions, from this little deal. Are you interested?"

"Count me in."

Within six months, Dr. Ghadre, who supervised the operations and research and development arms of YAF, was tasked with the project. However, it was quickly apparent that he wasn't able to move the project along quickly enough to satisfy the demanding Mr. B. So, Bhatti reassigned it to another doctor, Dr. Matisha Malok. Malok became the director of what eventually would become known as the Dark Labs Dept. As for Malok, he was a cousin of Bhatti's and had gone to the same medical school. In all respects, he was just another member of the bigger Bhatti crime family.

But few, other than Bhatti and Ghadre, knew what Malok and his team did deep in the bowels of YAF's headquarters. In fact, the operation was largely "off the books." Funding and expenses were not disclosed—not even to the banks of their auditors.

"Matisha," asked Bhatti, looking over reports in her office, "how are we coming on the therapeutic?"

"The M66 serum?" said Malok.

"Yes, of course. What other therapeutics are you working on?" she answered caustically.

"Not as many as I would like," he sniped back. "But as for 66, we're still not able to produce the near-term results we need to make it saleable to anyone in Parliament, let alone meet the specs given to us by Labac."

"Do you have the updated vials from Labac to test on?"

"They've sent a thousand to us, but every one of our serums has failed against it. I think the pathogen is mutating and creating problems for our cure."

"We promised our investors we would have something ready by the end of this year. It's got to get done! You've *got* to come up with something."

"What about the substance that was uploaded into the Global Compound Database? I thought you were getting a sample of that?"

"We're working on it, but in the meantime, you need to figure out something in case that doesn't pan out. Project Encore is expected to go live on January 1. We have to plan for what we're working on right now to be ready for the rollout. So, proceed on that premise. They'll want millions if not billions of doses no later than the end of March when things begin to warm up outside in America. I don't want anything to be out of place. Do you understand?"

"Yes, Saloni."

But Bhatti was growing impatient. Even though she was in the middle of several other battles, she was intent on retrieving the magical elixir that allegedly cured a dog in the U.S. and offered them a glimpse into a new, wildly profitable, line of drugs to combat aging and, possibly, give them a pathway for a cure for Labac's pathogen. If they could find out what was in that elixir and corner that market, they—she and her company—would be worth, not billions, but *trillions*.

Bhatti shifted gears as she put a call in to her head of security.

"Where are we on that black elixir from the U.S.?" she asked Chip, bitterly. "This is taking too long. I want that vial now!"

"Our assets in the States. operate more carefully than we do here, doctor. It's hard to get things processed quickly. They've got FBI and local authorities all over them right now."

Broad chested but narrow shouldered, Chip was a handsome Indian with dark, deep-set brown eyes, wavy black hair, and a killer smile that could charm the panties off many a young woman. He was smart, cunningly so, and he was well aware of the wide latitude he had to accomplish his directives. But even that had its limitations.

"We're moving too slowly!" barked Bhatti. "I want that vial no later than this Friday. Make arrangements for someone to fly it here if they have to! Do I make myself clear?"

"Yes, doctor."

"Good. Then, Friday I'll expect it in a package on my desk with a bow on it. Got it?"

Right after the call, Dr. Ghadre was unfortunate enough to come into her office.

"Dr. Bhatti," said the doctor, "we have a problem."

"No, we don't, Ghadre. As I told you before, *you* have the problems—not me. And I don't want any of yours to become mine either—especially not right now."

"I received a warning from our mole inside the Ministry of Health. He told me there will be a surprise inspection of our lab within the next two days."

"What?"

"Yes. That's why it's *our* problem," said Ghadre. "We don't have time to cross-reference all the data to ensure it's all consistent. They are apt to find incongruities in the results."

"That can't happen," said Bhatti.

"I know that can't happen. That's why I'm trying to tell you that we have a problem."

Bhatti was quiet. Finally, she said, "I'll make a call."

Ghadre left the office, and Bhatti reached for her personal phone. Looking up a number, she pushed the autodial.

"Hello?"

"Hello, Mr. Aiyar. This is Dr. Bhatti. I have a favor to ask."

*****

CH 17 – Great Release

It was with great fanfare that the current president, Clarice Carpenter, and her administration announced a new program to combat what she claimed was the next disaster to destroy billions of lives worldwide. It was the latest warning from the CDC, the Center for Disease Control, on the new pandemic sweeping the globe.

Born and raised in California, Carpenter's victory had been a surprise. Trailing by more than eight points going into election day, she had shocked everyone by winning every crucial state needed for the electoral majority. In those states, the margin of victory had been a fraction of a percent.

Blonde, blue-eyed, slim and athletic, her comely appearance was thought to have given her the edge over her older, male opponent. But as the campaign had rolled on, her gaffes and insensitive remarks had almost certainly doomed her chances of a victory. Oddly, they had not.

"This is a pressing matter," said Carpenter, using her well-practiced 'serious' look before the legion of cameras. "We now have two cases confirmed in the United States—in Arkansas—and we fear it will quickly spread. I have instructed the CDC to be on high alert as well as the Department of Health and Human Services. The governor of Arkansas is also helping us coordinate efforts. All the experts are afraid the contagion may explode, and I share their concerns. This is a new strain of malaria—a very deadly strain."

Although there had been nothing in the news about the malaria parasite resurfacing prior to the CDC announcement, the president's press conference with her Secretary of Health and Human Services by her side was meant to press home the urgency. Carpenter's HHS Secretary went on to tell the claque press and, thereby, the American people about the dangers now faced by the virulent strain originally discovered in northwestern India.

"This virus has come ashore to America, and we must do everything possible to fight against it," said Herschel Tomlinson, HHS Secretary. "And the best way to do that is to eradicate the source—the mosquitos that carry the disease. That is why we have contracted with a cutting-edge technology firm that specializes in producing sterilized mosquitos. These insects will mate with those carrying the disease but be unable to produce any more. With their short lifespan, the deadly mosquitos will die-off quickly, leaving no offspring to continue propagating this pandemic."

The president then returned to the podium to take questions.

"Madam President, what is the exact parasite that is causing the deaths?" asked a New York reporter.

"I do not know. I will let Dr. Abramson answer that question."

Dr. Abramson was from the CDC and stood behind the others near the podium.

"This would be the *Plasmodium falciparum* and is transmitted through the bite of the *Anopheles* mosquito as we all learned in grade school. The infected mosquito injects the parasite into a person's bloodstream when it bites. Then the *P falciparum* travels to the liver where it reproduces. It's a nasty little bug."

"Madam President," began another reporter—one from an independent, but pariah, news organizations, *BreitLink News*, "I understand that there have been no hospitalizations or deaths as a result of this virus. Why are you taking such extraordinary measures?"

"I have made it my career to address issues very early on and not let them grow to the point where they're much harder to remediate. I have been very successful doing that. This is no different. I'm told by my experts—by key scientists in the field—that West Nile is not to be taken lightly. We must do everything we can *now* to prevent the spread of the disease, and, as President of the United States, I will do just that. I have issued an Executive Order requiring the release of infertile, genetically altered mosquitos into the major urban areas of the United States. As Secretary Tomlinson said, we have a contract with a major bio-lab which provides mosquitos. This is the best way to neutralize the threat to our citizens."

In fact, the contract had gone to an Indian company called Labac which had already begun low-level flights over all major cities in the U.S., releasing billions of genetically altered, sterile mosquitos. At the government's request, the flights had been made during the cloak of night and without any forewarning to the state governors or the city mayors.

"But Madam President, why are urban centers being targeted where there are low levels of mosquito populations? And, as a follow-up, why weren't the governors and mayors advised?"

"To your first question, I think the answer to that is obvious. To the second, they were advised."

"No, I'm afraid it isn't obvious," said the *BreitLink* reporter. "Will you answer the question?"

"I don't know where you went to school, but it clearly wasn't an Ivy League one," she shot back, rolling her eyes. "You see the problem we have in this country is the spread of disinformation by people like you. People who don't understand or can't understand the simple science of things. Why don't you come back to the White House when you get your GED."

Carpenter seemed satisfied with herself for putting the young man in his place. Yet, when it leaked out that the reporter had actually attended the same college she had—Stanford—she made no apologies. "That story is old," she told another reporter later. "It's time to move on."

During the next four months, genetically modified mosquitos were released in every major city. All told, Washington and the states spent billions on the program, and all those profits had rolled into one company: Labac—a company in which many of the major lawmakers had an equity interest.

As soon as the president's press conference finished, the nightly news programs were on fire, spinning the story to generate the most fear and greatest viewership possible.

"This is Brett Major for *WBC Channel 7 News*. Tonight, we have a special report on the latest outbreak of a disease arising from mosquitoes. We learned today, the Carpenter Administration has spent billions in developing and releasing sterile mosquitos to fight the spread of a new disease in America. Todd Lancaster has more. Todd?"

"Thanks, Brett. The CDC in Washington released a report today about an outbreak of a very deadly disease thought only to plague countries in hot, moist climates near the Equator. The president echoed these fears in a press conference. That disease is malaria."

Lancaster continued talking about the problem and the rise in cases as the scene cut to video clips of packed emergency rooms at hospitals and crimson ambulances screaming by with their lights flashing and windshield wipers furiously trying to fight off the pouring rain.

"Like at this hospital in Fairfax, Virginia, doctors are seeing a flood of patients arriving at the doors of their emergency rooms complaining of fever, aches, and pains followed by bouts of sweating and cold chills. Scientists around the country agree that this is a strain that should be taken seriously."

The picture then shifted to an interview clip. The man was middle-aged, heavy-set, and wore a dated, brown wool suit.

"It's a good thing we are releasing these modified mosquitos," said Alan Jurgenson, whose title, Director of the Virginia Board of Health, scrolled below his image. "Our team of scientists are finding that the pathogen borne by the *Anopheles* mosquito is very deadly. The CDC tells us that the mortality rate for those bitten could be as high as seventy-eight percent."

"And when do you believe you will have a cure?" Lancaster asked the doctor.

"Although we are not working on a cure from this facility, I know a cure is being researched at other bio-labs here and abroad. It is only a matter of time when we will have something to roll out to the public," said Jurgenson.

Cutting back to the reporter, Lancaster concluded by saying, "This is something that we will be hearing more and more about as the days pass—especially until we have a cure in hand. This is Todd Lancaster reporting for *Channel 7*."

*****

CH 18 - Kiev

2018

Two days earlier, Ben had said his goodbyes to his family. Now he was sitting in his room at the Presidential Hotel in Kiev, Ukraine, going over the encrypted information he had on his data stick. He was supposed to get a call from his contact, Uri Biendar at precisely 1630 hours; however, it was now 1640, and he had not yet heard from him.

Finally, at 1653, his cell phone rang.

"Hello?" Ben answered, waiting for the designated response.

"Yes, snow is coming, and winter is near," said the voice.

"Yes, but the leaves have not yet turned," Ben responded as instructed.

"I am in the bar in the lobby," said the voice. "You will find me near the back, admiring the beautiful Dnieper River."

Ben took the cramped elevator to the mezzanine floor where he got off and walked briskly across the highly polished, glistening marble tile in the lobby. Passing the front desk, he found an expansive array of low-cut chairs and drink tables spread out near the bar and spotted a middle-aged man sitting towards the back by a window with a stunning river view.

"Uri?" Ben asked.

"Arthur?" replied the man.

"Yes," Ben said, answering to his cover name. "It's good to meet you."

Ben always traveled under an alias when conducting agency business. In this part of the world, he was known as Arthur Maddington—someone who brokered arms sales between governments and also between governments and rogue elements within countries. All of it was under the purview of the CIA, and it often involved illegal as well as legal transactions.

"I assume you've been briefed and are up to speed with the allegations and what is being done here to undermine the work being done at the labs," said Ben, getting right to business.

"Yes," said Biendar. "Perhaps we should take a walk."

"Of course," Ben answered, not bothering to take a seat.

Ben's contact looked just like his picture. He was only slightly older, and he wore a wedding ring—although in the business of espionage, rings mattered little, one way or the other. Already balding, Biendar seemed amiable and more carefree than most in the business. However, Ben had learned that everyone involved in the craft was a Thespian as well, and in most cases a Janus—someone who could play diametrically opposite roles in a moment's notice. As such, he was aware that a colder and more calculating persona of the man lay just beneath the surface.

The two men hailed a cab and were later dropped off at Navodnitsky Park a short distance away. There, among the glorious fountains and carefully pruned trees and bushes, they talked.

"You know, Arthur, this business we're in—it's a dangerous game. Here in Ukraine, there are always those trying to take power while others are trying to hold onto it. Power and people constantly shift from one side to the other. It happens so often that it's sometimes hard to know not only who is on what side, but how many sides are playing in the same game."

"We have the same thing in America, even though it's not always out in the open like it is in other places."

"Here we have outside influences," said Uri. "They have money; they have power. Just look at what happened after our 2014 elections. Your people helped overthrow the sitting president and install one more favorable to your government. I was not happy with this."

"There are many things we have no control over, Uri. I only worry about the things I can control."

Uri smiled. "You're right, my friend, and there are plenty of people here who would have their grandmother off'd just for a few US dollars. It only validates a saying we have."

"Which is?"

"We'd sell our own mother for a few kopeks.'"

"Sometimes people are ordered to do things," said Ben. "Threats against your family work just as well as payoffs, you know."

"You're right. People are ordered to do things and then even when they do them, they're found dead a few days later. Tying up loose ends, they say. There is no honor among thieves. It's a matter of covering your tracks so you don't get caught and don't wind up dead."

Ben nodded, hearing enough of the cliches Uri was throwing out for him.

"So, I'm here to find a rogue officer within the US army ranks," Ben began. "What I need from you are the names of officials in the Ukrainian government who are meeting regularly with a US colonel named Williams – AK Williams. I also need to know of any Russians or Chinese who may be working with him."

"And why is this important?"

"There are people in Washington who believe he is working to destroy some high-security bio-labs here in Ukraine. These labs are vital for the security interests of this country, the United States and our western allies."

"Why is it so vital?"

"They want to eliminate our capacity to develop vaccines or cures to resist a new virus they're planning to release. It would be extremely potent and could be capable of wiping out much of Western civilization."

"And you're sure about this?"

"Yeah. We have solid intel on it," said Ben.

"But if the Russians and Chinese do that, won't they be endangering their own people too?"

"I can only suppose they've already developed a vaccine or cure for it. They've likely inoculated their people against it."

"We would know that, though. We would see evidence that they are giving out mass vaccinations to the people, but I have heard of none of that."

"My understanding is that it's been put into the food supply. The people aren't even aware of it," said Ben.

"I don't believe you."

"It's true. It's possible to develop genetically altered foods that can change someone's immune system."

Biendar crossed his arms and shook his head. "I guess technology is moving faster than any of us could have imagined. But you say there are bio-labs in my country. I am unaware of any such labs."

"These labs are doing good work, researching and developing new vaccines and therapeutics to combat the lethal contagions the Russians and Chinese intend to let loose on the world."

"Who is running these labs?" asked Biendar.

"They are being run by multinational groups."

"That's pretty vague."

"That's all I can give you at this point," said Ben.

Biendar smiled. "But where's the money in all of this? There is always a money trail."

"I'm told there are sources outside Ukraine that are funneling millions here to bribe Ukrainian officials and, apparently, the colonel to take out the labs. We can't let that happen."

Biendar nodded. "It doesn't take much money to create sides these days. Anything is possible."

"From my experience, we're only characters in a long novel and don't get to experience all the chapters. We only find out the truth when the author brings the story to an end."

"If the author lets us live that long," said Biendar.

Ben laughed. "Good point."

"I understand," said the Ukrainian, now smiling. "I will find out what I can. I'll be in touch."

*****

CH 19 – Retrieving the Elixir

Shannon was not feeling well. She had attended an outside party the prior week and had not felt the same since. When she didn't improve within a few days, her mother, Faye, decided to take her to the doctor.

"Well, I think she's got this new malaria that's been going around," said Dr. Oglevee. "The standard malaria is treated with chloroquine phosphate, but we aren't able to prescribe that anymore. Instead, we normally would use an Artemisinin-based, combination therapy or what we call ACT."

"All right, then. Let's do that," said Faye, hesitant to question the doctor.

The doctor shook his head. "Unfortunately, the ACT isn't working on this strain of the disease. We really don't have anything that will fight it, yet."

"What?" Faye answered.

"What about the chloroquine?" Shannon asked, looking pale and anemic.

"Like I said, we can't use that."

"Does it work?"

"Yes, it has worked in the past, but …"

"But what?"

"I'm sorry," said the doctor. "I can't risk my license to prescribe that to you."

"But my daughter is sick!" shouted Faye.

"No, I'm sorry. We have to wait for some new drugs or therapies to come out that can fight this thing. In the meantime, you'll just have to keep her in bed and let her rest. This will take time."

Frustrated, Faye took Shannon home and put her back in bed. She worried about her only daughter and watched the evening news religiously to see what updates or breakthroughs might be in the offing.

***

The next day, Will went to Shannon's place to retrieve the trunk. He had talked with her earlier in the day, and she had said that anytime would be fine. Unfortunately, Faye was home when he rang the doorbell, and she greeted him with a stiff and frosty tone.

"Will? Why are you here?" asked Faye with the look of a strict school marm.

"Hi, Mrs. Evans. I was just in the neighborhood and ..."

"I'm afraid Shannon's not feeling well," she said. "Is there something I can do for you?" The chilly reception did not go unnoticed.

"Yes," Will continued, undeterred, "I spoke with Shannon this morning. And I don't know if you know, but she is keeping a trunk of mine. She said I could come by and pick it up."

"You mean, you *asked* my daughter to keep that wretched trunk for you?" Faye was beside herself, particularly after the horrific experience she and her husband had been subjected to in Egypt because of Will and his Gramma's trunk. They had barely managed to make it out alive.

"I'm sorry, Mrs. Evans. I know I shouldn't have. It was wrong of me. I'm just trying to get the trunk, so it doesn't cause you or your family any more harm."

"She told me about it, Will, and I told her to get rid of it. She's sick—really sick. And I don't know if it's the malaria bug or that stupid trunk of yours that's causing it." Faye stopped and unfolded her arms. "Yes, get that damned thing out of my house! I never want to see it—*or you*—again!"

Will came inside, and as he made his way down the hallway toward Shannon's room, he said to her, "Mrs. Evans, you know that I never wished any harm to come to Shannon or any of your family. I mean that."

"Her room is right down here," Faye answered flatly, going to the door and lightly pushing on it.

Will followed her into Shannon's room where her daughter was sleeping comfortably and unaware that they were there.

"What's wrong with her?" Will asked, taking in the sad image of his close friend who was curled up on the bed in a fetal position, looking frail and helpless.

"The doctor says she has that malaria bug that's going around. They say there's no cure--not yet anyway."

"What?"

"There's supposed to be a cure on the way, but we don't know when. She isn't doing very well, as you can see. I'm afraid for her, Will."

"Well, when she wakes up, will you let me know?"

Faye didn't answer him but let him find the trunk in her closet and quietly pull it out. After he had dragged it outside, Faye said, "Goodbye, Will. Don't come back." She immediately slammed the odor on him. From there, Will labored to get it down from the raised porch. There, he opened the lid.

"Crap!" he said aloud. *They're not here,* he thought. *Well, I'm not going back in there. I'll just have to get this out of here somehow and figure out what to do next.*

Will hung his head forlornly. He needed the elixir, but now he was very concerned about Shannon. There were so many things going on that he didn't understand, and they were all happening at once. He only wished Jack were around to talk to, but he had no idea where he was.

***

Only an hour later, Faye called.

"She's up. She wants you to come over so you can talk. She said to bring something to pour some liquid into. I don't know what that means, but she said you would."

"I'll be right over," said Will.

Will rushed back to the house, and once again, Faye took him to Shannon's room. This time, she was awake, but she looked terrible. Her eyes were sunken, her face was drawn, and she was white as a sheet.

"You don't look so good," said Will, shocked at her appearance. She looked ten years older with age lines beginning to show on her forehead and around her eyes. Her cheeks were sagging as was the skin under her chin.

"Thanks," she muttered in response. "That makes me feel even better." Then, Shannon turned to her mom. "Would you mind?" she asked in a not-so-polite tone.

Faye huffed and left the room but left the door ajar.

"Will, thanks for coming to see me," Shannon said, sitting up straighter in bed. "I guess you got the trunk. Mom said you'd come over for it."

"You're sick."

"Yeah."

"And you have no idea what it is?"

"The doctor said it's that new strain of malaria. I went to Adam's party last week and ..."

"Oh," Will blurted out, surprised. "Uh, well, was it fun?" he added, not knowing what else to say.

"It was okay. There weren't a lot of people there that I knew. You know Adam, right?"

"Uh, yeah. Good guy. I didn't know him in high school, but I've run into him a few times since. Are you two …"

"What?"

"Are you two dating then?"

Shannon shook her head. "Heck no. We're just friends, Will. Nothing more. I just went 'cause he asked me to. That's all. But that's where I think I got this thing. We were outside by the firepit most of the night. There were a lot of people there, and, apparently, a lot of mosquitos. I didn't know they'd released billions of them around here."

"Well, it was a swamp at one time …" said Will. "… back in the eighteenth century before the Revolutionary War. They built our nation's capital on a swamp. Go figure."

Shannon laughed. It was a feeble one, but Will was encouraged by it.

"You're probably looking for those jugs that were in the trunk …" she said. "… the black and white ones. They're the ones with the black elixir you said you needed."

"Yeah, I did notice they weren't in the trunk when I picked it up."

"They're in my closet in a box marked *My Stuff.*"

"That's original," said Will, getting up and walking to where she was pointing.

"Will, I'm really not in the mood. Just go to the box. Inside should be both bottles. But Will …"

"Yeah?"

"If that's the stuff these people are willing to kill for, I think it's better to keep some here just in case they come looking for it at your house. You can claim you don't have anymore, and when they don't find anymore, they'll leave."

"That's why you wanted me to bring these," Will said, holding up two test tubes that he had pilfered from his Chemistry class.

"Yes," she said. "I think it's prudent. Don't you?"

"I guess so."

Will pulled the corks from each of the jugs and laid them on Shannon's nightstand. Then he began pouring some of the elixir from each into the tubes. After reapplying the stoppers, he put the test tubes back in her box.

"What are you doing?" she asked.

"I'm leaving you the tubes, like you said."

"No, Will. *You* take the tubes but leave the jugs here. This is the safest place for them—not at your house. You have what you need in those tubes to get Max back. Let's not get stupid about this."

Will knew she was right, and he replaced the test tubes with the much larger jugs.

"Are you going to contact the dognapers, now?" she asked.

"We're waiting for them to contact us," said Will.

"When are you going to get the police involved?"

"I don't know. They're not going to be interested in a dognapping caper. I think they'd just mess things up for me."

Faye re-entered the room. "Will, it's time you leave. Shannon needs her rest," She looked at the jugs on the nightstand and the test tubes in his hands filled with black-ish elixir. Shaking her head, she said, "I don't even want to know. Just leave Will. Just leave."

"Will, call me," said Shannon, sitting up in her bed.

"I'll check on you to see you how you're doing. Hopefully, you'll be better soon," he said.

Will left, and Faye closed the door. Once they reached the front door, she said again, "Will, I don't want you contacting my daughter. Do you hear me? Now, leave and don't come back."

Will left with a heavy heart. The thought of not having Shannon in his life was almost more than he could bear. So, he shifted his thoughts to Max. *I need to save my dog right now,* he thought. *I can only do one thing at a time.*

*****

CH 20 - Luoyang

1964

The old trunk had been useful, carrying their trove of relics from one part of the globe to another. However, the black mandarin wood from Sri Lanka had begun to show signs of weakening, and Luka feared it might not last much longer.

"It's a good thing we have this new trunk," said Luka, running his hand over it. "It's like a tank. Nothing can damage this one!"

"I wouldn't say that," said Brandon. "It's made of stone, so it's very heavy and, if you drop it from high enough, I'm sure it will break wide open."

Luka pounded on it with his fist. "Seems pretty tough to me," he answered. "We'll keep our stuff in here from now on. It will be safe."

Tulia, on the other hand, was not so sure. Looking at Brandon, she said, "I think I'll hold on to the wooden one—just in case."

Brandon only stayed a few days before returning to London. Meanwhile, Luka and Tulia finished their plans to go to China. However, when it came time to take the children to Chicago and be dropped off at Tulia's cousin's place, she hesitated.

"I thought this was a good idea," said Tulia, "but now I don't know."

"What are you worried about?" asked Luka. "Melena is a good, reliable person. You said so yourself. Heck, she and her husband, Ray, have raised four kids themselves, and they all turned out alright."

"But they're all the way up in Chicago," she answered. "That's a long way."

"It's not far at all, Tulia! We're going to China, for god's sake."

Melena was, indeed, a good egg. Tulia's mother, Dumitra, had two siblings in Romania, but her sisters were older—Irina and Sorina—and each had sizeable families of their own. Sorina still lived in Laşi, Romania, with her family. But it was Irina who had married an American and moved to the United States well before the opening salvos of World War II. Her daughters, Tassa and Melena, and her son, Stephan, still lived in Chicago.

"You're right, Luka. I shouldn't worry. But that's what mothers are supposed to do!"

After taking the children to Chicago, the pair flew out of O'Hare airport, and three days and multiple legs later, their prop plane finally touched down in Beijing, China. Although many in the United States still referred to the Chinese capital as Peking, its official name under the communist party was Beijing. But what lay ahead for them from there was an arduous journey from the capital to the city of Luoyang where Luka and Tulia would meet a man who claimed to have bi-cong discs for sale and perhaps other mysterious treasures.

The trip from Beijing to Luoyang—over five hundred forty miles—would not be easy, and it would take three full days traveling six hours per day. The only means to Luoyang was via a series of crammed, regional buses that traveled on rock-covered, two-lane rural roads which occasionally narrowed into a single, rutted, dirt lane.

Tulia and Luka threw their travel trunk, called a steamer, onto the top of the dilapidated 1940s vintage Chinese bus in Beijing and watched as the driver lashed it to the rails. At that point, they could only hope it didn't bounce off the roof and into a bottomless pit along the way. In that event, there would be no way to ever recover it.

In 1959, Luoyang was a backwater city within a backwater country with few modern, Western conveniences. The city's importance since its heyday two thousand years earlier had declined significantly, and by the twentieth century, it held fewer than one hundred thousand people—small for China. During its salad days, it had been a significant cultural center and capital for the Zhou Dynasty, when, for over five hundred years from 770 to 256 BCE, it had been the center of many trade routes to the West. By the 1950s, it had become merely an agricultural hub—one of hundreds that kept food supplies funneled to the big cities on the East Coast where the power and influence of the Communist Party lived.

When Luka and Tulia arrived in Luoyang, they got off the bus and collected their trunk and other luggage which had already been unceremoniously tossed from the top of the bus to the dusty ground. After watching the bus roar off to its next destination, spewing thick diesel fumes behind it, they struck out to find a place to stay. All around them were the imposing peaks of the Taihang Mountains which, as legend held, contained even greater secrets from China's ancient past.

The small, two-room boarding house they finally found was the only inn available, and it lacked even rudimentary conveniences that Luka and Tulia were used to like running water and indoor plumbing.

"Straw cots?" Tulia muttered, shaking her head. "I don't mind 'roughing it Luka,' but this is ridiculous."

"Wait 'till you see the outhouse," Luka said, laughing.

Once settled, Tulia went to the innkeeper's room downstairs. "Hello, we want to go to the Shaolin Temple. We are supposed to meet someone. Do you know how we can get there?" she asked.

"Shaolin," answered the owner, only understanding the single word of English. He nodded and smiled before leaving her without saying another word and without coming back. It was clear to her that getting help would be harder than they thought.

It took another day, but the two travelers were finally able to find their contact in town: an artifacts collector and archeologist known as Zhau Suyin who was said to live near the Shaolin Temple. There were no telephones or other modern forms of communication in the village, so they set out on foot to find his place of work. Using the address which Tulia had scrawled on a piece of paper they carried with them, they asked enough people in town to find the small, thatched home. Knocking on the only door, they waited, and finally, a small woman of not more than five feet answered. With long, graying hair tied in a braid down her back, she bowed respectfully as she saw they were not Chinese.

"*Wǒ kěyǐ bāng nǐ ma?* (Can I help you?)" she asked.

Tulia looked at Luka and shrugged, not knowing what she was asking.

"Zhau Suyin?" Luka asked, pointing inside.

The woman nodded and left the door. Soon, a slight, middle-aged man of about forty approached the entry.

"May I help you?" he asked in perfect English.

"Ah! Mr. Zhau. It is good to meet you. I am Luka, and this is Tulia. We've corresponded with you about the bi-cong discs."

"Oh, of course," said Zhau, smiling. "Please come in."

Zhau gestured, directing them to have a seat on two pieces of decrepit furniture that were mildewed and severely rotted. One had a torn pillow with its stuffing bursting from the side, while the other had a broken leg which was propped up by a stack of three, hardback books.

"Did you just arrive today?"

"Yes," said Luka. "We just got in. It was a long journey from Beijing."

"Of course. Many buses, I assume."

"Yes, too many," quipped Tulia.

"Well, as you can see, our people have been through much in recent years," said Zhau, pointing outside. "Only recently have we formed a collective just outside the city. Before that, the land of the wealthy families was seized and redistributed to everyone as a single group. However, no one farmed it, and it fell into disuse. Crops were largely not planted, and those that were, were not harvested. Our people starved. In Luoyang alone we lost four thousand people during the past five years."

"That's awful!" exclaimed Tulia.

"Yes, it was a terrible time, but it's not something we are allowed to talk about."

"I read that millions throughout China have died from the food shortage during this time," said Tulia.

"The number is far higher," said Zhau. "Some say up to forty or fifty million."

"My god," murmured Luka.

"Yes. It was all due to our leadership."

"You mean your Chairman. Chairman Mao," said Tulia.

"I cannot mention names, or my wife and I will be in danger. You must understand that is how things are here. No one may speak against the authorities, or they will disappear. I do not wish to disappear, and if you know what's good for you, you won't speak of such things either."

Luka nodded. "I understand," he said. "I lived under Stalin's rule until he died in 1953. Things did not improve greatly after that, but at least people were no longer dragged from their beds and shot in the middle of the night."

"Ah, yes. The utopia they call communism," said Zhau. "But again, we must be careful. The walls have ears. I believe our neighbors spy on us; they will turn us in if they overhear something or we get on their bad side. That's why my wife and I keep to ourselves. We don't wish to be seen as a problem in our community. It is those people who disappear."

"Yes," Luka answered.

"Well, enough of that. Please tell me what you are looking for," said Zhau. "You say you are interested in bi-cong discs. Is that right?"

"Yes," said Tulia, "I remember seeing one when I was at the University of Bucharest. It was on display at the museum in the city. I found it fascinating."

"Ah, yes. I simply call them bi-discs. They are more common than other relics, especially here."

"They are common?"

"Yes. There are other things that are much more rare."

"What?"

"We call them Dropa stones."

"Dropa stones?" asked Tulia. "I don't know of these."

"Dropas are very, very strange discs that belonged to a dynasty well before any other in China."

"Before the Zhou Dynasty twenty-five hundred years ago?" asked Tulia.

"Oh yes," said Zhau. "Even before the Xia Dynasty four thousand years ago."

"Before? I thought the Zhou was the first dynasty," said Tulia.

Zhau winked at them. "So does everyone else, but it is not true. There were other dynasties before. There is one that goes back, not four thousand, but *twelve* thousand years."

"Twelve thousand? That's not possible."

"Yes, it is fact."

"What was that dynasty?" asked Luka.

"They called it the Di yi Dynasty, and there are relics from that period. There is a man in a small village near Xianyang. He claims he has such a stone—a Dropa stone—from that era. He says it came from Nepal or someplace near there."

"How did he get it?" asked Tulia.

"I do not know, but we can ask him if you will travel with me tomorrow. Will that be acceptable to you?"

"Let us know what time to be here," said Luka without hesitation.

*****

CH 21 – Mr. Big

"When do you expect to have the anodyne ready?" The voice was garbled intentionally in the event listening devices had been surreptitiously installed to record the call.

"We're working on that," answered Saloni Bhatti. She only knew him as Mr. B but referred to him as 'Mr. Big.'

It was a monthly call between Dr. Bhatti and the man to whom she reported. He was a major investor in her company but kept a low profile and was as secretive and mysterious as the organization for which he worked.

"Then what is your progress?" he asked, not yielding to the brush-off. "You said that last month. If you can't figure it out, then we'll find someone who can."

"Mr. B, we will find a cure. I told you at the beginning of this project that it would take time. Research and development of therapeutic drugs takes time."

"This is the most important thing the Circuit is working on. Do you understand? It's what we've been working on for two hundred years, so we cannot screw this up! We must meet the timeline we agreed on!"

"I understand, Mr. B," said Bhatti. "I have a new source which we believe will lead to a breakthrough. We should have a sample soon. If things go well, we should be able to reverse engineer the compound and re-create it in the lab."

"Is it DNA or RNA based?"

"I don't know," said Bhatti. "We are prepared for either. Our labs work with both, so we can go quickly in either direction if we need to. What about your part?"

"What about it?"

"Well, we need the disease spread widely around the world so that my cure is warranted, don't we? It makes little sense to have a cure and not have a disease or pathogen that requires curing. Am I right?"

"That was completed two years ago. The pieces have been in place for some time to be able to disperse it globally. We now have willing partners in this. You are aware we are using non-profit foundations as the cover for the operation. They have successfully secured contracts with national governments to assist us. In preparation, we have produced billions of delivery systems in facilities worldwide. Those are being released as we speak, taking care of your problem. I assure you, there will be plenty of need for your cure, Dr. Bhatti. But that's why it's imperative that you have your jabs ready for shipment. You need to do *your* part. Do I make myself clear?"

"Yes. I understand."

"Good. So, when we discuss this again in two weeks, I'm sure you'll have better answers to my questions. All I want to hear from you is 'Yes, we tested it, and all systems are go for launch.'"

"I didn't realize we were sending missiles into space," said Bhatti, sarcastically.

"If you don't have your cure ready, I assure you that you will be the first I strap to the side of one and send up."

The line went dead, and Bhatti knew he wasn't bluffing. The thought of her screaming as the rocket fired up its thrusters sent a cold chill through her body.

*****

Part 2
CH 22 – Ferreting Out the Truth

Kierney carried many different passports which held many different nationalities and names. While in India and other UK-related countries, he went by the name Al Kierney; in other countries it was someone else. Although the State Department surmised Kierney might be his real name, they said they didn't know for sure. Most recently, there had been an Interpol BOLO (Be on the Look Out) for him under the name Juan Aquilera in Peru and Ecuador, suggesting he had traveled there recently. This information was immediately passed along to Jack in the field.

Yet, Jack was also made aware of other facts. Within his dossier, he read that after the destruction of biolabs in Ukraine during the Russia-Ukraine Conflict in the early 2020s, new locations were found for the work. Interest shifted to an area already well established for big pharma experimentation: New Delhi, India. It was a huge metropolis with millions of people—just the place for activity of this kind to get lost in the shuffle. At the same time, it was the worst place in the event of an accidental or intentional release of a lab contagion.

Other information offered to him included a list of the known biolabs in Delhi—at least those working with military-grade specimens. However, since these were already well known, the State Department and CIA believed that Kierney might plan to attack other labs that were less well-guarded. These were known as Cavelabs. They were technically legal laboratories, but ones with shady management or operations that were tied to underground groups. Essentially, they were black market labs where anything and everything could be developed with little oversight or accountability, but ones the CIA believed offered the best chances to develop promising new drugs. These Cavelabs were the ones on which Jack was to concentrate his efforts.

Jack landed at Indira Gandhi International and immediately got to work, taking to the streets of New Delhi to find answers. Although Mumbai was generally considered the pharma capital of India, Delhi was a close second. There were hundreds of companies and thousands of labs throughout the country, and pinpointing possible Cavelabs would be daunting, even with the CIA data he had been given.

Jack's partial list of Cavelabs had come from military sources. These included labs that supplied the Indian armed forces with services, all ranging from processing routine medical lab tests to Level Four bio-hazard research. Since the top labs were heavily guarded by military units or by local police, the bigger concerns for the State Department were the Cavelabs that were less secured and easier targets for Kierney. If they were conducting bio-hazard research under such lax conditions, Kierney, they believe, could take advantage of it and cause immeasurable damage.

For Jack, this mission was made more difficult than was necessary. Unlike his mission to Shanghai a year earlier, he had been given no diplomatic immunity in India. The new State Department had told him such immunity was unnecessary. In reality, Jack knew they didn't want to grant it because they didn't want the risk of being implicated should the mission go badly. They wanted to be able to disown him as a "rogue" agent if things went south. No, this time, Jack was on his own.

His first stop was to meet with Uri Biendar, and it wasn't long before the now-bald-headed Biendar contacted him at his New Delhi hotel. Sitting at the bar, they both ordered martini's—for Uri one with vodka, no olives, and for Jack, one with gin, four olives.

"You like your olives, I see," said Biendar smiling and taking his first gulp.

"Yeah, I like my martinis with olives and a splash of gin," said Jack. "You don't like olives?"

"Ah, I can take 'em or leave 'em. Mostly, I leave 'em."

"So, tell me something, Uri. Tell me what you know about the bio labs in New Delhi. Talk to me."

"What do you wish to know? I only understand that you're looking for some as well as a large sawmill in India. They don't have many of those as you know, so it may be difficult to find one." Biendar was talking in code, but Jack knew exactly what he was referring to.

"Perhaps, but I'm told you were the best place to start if I wanted to find one."

"My understanding is that there is a mill that has been very unruly and poorly managed. It is causing a lot of people a lot of problems."

"Where can I find this mill?" asked Jack.

"I don't know which one it is or where, but I will get you the location as soon as I start digging. Is that the only thing you're looking for right now?"

"What about the owner of the mill?"

Biendar took another big gulp, nearly draining the rest of his martini. He raised his hand and motioned for the bartender to bring fresh refills for both of them. "We should find the owner when we find the mill, don't you think?"

Jack smiled. He'd been in the business long enough to know when he was being baited. Most times, he acted as if he didn't know and chased the bait to see where it would lead. In this case, he thought another approach was in order, given the age and experience of his contact.

"Not necessarily. It's my understanding that the two are linked only by the owner's interest to destroy the mill."

"Ah, that sawmill," said Biendar, giving a pause to see if there was any further reaction from Jack. But when there wasn't, he added, "For that, you may wish to talk to your Chief of Mission here, Mr. Herron. He may have some information that I cannot provide."

"Like what? Is it related to the sawmill?"

"Yes, or the owner you seek. He is likely to know much more than I."

"But you will get me what you can find out, right?"

"Of course. We will talk again soon. I should have more information for you so you can complete your transaction and find your way home." Biendar downed the rest of this martini and left the bar.

Jack was left to nurse his drink. He was thankful for the short meeting. Sometimes encounters could last hours as the contact would have many drinks and possibly dinner—all paid for by Jack's State Department—before releasing his or her information. By that time, Jack typically had to pour himself into a taxi to find his way back to his hotel room.

The next morning, Jack hopped on his computer. He had done some work before leaving Washington but hoped to gain more insight into the nature of the Cavelabs once he arrived on Indian soil. Given little more to go on by Biendar, he began looking at Indian pharma companies with government contracts—not only with India but indirectly with parties dealing with the US government. Finding these might lead him to those who owned the Cavelabs or to the group led by Sawmill Kierney.

Online there were many websites of pharma companies operating in New Delhi. It wasn't easy, but by following the trail of published government contracts issued by the Indian Parliament during the previous ten years, Jack came up with a list of "new" non-military contract recipients within the pharmaceutical industry. *This,* he thought, *could be my new Cavelab list.* There were fewer than a dozen which had any significant size—those over two thousand crore in revenue or about $200 million, but all had operations within New Delhi.

Going to several of these Cavelab companies under the guise of one Roger Mankoviz, a chemical salesperson working for a CIA shell company called Dalco Inc., Jack began talking to operations and technical staff to find out more. It was a time-consuming process, and one of elimination rather than identification. In his undercover role, Jack even wore a fake mustache and thick, black-rimmed glasses to alter his appearance.

"So, you're happy with your chemical supplier?" Jack asked, talking to the purchasing agent of Ramco Labs, a major company in New Delhi.

"Yes, quite so," the purchasing manager, Amahi, answered cheerfully. "They have high quality and excellent delivery schedules. I really don't think there will be anything you can do to beat what they offer. They've supplied us for many years, and the owners are quite happy with them."

"Well, we *can* beat the prices you have for some of your drug compounds. For those on this sheet, we can probably reduce them by 3.4 percent. That is a sizeable savings over a ten-year period."

"Perhaps, but, like I said, we are fine with the reliability of the products and their quality. It's not worth it for us to change, but thank you for stopping by."

"May I ask you another question?" Jack asked as he was readying to leave. "Do you have any competitors in the area who have grown significantly from government contracts during the last few years? You know, someone that you think may be using insiders in Parliament to ensure contracts are directed their way?"

The purchasing agent paused. "You mean bribery?"

"Well, let's just say they make payments to facilitate the government's decision in their favor. You know ..." Jack said.

"I don't usually say anything negative about others," she said, "but there *is* one who is causing us problems."

"Oh, really? Would you mind telling me who? I'd like to avoid them if I can. We don't like doing business with companies that aren't ethical."

"I understand, but I don't feel comfortable ..."

"I just wondered if it were one that I had on my list. I wouldn't stop there and offer my services if I knew they were doing something illegal. That's not the type of company we are, you know. I wouldn't want to help someone like that at your expense."

Jack smiled at her, hoping to disarm her further.

"Well, if you must know. I've heard things about *two* companies, but I don't know for sure which, if either, is involved."

"Which ones?"

"One is called YAF. I'm not sure what it stands for. The other is called Labac Labs, Ltd. or L3."

"So, you think they're making payments under the table?"

"That's what we think. YAF has gotten five of the last six contracts from Parliament. You must understand the culture here. We have become a powerful, first-world country, but we still fall back on ancient customs. One of those, unfortunately, is graft and corruption. They've tried for years to get rid of it, but it persists. Money talks. It always has and always will."

"Sadly, you're right."

"But more than that. We've hired employees who have worked for YAF and Labac. I say 'worked' but that turned out not to be true. They were still on their payroll and were sent here to infiltrate us and steal our company secrets. In another case, we discovered the person was sabotaging our production runs. We had terrible quality issues during that time because of the tainting of our products. We fired all these employees, but you can't bring charges because of the government labor regulations."

"I see," said Jack. "Well, I'll be sure to steer clear of YAF and Labac Labs, then. Thanks for your time, and if you change your mind about our services, here's my card."

These were the best tips he'd gotten all week, and he started immediately to find out more about these two companies.

*****

CH 23 – The General

2018

Ben loved to smoke, but in the states that was nearly impossible. However, in the Ukraine, it was still common, and he eagerly took out a filtered Credo—one made in the US but distributed in the Ukraine and elsewhere. He lit it, waving his hand back and forth to extinguish the match before inhaling the first puff. He felt guilty; he knew it was horrible for him, but the nicotine calmed his nerves when he was on assignment. It was the one thing he looked forward to every time he left the country.

Having met earlier with Uri Biendar, he was now scheduled to meet with General Matviy Pipenko. Even though he believed Pipenko to be an enemy of the United States on a political level, the Ukrainian military was considered an ally. As for Ben, he was allegedly there to discuss a pending arms sale by the U.S. to Ukraine—one that was to be made "off the books" and without the direct involvement of Congress.

"Ah, Mr. Maddington, it is good to meet you," said the general, knowing only Ben's alias. "I don't normally meet with individuals I don't know well. But you come highly recommended, so I thought, 'what the heck.'" He laughed.

Pipenko was a large, barrel-chested man with an even bigger belly. He enjoyed life and played it to the edge. Having risen through the military ranks with a combination of cunning and manipulation, he knew it took more than talent to get to the top. Blackmail and bribery were not outside his wheelhouse, and it wasn't beyond imagination to believe he was capable of and had committed things far worse.

"You haven't met me before because I prefer beer over vodka," said Ben, breaking the ice.

"Ha! We don't drink that beer piss here. We drink the vodka, just like our Russian brothers and sisters." Pipenko turned and raised two fingers into the air signaling the waitress to bring them two shots. "So, when will I get my shipment?" the general asked, as the shapely attendant placed two shot glasses in front of them along with the remainder of the clear, fresh bottle.

"It's coming," said Ben. "It's coming through Ankara. It should arrive at your port at Odesa within the next few weeks."

Pipenko poured two more shots from the once-full bottle and downed his quickly before refreshing his glass for a third.

Ben took his too and watched as the general poured another for him. He knew how things like this worked and had planned for a long night.

"General, I've heard some things about one of our colonels, Colonel AK Williams. Do you know him?"

"Williams, yes. I know the colonel. Sharp man—very shrewd. Why?"

"I heard he may be in the black market for some MANPADS and ATGWs. Why would he need those?" Ben was referring to man-portable air defense systems and anti-tank guided missiles.

"I have no idea. I would think he could get those from his own government. Are you Americans running out of weapons?" Pipenko smiled.

"No, but we could be running out of money to make them," said Ben laughing, and taking another shot. "I agree. I think he would order what he needed through military channels. That's why it's perplexing to us."

"I wish I could help, but the colonel is a very mysterious person. Do you know him?'

"No, not at all."

"Well, he's a bit of an odd duck, as you say in America. I don't know how he got to his rank."

"What do you know about bio-labs here in the country?" Ben asked.

Pipenko suddenly grew quiet.

"General? I've heard these bio-labs are involved in researching vaccines and cures for global diseases."

The general's good-humored demeanor returned quickly. "Oh, that! Yes, of course, we have several labs in Ukraine doing good works. They are developing new cures from what I understand."

"What about new viruses?"

"New viruses?"

"Yes, I've been told they are developing those too."

"Oh, it's not what you think. They're only working on those to defend against other countries that might be creating them to harm the rest of the world," he quickly added. "You know, like China."

"So, they're developing viruses too?"

"Yes, of course China is doing this. They've been at this for a long time."

"Do we know at what stage of development they are with these things?" Ben asked.

"No, but that is why we have our bio-labs. We are only creating new strains of viruses so we can make cures for them. Then, we'll have them stockpiled so they can be distributed in case China releases one of their pathogens."

"What about the Russians?"

"What about them?"

"Are they developing viruses too?"

"Perhaps, but not like the Chinese. There is a race between them, from what I understand. You know that your government is involved too. You've been funding our labs for years and overseeing most of the work."

"That's why I need to find the colonel. I'm trying to make sure he doesn't interfere with that work."

"Colonel Williams? I would say yes. I think he's trying to sabotage the efforts here in Ukraine. I have information that suggests he's running his own militia of sorts outside the U.S. chain of command. We jokingly call it William's War. He's gone rogue on you, and that's why they sent you here."

"So, is he planning to bomb some labs?"

"He already has. He blew up one in Mumbai and one here in Delhi last year. I can get you evidence," said the general. "But in the big picture, why are you so concerned about Colonel Williams? He is only a pawn in a bigger war."

"Even if he is, he's looking for weapons outside the normal channels. He could create a major international incident. I need to know where he is," said Ben.

"But *you* deal outside the normal channels," countered the general.

Ben smiled. "Sure, but these are outside of my outside channels, and I don't like that. Besides, I don't like competition," he said laughing. "I want to know who might be trying to undercut me in the marketplace. You understand that, right? It's just business."

Pipenko chuckled. "Of course. You American capitalists. It's about money."

"Yes, always."

"But what is money? Huh? When you have complete power, you don't need money. You can get whatever you want, whenever you want. Money is for those who must still pay for their power. When you have the kind of power I have—political power—you don't need money."

"I get that," said Ben. "I'm just trying to scrape by on whatever I can get. That's all."

"As for Colonel Williams. I don't know where he is now, but for a few dollars, I can get that for you."

"I thought you just said money wasn't important to you?"

"Ah, yes, but you still need it to buy vodka once in a while."

*****

CH 24 – Hazen Park I

"What do we do now?" asked Raya, sitting at the kitchen table with her son. "We haven't heard anything from the dognapers in days."

"We just have to wait," said Will. "They're supposed to call later today and give us instructions."

"What time?"

"I don't know. They wouldn't say."

The hours passed. Will checked his phone every five minutes to make sure he hadn't missed a call, and Raya tried to keep herself busy by listening to a murder mystery podcast on her earbuds.

More time passed, and the sun had long since set. Both Will and his mother thought it was over—that they were going to lose their beloved Max. But at 9:30, they heard the sound of Will's phone.

"Hello?" Will answered, jumping on the call.

"Do you have the black serum?" The voice was foreign—Will thought most likely Indian. It was halting and clipped.

"Yes," answered Will.

"You will take it to this address. You will leave it. Then you will ..."

"Wait a minute. No, we will not just leave it and hope we get our dog back. We will get Max at the same time we give you the black stuff."

"That's not going to work."

"Then, you won't get the serum."

"We will have to kill your dog."

"Either way; you won't get the vial."

There was a pause on the line.

"We will exchange the dog for the vial at that address. You must not have anyone with you, including the police or anyone else. Just you."

"There will be *two* of us."

"Who?"

"My mom. She insists on coming."

"Be at Hazen Park—corner of Reno and Tilden. Take the Hazen Trail. You'll find us. Be there at 10:30--in one hour. At 10:31, we leave." *Click.*

"Do you know where that park is?" Will asked his mom.

"No. We'll have to look it up."

They found the park. It was inside the city limits of DC, just off Connecticut Avenue—a major street. But there was just one problem. Although not a large park, it was secluded—very secluded.

"It's going to be very dark in the park, Will. It doesn't look like there are any street or trail lights in there. Two trails cut through the center of it—here and here," she said marking them with her finger on the screen, "but neither are meant for car. They're wide, but they're walking trails. We'll be vulnerable."

Will could see exactly what she was saying. Looking online from the street view, it was clear the park was not well maintained. It was thick with untrimmed trees and dense overgrown shrubbery, and once inside, there were no lights or easy means of escape.

"We can't bring help," said Will.

"Then what do we do?" Raya asked.

"Jack has one of those dashcam recorders in his car. It's the kind that can send images over cell towers. We can hook that up and beam the signal out of the park to someone, so if we get into trouble, they can come help."

"Our next-door neighbor is a cop," said Raya. "I'll ask him if he'll help us."

"I don't think that's a good idea, Mom. He'll want to bring some squad cars. That'll draw too much attention. We can't risk that."

"Let me ask him. I won't give him too much information—just enough to see what he says."

***

It was getting late, and Will wrapped the vial of dark black elixir in a bag his mom used for giving wine bottles as gifts at parties she attended. Then, with the dashcam set up in the car, they set out.

The park was only ten minutes from the house, and as they approached the corner where the park entrance stood, they could see how dark it was.

"Will things even show up on that dashcam?" Raya asked. "I think it's too dark for that."

"I dunno," Will answered. "But here it goes."

Will's palms were sweating as he turned on the camera and began the slow drive into the park. There was a large sign at the entrance that gave the park information.

Hazen Park
Open: sunrise to sunset
No visitors after dark allowed.
Violators subject to fines and arrest

Passing the sign, they continued into the park until they reached the end of the blacktopped road where they found ten lined spaces for visitors to park. To one side were two brown posts spaced about eight feet apart—just enough for a car to squeeze through even though another sign specifically read, "No Unauthorized Vehicles."

"This is where that Hazen Trail starts," said Will. "I think we're supposed to walk back in there …" Then, he turned to his mom, "But there's no way in hell I'm *walking* back there."

"Then what are we going to do?" Raya began.

But before she got an answer, Will re-engaged the car and drove between the two posts and onto the creepy trail.

The trail was a dirt road with two worn tracks where many years of car tires had driven with a worn, grassy strip in between. It was eerie driving the car along such a narrow trail, and Will only hoped it wouldn't narrow so much that he'd become trapped with no way to turn around and no way to escape.

"Where is our neighbor tonight?" asked Will. "I thought you said he agreed to help?"

"He said he'd be on duty, but he rigged this camera to stream directly to his precinct car. He said he wouldn't get involved in a missing dog issue, but if we found ourselves in danger, he would come."

"Great, so he's already seen us violate park rules by entering after dark and going down this trail. The first thing he'll do is handcuff us and take us away!"

"I suppose, but I don't think he'd do that. He's not that kind of guy."

The car moved at a snail's pace with its headlights on full. Overhead was only a sliver of a crescent moon which offered them little aid if something happened to their own lights. To Will, it felt like walking through a graveyard at midnight—someplace he never wanted to be, especially alone.

They rolled down the windows just in case there was a sound that might alert them to someone nearby. But there were only crickets chirping for a mate and the occasional hooting of a barn owl in the high trees. However, their trail paid no attention to any of it and continued to lay a path ahead as far as their highlights would let them see.

"Do you see anything?" asked Will, worried he'd missed a sign, a turnoff, or some other indication they were on the wrong route.

"No, I didn't see anything." Now, Raya was worried too. She wrapped her fingers into a knot on her lap, keeping a vigilant lookout for anything out of the ordinary.

When they came to the end of the trail, Will's greatest fear became realized. There was no exit out of the park. They were trapped.

"What do we do?" asked Raya.

"What time do you have?" Will answered urgently.

"I've got 10:32."

"They said they'd leave at 10:31," Will said.

"Let's backup and go back along the trail," said Raya nervously. "I think they're playing a game to throw us off-balance and take us by surprise."

Will put the car in reverse and began backing up, retracing the dirt trail which they'd taken through the park. However, this time he only had the dim, backup lights to illuminate the way.

Then, Raya noticed something.

"Will, the dash cam. It's all snowy."

Indeed, the picture was white. There were lines of static running through it as if it was stuck on a bad channel. Raya lightly thumped it with her fingers hoping to clear it, but nothing changed.

"Let me try switching it," said Will, turning toward the front of the car.

"Look out!" yelled Raya.

Even though Will was driving slowly, he wasn't prepared for what happened next.

*****

CH 25 – Road to Xianyang

1964

Travel outside Beijing, Luoyang or any other major city in China was not easy. The roads, when passable, were largely dirt and held deep ruts which could flatten tires quickly. That would be a major problem too, as there were no places along those routes to get tires repaired or replaced, especially in the rural outback. To return to a major city, one would need to know a friend in a nearby village who could offer assistance or to pray there was a frequent bus that had a route along that stretch of road. Otherwise, reaching a place that could help might take days or even weeks.

However, Zhau had assured Luka and Tulia that his truck—a Nanjing NJ130—would go over or through almost anything. Yet, after seeing the black, six-year-old truck, Luka had his doubts. Wisely, however, he kept them to himself.

It was July, and the temperatures that week had hovered in the mid-90s F — hot for that part of China. The road out of Luoyang was all dirt; in fact, it was three hundred seventy kilometers of dirt to Xianyang. Averaging not more than thirty-five kilometers per hour plus stops, it would take them nearly nine hours to reach it without stops. Zhau had planned to be back in Luoyang by late the next day. But they were lucky in one respect. Zhau had a large family with many friends in the expanded geographical area. And although the truck could allegedly run through almost anything, it still needed working fan belts to operate. Unfortunately for this crew, their belts went on strike and refused to work anymore.

It was a broad, flat plateau with waving prairie grass for as far as the eye could see. Like Montana in the US, the plain was spectacular in its breadth and scope. The immediate feeling was one of freedom and mental catharsis with the big sky country eliciting a sense of power and self-determination. However, when the fan belt broke, the radiator quickly overheated, and white steam began pouring out from under the hood.

"Now what?" Luka asked, annoyed by the incident.

"We're quite a distance from Sanlizhen," said Zhau, "but it's only about twenty kilometers to the next town of Banjieshan from here. I have extra coolant and diesel in the boot. There is enough coolant to get us there, but we'll need to make several stops to let the system cool, so we don't burn a piston. It will just take time. Banjieshan is on the steps of the mountains over there." Zhau pointed to the beginnings of the mountain range which appeared as a low, purple-gray ridge on the horizon.

"How long then?" Tulia asked.

"Oh, I would say it will take a day to walk one way—two days round-trip. Or it will take half a day to drive slowly with stops."

"I guess we drive," said Luka.

Every fifteen minutes, they stopped to let the engine cool, and it took another thirty minutes to get the temperature down to where they could continue. But eventually, the village of Banjieshan came into view, and by nightfall, their truck sputtered and lurched into the central square before giving one last belch and dying.

"I'll find my cousin," said Zhau. "He'll be able to help us get back on the road with full power again."

Zhau tracked down his cousin, Huan, and was able to convince him to put them up for the night. Meanwhile, his family was gracious and accommodated them with a hearty Chinese meal of steamed buns filled with mutton, zongzi, and steamed vegetables. After supper, the family's five children—aged three to eleven—put on a little show they had put together on their own. Singing while Zhau's cousin played a four-string Pipa, or Chinese lute, they joyously danced—thrilled at the chance to show their talents to outsiders.

After the children were in bed, Luka and Tulia sat down with Zhau and Huan to share a late-night cup of green tea. Huan was not as educated as Zhau, but he had a keen intellect and understood what was happening in his country.

"We have had hard times," Huan said, his words translated by Zhau. "Not enough food has been grown, and what is grown is stripped from our families and our village to take elsewhere."

"Have there been many deaths in your town?" asked Luka.

"Yes. I would say a quarter of the people have died within the last five years. We try to give our food—to share what we have—but it's often not enough. As you can tell from my children, they barely have enough to eat. Many days, my wife and I go without a meal so they can have something."

The next morning, Luka and Tulia stayed at the hut while Zhau and his cousin looked at the truck. Rain came down in sheets, sometimes pelting the ground sideways as the winds gusted, unobstructed in the open plain. However, despite the deluge, Zhau and Huan were able to figure out what was needed.

"Well, what did you find out?" asked Luka when Zhau walked through the door, water dripping from the black visor on his rain hat.

"It's not good," Zhau answered. "My cousin does not have a belt for this truck. He said we need to drive to Xi'an, which is another day, round trip, to find one. You will be here for a while."

"Does he have a truck?" asked Tulia.

"No, but the town governor does. He's a member of the Party so he has access. It will cost you though. Members don't do things without being well compensated."

"That while you starve," said Tulia.

"I'm afraid that's the way the system works," said Zhau.

The rain turned the dirt roads into muddy, marshy canals, slowing Zhau and Huan as they made their way to Xi'an. The rain continued unabated for the next two days in Huan's village of Banjieshan as well, creating unappreciated idle time for the couple from America.

Tulia ventured out into the rain, cloaked with the only raingear the family had which consisted of a simple straw cape donned over the head that kept most of the water from soaking into her clothes. She waded through the streets to kill time and observe what village life was like. But it wasn't until the next day that the clouds parted, and the rain stopped. It was also the time when Zhau returned from Xi'an with the parts he needed to fix his truck. Repairs proceeded just as slowly as everything else had during their journey, but by the fifth day, the NJ-130 was almost ready to resume its travels.

"Just need to put the chains on." Exclaimed Zhau.

"Chains?"

"Yes. Without chains on the tires, we will go nowhere in this mud pit they call a road."

Once the chains were strapped on, everything was in order, and the party ready to leave.

"Climb in," said Zhau chipperly, as if nothing had happened and this was merely a normal part of living in China. "We go."

While Luka put the baggage into the truck, Tulia went back into the house.

"Thank you," she said to Huan's wife, Jiao, even though she didn't completely understand. "Here, take this. You need it more than we do."

Tulia handed Jiao a wad of Chinese bills. It wasn't going to make them rich, but it would help them stave off the punishing food shortage and, quite possibly, save their lives.

Tears welled up in Jaio's eyes, and she grabbed Tulia, hugging her as if she had, indeed, saved their family from ruin.

"*Xièxiè! Xièxiè!* (Thank you! Thank you!)," she exclaimed, bowing deeply and clasping her palms together as if in prayerful thanks.

After also thanking Huan, Luka and Tulia once again set off for Sanlizhen. With the truck still belching purple smoke, they pushed through the thick mud and on to their next stop.

"I was just on this road," said Zhau as they drove.

"You took *this* road to get your part?" asked Luka.

"Yes. We got the part in Xi'an. That's close to where Sanlizhen is."

"Then why didn't we just ride along with you, then?"

"The Party boss would never allow you to ride in his car. You are not Chinese."

Tulia could tell Luka was upset, and, taking his hand, said, "Calm yourself, Luka. Getting upset isn't going to change anything."

Luka took a few deep breaths. He knew she was right. It was only a few extra days. *We will get there eventually*, he thought to himself.

*****

CH 26 - Hazen Park II

There was a blur of motion directly in front of the car as three men wearing black from head to toe rushed out of the woods; all were armed with AR-15s. They pointed their weapons at the car while one forced the passenger side door open, yanking Raya from the seat and throwing her to the ground.

"Get out!" shouted another, pushing the muzzle of his rifle against the driver's side window. The voice was Indian and familiar. It was the same one Will had heard over the phone.

Will obeyed, slowly opening the door and putting his shaking hands up before getting out. The car was still running as the man leaned into the front seat and began ripping things apart—opening compartments, feeling along the seats and under the dash. Moving to the passenger side, he grabbed the glove compartment latch and ripped it off its hinges to find the vial. Then, he searched under each of the front seats before scouring the back seat and the seat pockets.

"Where's the vial?" he asked angrily, turning back toward Will. But before Will could answer, the man said, "Give me the keys." Once he had them, he popped the rear boot, and again began tearing apart the insides, lifting up the spare tire and pulling off the side compartment cowls. He found nothing.

All three men were completely covered in black garb, including black masks, making it impossible to see their faces.

"Where's Max?" Will asked, defiantly.

"I'm not playing games, kid! Where's the vial?" growled the man.

"I'll tell you when you show me Max. That was the deal."

It was a standoff, but Will did not give in even with a pistol pointed at him. Finally, the man raised his hand, and instantly a fourth man came out of the woods with Max on a leash. He was panting and pulling hard on the restraint trying to reunite with his owner. Yet, the fourth man yanked him back harshly, uncaring how much it might hurt him.

"Hey, that's my dog! Don't do that to him!" shouted Will.

"The vial," demanded the man who had rifled through their car.

Will went to the trunk and opened another compartment just behind the back seat. From there, he removed a small bottle. As he turned to hand it over, the man ripped it away and punched him in the face. Will fell back into the trunk which closed immediately over him.

Momentarily stunned and with pain shooting through his nose, Will called out, "Hey! Let me out!"

"You let him out of there!" Will could hear his mother screaming outside. "Let him out right now! And give me my dog!"

Then, there was considerable commotion and scuffling going on, but Will couldn't tell what was happening. For him, he only saw darkness and heard the muffled noises of people fighting.

"Let me out!" Will yelled, banging on the underside of the trunk lid.

In the background was the mad barking of Max but then an eerie quiet. There was no sound of his mother, his dog or the men. It was then that Will became scared out of his wits. *What's happening out there?* he thought. *What's happened to my mom? To Max?*

Minutes seemed like hours, and inside the dark trunk Will was getting hot and dehydrated. He had continued calling out for his mother but had heard nothing.

"Mom! Mom!"

Will finally remembered there was an emergency latch inside every trunk just for such occasions. He groped around and found the plastic handle before giving it a yank. As the lid popped open, the cool air of the night blew in letting him catch his breath. Not far away, he heard sirens coming in his direction.

"Mom? Mom? Where are you?" he shouted, climbing out of the back.

Will dug out the slim flashlight he always kept in the trunk for emergencies and used that to illuminate the area beyond the reach of the car's headlamps.

"Mom?"

"I'm over here," came a feeble voice. Raya was not far from the car but was doubled over and in obvious pain. "I have him," she said, "I have Max. He's okay."

When Will found them deeper in the bush, Raya had Max clasped tightly in her hands, his tail wagging vigorously. He jumped up on Will for attention, and his human friend gladly obliged.

"Max," shouted Will, almost ignoring his mother, "you're okay!"

131

Max continued to swarm Will, demanding to be petted, so Will rubbed his head, his neck, and his belly while the short, white tail continued to swish back and forth.

"And what about me?" Raya stammered.

Will went to his mother and kissed her. "Are you alright? Are you hurt?"

"Just beat up a little," she answered. It appeared she had some scrapes and scratches on her face, and her nose was bleeding slightly. "I'll be fine. How are you?"

"Better than you from the looks of things."

The lights of the police cars appeared within minutes, and after the sirens muted, the officers got out with their hands on their holsters.

"Raya are you hurt?" asked one of the cops, presumably their neighbor.

"Kent, I'll be fine," said Raya. "They went that way into the woods. They're dressed all in black—they'll be hard to spot."

Officer Kent pushed a button on a mic next to his badge to activate the radio and called in backup to head north in the direction Raya had pointed.

"What happened?" Will asked his mom, picking Max up and stroking his head.

"After they shoved you into the trunk, they beat me up," said Raya. Then, they dragged me out here where one of them told another to shoot our dog. I screamed at them, and at that point, they heard the sirens coming and didn't want to stick around. They took off through the woods."

"The connection on the dashcam must have come back," said Will.

"Yeah, we got worried when the line went dead," said Officer Kent. "We tried several other channels and finally found one that was clear. It's a good thing we were just outside the entrance to the park. When we saw what was happening, we got here as fast as we could."

"Thank God," said Will, rubbing the bump on his head.

"We'll need a police report," said the officer. "Do you mind coming down to the station?"

"No problem," Raya answered. "We just appreciate the help."

"And getting Max back," said Will, as his dog happily licked his face.

"So, what was all this about?" the officer asked. "Surely it was about more than just your dog?"

"It's a long story," said Raya. "I'm not sure there are enough blank pages on the case report to cover it all."

*****

CH 27 - Breakout

"This is *WBC Channel Seven News*, and I'm Brett Major. Tonight, we begin with continuing news about something officials say is quickly becoming a repeat of history. There are reports that the new strain of malaria that has hit the US is creating wide-spread panic—panic that hasn't been seen since 2019 when the Wuhan virus struck the world. At that time, the Chinese Communist Party was accused of withholding information on the virus, leading to a global pandemic. This time, the WHO and officials worldwide are responding more quickly. However, they also warn that this strain may be ten times more lethal. Todd Lancaster has more."

The screen cut away from the anchor and showed hospitals in Chengdu, the fifth largest city in China with over twenty million people. The footage was grainy—clearly taken without the permission of CCP authorities. In the film, the emergency rooms were spilling over with patients on gurneys and wheelchairs waiting in hospital lounges while even more queued in the parking lots outside. Doctors and nurses were suited-up as if there had been a major HAZMAT spill nearby—covered head to toe in white suits with full hoods, gloves, boots, glasses, and heavy-duty respirators.

Lancaster explained that the epidemic had first been noticed in that Chinese city only five days earlier when a woman came into the hospital with malarial symptoms. Since then, there had been thousands infected. The report continued with an interview with a fully masked and suited employee of the hospital, making it impossible to identify them.

"Our CCP leaders have yet to issue a statement," the employee said, his words translated from Chinese into English. "They say there is no problem. Even the country's top health ministers claim there is no problem. Yet, how do you explain this?" he added, pointing to the chaotic scene around him.

Lancaster's face reappeared on the screen.

"The word from the Party leadership and the aging Chairman Xi is that the film showing patients overflowing in the hospitals is one taken in 2020, not 2038, and that the people promoting this myth will be tracked down and arrested. It's hard to know what is actually going on, but we will continue to cover this story as it unfolds. This is Todd Lancaster reporting."

***

As with the COVID outbreak in 2020, the facts and the truth were hard commodities to come by. Stories were twisted and manipulated to fit the narrative intended by the source. And as the population watched and waited, anxiety grew from both about not knowing what was happening and, even worse, what was about to.

*****

CH 28 – Mine at Last

The small vial of black liquid, packed in multiple layers of bubble-wrap, arrived in New Delhi within forty-eight hours after the late-night incident in Hazen Park. Bhatti immediately took it to the Dark Ops lab on one of the subterranean floors. Fortified by extensive security, the clandestine lab deployed a magnetic lab card reader, a retina scanner, and a palm print analyzer. In addition, it was a negative pressure lab which meant there was an air lock that permitted negative pressure inside the lab as compared with that on the outside. In the event of a viral or toxic leak inside the lab, the contagion could not easily breach the airlock to the outside, remaining confined within the lab.

The lab also held several "case" rooms where tests were performed on mice or other specimens under controlled conditions. These were also negatively pressured as an additional safeguard against accidental release. Yet, beyond these precautions, extensive personal protective equipment or PPE was required in most areas. Even full HazMat suits were mandatory in some quadrants where the dangers and risks were highest.

"Here," said Bhatti, handing the precious vial to Dr. Malok. "You need to separate this into several samples so multiple people can work on it. Treat it as a Level Four HazMat substance and use all safety precautions. We don't know what it is, and we only have three days to figure it out. You know what needs to be done. I not only need to know *what* it is but how we can replicate it quickly."

"As I said before, it will be difficult," said Malok, gently taking the specimen.

"I don't care how difficult it is. Make it happen."

Malok put his staff to work analyzing the composition right away. Using infra-red spectral analysis, they began whittling away at the complex molecules contained within the sample. It was organic, but it seemed to have covalent bonds Malok had never seen before. Indeed, more than that, there seemed to be an ion that was unique and perplexing.

Early the next day, Bhatti was already down in Malok's lab inquiring about the project's status.

"Well, where are we?" she asked, her hands on her hips.

"I must tell you," answered Malok, "it's very strange—something I haven't seen before."

"But you can crack it, right?"

"Well, yes. But it will take time," said Malok. "We'll keep working on it and will let you know when we have something."

"What does the spectrograph show?"

"Here," said Malok, handing her the colored chart with frequencies at the bottom and the jagged line above it that showed the levels of each trace element."

"Tell me what I'm looking at."

Instead of covering each frequency band, Malok highlighted the areas of special interest, pointing to certain peaks and valleys in the line chart that related elements to each other and to the substance's uniqueness.

"What it tells me is that almost all of this comes from plants native to South America—that's what the origin looks to be," said Malok.

"Where in South America?"

"Primarily the western forests of Ecuador and Columbia. However, there are other substances—amino acids and proteins—that I don't recognize."

"Can you replicate it?"

"I think we can replicate 99.7 percent of it. The remaining 0.3 percent, I'm not sure, but we can try."

"Do more than try, doctor."

Malok now focused the work on replicating the serum and the methods and means to do that. After five days, he returned with a vial of black elixir that looked remarkably like what they'd taken from Will and Raya in the park.

Bhatti looked at the result and smiled. "So, this will work?"

"I don't know," said Malok. "We've tried it on our mice, and it seemed to reverse the effects of the pathogen we got from Labac."

"The latest batch?"

"Yes. It's the same as they put in the latest batch of sterile mosquitos they sprayed over Detroit and Philadelphia last week—the MQ 63s."

"All right," said Bhatti, "then it's time for a human test."

"It's too soon. We need to conduct more tests before we ..."

"Malok, either get out of my way or I will take you out. Your choice."

"What are you going to do?"

Bhatti pressed the button on her intercom. "Tell Dr. Ghadre to come see me in my office."

*****

CH 29 – Meeting with Herron

"Thank you for meeting with me," said Jack, pulling up a chair inside the U.S. embassy in New Delhi. "I know your time is valuable."

James Herron was the second in command at the embassy. He had served there for over twelve years, and under three different ambassadors during that time. A career diplomat, Herron was originally assigned to the US embassy in Russia in the early 2000s until he was transferred to the Ukraine in 2014 during the political upheavals in that nation. Then in 2021, before the conflict between Russia and Ukraine began the following year, he was moved again—this time to New Delhi.

Known to be a survivor who blew where the favorable winds wished, Herron was a grizzled veteran of diplomatic trials and tribulations and was accustomed to the backstabbing and duplicity that came with the territory. Herron was in his late sixties, but his thick head of gray hair defied his age making him appear closer to his mid-fifties, instead. He was clearly a man who closely managed his personal health and fitness. With thick, bushy eyebrows that sometimes seemed to obscure his upper eyelids, he had dark gray eyes and a sorrowful mouth which sagged at the tips. Tall and trim, he was always sharply dressed and exuded the posture and decorum of the position to which he had aspired for many years yet fallen short—that of full ambassador. However, ambassadorships almost always went to top party donors, and he lacked the financial resources required to be counted in that elite group—at least, not yet. He yearned to be inducted into that clique and waited anxiously for the right opportunity to come his way.

Herron saw Jack come into his office and rose to shake his hand, more out of protocol than from any attempt at civility or a modicum of respect.

"Mr. Morris," said Herron, having been briefed on Jack's real name and background. "Deputy Director Katz forwarded me your information, and from what she says you're looking to help us with our Kierney problem. Is that right?"

"Yes sir. I'm working with connections we have in India to track down his whereabouts. I'm hopeful that you'll be able to provide more for me to go on."

"You've been in touch with Uri, then?"

"Yes. We've met. I'll be looking into some other avenues as well, but Uri promised to have me logistics of Kierney's comings and goings and the people he's meeting with."

"What are your other 'avenues'?"

"I am contacting several of the biolabs that do business in New Delhi — ones that might be involved in the type of work Kierney is targeting."

"And why would you do that? From what Director Katz said, your focus is to be on finding and dealing with Kierney, correct?" said Herron.

"True, but I believe it's important for us to know which of these labs might be working on things he may target with his group. He may strike one of those before I can find him."

"You shouldn't waste your time on the labs, Mr. Morris. We are well aware of the biolabs here and are working with the Indian IB to ensure no incidents occur."

"You mean the Intelligence Bureau."

"Yes, of course."

The Indian Intelligence Bureau or IB was akin to the FBI in the United States.

"I thought there were some concerns about people working within the IB."

"Oh?"

"Yes, I thought some were thought to be compromised by the Russians and-or the Chinese. Is that not true?" Jack asked.

Herron smirked. "Where did you get an idea like that?"

"So, it's not true?"

"No, of course it's not true. We wouldn't work with them if we thought they were compromised."

Jack knew that was far from the truth. The CIA often worked with suspect groups even if they knew they were working both sides of the table. It was all part of the delicate dance that all intelligence agencies did with each other and with third-party players in the field. There was always someone inside who was on-the-take to some degree.

"No, I'm sure you're right," said Jack, only agreeing to agree.

"But I stress to you that you should *not* contact any of these biolabs. This might tip our hand and make it harder for you to find Kierney. These labs have contacts outside too, you know."

"I understand," said Jack. "Do you have any information for me about the whereabouts of Kierney? Do you know how many are in his organization? Where they are located? How they are funded? Etc."

Herron smiled. "Very good," he said. "You want me to do your heavy lifting for you, I see."

"With all due respect, sir. I feel that the sharing of information is important if we are to accomplish this mission. Isn't that why we're here?"

Herron's mouth pursed, and his eyes quickly re-evaluated the person he was talking to. He cleared his throat and then said, "Well, that's why *you're* here."

"I'm sure you wouldn't want me to write an unfavorable report about our meeting –the lack of cooperation, and the like."

Jack was agitated and took off the gloves. He wasn't going to let this twit of a diplomat stonewall him for the sake of ego.

"I may have some information that may be useful." Herron handed Jack a tiny, encrypted white fob. "I suspected you might ask for information, so here it is. However, I will not be available to answer any questions you have about it. You will be on your own. Between you and Uri, I'm sure you'll figure it out."

"Thanks. I appreciate the help," said Jack, giving an answer that could be taken either honestly or sarcastically.

Jack left the office and the embassy feeling uncertain about the degree of "help" he had been given by the Chief of Missions. He had been in situations like this before, and they usually ended with his feeling that there were more sides being waged in the battle he was fighting. Figuring out who was on which side was always a challenge.

*****

CH 30 - Ben and Uri Redux

2018

Ben waited impatiently for Biendar to show. They had agreed to meet again at the same park in Kiev, but now thirty minutes after the appointed hour, Biendar was nowhere in sight. Ben rechecked his watch wondering how much longer he should stay. However, finally, Biendar arrived in a dark trench coat and wearing a wool, derby-style hat. He sat down on the worn park bench near Ben and, seeing his friend smoking, pulled out his own cigarette and flicked his lighter to get started.

"Well?" Ben asked, blowing out a blue-gray cloud from the side of his mouth. "What do you have for me?"

"Here," said Biendar, strangely offering him a cigarette.

"But I ..." began Ben, lifting his smoke to show he already had one.

"It's all in this one," said Biendar. "You will find the information you need. Just don't light it."

Ben took the cigarette and put it in his breast pocket. "Thanks. Is there anything special I should know?"

"Yes," said Uri, finally looking over to engage his friend, "you're being set up. It is true that your American colonel is involved in a shady business. As you believe, he is trying to 'out' these bio-labs you refer to, but they are not what you think. Your information is faulty, I'm afraid. The colonel is also not working with the Russians, at least not directly. No, this runs much deeper than that." Uri stopped and leaned toward Ben. "I will give you some advice, Mr. Maddington. You should walk away from this. You are fighting a war you cannot win. It is much bigger than you are, and if you persist, you will be crushed."

"I don't understand," said Ben. "I have a job to do. I can't return home until it's done."

"Consider this a warning," said Biendar. "In this country, there are no sides. There is only one machine that operates everything."

"It's corrupt. I get that, but ..."

"Oh, you don't understand the half of it," said Biendar. "I am risking my own life telling you these things. I probably shouldn't. But I like you, Mr. Maddington. So, if you know what's best for you, you'll figure out some excuse to return home. Trust no one as you maneuver through this minefield. But if you wish to exit it safely, you must leave the country while you can."

Ben shook his head. "From where I come, there is good and there is evil, and one must defend good and fight evil."

"Oh, you make it sound so simple, but I assure you it is far from it. You may think there are two sides to every conflict, but sometimes there are many. You will see that the world is not black and white, Mr. Maddington. There are many shades of gray, and if you think in terms of black or white, the task quickly becomes impossible. Those of a silver complexion by day can become charcoal by night."

"Uri, I was born in a small town in Missouri—a population of no more than two thousand," said Ben. "My dad was a farmer; my mom was a homemaker. She took care of us kids. We were taught what was right and what was wrong. There was no gray or in-between in our household—that's the way my dad worked his whole life. But you're right. I've learned doing this job that, surprisingly, most don't follow those rules. They ignore them and make up their own—ones they think will line their pockets or further their power. Still, that's evil too—there is no gray there."

"The world has changed, Arthur."

"Yes, I'm realizing that more and more every day."

"Good luck, then" said Biendar, getting up. "Oh, and if you need anything more, you know where to find me."

****

CH 31 – First Test

Dr. Ghadre went to Bhatti's office, but her secretary redirected him to go to the restricted laboratory area on the lower floor where the dark ops work was conducted. Although no longer cleared for the area, he took a single-purpose elevator to B6 where he was greeted by his colleague, Dr. Malok.

"Is Dr. Bhatti here?" Ghadre asked.

"Yes, she's waiting for you. She wants to show you something."

Malok placed his magnetic security card against the reader and then pressed his eye into the retina scanner. Instantly, the first air lock released, letting them both pass through. The second reader required a palm print, which Malok also supplied.

Once inside, Malok asked, "It's been quite some time since you've been down here. Is that right?"

"Yes, about a year, in fact. I've wondered what projects you have been working on down here."

"Let me show you some things before Dr. Bhatti arrives."

Malok took Ghadre up and down the hallways and then into another high-security elevator where they dropped three levels to B9—the deepest subterranean floor. Getting off that lift, they found yet another set of locked doors guarding a restricted area that had biohazard level 4 warning placards posted everywhere—the highest of all levels.

"Why don't you wait in here," said Malok, opening one last door. "Dr. Bhatti will be right with you."

Ghadre walked into one of the testing rooms. It had triple-pane, break-proof windows all around it and a table where several empty cages and various pieces of lab equipment sat idle. None of it was operating, suggesting it had recently been cleaned out, awaiting the next batch of testing to be initiated. In the ceiling and around the perimeter of the room were several vents—all closed and appearing to be in disuse. Next to that room was another—a master control room with several panels of colored lights and digital monitors showing different graphs and charts. Ghadre could see several other testing rooms branching off on the other side of it that were much like the one he was standing in.

It suddenly occurred to the senior scientist that there was no one else on that floor—the rest of the laboratory was empty.

Then, the elevator opened, and Bhatti appeared. But when she got off, Malok got on, leaving his work colleague behind. Bhatti walked past the room where Ghadre was waiting and opened the door to the master control room next to it. Ghadre went to open the door to his room, but it was locked. He tried again—but again he couldn't budge it.

"You wanted to see me?" Ghadre asked, wondering why she hadn't come into his room.

"Yes, Dr. Ghadre. I know how much you want to be part of the experimentation of our products at this company, and I finally thought you should have some first-hand experience with it."

"I don't understand," he answered with increasing anxiety.

"We have been working with a sister company, Labac, to develop an antidote to a pathogen they've found in their sterile mosquitos. You see, the mosquitos were first sterilized but then given a toxin to carry—to transmit— to the general population. It is being misdiagnosed as a new malaria, but it's not—not at all. The parasite inside them has the effect of aging a person rapidly after they've been bitten by the mosquito and the parasite injected into the victim's bloodstream. Like I said, the toxin—or parasite—has similar effects to those of malaria, making it appear as a strain of the organism, but it's really a synthetic organism that changes the person's DNA and, in the process, causes him or her to age. Have you heard of progeria?"

"Yes, of course. It's a genetic mutation that causes rapid aging in children. They usually don't live beyond their teen years."

"Yes, and the lab-created version makes this process even faster. We're studying the effects with this little experiment, but with billions of the mosquitos already released and the advanced progeria-like disease beginning to spread, we've been asked to create a cure. And, we believe we have that cure."

"Wait. You mean you intentionally released this pathogen into the population?"

"No, we didn't. Labac Labs did and with full approval of the Indian Parliament, the UN and other nations around the world."

"Why would they do that?"

Bhatti laughed. "Two reasons. The first is money, of course. If we create a problem and are then tasked to create a solution to that problem, we can sell it for trillions to governments around the world looking for our panacea."

"And the second?"

"There are too many people in the world, doctor! The GEF and the UN want an 80 percent reduction in the world population within the next five years. They tried back in 2019, but the virus then wasn't deadly enough. They told me they aren't going to make the same mistake this time."

"So, you have the cure? Won't that prevent *all* deaths?"

"We're not that stupid. We're going to mix placebos with real doses to cloud the picture so no one will tie the effects back to our cure. You see what we've created is pure genius. It seems to cure the disease by killing the pathogen, but it also contains other nano-creatures that cause damage long-term. They won't be detected at first, but as more people die, they will blame the deaths on the initial disease instead of the cure we released. It's quite a brilliant plan even if it is similar to what they did in 2020. In the end, we make money, and the population goes down. Everyone wins." There was a morbid glee in her voice—something crazed and sociopathic.

"Everyone wins except the ones you kill and their families."

"Yeah, there will be those for sure."

"You're mad," said Ghadre disgustedly.

"No, no. I will be rich, Dr. Ghadre—worth trillions, not billions!"

"And how many millions will die?"

"Again, you underestimate. It will be billions, not millions, that will die. But right now, we need you to help us with a test. Don't worry, this won't hurt a bit—at least not right now."

At that moment, black swirling clouds began pouring from the vents in the top of the room. They came in by the millions if not tens of millions. The air became so thick with them that Ghadre couldn't see or breathe and began coughing, covering his mouth with his sleeve trying not to suck any into his lungs.

Mosquitos! he thought, panicking. He glanced around the room, but there was nowhere to go and no one on the floor to hear him scream. Within minutes, his body had become a human pincushion. *****

CH 32- Xianyang

1964

After making the repairs to the fan belt, Zhau and company finally made it to Xianyang—nine days after starting out.

Xianyang or Xi'an Proper—which was the city center—was one of the largest cities in China. After Shanghai (over 6.4 million), Beijing (4.6 million), Tianjin (3.2 million), and a few others, Xianyang held over 800 thousand and ranked fifteenth in city size at the time. By 2035, it would become nineth on the list and have over 10.4 million inhabitants. Within the city, there were great expanses of shanty towns—all looking dilapidated by Western standards—but housing as many as a dozen people in each cramped, squalid home. The town's roads were laid out on a grid, except where there were hills. There, the roads meandered to the contour of the land undulations. Merely ten miles outside the city were the beginnings of hills which lead to much more rugged terrain. Yet, this region was still over one thousand miles from the truly high mountains—those of Nepal and the world's highest peaks, the Himalayas. At the same time, Zhau's destination was only a short distance southeast of town where a much smaller town—that of Sanlizhen—was situated.

Once they arrived in the small village, Zhau went directly to his friend's humble, wooden home which was built next to a meager slip of a creek on the outskirts of the purlieu. The home was a mosaic of bits and pieces of planks, and the roof was thatched meagerly with thin tree limbs and mud.

Zhau knocked on the door, and soon an elderly man answered. Short and frail, the man squinted at his visitors, his eyes afflicted by the pernicious creep of cataracts. His hair was peppered gray, and his beard long—down to his chest—but pointed and well-trimmed.

"*Sheu, Zhēn gāoxìng néng jiàn dào nǐ?* (How are you?)" asked Zhau, bowing deeply.

The old man smiled, cupped his hands together and returned the bow. "*Zhau. Yǐjīng tài jiǔle.* (It's been too long)," he answered.

Both men talked in Chinese, but Zhau translated for Luka and Tulia as they went along.

Sheu invited them inside where they sat on tightly-woven, straw mats placed close together in one of the dwelling's two tiny rooms. The larger of the two

147

doubled as the kitchen where there was a rustic fire pit and a cast-iron, woodburning stove.

After talking for nearly an hour, Zhau looked over at Luka and Tulia. "So sorry," he said, bowing his head, "Sheu and I go way back. He is not a fan of the communist party but has kept a low profile, so he won't be arrested or even executed."

"They do that way out here?" asked Tulia.

"I'm afraid so—even out here in the rural areas. Mao has an iron fist over the entire country. *Anyone* who speaks ill of him or the party is subject to charges of treason and execution by hanging. It is something few here are willing to do. Our leader has an expansive network of party members who keep tabs on what happens everywhere and report back. Nothing goes unnoticed."

Luka sat uncomfortably next to Tulia. In a moment of *déjà vu*, he realized he was back in it—in a country that tortured and imprisoned its people to terrify them into silence and passivity. He and Tulia had left that world years earlier. It had been a horrible thing then, and it was still a horrible thing now.

"But not to worry," said Zhau, smiling again as he stood and put his arm around his friend. "Sheu is a brother. He will not betray our trust, nor we his."

"You said he had a Dropa stone," said Tulia. "Does he still have it?"

Zhau translated, and Sheu nodded before leaving them. After a few minutes, he returned carrying a coarse burlap bag that looked like it had been kept in a dirty barn with the drove of hogs. Quickly, he uncinched it and extracted the stone, laying it flat on the floor in front of them.

It was nothing like what Luka and Tulia had imagined. Only as large as a small dinner plate, it had a hole in the middle and fine grooves like an LP record on its surface. Also on the surface were strange, hieroglyph-like symbols that held some meaning, but Tulia had no idea what it might be. It was nothing she had ever studied or seen before.

"This is it?" exclaimed Tulia. "I guess I was expecting something ..."

"Something more exotic?" asked Zhau. "It does look like a piece of round rock all right."

"Like a millstone," said Luka, picking it up and examining it.

"Does he know what those symbols are?" Tulia asked, pointing to the strange figures.

"Let me ask him," said Zhau.

Zhau spoke for several minutes to Sheu who listened and nodded before answering. This exchange continued until Zhau finally turned back to the couple.

"He says that he got the piece of stone in Nepal when he was a Sherpa for a group of foreigners trying to climb the peak of Kanchenjunga. He said no one made it to the top, and, sadly, many died in the attempt. However, he said he was in the small village of Phurumbu near the Temple of Pathibhara Devi where they had stayed the night. He said the innkeeper asked him if any in his climbing group might be interested in some special stones he had. He claimed he had over a dozen, even though Sheu says he only saw one. He tells me he thinks there have been seven hundred sixteen discovered in the middle of the desert plains of China—a place called Bayan Har Shan. Sheu asked the others in his group if they were interested in buying the stone, but none were. So, feeling sorry for the man, he bought the stone from him. Now he wants to sell it. He needs the money for his family during this time of famine."

Zhau leaned in and added, "As to whether it's authentic or valuable, I have no idea. I make no representations to that and will leave that to you."

"What does he say the man in the village told him about the stone?" asked Tulia. "Does he know how old it is?"

Zhau translated and listened to Sheu who spoke quickly in his native tongue. When he finished, Zhau said, "He says the man who sold it to him believed it was used to store information somehow. He has heard about the records and record players you have in the West and think it's something like that."

"Except it's old," said Luka.

"Yes, he says it is probably thousands of years old."

"Does he know how many?" Tulia pressed.

Again, Zhau and Sheu bantered back and forth for a moment before Zhau continued. This time he had a wry smile on his face—one of either incredulity or astonishment.

"He was told it was created by ... by an alien group over twelve thousand years ago. It was intended to hold and store information on the cultures of the day. They didn't have written language back then, so the aliens provided these stones as a way to keep a record for them. If you are able to decipher what's on the stone, he says you will learn about a civilization that preceded anything known to date on this planet."

Luka laughed. "Aliens? You mean people from another kingdom here?" Luka asked.

"No, not from people here. Rather, from people out *there*," said Zhau pointing upward.

For Luka, he thought he'd heard just about everything, but even this was too much for him to keep bottled up inside. And again, he laughed.

"What's so funny?" Tulia asked him, giving a stern look.

"You don't think this is funny?" Luka answered, still grinning. "We travel a week to get to China and another week to get here only to find out it's all about little green men. Don't you find that funny?"

Tulia shook her head. "What makes you so sure it's not?"

"Come on, Tulia. It's a hoax. This man wants us to spend a large sum on a rock with a hole in it. I can find millions of them in the middle of the plains out there. We can pull the truck over on the way back, and I'm sure Zhau can help us find a dozen or maybe two or three alongside the road. It doesn't mean anything."

"What about the symbols?"

"What about them? I could make up a bunch of lines and circles too and call it a symbol of something. But it doesn't mean it is."

Tulia remained unconvinced.

"What does he want for it?" she asked Zhau.

"He says he wants two thousand new yuan." His tone was flat and matter-of-fact.

Luka had done enough research to understand the Chinese words for the various money denominations and had clearly heard the man say *fen*, not *yuan*. This was a big difference. There were ten fen in a jiao and ten jiao in a yuan, which meant, that two thousand fen were only twenty yuan—not two thousand. In US dollars, it was seven *hundred* versus only *seven*. The huge difference, it was clear, would be pocketed by Zhau.

"I see," said Luka, playing his hand. "Well, we're willing to give him the two thousand *fen* he is asking for and another thousand *fen* to you for your commission. How does that sound?"

"Did I say two thousand yuan?" said Zhau. "I think he meant jiao."

"No, he didn't," said Luka. "I know what he said, Zhau. So, if you still want *any* commission from this deal, I'd suggest you start leveling with him and me. It's my final offer."

Zhau nodded and told Sheu whose face lit up with excitement. He jumped up and began bowing many times, over and over, in appreciation.

Luka handed the twenty new juan to Sheu and ten to Zhau. Then, Tulia nudged him, coaxing him to give Sheu more for his family, which Luka did.

On the way back from the meeting, Tulia looked more closely at the stone. *It is strange,* she thought. *It's nothing like I've ever seen. I wonder what information the grooves hold and what those weird symbols mean.*

Only time would tell.

*****

CH 33 – News Update

"Now, with Brett Major--this is *News Seven* at seven," said the announcer introducing the night's broadcast.

"Good evening. The latest news on the ongoing malaria outbreak is not encouraging. What worries officials is that this contagion affects the brain rather than the respiratory system, and it may be extremely lethal. Todd, bring us up to speed on the latest."

"Brett, although the Administration continues to announce that it is actively working with labs around the world to develop a cure for this contagion, a secret report obtained by News Seven today suggests that the cure widely anticipated from YAF Labs is taking longer to refine and test than first believed. Although already approved for rapid deployment by the US Health Department and the FDA, the vials are only now being tested on human subjects. This process can take years. However, quicker, more-expedited protocols are expected to shorten this timetable drastically.

"In the meantime, the US government has already placed an order for one hundred million doses but when it will take delivery is anybody's guess. Reports from the World Health Organization show that as many as seventy thousand in the US are infected and another seventy million may be asymptomatic—that is, they may have the disease but aren't showing signs. Under the extraordinary and controversial powers of the World Health Treaty signed in 2024, the WHO is starting to force countries around the world to begin lockdowns and close their borders. As we've cited in previous broadcasts, no government that is party to the treaty—including the U.S.—can disobey mandates from the WHO."

Lancaster appeared once more on the air after playing a medley of horrific scenes of panicked people throughout the world.

"As you recall, the Coronavirus of 2019 infected more than two billion worldwide and killed tens of millions according to the World Health Organization which is the premier authority on such matters. Although the mortality rate was about one percent for the virus in 2019, the WHO estimates that this pathogen could have a mortality rate of over 66 percent, and over 78 percent for those older than seventy.

"Brett, we will continue to update this story as more information is released by the WHO, the Administration, the UN, the GEF and other bodies."

Faye turned off the TV. Heartened by the sudden recovery of her daughter, she felt less anxious than she had in a long time. Still, she worried about her husband, herself, and others in her extended family. News of hospital room overcrowding, videos of people falling over dead in the streets, in state-run grocery store aisles, and other state-sponsored venues were widely circulated.

A cure can't come too soon, she thought.

*****

CH 34 – Symptoms Worsen

"Todd Lancaster has an update for us on the malaria scare. Todd …" It was Brett Major, the anchor for Channel 7 News.

"Thanks, Brett. The infections of malaria are spreading—this according to the latest CDC report. Lockdowns similar to those in 2020 are being considered to stem the disease, but there has been no decision made yet. As for a cure, there is news today of a new therapy being developed by a company in India. This drug has apparently shown great promise in killing the parasite causing the disease and was developed in record time. The company said that clinical trials have been extensive, and if approved, could be made available within the next few months."

"And what about stories that the recent release of genetically modified mosquitos might have had something to do with this outbreak?" asked Brett. "Is this just disinformation?"

"Yes, Brett. Most certainly. Secretary Hoshia issued a statement saying that Labac—the company that created the genetically modified mosquitos—claims there is no possibility – zero – that its mosquitoes had anything to do with the latest outbreak. Scientists have also confirmed this. YAF, the company in India that has developed the new therapy, is known for its ability to develop breakthrough cures and treatments, and its testing has shown a 100% success rate. As I said, Secretary Hoshia noted that the new drug should be available as early as August."

Faye had been watching the newscasts every night since Shannon had gotten sick. Each night she hoped they would announce a breakthrough, and that night she heard what she had wanted to hear: Shannon's cure was on the way.

"… a few months" murmured Faye. "I just hope that's not too late!"

***

During the following weeks, Shannon had her ups and downs. Some days she felt well enough to get up and do things around the house; other days—most days—she felt too drained even to get out of bed. She looked horrible. Her face was drawn and gaunt, and the circles under her eyes were growing darker as the sockets seemed to recede farther back into her head with each passing day. Indeed, her skin was turning grayer and more scaley too, aging as if she had suddenly contracted the rare and degenerative disease known as progeria. More dramatically, her mood was changing. Normally happy and light-hearted, she had grown somber, depressed and withdrawn.

"Who's been in my room?" Shannon screamed uncontrollably as such irrational outbursts were also becoming more and more common.

"What's wrong?" asked Faye, sighing as she trudged upstairs.

"Someone has been in my room, Mom?"

"It wasn't me. I haven't been in your room."

"Well, *someone* has."

"Why would you say that?" asked Faye, trying to be patient.

"I ... I ... something is missing," began Shannon.

"What? What's missing dear?"

"My salve. It's not there."

"I don't know, Shannon. We can get more at the store."

"No! No!" she cried. Then, hesitating, she blurted out, "It's the potion—the elixir. You know, the one from the trunk that Will took."

"I thought he took all that from you!" her mother said, raising her voice.

Shannon groaned. "No, I kept the jugs. I told him I should keep them—to keep them safe."

"To keep them safe? From what? I don't know why you would have done that."

"Look in the closet, Mom. Maybe I put them in my Memory Box."

Shannon's Memory Box was a collection of odds and ends from her childhood—mementos, awards, newspaper articles, and other remembrances from her past.

"Here they are," said Faye, pulling out the box and finding the jugs. "You need to get rid of these."

"No, Mom! I need some of it."

"Of what? One of these liquids?"

"Yeah, Mom. I need the black jug. Give me the black jug."

"You're not getting any of this, Shannon. I'm not letting you. You don't know what this stuff is. Have you been taking this?" Faye held up the jug, swirling the black liquid inside.

"Yes! Now, give it to me!" Shannon shouted. Like an addict seeking relief, Shannon was getting visible irate.

Faye took her daughter and held her, letting the tears roll down her cheeks but trying not to sob and reveal how worried she was.

"You'll be all right, child. I know you'll get better soon. The cure is on its way. They said it should be ready soon. Then we can get that for you, and everything will be better."

These were words that meant less and less with each passing day, but it made Faye feel better to say them, offering what little comfort she could. It became even more bleak when the date of release for the "promised" cure continued to be pushed back. Shannon got out of bed and followed her mother as she left with the jugs. She watched as Faye went into her own room and placed the elixirs high on the shelf in her closet.

Neither Faye nor John saw Shannon the rest of the evening, but both were worried stiff about their daughter. Faye talked in whispered tones as her husband and she sat on the lumpy sofa and watched an old rerun of the 1995 horror movie *12 Monkeys*.

"I'm taking her back to the doctor," said John, having trouble concentrating on the movie.

"John, he already told us there was nothing we can do until the new cure comes out. And you and I now know it won't be released for another month or so. We just have to wait."

"But the disease isn't waiting, Faye. It's killing her. We can't wait. We have to do something."

"... and after the doctor tells you the same thing he told me, then what are you going to do?"

"I'll find another doctor," said John. "There are homeopathic doctors out there, you know. They use natural remedies instead ones made up in a lab someplace."

"If you think that will help, then be my guest. I've done all I can. You try to find one that hasn't been decertified," Faye said, frustrated as she lay back in her seat.

"It's a travesty what they've done to doctors who try to cure using natural agents instead of the stuff pushed by the big drug companies. You can't find anyone anymore who will even consider alternatives."

"Well, then you find someone, John."

Later that night, when Faye went up to bed, she found Shannon's door still closed. She thought about knocking and going in to check on her but decided it was better to leave her alone and let her rest.

The next morning, Faye rose to go downstairs and make her usual breakfast—oatmeal and orange juice—while John grabbed his coffee and headed to work. After he left, she went back upstairs to check on Shannon. This time, she knocked on her door and opened it.

"Shannon, are you up? I just ..." but she stopped mid-sentence.

Sitting straight up in bed with her eyes open and staring at a spot on the far wall was her daughter. No longer gray and gaunt, Shannon's face was now rosy and radiant as if she'd just turned sixteen. Shannon turned to look at her mother and smiled—her face oddly calm and serene.

"How are you today, Mom?" she asked chipperly.

"Uh, well, how are *you* feeling?" asked Faye. "It looks like you're doing a lot better. Do you feel okay?"

"I feel great!" Shannon answered, stretching her hands above her head. "What's for breakfast?"

*****

CH 35 – Post Attack

After the room was sucked clean of the mosquitos, Dr. Ghadre lay unconscious on the floor. He was carried out on a stretcher and placed in another room—one nearby that looked like a critical care unit of a hospital. With monitoring equipment all around him and hoses running into his arms and nose, he was completely immobilized. But in addition to the life-sustaining equipment, there were other devices that were measuring the changing effects of the mosquito bites on his DNA.

Swollen beyond recognition, his face was half again larger than its normal size as were his arms and legs. He had suffered thousands of bites from the aggressive vampires, and they had drained nearly a pint of blood from his system. High over his head were bags of saline and blood plasma as well as one other—one more unusual. In a small pouch was a strange, black, viscous liquid which dripped rhythmically into a tube leading to his arm.

"How are you feeling, doctor?" asked Bhatti coming into the room.

Ghadre rolled his head slowly toward her. His eyes recognized her, but he couldn't speak.

"We should be able to tell soon whether the black serum is reversing the effects of the mosquito micro-injections. Your DNA continues to be modified by the toxin from the mosquitos. At the same time, we are administering our latest version of the 'wonder' drug who hope will reverse the effects. We're still not sure how or even if the black liquid works on this pathogen. If what worked on the lab mice works on you, then it will keep you from dying." Chillingly, there was diabolic joy in her voice as she seemed to revel in inflicting pain on someone else.

"What have you done?" muttered Ghadre, barely coherent.

"Well, you must have forgotten our little conversation before the test began. I told you that our partner lab, Labac, created and released billions of those mosquitos into the world during the past several months. They also provided an additive to put into my serum even though I don't know what it is. But that's for those people high up in our own food chain to know—not me. They've directed all this as part of their global mission 'to change and reset the world.' As I understand it, these mosquitos contain a genetically modified parasite which gives the symptoms of malaria but also changes one's DNA. Fearing a lethal malaria outbreak that is resistant to everything we have on our pharmacy shelves, the world is frantically searching for a solution, and, I believe, we have it."

"What will happen now?"

"If this works as planned, people will clamor to get our exclusive cure, and we will make trillions! But as for you ..." she stopped and shook her head, "... I'm not at all sure. You are old, Ghadre. If you're lucky, you will survive this, and even if you don't, we'll register you in the 'cured' column. Our tests always show that at least 96 percent of our subjects are cured."

"You can't do that."

"Oh, doctor, I can, and I have. In fact, Dr. Malok and I have been manipulating test results for years. We have very powerful backers in the parliament, you know. They are also investors in YAF. They wouldn't object even if they knew the full extent of what we are doing. No, I'm quite confident that we won't be touched."

"You *bitch*!" Ghadre said under his breath.

"Ha!" said Bhatti. "That's the best you can do? I've been called far worse— even by my dying father whom I had killed so I could inherit all of this. Killing him was probably the best thing I ever did. He was worthless. He couldn't build this company to save his life. It took his daughter to do that."

"You're pure evil. Do you know that?" Ghadre gritted his teeth. The pain was growing quickly—far beyond the discomfort of the bites.

"Oh, your words hurt me not," said Bhatti, mockingly. "I worship Satan every day, as do most of my other colleagues here. However, you were never one we could corrupt. It's an honor and virtue thing with you, isn't it? I suppose there are still some of you out there. However, your choice did have some downside, didn't it?"

"Your father was no saint, but he would never have done what you are doing. Never!"

"Yes, he was more virtuous, but that was his weakness. How do you think one gains power? It's through force and terror, as it has for millennia. That is exactly what my handlers do to me, and, in turn, that's what I must do to you. Anyway, we'll know soon enough whether this thing will work. You'd better pray to your god that it does. It's better to live a little longer than to die a rather quick, but horrible death. Don't you think?"

Within a few days, Ghadre did get better, and the redness and puffiness around his head and limbs abated. But beyond that, there was something else: he suddenly looked younger too. By the end of the second week, he appeared at least twenty years more youthful—like someone in their fifties instead of their seventies. The transformation had been amazing.

"This is quite something!" said Bhatti, looking at the doctor who was still secured in one of the clinic recovery rooms downstairs. "Not only do I think we have a miracle cure for the malaria, but I also think we may have found the Fountain of Youth! Do you know what the world would pay for that? Multiple trillions! I may even win a Nobel Prize!"

Bhatti turned to Malok who was standing beside her. "Contact Mr. Big. Tell him it works. It's all a go."

"And what about testing other subjects?" asked Malok.

"No, we need to stop while we're ahead. Our success rate is 100 percent. Why should we go and spoil that?"

*****

CH 36– The Micro Dot

2018

Ben had the equipment he needed to review the data on the microdot he was given by Uri. He wanted to be sure that the data on it appeared to be valid before taking the risk of sending it on to Washington and having it quickly dismissed. It would be up to those at Langley to scrutinize and authenticate it.

However, based on what Uri had told him, he knew he had a problem. If it were true that there were double-dealings and blackmail going on both there and in America, then what was on the data stick could lead to further death and destruction. Someone on the wrong side of that information would want it buried, and if that person was one of prominence in Washington, there could be many casualties of the war to come.

Uri had warned him. "Trust no one," he had said. "Chameleons care not what background lay behind them. They can adapt to any new condition at will."

Then, to whom could he turn?

Having started his career at the State Department, Ben had contact with many people with high security clearances. It was always a risk going outside the agency, and if the wrong people learned of it, he could be fired or worse—possibly brought up on charges of disclosing national secrets. It was all a game—one that some played with impunity while others were nailed by the smallest infraction.

"Allen, it's Ben Curtis." Ben decided to contact a colleague and friend, Alan Larkin, whom he had met at the Agency. He used a backchannel known only to a few at the agency to reach him on a secure line.

Larkin was the Director for the Bureau of Political and Military Affairs within the department. Although he did not report directly to the Secretary, he was only a few levels down and only a few steps away from that office. Larkin had supervised Ben while he was on a mission at the CIA a year earlier. Larkin was then transferred to State. Ben had always had a good relationship with Larkin, but his transfer had been a surprise. Rather than a demotion, it had been a two-level promotion from his position at the Agency.

"I thought that when I get back to the states we could get together for a drink. It's been a while," said Ben.

"Yes, it has," said Larkin, his voice sounding warm and happy for the call. "We need to catch up. What's going on in your world—at least anything that you can tell me about?"

They chatted for a while before Ben got down to business, still careful with his words.

"Allen, I received some information while overseas. Of course, it's sensitive, and I'm afraid, troubling."

"Oh."

"I've been given evidence that what's been going on in some labs in Ukraine has not been on the up and up."

"What do you mean?"

"I mean that there has been activity in those labs—work funded by health agencies of the U.S. government—that is not authorized by Congress. There also appear to be rogue elements in our CIA who have enabled the development of bioweapons in those labs. The matter is of grave concern with the Russians who, as you know, share a border with Ukraine."

There was an awkward silence on the other end of the line.

"Allen? Are you still there?" Ben asked nervously.

"The Ukrainian situation is certainly becoming more volatile," Larkin finally answered. "But I was unaware that it was so serious. I thought the rogue agents over there *were* the Russians. Who gave you this information?"

"I can't get into that on the phone."

"Does this have to do with the pandemic?"

"What pandemic?"

"Oh, I thought you were referring to ... never mind."

"Is something being planned?" asked Ben. "This is the second time I've heard something about a global pandemic."

"I can't comment, Ben. I had only heard that you are working on a project related to that. That's all. What I will tell you, however, is that there are forces at work, and they involve more than just Ukraine."

"Who?"

"Let's just say that if things go wrong, we could be looking at a third world war. They are playing with fire."

"Does this involve those bio-labs in Ukraine?" Ben asked.

"Yes."

"Does it involve a certain colonel here who has gone rogue on us?"

"I can't comment on that."

"But I was told …"

"Ben, whatever you were told, understand this. There are multiple sides to this possibly catastrophic issue. I wish I could tell you more, but I can't. My word of advice is this: drop it."

"Drop it?"

"There are powerful people in this world, Ben. I don't need to remind you of that. If you think your information will cause a problem, then bury it."

"That's your advice, then?"

"I shouldn't get myself involved in this. I have a family too, you know. I've given you my advice. I'm sorry, but I can't help you any more on this one." Larkin cutoff the conversation, saying, "Ben, I wish you well."

After Ben hung up the line, he was left empty and feeling abandoned. Hoping for some morsel of support, he felt as if he were being left holding the proverbial bag.

In the end, Ben made up his mind what to do next, and it would be the most important decision of his life.

*****

CH 37 – Troubling Call

After Jack's conversation with Herron, he received a message from Katz in Washington. It was strange to be contacted during a mission, but it was an encrypted message over a private server. At the appointed time, Jack dialed the number using a multi-mask algorithm that bounced the line through a Tor-like network of multiple secure, global servers used by the Defense Department. At the other end, Katz picked up.

"Hello," she answered.

"Yes. You asked me to call," said Jack.

"Yes, I got a message from our contact in New Delhi based on the meeting you had with him. He wanted to convey to me your discussion and his strong opinion about the course you are taking. In this case, you're looking into other operations there that you believe are important to the project." Her words were intentionally vague in the event their conversation was breached and begin recorded.

"Yes, I did mention that to him."

"Well, I agree with him that you are *not* to pursue those under *any* circumstances. Am I clear? We both fear you may jeopardize our ability to accomplish our goals there. It will open a Pandora's Box and subject us to greater scrutiny than we need without aiding us in the least. It is likely that you will get disinformation that is harmful rather than information that is helpful."

"I see."

"Do I make myself clear?"

"Yes, quite clear. I should cease and desist in pursing those avenues, then."

"Yes, immediately. You need to find your objective quickly, take care of things and return to Washington as soon as possible. That is your responsibility and your *only* responsibility."

"And the contact from outside the country that I have been involved with will be able to provide me with what I need?"

"Without a doubt. He is extremely trustworthy and will give you that."

"All right then. Thank you for the clarification."

Jack hung up the line, but he felt a growing unease. Nowhere in that conversation had she said anything about it helping him in his mission. The *team* aspect of the mission seemed no longer to apply. I now appeared to be an antiquated value system of an Administration from a time long-since passed.

Jack was on his own, and somehow, he had sensed that ever since the mission had started. It was a feeling that someone else in the Curtis family had experienced nearly twenty years earlier.

*****

CH 38– Reprieve

As Shannon devoured three eggs, over-easy, two strips of turkey bacon, and two pieces of whole wheat toast, Faye looked on in amazement. Only the day before, her daughter looked as though it might be her last.

"So, what happened?" Faye asked. "You just got up and felt better?"

Shannon took a deep slurp of orange juice and wiped her mouth with her napkin.

"Something weird happened in the middle of the night," her daughter began. "It was the weirdest dream."

"What?"

"I heard my name being called, and I sat up in bed looking around the room. But there was no one there. My door was shut, and I didn't hear anyone moving around upstairs or creaking the floorboards downstairs. Then, I heard my name again."

"It was a dream, Shannon. I wouldn't worry too much about it."

"But the second time I heard my name, I saw something in my room. It was a misty cloud—kinda' like the one Will talks about when he talks to his Gramma."

"Oh, no, … don't start with that!"

"No, really, Mom. That's what it looked like. It told me to get the jug—that I would find my cure in that jug."

"You're beginning to sound like a …"

"Like a what, Mom?"

Faye was thinking about addiction, and that it sounded like what an alcoholic would say about finding the bottom of his or her bottle.

"Nothin'. As you were sayin'."

"That was it, but you're right. It was only a dream."

"So, just because you had a dream, you've had this remarkable recovery? I don't understand."

"Uh, well, …"

"Shannon. What did you do?"

"I ... I did as my dream told me to do."

"You did what?"

"I went to your room last night while both of you were downstairs. I got some of the black liquid—the elixir."

"What?" screamed Faye. "I took that away from you so you wouldn't get to it!"

"It helps me, Mom! You can see it yourself. I'm fine now," Shannon answered.

Faye cast a skeptical eye on her daughter.

"You looked like hell yesterday. I don't understand it, but it can't be from that jug. It's infernal! It's damned, it is! I want you to stop!"

Shannon was quiet. Then she said, "But if I don't take it, then what?" There was an awkward silence between them. "When is that vaccine or cure coming that you talk about?"

"They said in another few weeks."

"If I regress again, then a few weeks may be too long. You and I both know that. Just let me keep taking it until the cure comes. Please!"

Faye looked at her daughter and saw the miraculous recovery she'd made. She couldn't explain it, but at the same time, she wasn't sure that she feared the strange black elixir in the jug even more.

"Maybe you won't need any more," Faye answered. "Maybe that's all you'll need."

"Maybe."

"All right. But only if you really need it and only for the next few weeks—until the shots are ready."

***

Two weeks passed, and Shannon found that without daily doses of the black elixir, she started to regress. Each time, her regression was faster and deeper.

When Faye next checked the black jug, she found it only half full.

"Shannon, how much of this are you taking?"

By now, Shannon's face looked as though she'd had thirty years of plastic surgery. She didn't look like herself, regardless of how young the potion was trying to make her.

"You're addicted to it, aren't you?" asked her mom.

"No! Of course not! It's just taking more to get me get back to normal."

"No, it's not, Shannon. It's killing you!" Faye got up from the kitchen table. "I'm going upstairs and pouring it all down the drain. It's for your own good."

"No, Mom. If you do, then I will certainly die. You saw what happens when I don't have it. I'll look ninety in a week. I'll be dead soon after. We both know it."

Faye broke down in tears, sobbing beyond consolation. Shannon put her arm around her mother, but it offered little solace.

"I just don't understand. They said the cure would be ready any day now, but every time I ask, I get the same answer—'maybe tomorrow.' We can't wait until tomorrow anymore. We can't." Faye swirled what remained inside the jug. "How long do you think you can hold out with what's in here?" she asked.

"I don't know—maybe for another week?"

"That was the same stuff Will's dog ate, right?"

"I think so. We're not really sure. That and the dream are what made me think to try it," said Shannon. "I didn't know it would react differently in me."

"I ... I don't know, Shannon. All this is too strange for me to understand. I think we should take you to the doctor to see if there's something more we can do. Get dressed."

The two of them drove to the doctor's office, and they managed to squeeze into a time slot just vacated by another patient who had just cancelled.

Dr. Oglevee took her vitals and recorded them all on his laptop. Then, he sent them to a nearby lab where they took some blood samples and ran them through some quick screens, but other than confirming she had the malaria-like pathogen, no other answers were forthcoming.

"Well?" asked Faye. "What did you find?"

The doctor shook his head. "Inconclusive—just as before."

"Inconclusive? What's that supposed to mean?"

"What I mean is that your daughter shows only the signs of the malaria-like disease we've been finding everywhere. We still don't know what it really is, though. There seems to be nothing in her blood work or in the DNA tests we ran earlier that would explain why she should be aging so quickly—like having progeria. She doesn't."

"Then as her mother, what the hell am I supposed to do for her!"

Indeed, during the few hours between the time they had arrived and then, Shannon had aged another year or even two.

Oglevee shook his head. "I don't understand it. But I tell you what. Let me order some more blood tests to see if anything shows up on those. They are only for rare and unusual disorders, but perhaps we'll find something there."

"This whole thing was caused by those damned mosquitos they let loose everywhere," said Faye. "*That* was the cause, you know. *That's* what they're saying on the Internet."

"We talked about that the last time you were here. Since then, the consensus of leading scientists, the WHO, the CDC and others is that it's *not* coming from the sterile mosquitos they released. They said that was impossible. What you're hearing on the Internet is fake news—tin foil hat stuff. You need to turn that off, Faye. It's not helping you or your family. They are scare tactics and intended to deceive you. Don't fall for them!"

"All right, then what *is* causing it?" asked Shannon.

"We don't know. But the current theory is that it's coming from *other* mosquitos—not those that were sterilized. They're saying now that we need to release *more* of the sterilized ones to get rid of the ones—the native ones—that are the real threat," said Oglevee.

"Isn't there *anything* you can give her now?"

The doctor shook his head. "No, I think it's prudent to wait for the cure."

"When?"

"They issued an EUA for it, so I think it should be coming out within the next few weeks."

"A what?"

"An EUA, an Emergency Use Authorization. They're saying *everyone* should get it to prevent the disease. It had an efficacy rate of 99.9% during the rigorous testing they've done. This is a no-brainer, Faye."

Indeed, it was only a few nights later that the breakthrough cure was proclaimed.

President Carpenter stood at the podium in the Press Room of the White House and beamed with triumphant satisfaction.

"We have wonderful news to report today," she began. "My Administration has been working diligently with companies overseas to develop a cure for the disease that is afflicting millions across this country and the world. Because of my efforts, we have developed—in conjunction with cooperating companies—a cure that will be rolled out within the next thirty days. These shots will be mandatory for *everyone*. If you don't get the shot, you won't be able to leave your home. Cure cards will be electronic and checked by the police on the streets. Those without a shot will be taken to a FEMA quarantine camp until they agree to the shot. They may be detained indefinitely if they refuse. This is too deadly of a disease to let it go without treatment or prevention. Scientists believe that unless we give the shots to everyone, hundreds of millions could die. And while the mortality rate now is low, scientists believe it could reach 95% if we don't take these measures."

"Madam President, what's the name of the drug?" asked a pool reporter.

Carpenter leaned to one side and listened as one of her advisors spoke into her ear.

"It's called *iuventuris*, I believe," she muttered. Then, after she was corrected, she said, "I mean *iuventutis*. I think I'll just call it the IUV."

"Madam President," cried a reporter, raising her hand, "why all the hoopla when only fifty-two people have died from this disease during the last six months and, of those, most were obese and in poor health. Isn't this the same failed approach taken in 2020 with COV 19?"

"Absolutely not!" the president barked back, stuttering with anger. "This is a serious disease! It cannot be taken lightly. If we ignore the potential of this, we could lose our families, our friends, and our neighbors overnight. Is that something you're willing to do? Is that something you're willing to risk? I'm not, and I know the American people aren't either."

Shortly after finishing her statement, she left the room—not taking any more questions.

"Well, that's good news!" said Faye, watching the newscast from her sofa. "They have the cure, finally! We can all go down to the clinic and get our shots next week."

Her husband, John, sat across from her in his usual spot, a recliner otherwise known as his "master control chair." He took a sip of beer and nodded in agreement. "I think you should go tell Shannon," he said.

Faye jumped off the couch and bounded up the stairs, entering Shannon's room without knocking.

"Shannon, darling! I've got great news! The cure – it's ready, finally!"

Shannon smiled weakly. The effects of the elixir were, by now, almost non-existent, and the toll taken on her body was evident. "I'll hang on as best as I can, mom."

"Only a little longer. We've got this."

Her daughter rolled back over. There was little they could do one way or the other. Shannon's fate was now up to Father Time.

*****

CH 39 – No Way Out

2018

The data from the microdot was sent to Washington and processed. The results were compiled in a report and put on Dwight Eichenberg's desk for review. He was frowning.

"This is what Uri gave you? Are you sure?" Eichenberg asked.

"Yes," said Ben, talking to him via a secure video link. "That's what he gave me. I validated much of it while I've been here, contacting others in sensitive positions—discretely, of course."

"Of course. But this isn't what we sent you to find out. We asked that you look into Colonel Williams, our Wesbaden commanding officer, and the rumors he either has or is planning on breaching certain hazmat bio labs there."

"What's on the data stick suggests there may be others involved in that," said Ben.

"I think they are trying to confuse you," said Eichenberg. "Don't be manipulated by forces there that wish to obfuscate the matter. They are masters of making the truth appear as a lie."

"Sir, the data points to others in our government who are behind the bio-labs in Ukraine and that they are not developing cures, as you believed. They are developing bio-weapons, sir, and it appears that Colonel Williams is trying to stop them from doing that. Isn't that the truth?"

Ben waited nervously. He had posed the question as if his boss knew nothing about what was actually going on there. He had hoped Eichenberg would be surprised by the news and ask him to help ferret out those responsible.

"I think we have all we need from you Ben. Thank you."

Ben sat uncomfortably, expecting more but getting nothing in return. He had gone out on a limb, believing in the system and those in charge. As a youth, his father had told him to trust and obey the wisdom of adults, especially his parents, teachers and others in the community with authority. It had been indoctrinated into him, and now he found it hard to let it go.

"That's it?" he asked, shocked and surprised.

"Yep. Thanks." Eichenberg looked away from the screen before it went black.

Ben's worst fears were being confirmed. He had a sinking feeling as he turned off his screen, feeling trapped with no place to go and no one to turn to.

***

Ben stayed in Ukraine for another three days, awaiting the final instructions and arrangements to come home. "You will be reassigned shortly," was the cryptic message that had come to him shortly after his call with Eichenberg.

But while he waited, Ben made one more contact—one he had been meaning to make ever since he had arrived in Kiev.

He used a disposable phone to make the call, and when he had finished dialing, he waited for someone to answer.

"Wiesbaden AFB. How may I direct your call?"

"Yes, may I speak to Colonel Williams?"

*****

CH 40 - Rollout of the Cure

Finally, the cure was here. It had been announced with great fanfare by the Administration and the Army which was called in to help administer the shots. As for the citizenry, the scramble was on to get the shot.

Initially, the Department of Health and Human Services, HHS, stated that only one hundred million doses would be made available. However, this created panic within the country as people gamed the online sign-up systems to make sure they got in. Finally, the Administration changed their story and said they had well over five hundred million doses—more than enough for everyone. At a cost to the taxpayers of over $10.3 trillion, it was the most expensive purchase of drugs by the US government in history—and nearly all of it went into just a few pockets: YAF, Labac Labs, politicians, and Mr. Big and the Family.

"How are we doing on the IUV production levels?" asked Bhatti, beaming as she reviewed her manufacturing reports.

It was Dr. Malok who kept her informed of the massive numbers of shipments being made all over the world. Demand had skyrocketed almost overnight when the announcement of a cure was made.

"We've sent five hundred million to the US, ninety million to Canada, three hundred-fifty million to the EU, …" he continued rattling off the numbers by country and region.

"And this month's profit estimate?" she asked.

"YAF should clear $25 billion this month before splitting the profits with Mr. Big, Labac, and all the government leaders we made promises to."

"How much will go to Mr. Big?" she asked, referring to the top sixteen families that ran the global cabal and, essentially, all things going on in the world. "What is his cut?"

"In addition to the $8.2 billion in bonus money they get, they also own 80 percent of your company—either directly or indirectly. That brings their cut to $21.6 billion this month alone. We anticipate this level of profits will only rise as we promote boosters for the next two years."

"So, what are we left with?" Bhatti asked.

"You should still make $3.4 billion. Not too bad for a month's work."

"Yeah, I can make it on that."

"That's about $40 billion for the year."

"I think we should be buying up all the gold we can. $40 billion isn't going to be worth what it once was if inflation kicks higher."

Meanwhile, in nations around the world there was a mad scramble to get the shots. By the end of the fifth week, nearly 82 percent in the US had been jabbed, and threats to those unjabbed were growing more dangerous every day.

"President Carpenter announced today that governors in all the states must comply with her order to begin arresting those not inoculated against this deadly disease by the end of the month or face not only the withholding of *all* federal funds but also the invasion and takeover by military force. This would be devastating to those states and their governors if they don't comply. It would mean the end of … well … that is something that goes without saying." The reporter couldn't bring herself to finish the sentence: *… the end of federalism and our democracy.* "Therefore, the president expects every state to carry out its Constitutional responsibility to ensure her orders are obeyed." The fact the *US Constitution* did not mandate such a thing was irrelevant. What was reported by the media had become truth— whether it was or not. The message needed to be given, and the Administration was firm that it was the media's responsibility to ensure it was delivered.

Several lawsuits were filed in federal court against the Executive Orders, but none believed they would result in any action by the already compromised federal judiciary to force a retraction. Even the Supreme Court had long been threatened by forces outside the control of the citizenry it represented and had surrendered its powers under the *Constitution*.

***

During the first few weeks following the shot deployments, there was a tremendous improvement in the rate of illness. Hospitals and clinics were reporting significant declines in the number of "malaria" cases being recorded. In addition, doctors' offices were reporting a huge rise in the number of cases—some in severe or grave condition—being restored to health with no signs of adverse effects.

It appeared to be a monumental success.

Of the 2.1 million cases of the new strain of malaria, 89.1 percent had improved with the new treatment within the first five days of getting the jab. What was not reported was the increase in the number of cases of the disease. As the releases of "sterile" mosquitos all over the country continued, the spread of the disease rose. Yet, arguments were made in most state legislative chambers and Capitol Hill in Washington calling for even more sterile mosquitos to be purchased and released. It was a vicious, self-replicating cycle—masterfully planned and executed at the highest levels.

"Only by releasing more sterile mosquitos," said Cynthia Misken, the head of the CDC, "can we mitigate the risks entirely by making sure the mosquito population is eliminated. Adding more sterilized mosquitos is the only way to achieve this."

Yet, as billions more of the flying vampires were released into the public square, another 15,000 cases of the disease were being reported each day.

It wasn't until the third week after the shots began being administered that those treated were found to be regressing. This trend was showing up in the major hospitals and clinics, but with the help of the media it was not covered. Instead, hospitals were incentivized to treat those patients who seemed to be developing *Pre-progeria* symptoms—those of pre-mature aging—with even greater doses of YAF's IUV drug. The official narrative was that this strange regression was something new and had nothing to do with the latest strain of malaria or its treatment. Even though the correlation between those "cured" by the new drug and the later discovery of pre-progeria was nearly 99.8 percent, anyone suggesting such a link was banned from all social media. Some were even arrested by a new military police group—the Patriot Force—assembled by President Carpenter just for that purpose.

Indeed, it was a crackdown like no one in the country had seen before. Yet most had no problem with it as they accepted being told that it was all "for the greater good." It was a phrase used by the president and repeated thousands of times throughout the country by the media to reinforce the message. "Why wouldn't you get the shot if it prevented your elderly and feeble grandmother from dying? Are you so callous and inhumane that you wouldn't do that for her?"

Meanwhile, Shannon, too, continued to regress, and her mother again began to worry. After a week, her daughter looked as bad, if not worse than, at any time prior to taking the black elixir.

"Shannon, you're coming with me to get your booster shot! I'm not taking no for an answer, young lady!" Faye had said.

"No, Mom. I won't."

"Yes, you will! You must!"

But at this point, Shannon was too weak to comply, even if she had wanted to. Her resolve to continue the fight was failing, and she knew no amount of the new "cure" would do anything more than what she had already gone through with what was left of the elixir in her closet.

*****

CH 41 – Poor Dr. Ghadre

Dr. Ghadre had been quarantined in a little room down on B4 of the YAF building for over a month. Fed little more than bread and water, he continued to be monitored as his condition suddenly began to decline.

As with Shannon and a rapidly growing number of the global population that had taken the jab, the scientists at the lab found that Ghadre's body was reverting and aging very quickly. When they had re-administered the serum, he had again improved, but these periods of recovery were becoming shorter and shorter. He now had to take more and more of the black serum just to get back to his previous condition.

"He is failing," said Malok. "What should we do?"

"With Dr. Ghadre? Nothing. I don't think there is anything we can do. But this presents us with a great problem as well as a great opportunity," said Bhatti.

"I don't understand."

"Send out a press release with our manipulated data that shows how the first dose was 99 percent effective but add that its effectiveness wears off over time. Show our follow-up testing and state that we recommend regular boosters every four weeks to keep up the body's immunity to the disease."

"You don't think anyone will ask for proof?" asked Dr. Malok, becoming increasingly worried about the house of cards they were building.

"What if they do? By the time the world figures it out, we'll be so rich we won't care. All our money will be offshore and hidden away, and, if we need to, we'll have enough to buy off anyone who gets in our way."

So, the requirement for boosters was propagated far and wide, and as a result, the demand for IUV increased dramatically. That, combined with the governmental contracts for more sterile mosquitos, meant the Indian corporate consortium YAF-Labac was going to reap huge profits very quickly.

However, Dr. Ghadre was not so lucky. His condition worsened even with daily injections of the black serum. Eventually, after little more than six weeks, his major organs began to fail. By this time. his pate was bald, his face looked like a shriveled prune, his skin had age spots covering most of it, and he had completely lost his memory and his mind. He looked like he was 105 years old or older. Unable to feed himself or regulate any other bodily functions, he was left to die.

"What will we do when the serum doesn't work for anyone anymore?" asked Malok.

"Nothing. The Families will have what they want—a population decline of about seven billion people—and we'll have what we want—trillions in cash."

"What if one of us or our family members comes down with it? What then?"

Bhatti thought about this for a moment. "You need to come up with a cure, then."

"A cure for the cure?"

"Precisely. Start working on it. We'll keep it for those of us who may really need it. It will also be worth a lot of money too—perhaps a quadrillion! Think of that! No one's been worth that before!"

Her eyes danced in a madness Malok had never seen before. It was a dark energy that had possessed her—taking her over completely. She cackled uncontrollably at the thought of others' misery and torment. She had become a monster of her own making and had sunk so low even her soul was in jeopardy of eternal damnation.

*****

CH 42 – Strange Box

1964

Sheu's guests spent the evening talking with him as Zhau translated. Fresh candles were brought out for the occasion, and by the time all were ready for bed they had burned more than halfway down their wickets.

The following morning came early, and Sheu had a big breakfast of some rice dumplings and congee, a rice porridge ready for them. After generous pourings of green tea, Sheu motioned for them to take their seats.

"What is it?" Luka asked.

"He said he wants to show you something," said Zhau, seemingly confused as well.

"What?" Tulia asked.

Zhau shrugged. "I don't know. He didn't explain it to me either."

Sheu returned to the table holding something in his hands. It was large and gangly looking. At the same time, it appeared ancient although not as old as the stone Tulia had purchased just one day earlier.

"Zhè shì nín kěnéng huì gǎn xìngqù de qítā nèiróng," said Sheu. He pushed the piece toward Luka, who wasn't sure what he was supposed to do with it.

"What's this?" Luka asked before Zhau had a chance to explain.

In Luka's hands was what looked like a rusted machine. Caked with dust and grease, the machine appeared as if it had come from an old machinist's mad laboratory. Covered with the same strange symbols that had graced the stone surface of the Dropa disc, the metal box was heavy and measured six by six inches square but only two inches thick.

"My friend said if you can figure out how to use this," Zhau said, translating Sheu's words, "you may be able to decipher what's on the stone."

"And where did this come from?" asked Luka.

"Sheu claims the man who sold him the stone also gave this to him, but he was never able to figure out how to use it."

Luka scrutinized the strange object, and there didn't seem to be any slot or other way to put a stone disc inside the box. Neither was there a "record-type" spindle or indented space on top to place it.

"I suppose he wants us to buy this from him too," said Luka.

Zhau started to nod, but Sheu shook his head, understanding what Luka had said. He answered something more in Chinese, and Zhau listened. But after Sheu had finished, Zhau thought better about changing his words.

"My friend said no. He does not seek anything more but is willing to give it to you for you to try to decipher on your own. He said it is important for you to have it."

Tulia reached into her purse and pulled out twenty more yuan. "Here," she said. "You need this a lot more than we do. Here. Take it. It's also for your gracious hospitality."

Sheu shook his head, but Tulia insisted, placing into his palm and closing it. Sheu bowed and said his thanks countless times in gratitude.

The trip back from Sanlizhen was, to Luka's and Tulia's relief, uneventful. They did spend one more night at Zhau's cousin's place as a rest stop but made it back to Luoyang without incident. After giving Zhau a nice tip as well, they took their bus back to Beijing and then on to America aboard one of the new Boeing 707 Cruiseliners.

When they reached Chicago, Melana stood at the gate as they disembarked. Next to her was Natalia with Leonid snuggled in a blue, cotton blanket in his baby carriage. Natalia ran to Tulia once she spotted them coming in through the outside door off the tarmac. She jumped into her mother's arms where she got scores of kisses. Luka gave his daughter a peck on her forehead and then tickled Leonid as he lay fussing in his stroller.

"*Cum a fost călătoria?* (How was the trip?)" Melana asked in Romanian.

"*Da, a fost minunat!* (Yes! It was great!). I'll have to tell you all about it," Tulia answered, switching to English for Luka's sake.

"Did you find what you were looking for?"

"That, we're not sure," said Luka. "Only time will tell."

As they drove back to Indianapolis, Luka began shaking his head.

"What is it? What's wrong?" asked Tulia. "Did we forget something?"

"Perhaps we did," said her husband. "I now realize how much I missed those two rug rats back there."

Tulia looked behind her into the backseat. Both children looked like pure angels to her as they slumbered without a care in the world.

"Yes, so did I."

"I don't know if we should ever leave them again, Tulia."

"Perhaps that was our last adventure, Luka. And perhaps it's for the best."

Tulia pulled out her bag and looked once more at the strange disc and the even stranger metal box. Taking her fingernail, she scratched the surface of it trying to remove some of the grime. But beneath the rocky exterior, she spotted something different.

What? she thought. *What is this?*

*****

CH 43– Addiction

Shannon went to the secret box in her closet; this one was where she kept her high school trophies and memorabilia. It was also where she kept the two, colored jugs from Gramma's notorious trunk of treasures. While Faye had not wanted her to continue using the black elixir, she had sadly acquiesced, realizing it was the only thing keeping her daughter alive until the cure was available. But now that the alleged cure had been released, Shannon had resisted it, leaving her mother in a quandary.

"No, mother. I won't!" said Shannon, in defiance.

"You must, child! If I have to stick the needle in your arm myself, I'll do it!" said Faye, storming out of her daughter's room.

By this time, Shannon was shaking so badly that she could hardly get the black jug out of the box. Ever since the first dose, it had taken more and more of the serum, and more and more often, to bring her back from the Reaper's scythe. Now, she was taking sips constantly throughout the day, like a poor, addicted wino clinging to a brown bag on a dirty street corner. But Shannon was not oblivious to her condition. She realized what was happening. She was suffering from acute withdrawal and had quickly become addicted. It was all she could think about during the day—needing her next fix. First thing in the morning, throughout the day and last thing before she went to bed. It was non-stop.

But now when she lifted the black jug, it seemed light--almost empty—and panic began to set in. She knew she would need more and soon.

Shannon sat at the kitchen table staring at the jug she had enveloped with both of her hands. She laughed. *A cure that kills,* she thought, amusing herself. But the amusement quickly vanished, and the reality returned that she was an addict and was likely dying. It was something she couldn't fight, and deep down, she knew it was, indeed, killing her—slowly.

How quickly it had consumed her. How quickly it had controlled her body and mind. What would she do when she ran out? What would she be willing to do to be calm again? She put her hands to her head to stop the thoughts from racing through it, but nothing helped. She had never felt so alone in her entire life.

"Will!" she called out. Her parents weren't home, and her mother wasn't there to chastise her for wanting to be with the one boy she needed then.

Someone who always seemed to understand her. Someone who had been through much with her. Someone upon which she counted and could always depend.

She tipped the black jug for one more sip, but this time nothing came out. She tapped the bottom, trying to coax a few more drop from its cavity. Yet there was nothing left. The black bottle was empty.

*****

CH 44 – Colonel Williams

2018

Although it wasn't easy to convince the colonel's attaché to allow a conversation with her boss, Ben managed it. Hesitant, the colonel finally agreed only to a phone conversation. Ben wasn't even sure what he wanted to accomplish by having the discussion. He had been sent to Ukraine to find out about the colonel's band of renegades and to eliminate them. Colonel Williams was intended to be the first casualty but only if he could arrange to meet with him in person.

Ben's phone rang, and he picked up.

"Yeah," he answered, careful not to give away any information that wasn't necessary.

"Mr. Maddington?"

"Yes."

"This is Colonel Williams. I don't normally talk to civilians, but my attaché was convinced that you are someone for whom I should make an exception. I'm impressed. She never falls for easy lines like you gave her. So, with what can I help you? I can only give you three minutes, so make it quick."

"You are aware of certain biological laboratories here in the Ukraine that are working on cures for pathogens that could threaten mankind," said Ben, cutting to the chase.

"I thought you were a reporter with the *Mumbai Times*?" said Williams, now more defensively.

"No sir. I work for the same group you do."

"You're not Army."

"No sir. But we are on the same side."

"Are we?" asked the colonel, skeptically.

"I've been sent to talk to you about your intentions with regard to these labs. My supervisors believe you are planning to destroy those bio-labs to prevent them from developing critical cures or therapies for worldwide contagions."

"They do, do they?"

"Is that the case?"

Williams laughed. "Do you really think I would tell you if it were?"

"I must say there are many in Washington who believe you are working against those labs."

"What do you want?" asked the colonel abruptly.

"I just want to talk," said Ben. "I'm here to help those in Washington get a better understanding of the situation on the ground here."

"CIA doesn't get involved to get 'a better understanding.' I wasn't born yesterday, Mr. Maddington."

"I didn't say I was with the Agency."

"You didn't have to. Have a nice day, Mr. Maddington."

"Wait," said Ben. "What if I told you I believe those labs are *not* developing cures but rather developing the pathogens themselves? What if they're creating the next global pandemic?"

The colonel was quiet.

"Sir?"

"Yes. I think we should meet Mr. Maddington. Let me tell you where and when."

The meeting was arranged at a local café in Kiev during the early-afternoon rush in broad daylight. As Ben fully expected the colonel brought a couple enlisted men with him in the event this was a setup or other ploy to get the colonel off by himself, vulnerable to kidnapping or attack.

Williams was tall and broad-chested. He walked in with a swagger that only someone of his rank or higher could muster, and he came over to Ben immediately, pulling up a chair after motioning off his guards. Nearly bald, the colonel had a strong, square chin and high cheekbones. His eyes were steely blue, and his gold eagle lapels glistened in the light of the café.

"Maddington?" said the colonel, sitting down. "Let's start off by your telling me your real name and who you really work for, shall we?"

The colonel had counterpunched quickly, catching Ben off guard. However, Ben was trained in the event his cover was blown.

"Yes, colonel. I'm Ben Curtis, and as you rightly suspected earlier, I work for the CIA. That is why you couldn't find me anywhere in the files, as I'm sure you looked."

"Of course, Mr. Curtis. I already found you in the CIA files. Now, how did you come by the information you have on these bio labs?"

"I can't reveal my sources, sir. However, I do believe they are valid and believable."

"And I suppose you've been fed the lies about my going 'rogue' and plotting to destroy those labs."

"Yes. My superiors in Washington believe you are looking to falsify evidence about the labs to make them appear to be manufacturing a virus that could wipe out the planet. Then, you will use that evidence to discredit people in high places in DC before you blow them up."

Williams laughed. "That's good. Very good. Except it's not true."

"What parts?"

"All but the part about manufacturing a virus."

"Then my source is right."

"But they aren't the only ones. There are labs in China and India doing the same thing. Soon, they will release it, and it will bring the earth to its knees."

"Soon?"

"My sources tell me so, yes," Williams answered.

Ben nodded. Uri's microdot had claimed the same thing, even though it was uncertain from where the virus would originate.

"So, did you bring your weapon?"

"Excuse me?" Ben asked.

"They sent you to kill me, did they not?"

Again, the punch came hard and direct—just as the colonel liked it. He took out a cigar and lit it, blowing smoke into the tiny café.

"Do you think it will come from here?" asked Ben, ignoring the question.

"I don't know. But it's coming. The question I have," said the colonel leaning into the table, "is 'Why kill me?' If you eliminate me, do you believe the threat of stopping the release just goes away—because it doesn't. I'm not the only one trying to stop it. There are others working to do the same right now too. In fact, they may start a war over it."

"Who may start a war?"

"You will find out soon enough. Those back in Washington already know, I can assure you. But as for your mission to kill me, I would ask that you not. I am a patriot, Mr. Curtis, not a traitor. If you are looking for traitors to our country look no further than the agency that employs you. Do you suspect your superiors aren't telling you the entire truth? Then you would be right. Go with your instincts. Just be aware that you can trust no one. No one."

"What about you?" asked Ben.

"What about me?" Williams answered, blowing out another smoke ring. "I am lucky to be alive, Mr. Curtis. There have already been two attempts to take me out. But both were carried out by Ukrainian troops. They tried to stage them as accidents. So, you see, you are not the first."

"Why would they want you killed?"

"They want my evidence on their labs—the bio labs. They are working with the Deep State in DC. Both need this to go away or at least re-submerge into the swamp where it thrives. Their best way for that to happen is for me to go away."

"To be killed?"

"Having failed at their earlier attempts, I thought they were merely reassigning me. There was a letter that I received just before you reached out. It suggested such, but it came from an unlikely source, so I didn't give it much thought."

"What was that?"

"The State Department. From an assistant director there ... Allen Larkin. Do you know him?"

Ben froze. It was his worst fear confirmed. *Trust no one* were the words that echoed in his mind. Now, he understood. Those who played in the spy arena were very good at their jobs—very good indeed.

"I don't," Ben answered, fumbling for words. "What do you plan to do?"

"I have my plans, but it wouldn't be prudent for me to tell you. Now would it?"

"No, I don't suppose it would."

The colonel left the meeting with his two guards. It would be the first and last time that Ben would meet with the colonel.

*****

CH 45 – Sales Call

At first, many other drug companies in Delhi were eager to rat out YAF and their nefarious practices, but as time went on, there was pressure coming from powerful people in the country to snuff it out. In time, Jack felt uneasy in the big city of more than forty-seven million people. Even for him, an experienced agent, it felt like there were eyes watching him all the time—as if he were visiting one of the communist or totalitarian countries in the world.

"I don't know where you got that idea, Mr. Mankoviz," said Param Sachdeva at one of the big pharma companies. Jack had stopped by the facility earlier in this visit, but things had decidedly changed since that time. "I think there must be some misunderstanding. We would never say negative things about our competitors, especially YAF. That's not the way we do business in India."

Jack got that same treatment several times as he made his rounds trying to sell raw chemicals to and collect information on the industry. The responses changed abruptly and so did the degree of cooperation.

"Sorry."

"I'm sorry."

"So sorry, we can't help you."

Fearing his cover had been blown, he reached out to Washington for answers.

"We have no intelligence from anyone that your cover has been compromised, Jack," said Katz, his boss.

"Well, then I don't know how I can make any progress with this thing."

"I trust you still aren't snooping around labs there in New Delhi. I told you to leave that alone. We need you to take care of Sawmill. Nothing more at this point."

"Just trying to do the job," Jack replied.

"Good. Then get this wrapped up."

Defying orders, Jack took one more crack at YAF. Walking into one of their in-town laboratories, he announced himself at the front desk.

"Yes, I'm Roger Mankoviz of Synt RX from the United States, and I was in town calling on several of our accounts. We sell raw material additives, vitamins, and other chemical compounds used in your manufacturing of pharmaceuticals. I was wondering if I could talk to someone about our pricing."

Although the company's purchasing department declined to see him, he managed to strike up a conversation with another vendor in the lobby—a man who sold YAF their lab glassware, including pipets, test tubes, beakers, and other equipment essential for drug research and development. Oddly, he was from Derbyshire, England, where Jack's mother had been born.

"You don't say," said Jack. "Why, my mother was from Derbyshire."

"Really? I haven't been to Derby for many years now," said Walter Peabody, the sales rep for the glass company. "My parents moved here to New Delhi in the 1990s, and I was born here. I married a beautiful Brahman woman who is the love of my life. With my family living here, I wouldn't think about moving back."

"I understand," said Jack. "I feel the same way about America. Say, I've been trying to see someone in Procurement here but am having a hard time of it. Do you have any suggestions?"

Peabody laughed. "Oh, for you, that's easy. The head of the department is Jerome Patton. He's one of the queen's men too. He'll see you. Just tell him you're a friend of mine. But he's over at YAF headquarters which is a short cab ride from here."

Jack stopped by the huge headquarters building of YAF—one that had doubled in size since the outbreak of the alleged "malaria" pandemic worldwide. The soaring atrium in the lobby extended up twenty floors to a glass ceiling, and there was marble everywhere; everything was white. Exotic palms and banana trees sprang from huge white pots sitting strategically near expansive glass panels to soak in the Delhi sun. Yet, at that time of day, the windows automatically turned dark from a piezo-effect glass installed to shield the lobby from the ferocity of the sun's rays beating down.

Very impressive, thought Jack, looking around the vast entrance. *And I know where they got the money for all of it.*

Jack did as Peabody had instructed, and as if choreographed to perfection, the pretty Indian woman at the front desk informed him that Mr. Patton would be down promptly to see him. It took no more than fifteen minutes when Jerome Patton emerged from between two golden elevator doors and strode quickly past the three guards stationed at the front desk and into the lobby.

"Mr. Mankoviz, it's nice to meet you," said Patton, extending his hand.

"Call me Roger," said Jack.

"This way," said Patton, gesturing toward the bank of golden escalators. "So, you know Walter Peabody? He's a godsend to me. Don't get me wrong. I love India and the people, but after a while, I do miss my home of England."

"How did you find yourself here, then?" Jack asked, nicely sidestepping the question about his relationship with Peabody.

"Opportunity, I suppose," said Patton. "I was younger; more naïve. I thought coming to India would be exotic and freeing. It was. But now that I'm older, I'm thinking more about returning to the king's country."

They rode the elevator to the third floor, skipping the second, before getting off. Then, they went through a series of secured doors until they reached a fishbowl conference room that was surrounded by heavy plate glass and rimmed with several large white monitors hanging around the perimeter.

"We have grown quite a bit during the last six months," said Patton. "I've been at YAF about a year, and I've never seen anything like it."

"It's your *iuventutis* drug that's making the difference," said Jack. "It's doing wonderful things for people, I understand."

"Yes, it's an amazing therapeutic," said Patton. "It's been a blowout drug for us. We can't make enough of the stuff. It's keeping my department busy. That's for sure."

"Yes, it must make you feel good. How does it work, actually, when nothing else seems to?"

Patton laughed. "I'm not a scientist. I can't help you with that."

"Do you know what chemical compounds are used in it?"

"I buy all of it; so yes. But for me they're just chemicals. I'm not privy to the secret formula that makes the thing work. We also get some ingredients from Labac Labs, a sister company, although I don't know what's in that stuff. Around here, it's like asking for the formula for Coca Cola. It's not for public knowledge. All that comes out of our Dark Lab."

"Dark Lab?"

"Yeah, that's what we call the lab in the basement. There are several levels down there where they work on the really secret stuff. You have to give your first child and a liter of blood to get into it."

"Interesting," Jack answered.

As they talked, Jack glanced around the floor. There was glass everywhere, so it wasn't hard to see the offices from one side of the floor to the other. All the cubes were filled, as were most of the private offices. People were scurrying about here and there busy carrying laptops to meetings or retrieving documents for scanning and processing.

"So, the IUV drug came from your Dark Lab?"

"Yes."

"Do you happen to know anything about the trials that were conducted—Who they tested on? How many people were tested? What the results might have been? You know, the usual stuff."

Patton laughed. "Again, I'm just the purchasing agent. What I can tell you is that your pricing is quite competitive. I think we may need to look at what you can do for us. Can you send me samples?"

"Absolutely," said Jack, knowing he wouldn't be sending anything, but buying time for himself to get more information. "I'll send over a list of everything we offer, and you can choose what and how much of each you'd like for testing purposes."

As Jack got up to leave, he asked, "Oh, one other thing. Do you know if your sister company, Labac Labs, has any chemical needs? Do you purchase for them too?"

"But they work on sterilizing mosquitos. I don't know what chemical needs they have, but you're right. I'm sure they do. I just think they would need different chemicals—you know, for the genetic modifications they're doing."

"Of course not. Not the same ones, but perhaps others? Do you buy for them or is there also a central purchasing group for both companies?"

"No, they buy their own."

"Do you have the name of their agent, by chance?" Jack asked.

Patton provided the information, reluctantly handing him the business card of the Labac purchasing agent. But by the end of the meeting, Jack had established a good rapport with Patton—one which he could leverage in the future, if needed.

***

Jack returned to his hotel room and found the sheets of his bed already turned down by the housekeeping staff with a small chocolate wrapped in a gold-colored aluminum foil gracing the top of his pillow. He changed into his PJ bottoms and opened his computer to cull through the day's news and the throng of emails he had received during the day.

Yet, as he sifted through his emails, he found one that caught his eye. It had been sent anonymously by someone using an encrypted email address that was only a series of numbers and letters. The article attached was entitled, *A Connection Between New Malaria and Labac Labs.*

The piece discussed the correlation between the new disease and the government's program to release sterilized mosquitos into heavily populated urban areas. Since malaria came from the *Anopheles* mosquito, whether sterilized or not, the connection appeared logical. Even though the sterilizing company, Labac Labs, as well as the greater scientific community had dismissed the allegation as "completely unfounded." The company claimed all its mosquitos were somehow tested for the single-celled, *Plasmodium* parasite that caused malaria, and none—absolutely zero—had been identified with it. To assert that every one of the billions of mosquitos had somehow been tested was a ridiculous claim on its surface. No contention could be made without extensive qualifiers.

Indeed, several studies had been conducted on the released mosquitoes. Two teams of scientists reported capturing specimens right after their release by Labac Labs. These were then tested for the pathogen. One study revealed that over 73 percent of the Labac sterile mosquitos had the parasite, or at least tested positive for the traits of the disease. In its damning conclusion, the research author went on to suggest that such a high percentage *"could only be intentional."*

Jack searched to find other articles on the Internet, and although many titles were blocked, marked "Unavailable" or were removed as "Disinformation," he did access a few. These also referred to studies that involved capturing mosquitos released from the government programs. One in Miami studied released mosquitos and found them to contain not only the parasite but also a synthetic nanotechnology that resembled an amoeba. However, they were unable to identify what it was or why it was in the mosquitos. No such organism had ever been found in mosquitos before. When exposed to temperatures above 98.6 Fahrenheit, the structures grew exponentially into long fibrous "tendons" that seemed to block major pathways in the human body's circulatory system.

Taking another angle, Jack looked into government contracts with YAF and Labac. What wasn't surprising was the amount of profits made by the two companies during the previous twelve months. They were massive.

Contracts with national and local governments were in the billions, initially to fight the West Nile virus, and then later to obtain a cure. Both programs garnered tens of billions for their manufacturers.

Create the problem; react as the public demands; then, create the solution. But from each process, profit handsomely. *Masterful*, thought Jack.

Other articles also revealed how the mosquitos were not all sterile. Statistically, 100 percent sterilization was virtually impossible. Even a one percent error rate on ten billion mosquitos would mean that one hundred million would be able to reproduce. With that flaw and the mosquito's rapid reproductive cycle, there would quickly be millions more created in fertile condition, exacerbating the threat. Adding a hundred million more to a native population of a billion fully functioning mosquitos in the environment was a recipe for disaster.

When Jack looked at the geographic dispersion of the Labac mosquitoes and overlayed that with the outbreak of New Malaria, he found the results striking. In nearly every case, the highest instances of New Malaria were reported in the cities with the largest releases of the Labac mosquitos: New York, Los Angeles, Chicago, Philadelphia, Dallas, Jacksonville, Cincinnati, Miami, and Washington, D.C. With governments calling for more mosquitos to be released while at the same time clamoring for IUV doses, YAF and Labac had created a perpetual money machine, and it was printing faster than anyone could have imagined.

But what Jack lacked was a connection between the two companies: YAF and Labac. *It must be here*, he thought. But there seemed to be nothing online. It had been buried deeply, hidden or even expunged. So, this time he scheduled a meeting at Labac to see what he could dig up.

Jack found the Labac lab, which was located in a suburb of New Delhi. The combination of a new receptionist and laxer security made getting to someone much easier than it had been at YAF. In fact, rather than a purchasing agent, the receptionist contacted the Director of Lab Operations for him. The director, Dr. Eeshan Umar, was also relatively new to the company, having been hired directly from another lab: YAF.

"Dr. Umar, thank you for taking the time to speak to me," said Jack. "I've been talking to Patton at YAF about the prices of chemicals they're buying, and he suggested that I talk to you. But before I do, I was wondering what you could tell me about your mosquito program and New Malaria strain that's been found in them."

Jack was fishing. He had no information that anything like that was going on at the lab, but he thought he would try.

"New Malaria?" asked Dr. Umar.

"I don't recall the exact name of the project, but Dr. Bhatti said she was working on a cure for your New Malaria problem. Is that right?"

"There is no problem with our mosquitoes. There has been no link of the new contagion to them. I don't know why she would ..."

"Oh, then I'm confused. I was told that YAF developed the IUV drug in connection with your mosquito program."

"It wasn't in *connection* with the program."

"But there are government contracts that both your companies share. Isn't that right?"

"Yes, we work on contracts together."

"But this was not one of them?" Jack asked.

"Listen, all I know is that YAF found a substance that seemed to work on the New Malaria problem. It was independent of Labac."

"I understand. Just one more question. You came to Labac from YAF, right? Was that because of the similarity of the work?"

Omar was surprised by the question and muttered, "I don't know what you mean?"

"Well, it would make sense that Labac would hire you, but only if you had experience working on similar projects. Right?"

"Labac develops genetically modified insects and animals to solve ecological and other problems. YAF develops therapeutics and vaccines. Those are quite different."

"Then why would Labac hire you?" Jack asked.

"It is true that YAF's therapeutics are genetically driven. I worked on that aspect. It's a significant upgrade from the old mRNA we used back in the 20s. I'm pretty proud to have made the discoveries that have led to their success."

"So, the genetics related to the modified mosquitos *is* connected to the development of IUV."

Dr. Umar squirmed. "On the surface, it appears like there would be. But there isn't."

"When you were at YAF, you must have gotten something from Labac to be able to find a cure, right?"

"No. As I said, there is no connection with New Malaria and our mosquitoes. There would be no reason for Labac to supply anything to YAF."

"But people at YAF told me so. They said they got samples from Labac to work with."

Dr. Umar gave Jack a Stoic look—cautiously evaluating whether Jack was telling him the truth. And after an awkward silence, it was clear he bought Jack's argument.

"Whether YAF got the samples from Labac is irrelevant," Dr. Umar answered. "What is important is that we find cures for this contagion. Don't you agree?"

There it was—the connection. Labac and YAF were in this thing together. Together with government politicians and others in power, the circle had been completed.

"Yes, I couldn't agree more. Dr. Umar," said Jack. "I thank you for your time, and I will follow up with your purchasing agent to see if we can help you with any equipment or chemicals you might need."

Jack left the building. He didn't have an admission, but he had enough to fit the last piece to the puzzle. He was convinced, now, that what went on in these labs was not "for the betterment of mankind." These were nefarious activities intent upon bringing pain and anguish to the masses while at the same time making many people very rich.

Instead of Kierney being the evil, rogue agent trying to destroy "good" works in those labs, he, if true, was trying to destroy an evil tripartite bent upon destroying as much of the population as it could. It was about depopulation and money—it was as simple as that.

So, the question was, What should he do now?

*****

CH 46 - Outbreak 3

"Good evening. This is Brett Major. As the pandemic spreads from country to country, governments are imposing stiff new rules to contain it. Currently, the numbers show 2.4 million already infected and 305,725 deaths, although those numbers are expected to go much higher. But hope is rising, as the new cure from YAF Laboratories seems to be the drug of choice."

In the lower right quadrant of the screen was a table listing the number of cases and deaths as a macabre tally of the devastation claimed to have been inflicted on the country. The numbers changed by the second, spinning higher as the broadcast went on, intended to underscore the seriousness of the event.

Major turned toward another camera which also came with a new backdrop. The new one showed the YAF company logo together with a picture of a syringe.

"Although there have been reports of the effects of the YAF cure not lasting as long as was originally anticipated," Major said, continuing, "the protection should last longer than thirty days. The director at YAF, Dr. VK Malok, claims it is much longer than thirty days."

The story shifted to the doctor at YAF who was being interviewed by a BBC reporter.

"Can you explain the effectiveness period, doctor Malok?" asked the BBC reporter, standing in one of the labs that had been assembled purely as a backdrop for conducting interviews.

"Yes, the talk of thirty days is purely a regulatory matter," said Malok. "When the efficacy of a drug falls below a certain threshold, we must categorize it as if it had no efficacy at all. This is very misleading, of course. The drug has a much longer span of effectiveness than merely thirty days."

"I see. So, do you anticipate that boosters will be required?"

"Yes. This is not unusual. As you recall, regular boosters were mandated as part of the 2020 Covid protocol. This is really standard procedures at this point."

"Thank you for that clarification, doctor." The reporter then turned back to the camera. "As you can see, while this pandemic is expected to be much worse than the one almost twenty years ago, the same protocols will be used as they were very successful in wiping out Covid after only three years."

But as the reporter signed off, what struck most viewers was why the reporter failed to follow-up with the obvious question. "What is the threshold below which the efficacy of the drug comes into question?"

The answer lay deep in the limited trial results conducted by others on the drug, and it had been shocking. After only two weeks, the effectiveness was less than 20 percent, and after thirty days, it was actually *negative*. Indeed, those taking the jab were *more* likely to suffer and die than those without it.

Brett Major was unaware of the information, and as a talking head, he merely continued reading from the teleprompter. Had he known, it likely would not have made any difference. He still would have mouthed the same words that came over the screens in front of him. His $10 million per year salary depended on it.

*****

CH 47 - Ahab

By now, Shannon's condition had become critical. Without another dose from the jug, she was failing fast. Once a beautiful young woman of twenty-one, she now looked every bit of seventy, if not eighty.

"I can't let this continue!" screamed Faye, looking at her daughter. "I'm taking you to get a booster right now!"

Shannon was only semi-conscious when her mother placed her in the car, and they drove to the Emergency Room at Georgetown Hospital. Medics took Shannon in on a stretcher while Faye watched, helpless and forlorn. John met her at the hospital, and together they waited in the lobby for someone to come and talk to them about their daughter's condition.

Initially, the administrator had refused to admit her.

"I'm sorry, but your daughter hasn't had all the boosters we require for admittance. We can't accept her."

"But she got the first one!" screamed Faye.

"I'm sorry, but it's too late for that. She had her chance. We can't risk ..."

Faye had leaned over the desk with a look of determination and anger. "You *will* admit her. Do you understand me? Or so help me God, I will ..."

After two hours, a doctor pushed open the double-swinging doors in the Emergency Area. He was talking through his blue medical mask when he said, "Your daughter has genetic signs of progeria. It's unusual to show signs this late in life—usually they show at birth—but we've seen a lot of these lately."

"Then she needs to get another booster, right?" asked John.

"Yes, I think that is essential," answered the doctor.

Nearby, a woman sitting on a chair jumped up. She wore gray sweatpants and an oversized t-shirt. Although dressed like a college co-ed, she was middle-aged and looked like she had been through a rough time. The dark circles under her eyes punctuated her already-disheveled appearance. With short, blonde hair tied back in a make-shift ponytail, the petite, wafer-like woman was animated and unafraid to throw herself into the middle of the controversy.

"Did you do a blood test?" the woman asked the doctor.

"Are you a doctor?" asked Faye.

"Yes, as a matter of fact, I am," the woman answered.

The ER doctor bristled at the interruption. "This matter doesn't concern you," he said brusquely. Then, he turned his back on her to re-engage Faye and John. "We should leave here to discuss this matter in private."

"I saw your daughter when she came in," the woman continued. "My daughter was the same way, and they ended up killing her."

"What?" asked John.

"Yeah, they overdosed her with that IUV crap and ended up killing her. They didn't bother to take another blood test to see what her antigen levels were. They didn't seem to care. When I protested, they had guards take me out of the building, and I wasn't allowed to come back in. They killed her—they killed my daughter!" The woman broke down in tears.

"I'm sure that's not the case," said the ER doctor. "You were just too close to it as a mother and doctor. This happens all the time."

"Did you do a blood test on our daughter?" asked John.

"No, there's no need."

"Why?"

"Because I'm the doctor in charge of your daughter's case, and I see no need to incur the time or expense of a blood test. We already know she needs another IUV shot."

"Don't listen to him! Don't!" the woman cried out.

"I want a blood test done," said John adamantly.

"I said it wasn't necessary," repeated the doctor.

"I'm her father, and I'm asking for it."

"I'm her doctor, and I can deny that request!" the doctor shot back, crossing his arms.

John didn't reply but went to the front desk. "I'd like to have this doctor removed from my daughter's treatment. I want to talk to the head of medicine here or the hospital administrator."

The doctor heard what was going on and approached John. "Fine, I'll order the test. Now just back off!"

The ER doctor huffed and left, banging on the wall button to open the double doors. It didn't take him long to disappear.

"Why are you back here?" asked Faye, turning to the woman who had spoken up against the ER doctor.

"To get my daughter's death certificate," she moaned. "But I know what it will say."

"What's that?"

"That she died from that New malaria bull-sh*t they're pushing and because she didn't get the shot. But that's a lie. She *did* get the shot. And she got two boosters. The hospital gets an extra $100 thousand per case that's diagnosed that way. They did it intentionally! They killed her for the money!"

When a nurse finally brought the woman a white envelope, the doctor opened it and showed it to the Evans.

> Cause of Death: New Malaria C38.
> Patient had not received IUV injection

"See! I told you!" said the woman in a loud voice. "They killed her! They killed my daughter!"

Soon the guards came and dragged the woman out of the building. Later, Faye and John learned that the hospital and the AMA had stripped her of her license to practice medicine. Inflicting injury upon injury, the woman was crushed with grief. Hours later, police would find her body at home on her bed overdosed with alcohol and hydrocodone.

But John and Faye waited patiently—another hour—before the same ER doctor returned, still wearing the blue mask and still in a surly mood.

"Well?" Faye asked.

"She does show elevated levels of antigens and other proteins that suggest she's already had too much IUV. I don't understand that if you say she's not gotten all her boosters. Her genetic result is also negative for progeria. It's very odd."

"So, what would have happened if you would have given her more?" asked John.

The ER doctor wouldn't answer him. Instead, he merely said, "What's important now is that she get some rest."

"Some rest? What? She's dying!" shouted Faye.

"I don't know what to tell you, Ms. Evans. She doesn't have progeria. Her symptoms are like that, but her genetics don't show it. It must be some other degenerative disease we've never seen before."

"We don't have any history in my family or my husband's of anything like that," said Faye. "Can you test us?"

"Yes, but if we don't know what we're looking for, I don't know how we're going to identify the cause."

Faye shook her head. "How long, then?"

"How long …?"

"How much time does she have left?" asked Faye, holding back tears.

The doctor sighed. "Ms. Evans. I would plan on three weeks … at the most."

***

Faye called Raya the next day.

"Raya, I'm so upset with you I can hardly talk!"

"What is it, Faye?"

"Do you know what your son has done to my daughter?"

"No."

"He's killed her—that's what!"

Faye went on to tell her about Shannon and her condition.

"And it all happened about the time your son brought that trunk here to have her hold it for him. It's all your fault! You people are evil! I never want to speak to any of you again. Do you understand!"

Faye started to hang up, but Raya interjected.

"Faye, Faye, calm down. I'm sorry. I really am. What can I do? How can we help?"

"There's nothing you can do. There's nothing anyone can do. It's all because of your stupid son and his Gramma's evil trunk!"

Raya thought for a moment.

"Faye, if what you say is true, then perhaps what got us into this mess can get us out of it."

"What? What do you mean?"

"What if we try something?" she asked.

"No!" shouted Faye. "I don't want *anything* to do with you."

"What if there is a possibility to help her?"

"What?"

"Faye, I'll talk to Will. Maybe he can use the same means to get you-us out of this mess that got you-us into it. Will you give me an hour?"

Raya talked to her son, but while he listened attentively, he slowly shook his head as she talked.

"Mom! It doesn't work that way! Gramma doesn't come just because I call for her. She comes when *she* wants to."

"Well, this time she needs to come when *we* want her to. This is important, Will!"

Will left, going upstairs to give it a try. Standing by his bed, he called out, "Gramma? We need your help. Please come. Please help us. Shannon is dying, and we need to get her cured. We need you to show us how to do that, and if you can't, then call in the Big Guy. It's important."

Of course, Will was referring to Jesus as he was talking, and it was then that he realized what he was doing. He was praying, rather than trying to talk to his great grandmother.

"Lord," he then muttered, "I really need Your help. *We* really need Your help. Shannon is ... well ... she's ... You know ... and it's not her time, Lord. It's not! You need to help her! Please help her! If there is anything I can say. Please Lord. Please!"

Will grew quiet trying to think of what else he could say. He knew some people could pray for hours for things that were really important. It had been a long time since he'd prayed. In fact, the last time was right after his brother, Daniel, was killed. But afterward—after spilling his heart to the One Most High—he had heard nothing, seen nothing, experienced nothing. So, he had moved on. Yet, something inside him pushed him ... pushed him to try once more.

After finishing, he waited and shut his eyes. For whatever reason, he believed that this time he would have a vision or something that would tell him that the Lord was answering him—answering his prayer. He muttered a few more prayers and waited. But there was nothing. Nothing happened.

Will sighed. It was the same thing that had happened before. *How stupid,* he thought. *Why should I think there is a God anyway?*

He rolled over. Sleep came quickly.

***

That night, Will tossed and turned, but eventually his fits turned to sleep—a deep sleep. And in that sleep, he had a strange dream. In it, he was on the deck of an old, two-masted English whaling ship—one from the middle 1800s. The seas were violent with black waves crashing over the ship's prow and drenching all on board. Overhead were dark ominous clouds which had opened their bursars with heavy rains and powerful gusts that were quickly shredding the sails.

"All hands!" cried the first mate, directing the frantic and battered sailors to save the ship.

Will climbed the mizzenmast and secured one of the sails, lashing it to the cross spar while sailors tied down other unruly sheets and wayward items on the main deck. As the ship tossed up and down and listed from side to side, the winds and sprays became fiercer, and all on deck struggled to stay afoot.

"Captain!" shouted another young sailor high up the mainmast in the crow's nest. "There's somethin' brewin' down under. I can see somethin' in the water!"

"What is it?" came the answer.

A man with one leg came out from the captain's cabin. Dressed in a thick, woolen coat, heavy black boots, and a caricaturist brimmed cap, he gazed out across the deck with a scowl and an attitude. His thick gray beard curled around his mouth as he barked orders. He was one who looked familiar to Will although he was sure he'd never seen him before.

"Captain, sir. It looks to be a sea monster!" cried the sailor.

Will looked at the captain, his hands planted firmly and resolutely on the ship's round, spindled wheel. Across the top of it were the words *Pequod*

It can't be, Will told himself. *Was this the living story of Melville's* Moby Dick*?*

Yet, this scene was different, and what came next, totally unexpected.

"Where is it …," asked Ahab, "… my white menace?"

"No, sir. It looks black and has …"

Just then, black and long suckered arms came out of the depths from under the ship and began enveloping the hull. Quickly, the tentacles whipped around the slippery deck railings like rabid vines trying to strangle its centenarian arbor host. The sailors fought off the attacking arms, brandishing swords and long sabers to cut or gouge all that threatened them. However, their efforts soon proved futile as the tentacles freely grabbed many of the men, coiling around them and yanking them over the side to their deaths.

Will stood on the deck in shock, not knowing what to do next as chaos ran unfettered around him. However, as the violent scene played out in front of him, two black, slimy arms grabbed him from behind and began to squeeze. In his hand, he found a dagger—its sharp, silver blade gleaming in the moonlight from above. Instinctively, he began swinging it wildly against the creature to make it let go.

"Get off me! Let me go!" he shouted.

He looked over his shoulder and found the man they called Ahab standing calmly nearby, smoking his pipe and assessing what he should do next. Instead of being frightened, he seemed as though he had been through this test before. Engaged and determined, he stood tight to the wheel, watching as everything unfolded and hoping this time to change the outcome of an event he had experienced many times before.

"Keep it at bay!" the captain yelled. "Fight it with all your strength! Send that beast back to the deep where it came from."

Yet, the menacing black arms of the creature were gradually crushing the ship, splintering the heavy beams that feverishly pushed back against the water to keep it from rushing in and taking all aboard to their watery graves.

Will cut himself free from the monster and ran to the captain. "Should we abandon ship, captain?" cried Will.

At the same time, another sailor, called Starbuck, also hurried toward them. "Captain, captain! We must abandon ship!" he said, echoing what Will had said.

However, at that moment there was another commotion in the crow's nest above.

"Captain! There she is!"

"What?" shouted Ahab, thumping his ivory peg leg on the deck.

"Moby Dick, sir!" shouted the sailor. "She's right there!"

Ahab looked over the starboard side of the ship. Sure enough, there was the large, white body and the dorsal fin of the creature he most despised.

"Ship a starboard!" shouted Ahab, pointing in the direction of his ultimate adversary. However, the ship didn't move as the giant black squid, unaware of and unconcerned with the captain's order, continued to maraud the ship and its crew.

Will watched as the great white whale made a beeline for the attacking squid and their foundering ship. It struck the black creature head-on but did little more than annoy it. Then, circling around, the whale opened its long white jaws and bit into the squid's fleshy flat tail, forcing it to ease its grip on the old whaling ship. Finally releasing its prey, the giant black beast turned its evil, yellow eye to confront its new—or perhaps very old—enemy.

Will stood witness as the two enormous creatures battled—the whale nipping at the squid as the latter attempted to wrap its deadly tentacles around the whale's long, high snout. The ocean frothed and foamed from the turmoil, sending white-crested waves over the bow of Ahad's ship as the battle raged on.

But as the two thrashed in the turbulent waters of the darkened sea, the sun began to poke above the distant horizon. And when it had risen high enough and the clouds parted far enough, a full and divine light from the heavens burst through, pushing away the darkness and the chaos to reach the ocean's surface. But by the time the rays reached to calm the roiling waters, the two beasts had disappeared—back into the inky depths from which they had come. Suddenly, the seas calmed, and the winds abated. Serenity had returned.

"All hands," shouted Ahab, getting his men back to their duties.

"Where did they go?" Will asked as the captain reassumed the helm.

But it was Starbuck who answered. "There!" he shouted, pointing off the starboard side.

Will turned to see a wonderous image—a geyser of silver spray erupting from the sea and plume into the air. It was the great white whale which had returned to the surface. After another two spouts, the beast slapped its fluked tail, arched its back, and went back to the depths.

Will opened his eyes. He was groggy and surprised at the bizarre dream he had just had. However, the symbolism was not lost on him. He knew what he needed to do. He put his hands together and looked up.

"Thank you, Lord. Thank you."

*****

CH 48 – White Whale

"Mr. Evans, I really need to see your daughter," said Will, standing at the door of the Evans's home.

"No, Will. You've caused enough damage to our family. I can't let you in," said John blocking the way.

"Really, Mr. Evans. Please! I think I know what will help Shannon."

John sighed. "All right but be quick. Mrs. Evans will be home soon."

He let Will inside and took him up to Shannon's room. As before, she was in bed, wasting away. Looking close to ninety now, she was unable to move on her own. Her eyes were closed, her mouth open, and her breathing shallow.

"Honey, Will is here to see you," said her father.

Shannon still didn't move, so Will went to her bedside.

"Shannon, I think I know how to cure you. Listen to me. Where did you put the white jug?"

He waited, but Shannon didn't answer. She didn't even move.

Not waiting for her, Will went to her closet to find the jugs, but they weren't there.

"If you're looking for those damned jugs, they're gone," said John.

"Where are they?" Will asked.

"I put them out in the trash to be picked up tomorrow morning. Mrs. Evan didn't want them in the house."

Will ran downstairs and out to the garage where he knew they kept the trash cans. There he found the trunk and the two bottles he was looking for. He lifted the white jug from its place next to the empty black one and swirled it to see what was inside. To his relief, he heard a swishing sound as if it were nearly full and hadn't been touched. Racing back upstairs he re-entered Shannon's room.

"Do you have a glass?" Will asked Mr. Evans.

"You're not going to give her that are you?"

"This will help her. I know it will."

"I can't let you do that, Will."

"Do you have any better ideas? If we don't do something, she'll die. We have to try."

John stood still, frozen by indecision. Finally, though, he nodded. "She has a cup in her bathroom."

After retrieving it, Will poured a little of the grayish liquid into it. Surprisingly, when it hit the glass, it changed, turning a creamy white but of the same, thick consistency as that from the black jug. The thick elixir that dribbled out of the jug and into the glass looked like a rich, vanilla milkshake.

John helped Will lift Shannon's weak body so she could sit up. At first, the elixir dribbled down the side of her chin, but Mr. Evans held her mouth open so some of it could get inside. Then they helped her swallow it.

"Maybe we should just wait and see what happens," said Will. "It took some time for the other stuff to begin working."

But just then, they heard a car pull into the garage in back.

"Crap!" said Will, looking helplessly at Mr. Evans.

"Hurry," said John. "You need to get out of here before Faye comes in. She'll likely kill you if she catches you—and me too."

Will ran out the front door of the house and jumped into his car. He sped off not knowing whether what he had just done had cured, or killed, the one he loved.

*****

CH 49 – A Message

2018

When Ben had told Raya he was returning home, she had been ecstatic.

"That's great, Ben!" she had said. "What time will your flight get in?"

"I leave in two days. I think it arrives at Dulles at 5:35 in the afternoon."

"Can't wait to see you, hon! Also, the boys will be so excited!"

Meanwhile, Ben busied himself with department paperwork before his scheduled departure. Most of it had to do with mundane actions needing his attention, but there was a notice that he had a message at the front desk.

"Yes, sir?" asked the desk attendant at his hotel in Kiev. "How may I help you?"

"I think there is a message that was left for me. Room 1225."

"It would have been forwarded to your room."

"It wasn't electronic. I'm told it was a paper message."

"Oh, uh, let me check." The front desk attendant opened a drawer and rifled through a short stack of paper. Then, his fingers stopped about two-thirds of the way through. "Ah, yes. Here it is." The envelope was sealed and marked in bold block letters, 'Mr. Maddington.'

As he left the front desk, Ben ripped the side of the envelope and pulled out the paper which read:

> *Mr. Maddington,*
>
> *I have more information for you. Let's meet tomorrow evening at eight thirty at the same café. I will come alone.*
>
> *Colonel Williams*

Interesting, he thought, stuffing the paper back into the now-torn envelope.

Ben took the elevator back to the twelfth floor and walked briskly to his room. The hotel was quiet, and the hallway empty. After sliding the magnetic card over the keypad and opening the door, he went inside. Tossing the note and room key on the table, he went directly to the bathroom to freshen up before going back out for a late breakfast.

But as he leaned over the sink, he felt something slip around his neck. Violently, he was yanked back from the vanity, nearly being pulled off his feet.

"Ugggg!" he stuttered, grabbing at the choker collar that had been put around his neck. "Llll ettttt me goooo ..." he gurgled, fighting to breathe.

He looked into the vanity mirror. The man behind him was dressed all in black including a black ski mask. All he could tell was that the man was dark complexioned and had black eyes and a ruthless disposition.

Ben struggled, but the man only pulled the cord tighter. He could feel it cutting into this throat and closing off his windpipe. As he was trained, Ben backed up, slamming the assailant into the bathroom wall behind him before leaning over quickly to pound his groin. This stunned his attacker, giving him precious seconds to flip the man onto the hard tile floor. Then, Ben pounced, pummeling the man with his fists until he lay unconscious and bleeding from his mouth and nose.

Not knowing if there were others in his room, Ben ran, sprinting down the hallway to the stairwell. Behind him he could hear another door open, but he didn't look back to see what was happening. His heart pounded as he dashed down several flights of stairs, taking many at a time before jumping off to the next landing. Along the way, he opened a door on the nineth floor, allowing it to close slowly to confuse anyone following him.

When he reached the mezzanine floor, he exited the stairwell and into a short corridor lined with a bank of elevator doors. Across from him, one of the doors opened, and a pretty, young woman with a small, wiry terrier on a leash got off.

Ben followed close behind her, trying to give the impression they were together. But once outside, he tucked into another crowd hustling by and stayed tight with them until he reached a nearby hotel. Then, he ducked into the Fairmont Grande and dialed a number he had used in the past, hoping the right voice would answer.

"Hello?"

"Uri?"

"Who's this?"

"Arthur."

There was silence on the other end of the line.

"Hello?" Ben repeated.

"Is there something wrong? I thought our business was finished."

"Yes. Something is very wrong. I need to talk to you about what was on that stick you gave me. I'm heading back to the U.S. and need to clear up something."

"I'll meet you. When are you leaving?"

"Day after tomorrow," said Ben.

"Good. I'll let you know where and when."

***

They met at the same place where they'd had their earlier rendezvous. However, on this day it was overcast and rainy, and Ben stood holding a black umbrella over his head waiting for Uri to show. Several men walked past with their faces hidden by black umbrellas, but eventually one showed himself— it was one Ben recognized. It was Uri, but he wasn't smiling.

"Are you alright?" asked Biendar.

"I've been better."

"You must leave Kiev immediately. Both of us now are in real danger."

"What else have you learned?"

"The plot goes much higher and deeper than we knew. The Families are involved."

"The Families?"

"Yes, and their front organization--the GEF—has funded labs here in Ukraine and in China to develop and ultimately release a manmade virus intended to wipe out most of humanity. It's already been developed, and it worries the Russians. They believe the U.S. is behind it—and they are right. But the Families are making sure it doesn't just stop with the Russians. They want it to eliminate billions on the planet to free resources for them and their elite friends. They were waiting to refine the process so it could be genetically customized to target specific ethnic groups."

"Like the Russians or the Arabs."

"Yes," Biendar answered, his eyes shifting nervously from side to side.

"What kind of virus can do that?"

"Like I said, it's man-made, but their plan is to say it comes from bats. That's a lie, of course, but it will be picked up and spread far and wide by the news outlets who will be instructed to carry it. The Families with the help of the CIA and a dozen other intelligence agencies around the world will ensure the pathogen is distributed quickly—within weeks. Their plan is for tens, if not hundreds, of millions to die—maybe more."

"Why?"

"To force a global change—a Reset—they're calling it, where the global elite will steal all the money from the rest of us and put those who don't comply in concentration camps. It's a horrible thing. It will make the death camps of WWII look tame by comparison."

"I don't believe you."

"Then don't. Just don't blame me when they take your wife and children away after they torture and execute you in front of them."

"Who's doing this?"

"The GEF which does the bidding of the Global Cabal—the richest people on the planet. They're also referred to as the Pure Blood Families. Have you heard the name Bhatti?"

"No."

"The Bhatti family made a deal with the Devil which is the ultimate head of all the sixteen Families. In exchange, they will be funded with billions of US dollars to prepare this bioweapon for wide circulation. It will happen soon."

"And why would the US government support this?" Ben asked.

"All your leaders are in the pockets of Big Pharma which will 'come to the rescue' with a jab to cure or prevent the virus from spreading. But it won't do that. It won't be intended to do that. However, besides killing off a large part of the population, the Families will be set to make hundreds of millions, if not billions, and the billionaires may become trillionaires."

"Why come after us?"

"To make sure none of this comes to the surface. They can't let anyone know their plans. They can't have any light shed on it. The problem is that we know, and they don't have anything on us to blackmail us.

Ben immediately spotted a dark sedan driving suspiciously down one of the streets adjacent to the park. It was going very slowly and had already rounded the park twice before coming to a stop.

"We have a problem," Ben said, getting up quickly and nodding toward the mysterious car.

Uri got up and began walking away as the rain pelted his umbrella. Ben did likewise, but in the opposite direction. However, suddenly, another gray sedan appeared, and it took off after Uri.

Ben threw his hand into the air and hailed a taxi before hopping inside and slamming the door.

"Drive anywhere!" said Ben. "Just lose the sedan that's tailing us!"

The taxi driver panicked and accelerated madly trying to allude the sedan, but the second gray car gave chase. Flying through the streets, the cabby swerved in and out of traffic to get away, but nothing worked. The sedan was right on his tail. Ahead, a traffic light turned red, but Ben just shouted at him, "Go! Don't stop!"

He didn't stop, but neither did the gray sedan.

As speeds approached over seventy miles per hour, the taxi began to lose its grip on the wet pavement. Then, making a sharp turn at a busy intersection, the cab skidded, hydroplaning before flipping several times and crashing through the display windows of a popular department store. Glass shards flew through the air inside, luckily missing the few patrons who were shopping in the area. But the taxi struck and collapsed a stone support column on its pathway into the store—the impact of which sheared off the left side of the car where the driver had been sitting. He was killed instantly.

Dazed, Ben opened the door on the passenger side and tried to climb out, but the gray sedan rolled up behind them. The tinted window behind the driver's door glided down into the frame, and the barrel of a semi-automatic appeared. Bullets sprayed the taxi, riddling it with heavy rounds that ripped out huge chunks of the car's metal body as well as human flesh. Ben dropped face first onto the sidewalk. It was all over very quickly.

Squealing its tires, the gray car sped off as the pitter patter of rain continued to fall—a light, whimsical sound that otherwise would have been a minor inconvenience. Instead, it created a grotesque scene of rouge everywhere, washing the blood pouring from Ben's body to the street and then down and into a nearby sewer.

Ben's life ended before he knew what had become of Uri. It was a tragic conclusion to a mission that was intended to prevent the destruction and release of a lethal bioweapon upon the earth. In the end, Ben's life was snuffed out, an agent was eliminated, a husband was gone, and a father was no more. Ultimately, the lives of his wife and two young boys were also changed forever.

*****

CH 50 - The Families

It was an unusual meeting.

Rarely did the heads of the sixteen families gather in one place at the same time. The risks were too high—there was too much at stake. The world's political, economic, military, and societal systems were all run and controlled by them. They took solace in the fact that ideas of their very existence had been debunked and relegated to tin-foil hat conspiracists. It was, in fact, something they had fostered and in which they had reveled. *How ironic,* they thought, *that they had been able to control the very idea that they existed at all.*

It had been a brilliant concept, derived and developed during the nineteenth century. Although the pieces had been largely in place for eons, things did not coalesce until 1770 when one wealthy family commissioned Adam Weishaupt, an Apostate Jesuit-trained Professor of Canon Law, to revise and modernize the philosophy known as Illuminism. His twenty-five-point thesis outlined the course needed for the eventual takeover of global governments and, ultimately, the citizens of all nations. By implementing this course, this one family, with the help of many others that had also amassed huge fortunes, was able to rise to the pinnacle of the world's societal structure. They would rule after the destruction of all other authority—the fall of sovereign nation states.

"This meeting will come to order," said the chairman, speaking stiffly and with a formal air. "We have much to discuss and little time. I refer to the agenda outlined on the monitors before each of you, and the instantaneous translation of our discussion into French, German, and Arabic will be provided for you as you and your staff required. According to our By-laws, there may be no recordings of any kind of the discussions taking place here today. Now, after dispensing with the meeting formalities, we will proceed to the pressing issues."

The "formalities" were perfunctory and took little time. Long ago, the group had ended the practices of renewing their blood-oath pledges to one another. Not unlike the Cosa Nostra, these ruthless men were often willing to slit the throats of any nonfamily member to gain just one more nickel from the system. It was estimated that together these families had an accumulated net worth of nearly $700 trillion, representing 65 percent of all the net worth on the planet. By comparison, the bottom 75 percent of humanity owned less than one-half of one percent. Their slogan during the 2020s that "You will own nothing and be happy" had come to fruition.

"The main topic of today is the second run at the global pandemic or Pan2 as I call it. As you recall, our efforts in 2020 were unsuccessful. We only managed to kill off a few hundred million people during the 2020s—far from the six billion planned. I don't tolerate failure like this!" he said, raising his voice slightly. "We are in the process now of correcting that blunder and eliminating the 'useless eaters' from our payrolls. Thus far, the mosquito ploy, with the backing of world governments and the media, has yielded much better outcomes. Although underreported, the true number of deaths is closing in on one billion worldwide, and our supposed cure—sold brilliantly by our vassal presidents and prime ministers—has again come to save everyone from disaster." The chairman laughed heartily with most in attendance following suit. "That companion product will ensure that during the next year we should achieve a depopulation of approximately seven and a half billion—much closer to our target numbers. At the same time, the mosquito programs and IUV cures should bring in an estimated $56 trillion to our coffers—a nice bonus for our hard work. So, with that introduction, I open the floor to discussion and questions."

Another family patriarch, a white-haired octogenarian, began to speak. His speech was slow and purposeful and was translated from German into the other languages for the others to follow.

"Mr. Chairman, what will happen when the truth leaks out regarding what is going on? It is clear that our so-called 'cure' only lasts a short time before the effect of the pathogen, which you say is embedded in the mosquitoes, reasserts itself in their victims. Is this working as intended?"

"Yes, it is working, and we have planned meticulously for every eventuality—including the leaking of information. Our lab in India is prepared to manufacture booster shots globally as necessary to keep the process going for as long as we need. This will not only increase our profits multiple times but will prolong the plague and kill more people in the long run. It's a win-win. We believe that by this approach, we will be able to reduce the world's population by 90 percent during the next twelve to eighteen months."

"Won't this cause a disposal problem?" asked another member of the group. "There will be many bodies, won't there?"

"Yes, but that will be an issue for the *hoi polloi*, not for us. As long as we stay sequestered in our villas in the countryside and protect ourselves and our families, we will be fine."

"Is YAF developing a permanent cure? You know, one needed in case one of us or our family members contract the disease."

"This is also in the works."

"And China? What about the CCP?" asked the octogenarian.

"What about them?"

"They have fought us through the years for global dominance. Why are they going along now?"

"As you may recall, we cut them into the deal back in 2020. In exchange for allowing us this course, they would take a split of the world profits and be allowed to govern the people of the world on our behalf. We don't want the task of actually *governing* them. There are too many headaches and mundane issues that must be addressed. We can't forget our charter, as drawn up by Weishaupt—focus on the strategic level—where there is power and control. Once you have those, you need not worry about anything else. And how do we do that? Control three things: their health, their food and their freedom. Once we have absolute control over the first two, the last one falls into place very nicely."

"As for the cure, it is merely the illusion of one, correct? There is no Fountain of Youth serum they're talking about. Right?"

The chairman chuckled once more. "As you should recall from earlier meetings, we are close to perfecting our Transhuman technology which will allow those of us in this room and our families to live well into our 200s or longer. When completed, it will be implanted into our brains and will manage all aspects of our health. We need not worry about magical cures or potions. That is best left to the quacks and snake oil salesmen."

"You mean the pharma industry," joked one of the members.

"Very good. Yes, quite right," said the chairman.

"But the actual transhuman technology won't be made available to just anyone. Correct?"

"No, of course not. The average Joe won't be able to afford it anyway. Hell, many billionaires who think they are wealthy won't be able to afford it. This technology will only be made available to our Family."

"And what if we kill more people than intended and there aren't enough serfs to run the rest of society for us?" This question came from the youngest member of the group—a fifties-something Arabic prince. "We can't run the state without slave labor—even if we robotize most of the jobs. There will always be a need for some lower-level humans."

"That is true, but the majority of the work will be done by AI, artificial intelligence, young sir. AI will solve that problem. We will just use those AI robots and that technology to serve us. We also expect enough of the serfs to survive this period so we will still have enough to carry out the duties we need for our survival. Don't worry, we've covered every possibility. We've run billions of simulations on our quantum computers. There is nothing we haven't thought of in advance and prepared for. This *will* happen. The Great Reset is almost complete."

*****

CH 51 – "Meet Me"

A few days after his meeting with Labac, Jack got an urgent message from Biendar to meet with him. It was an odd message, received outside of encrypted protocols, asking to rendezvous with him at a corporate park on the outskirts of town in Nangli Sakrawati. It read:

I have information that is vital to you. Meet me at 22.30.

It took nearly an hour to find the park which was hidden away in the maze of streets that encircled large plots of land developed for commercial enterprises. And when Jack arrived, the parking lot was dark and empty. There were few functioning light fixtures on poles in the lot, and the ones that were working had half their bulbs illuminated. And of those, half flickered and buzzed annoyingly, rather than giving off any useful light.

The time of the meeting, 22:30, had come and gone, and by 23:00, Jack was ready to leave. He checked his Sig Sauer and replaced it in his shoulder holster before turning on the rental car's engine to leave. However, at that time, he heard the rumbling of another engine—one pulling into the parking lot and heading toward him. It was a dark Mercedes sedan with a high gloss finish that sparkled as it passed beneath each of the successive light poles. Yet, as it rolled to a gentle stop thirty yards away, its lights remained on, pointing directly at him.

Jack watched carefully, drawing his weapon from its holster once again.

Slowly, the driver's door of the sedan opened, and a dark figure emerged. Jack could tell by its outline that it was most likely Uri, who struggled to lift his overweight frame off the seat.

Jack slid his gun back into the holster and opened his door fully, hopping out to greet his friend.

"Uri," said Jack, "why did we have to meet so far away from my hotel? Was this really necessary?"

"I'm sorry," said Biendar, his voice quivering. "I didn't mean for this to happen this way. You don't …" He started to raise his hands in the air, as if to surrender, but the next few seconds were enough to break the calm.

Two shots rang out, and Biendar dropped to his knees before collapsing to the asphalt. He didn't move.

Jack ducked behind his car door and held his gun ready.

Bam! Bam!

Two more shots shattered his windshield and would have killed him had he been behind the wheel.

Jack returned two volleys back at the sedan before hopping into the driver's seat.

Bam! Bam! Bam!

More shots struck his car as he turned it on and threw it into gear. He stomped on the accelerator and headed straight for the black Mercedes. Only at the last minute did he veer to the side to avoid a collision, but he still managed to tear off the rear side door.

Bam! Bam! Bam!

Turning quickly as he passed, Jack saw a gunman in the backseat ducking down as the rear door was ripped from its hinges and flew across and over the hood of his car. The impact rocked the black sedan, forcing the attacker to shoot aimlessly from the backseat while Jack raced out of the lot and onto the nearby access road. Once he reached the main drive, he turned off his lights and sped quickly to the nearest major highway, NH 48, which would take him back to his hotel near the city center.

Shaken by the surprise assault, Jack collected himself, wondering what had just happened, and why. *Was Uri going to kill him and backed out or was it the person in the back seat who was holding him hostage? Why was his friend shot by this other person? How did they know each other, and why did they try to kill him?*

He felt he was getting close to something. He just hoped he lived long enough to tell someone.

*****

CH 52 - Back from Xianyang

1965

After they returned from China, Luka spent time analyzing the stone and the strange machine that came with it. Right away, both he and Tulia realized that decoding any message on the disc would be a long-term project. Tulia had discovered a slick, shiny surface under the hard crust of stone but knowing that didn't help them solve the mystery. Worse yet, the resources available in the small town of Indianapolis were much more limited than those they'd found in New York City.

As for the stone, she had taken to heart the suggestion that it was similar to a vinyl record and had tried to put it on Luka's record player believing it would somehow play. It was more than wishful thinking, and it ended up ruining his diamond stylus. Luka had not been happy.

"Let me work on it," said Luka, clearly displeased and taking the stone away from her. "I'll see if I can figure out how it works. If I can't, I'll ask some people at the company. They're really good at electrical things like this. They can probably look at it and solve it within a few hours."

The following afternoon, Luka came home and plopped himself onto the sofa, depositing the grey bag that contained the stone and the device on the end table next to him.

"Can't be done," he said disappointedly.

"What can't be done?" she asked, not on the same wavelength.

"I talked to my guys at work about the stone and that machine thing. If there's anybody on the planet who can figure out how to get the information off it, it would be Dan. He looked it over and said there ain't no way it can be done … not with what we have now. It's a rock. He said it can't contain any information like that—it's impossible."

Tulia looked dejected. "There is a way … but maybe he's right. Now is not the right time or place. Sheu said it was from a civilization well beyond ours. Maybe we haven't created the technology yet."

"But this machine should be able to do it if we could just get it to work."

"Let's just put it back in the trunk and watch for something to come along that might work," his wife answered. Then she paused. "In the meantime, we have a new adventure for you."

"What's that?" asked Luka.

"We're going to be parents … again."

*****

CH 53 – Restoration

Faye cried when she came home and looked at her child. Once exploding with vibrant life and potential, Shannon now looked ready for her funeral. Her head was shriveled and nearly bald, and it was shaking with palsy as her eyelids drooped and fluttered closed.

"No, child. Don't go!" Faye cried out, sobbing.

Shannon gave a feeble grin and opened her eyes once more. There was still a faint ember of life within, but that was fading quickly.

"Mother, don't cry. It's just my time. That's all. I'll be okay. I will," her daughter said.

"No, Shannon. You can't leave us yet! Please God, no!"

John consoled his wife the best he could. He was still hopeful the white elixir would do something to help, but even now his faith was waning.

"Let me rest," said Shannon. "I just want to sleep."

Faye knew that was the best thing for her, but she also feared that her daughter might never wake up. She sat by her daughter's bed faithfully all night, holding Shannon's curled and arthritic hand. *It would only be a few hours at the most,* she thought. *At least her suffering will be over.*

***

It was late in the afternoon the next day when Will got the call. It was from John.

"Will, you should come over," he said.

"What's wrong? Is it Shannon?"

"Just come over, Will. We're all here now. It's time."

John hung up, and Will dashed to the garage.

"Where are you going in such a rush?" asked Raya.

"I'm going to the Evans's," said Will. "Shannon is …"

"… is what?"

"I don't know," Will answered, choking up.

Raya insisted on going with him, and together they went to the house. Hurrying to the front door, they were greeted by John who had it open for them.

"Where is she? Is she ..." Will stuttered.

John merely pointed toward the bedroom. Then, he said, "Faye is there waiting for you."

There was a pit on Will's gut that made him feel as though he would vomit. Lightheaded, he walked upstairs to Shannon's room expecting to see her cold, gray body lying in the bed. When he entered, Faye was seated on the bed.

"Mrs. Evans?" Will asked, coming in.

Suddenly, Shannon popped up from behind her mother and smiled at him. Her face was pink and radiant, and although it hadn't returned to its twenty-year-old youthfulness, it was well on its way.

"Will!" Shannon exclaimed. "Did you come to say goodbye to me? Or to say hello?"

Will smiled. He felt as if the weight of the world had lifted.

"Shannon!"

He rushed to her side and kissed her on the lips. It was passionate, and it took Faye quite by surprise. When he pulled away, his heart was pounding with joy.

"I guess you've come to say hello, then," Shannon said, in mock humor.

"Oh, Shannon. You're okay!" said Will, fumbling for words.

Raya stood at the doorway and took John's arm and gave it a gentle squeeze. "There is a God," she said.

"Raya," he answered, "you should know by now, there's always been a God. It's just hard sometimes to hear what He has to say to us."

"I don't understand it," said Faye. "She was almost gone, and then a miracle happened. Her face began to pinken, and within an hour her eyes were open and alive again. Within the last hour or so she's been sitting up and talking. It's an absolute miracle!"

"Yes, it is," said Will, glancing over at John. "God works in mysterious ways sometimes."

***

Once Shannon was well on her way to a full recovery, Will began looking into the strange white elixir he had given her to cure her illness once and for all.

His Gramma had said that she and her husband, Luka, had gone to Ingapirca, which Will found on the map of Ecuador in the *World Atlas*. She had told him they had been given a strange jug by an old woman. However, she had not said anything about a second jug.

So where had that come from? Will asked himself.

Will put away the Atlas and went into the family room where his mother was sitting on the couch with her computer.

"Mom?"

"Yes," she asked, not looking up.

"I have to go to Ecuador."

The shock of the statement immediately got her attention, and her head snapped toward him with an expression of disbelief.

"What? You're going where?"

"I'm going to Ecuador."

She looked at him as though he were mad. "That's pretty funny, Will. No, really, where did you say you were going?"

Will explained what his Gramma had told him and that everything pointed toward his going to Ecuador to find ...

"To find what, Will? I don't understand you sometimes. You think you need to find more of the white serum, but you have no idea how, where or why. It that is?"

"I know it's in Ingapirca," said Will. "Gramma told me that much."

"But where? I'm sure Ingapirca isn't a one-house town with signs everywhere pointing to where you need to look. It's a needle in a haystack. You need to use some common sense, son. Really, I think you've lost your mind."

"People are dying, Mom. I think we can help them."

"What? With one more white jug?"

"Yeah, it saved Shannon. I'm sure it can save others too."

"Do you understand how much of that stuff you'd need to cure everyone? It's impossible, Will. And we only have less than a liter in that white jug you used for Shannon. That will hardly save ten people, let alone millions."

"I've come to learn that Gramma sends me on these journeys to do good in the world. Each time, we've helped solve a huge problem or avoid a major disaster. Right? Well, it seems to me that it's the same thing here. There's a major, global disaster going on and she wants us to fix it."

"I don't think so," said Raya. "You're not going down there to Ecuador."

"But Mom! I have to. Someone has to." Will stopped and took a breath.

"Why don't we take it to a lab and see if they can figure out how to make it? Wouldn't that be the more logical approach than traipsing off to South America?"

"It won't work."

"Why?"

"I think it has something to do with alchemy. Gramma mentioned this guy, a Frenchman named St. Germaine. When I was looking into him, I found this article which says,

> *In South American folklore, the natives would mix an elixir that came from an insect called the glowworm and several other plant residues and oils. The Indians of Peru would capture certain bugs and grind them into a fine white powder. Then, they would take the flowers from the cattleya plant—a type of orchid—add the root of the una de gato and the sap from a curcuma plant and heat it over an open fire. The white powder would be mixed into the concoction together with other ingredients. This was the potion that was said to be the Elixir of Life.*

"The Elixir of Life?" asked his mother.

"Well, it was what Ponce de Leon was searching for in what is now Florida back in 1513. Of course, he never found it."

"No. the Fountain of Youth doesn't exist. That's a fact," said Raya.

"Maybe the fountain doesn't, but maybe there is an elixir that does. Perhaps it's the white elixir in the white jug we have."

"We only know that it cures the disease from those mosquitoes," said Raya. "You're jumping to major conclusions to think that it's some Fountain of Youth potion."

"It says here, that after Ponce de Leon tried to find it, the search continued," said Will, continuing to read the article. "In fact, it was a Frenchman who supposedly found it."

"That St. Germaine fellow?" asked Raya.

"No, his name was Charles Marie de la Condamine. I believe he was born in 1700 or 1701 and lived until 1774. In 1735, he was sent to Ecuador to measure the diameter of the Earth at the equator. It was thought—correctly too—that the Earth was larger at the equator than it was from pole to pole. This flattening, as we know now, is caused by the centrifugal force of the Earth spinning. Even though Condamine and his group proved it to be true, another group that was sent to Lapland for the same purpose beat them to the discovery."

"Bummer."

"Yeah, bummer indeed. But here's the thing. While he was in Ecuador, Condamine took significant notes on local plants and animals. He returned to Paris in 1745 and published his journals detailing this ten-year journey in his book *Journal du Voyage fait par l'ordre du Roi á l'equateur*. In his journals, he claims he discovered a formula for the Elixir of Life. It was something the locals used on occasion to prolong the life of their royalty. However, without continually taking the potion, the body reacted badly and began to degenerate—aging significantly and quickly. That's why it was not used often."

"That sounds like what the black elixir is," said Raya. "What about a white one?"

"There was one man who is said to have perfected the formula in Europe at the time. *He* was the Cmpte. de St. Germain. Although he worked to develop the formula for eternal life, he claimed he never achieved it. However, legend contends that he did. It is said that he was born in 1710 and allegedly died in 1784; however, there are alleged sightings of him in 1812, 1829, and 1853."

"How can that be?" asked Raya. "He would have been a hundred forty-three by then."

"This says, there have been even more sightings of him later in the century and well into the twentieth."

"You don't believe that nonsense, do you Will?"

"There are many things I never thought I would believe, but now I never say never. But further in the article it claims there is an Elixir of Life and an Elixir of Death. Both can be found in the ancient Incan ruins." Will put away the article and pleaded with his mother. "Mom, the answer is down there, in Ecuador. I don't know exactly where, why or how, but it's down there in Ingapirca."

"You can only hope that Gramma will appear to you again and sort it all out for you," said Raya.

"Can we take the chance? How many people are dying of this New Malaria thing every day? Can we just sit here and ignore it? Soon, it could be someone else we know who is stricken? Are we just going to hoard the white jug for ourselves?"

"So, you want to fly all the way to Ecuador to some ancient ruins in Ingapirca and then what? You think something magical will happen down there, and all of a sudden, a tanker truck of the stuff is going to appear for you? You don't make any sense."

"I don't know. I just sense it. I'll find out when I get there."

"*We'll* find out when *we* get there."

"You're coming?"

Raya nodded. "I really shouldn't take the time from the university. But I can't let you go down there by yourself, and Jack isn't here to go either. When do you want to leave?"

"Tomorrow."

"Tomorrow? I can't leave that soon."

"All right, but we need to leave as soon as we can. This pandemic isn't going to wait for us.

*****

CH 54 – Finding Kierney

After watching the gunman shoot Uri in the parking lot and then turn on him, Jack was shaken. He knew he was on to something, but who could he trust?

It was late in the day, and Jack was supposed to send an encrypted message to Katz about his progress in tracking down and resolving the Kierney matter. However, instead of giving an extensive and thorough account, he sent a message that was short and sweet.

> *Still working out arrangements for completing the mission. Will advise as soon as things are finalized.*

The response from Katz was not what he expected.

"Kierney must be addressed quickly. He's blackmailing us—the world—to give him a huge sum of money not to blow up one of the bio-labs producing the cures for the malaria pathogen. If he does, it will release an even more deadly disease into the air which will blow into Russia and move east, killing millions of people. When it reaches China, it will kill billions."

The final pieces of the puzzle were now in place. Everything was starting to make sense.

So, why would a more *deadly pathogen be released?* he thought. *The only way that would happen is if the lab was* not *working on a cure or vaccine but was, instead, creating bioweapons.*

"It's about *global* security, Jack," said Katz. "Kierney is a terrorist."

Jack disengaged the secure line. *Global security or securing illegal activity going on in those labs?* he thought. He'd already heard about President Carpenter's move to buy billions of dollars of YAF's cure and knew of the vast amount of expenditures that had already been spent on sterile mosquitos. *Follow the money.* To him, it seemed as simple as that.

After he closed up his computer and began getting ready for bed, he got a strange call.

"Mr. Mankoviz, I was told you were interested in what is going on at YAF."

"Who is this?" asked Jack.

"I'm your 'someone of interest.'"

Jack sat back and took a breath. It couldn't be that easy, could it? "Mr. Kierney?"

"Tomorrow at Café Zombie. 2100 hours."

The line went dead.

Jack hung up the phone. The question he now had was whether he should bring his gun and end this affair quickly or go without it and see where the meeting might lead him. He decided against taking it—at least for now.

***

Café Zombie was a quaint little place in Shankar Market, Delhi, with three tables just outside and another four inside. There were several lively customers having pizza and green tea of all things, but Jack surveyed the area, making sure there were no obvious signs of an ambush. Of the people at the café, only one stood out as the possible caller who had contacted him only a day earlier.

But when Jack approached the man at his outdoor table, the patron looked up at him with surprise. He was a Caucasian—European or American—and he slowly lowered his English newspaper after being interrupted.

"Yes? May I help you?" he asked Jack with a distinctive British accent.

"Perhaps. I am supposed to meet an American at this café. Have you seen or noticed anyone like that here lately?"

The man shook his head, picking up his paper once again. "No, I'm afraid not." He then quickly resumed his reading.

Jack took a seat at one of the other tables—one where a quick escape was possible, if necessary. Five minutes passed, and there was still no sign of another non-native person at the café. Meanwhile, the man Jack had talked to earlier put a tip on his table and got up to leave. He walked by Jack's table, and without slowing, dropped the newspaper on the chair next to him before continuing down the street.

Surprised, Jack started to summon the man but instead casually pulled the paper from the seat. Snapping it taut to scan the front page, he watched as a folded white slip of paper fell out, landing between the spindly legs of his chair. He picked it up and read it: *Follow me.*

Jack glanced back in the direction of where the man had walked. He then waited a moment, and then rose, taking the paper with him.

He had walked less than a block when someone from behind tapped him on the shoulder. Startled, Jack turned around. It wasn't the same man that had been sipping tea at the café. Instead, this gentleman was in his early sixties, bald but physically fit and held his carriage upright and proper. He looked every bit like an ex-military man based on his size and bearing. He also held a cold stare. With keen blue eyes and a taut-lipped mouth, everything about him suggested that he was a no-nonsense kind of guy—one you didn't mess with.

But what really surprised Jack was that he recognized him. He had seen this man before—or at least a picture of him.

"Mr. Kierney," Jack said. "It's good to finally meet you. You're a hard man to find."

"You, dear sir, are not—not hard to find, that is. Let's walk. We have much to discuss."

The two men continued their walk down the street. It wasn't a wealthy part of town, and the neighborhood was less than completely safe, although each man could handle himself easily if he had to.

"So, Mr. Mankoviz, or should I say, Mr. Morris, why were you sent here?" Jack took a breath. Few knew of his assignment and the link between the two names. "Yes, I am aware of your status at the State Department and that you were deployed to find me. Well, here I am. What is it that you want?" Kierney continued walking as if it were just another stroll in the proverbial park.

"Well," Jack began, "since there are apparently few things you don't already know, I guess I should tell you that I was sent to find you and to dissuade you from acts of sabotage on the bio-labs over here. I am told that you are planning an attack on one or more in the coming weeks, and my … our … government will not stand for it. They wish you to cease your activities immediately."

Kierney pulled out a cigarette and lit it without offering any to Jack. "I see," he answered calmly.

"But then, you already knew that too, didn't you?"

"Yes."

"Then why did you want to meet with me?" asked Jack.

"My intelligence is good, Mr. Morris, and from it I have come to learn that you are married to one Raya Curtis. Am I right?" Jack grew tense. "I'll take that as a yes."

"Leave my family out of this," Jack barked back. "You touch my family and I'll …"

"Jack, Jack," said Kierney in a reassuring tone, "I am not threatening you or anyone in your family—quite the contrary. I am concerned for you and your family."

"Why should you care?"

"Let's just say I have a connection with your family—one that goes back many years. It was an unfortunate series of events, and I don't wish them to repeat themselves."

"I don't understand."

Kierney stopped and faced Jack, blowing his smoke out the side of his mouth so as not to offend his new acquaintance.

"Listen. You are involved in a matter that is much bigger than you think. It's much bigger, in many ways, than both of us. I signed up for this; you didn't. I'm urging you to return to the states. Leave this alone. It will not end well for you if you pursue it."

"You're talking about the labs and about what they're doing. You know you're not the first one to warn me."

"Yes. I'm sure you're already aware of the true nature of the things they are working on in those labs. They are not therapeutics for the benefit of mankind. Quite the contrary."

"Yes, I've come to learn that."

"Then you must also know that my intentions against the bio-labs are, if not virtuous, then valid and even necessary. If we have learned anything from the debacle of 2020, then we should recognize that our government in the U.S. is not what it purports to be. It is not what the Founding Fathers envisioned for us after over two hundred sixty years. It has become something unrecognizable—something antithetical to the true nature of democracy and freedom."

Jack didn't answer, instead waiting for Kierney's next words.

"So, if you already know that what I'm telling you is true, then you must realize that I am not a madman. I would not damage one of those facilities and risk the release of a dangerous pathogen that could, quite literally, wipe out mankind. I even suspect that you understand where the true danger lies. Am I right?"

Jack nodded. "But I have a mission, and I've been instructed to carry it out."

"Hitler gave orders to be carried out too. Did he not? Were the men who carried out those orders virtuous and good men for doing so?" Without waiting for a reply, Kierney said, "No. Of course not."

"Who are you?" Jack asked awkwardly.

"Who am I? Why would you ask that?"

"I don't know really. I just feel the need to know something about you."

"I see," said Kierney. "So, I suppose you are curious in that you've been sent to kill me. You want to know something about the man you've been tasked with assassinating. Is that it?"

Jack did not answer.

"Well then, I will tell you that I was a colonel in the U.S. Army. I served in several active theaters over the years, but my last one was in Ukraine back in the 2020s. People call me Kierney now, but back then I was Colonel AK Williams—Alan Kierney Williams. I was discharged in 2023 and followed the trail of the bio-lab as the CIA moved them from Ukraine to New Delhi after the collapse of the Ukrainian state and take over by the Russians."

"I see."

"So, what are you going to do, Jack? Are you going to kill me? If you are, then let's get this over with right now. I don't have a great deal of time either way. There are CIA everywhere, but there are some from the agency here in this city now who have one mission with two targets."

"Two?"

"Yes. Both men are talking to each other right here, right now. How does that make you feel? Betrayed?"

Kierney took his cigarette out of his mouth and flipped it to the curb, grinding it out with the toe of his shoe.

"I suppose I shouldn't be surprised," said Jack.

"No, you shouldn't. You're a smart man, Jack. Let's just hope we can keep you alive a little bit longer, shall we?"

"So, I must know," Jack began. "How do you know of my family?"

"Your wife, Raya. She was married to another agent who came after me many years ago. At that time, I was just starting to look into the true nature of the bio labs that were being funded by Washington. These were in

Ukraine, and it was before the war with Russia. I provided intel to the Russians to take out the dangerous bio-labs in Ukraine at the time. These were setup by the US and NATO and were linked to the Chinese lab in Wuhan which leaked the bio-agent of 2020. Before the labs were destroyed by Russia, they were moved here where they could operate under the protection of the Indian government. Of course, the fingerprints of the US and NATO are all over them here as well. Raya's previous husband, Ben Curtis, discovered the truth in 2018, and he was killed for it. I don't wish the same for you."

Jack stood in shock. He had known that Raya's former husband had been at the CIA and had died on a mission in Europe, but he didn't know the details—none of them did. Now, the truth had surfaced, and he was pained to be aware of the truth—a mystery that Raya had agonized over for years.

"Jack, if you really want to do this and see this through, then you will agree to meet me again. There is something I can do for you, and you can do for me. I can't vouch for your safety, but I can tell you I will do everything I can to ensure you aren't harmed—at least not here. Sound fair?"

*****

Part 3
CH 55 - To Ecuador

"You're not going to Ecuador!" shouted Shannon. "You can't leave me yet. I'm not fully recovered!"

Will knew Shannon wasn't quite herself yet, but she was far enough along that she was out of danger. Most of it was her sudden realization of how much he meant to her. The feeling was mutual. However, Will also knew how important it was for him to find more of the white elixir, or better yet, its source. This was the kind of mission his Gramma had prepared him for time and time again.

"I'll only be gone a few weeks. I promise," said Will.

It was little consolation, but Shannon understood. She had been through this drill with Will before, and during all the other times the stakes had been just as high.

Landing in Quito, Ecuador, Raya and Will took a cab to the hotel. The Dann Carlton was a huge building downtown that was high-end and very comfortable, but not exorbitant. On a professor's salary, they could hardly splurge for one of the luxury five-star hotels in the city—even in Ecuador. After checking in, Raya talked to people at the concierge desk about local dealers in Incan relics and where she could find one. But it wasn't the concierge but another, unexpected source, from which the information would come.

Within the hotel was a nice, continental-cuisine restaurant—one with an even nicer bar area. In the corner was a man sipping a fresh cerveza and lying casually with his arms stretched out across the back of his red-leather booth. With two already-empty glasses on his table, he seemed relaxed and comfortable taking in the comings and goings of hotel guests and other patrons who came, ate, drank, and left. But he seemed different even though clearly a local. There was something mysterious about him.

Lounging in a dark corner, only the whites of his eyes were clearly visible, and when Raya and Will entered, both noticed him immediately. The man puffed on the stubby remains of his cigarette, letting the cloud of smoke float away and dissipate into the rest of the room. With every exhalation, he watched Raya and Will carefully as they sat at the bar talking to the bartender.

"Who is that man?" Raya asked the young man behind the bar.

"He a regular," said the bartender in broken English. "He been here longer than hotel, some say."

Raya and Will finished their drinks, but as they got up to leave, the man tossed a few bills on the table and rose from his seat. He then proceeded to follow them out the door.

"Do you think he's following us?" Raya whispered to her son without turning around.

"I hope not," Will answered, trying to stay calm.

They walked to the curb to catch a taxi but noticed that the man lingered by the hotel entrance, continuing to watch them.

"I'm worried, Will. He must know that we're staying at the hotel. What if he wants to burgle our room while we're gone?"

Will turned to look at the man but saw he was now approaching them.

"*¿Qué quiere usted?*" Raya asked firmly.

As the light from the streetlight overhead struck the man's face, Raya could see he was very old. Thick and weathered, the skin on his face was cracked and wrinkled; yet, oddly, his hair was straight and black without a trace of gray. Standing only a little over five feet tall and of slight build, the man seemed to pose no physical danger and had nothing in his gnarled hands with which to threaten them.

"I mean no harm," said the old man in flawless English.

"Then why did you follow us out of the restaurant?" asked Will.

"I overheard you talking about Ingapirca. You said something about an ancient jug and an old woman. Is that right?"

"How could you hear us? You were clear across the restaurant from us," asked Raya.

The old man smiled. "I have seen a lot, and I have heard a lot. As you get older your senses fade, but your wisdom grows. It takes less to see and hear for one to understand if he is paying close attention. I understood enough to know why you are here and what you are looking for. You say that you seek something in Ingapirca. If you seek an ancient jug and an old woman, I think I might be able to help."

"You do?"

"Yes. But you cannot go there and expect to find what you're looking for. The old woman only appears if you are someone *she* wishes to find, not the other way around."

"I don't understand," said Raya.

"When the winds are blowing from the right direction, the temperature is extremely propitious, the moon and planets are in their proper synchronicity, and the stars are in a precise alignment—only then will she make herself known."

"That sounds like a bunch of astrology nonsense," said Will.

"Perhaps it is. Perhaps it isn't. But that is when you may encounter her. Even then, if she wishes to meet you, she will. If she doesn't, she won't."

"How will we know if all those conditions you say are right when we go there?" asked Will.

"You won't."

"Then why bother," said Raya. "The chances of all those things happening when we are there are slim-to-none."

"Perhaps yes. Perhaps no," said the man, now more enigmatic than ever. He smiled, revealing two gold front teeth. He looked the two over again and then added, "I think you should go. She has shown herself before, you know."

"To you?" asked Raya.

"Yes."

"Did she give you anything?"

"No. She said I was not the one to whom she was supposed to give anything, but that I was the one who would deliver the message when the right moment came. I didn't understand at the time, but I do now. Now, I think, that time has come."

"The old woman appeared to my great grandmother back in the 1950s," said Will, "or at least that's what she told us."

The old man nodded again. "Yes. It was some eighty years ago when the black jug last left Ecuador. But it has left many times before that that too."

"When?" asked Will.

"Centuries have passed. Many crises have come, and many have gone. There are many strange things that have come from the Incan Empire. Each has had an impact on world events. It may be time for yet another."

"And what about the white jug?"

"What about it?"

"We are looking for the cure," said Raya.

The old man smiled more broadly. "Ah, yes. The cure. The search for the Holy Grail, so to speak. Do you believe it exists?"

At the same time, Raya and Will blurted out their answers—each the opposite of the other's.

"Yes," said Will.

"No," answered Raya.

"Just as I thought," said the man. "Mankind has not been ready for it. He hasn't reached the level of Consciousness required."

"Consciousness? What does that have to do with it?" asked Will.

"A great deal. We all are evolving, you know. Not like a Darwinian evolution, mind you. No, no. It's something much more profound; more spiritual I would say. And it sounds as though you two may not quite be ready either."

Raya felt slighted by the remark, but Will came back with a question for the old man.

"You talk of being 'ready,' but what is that? Does it take a level of Consciousness to understand that millions are suffering around the world? That millions are dying because of this contagion? That there may be a cure that could save them? What part of all that is not at the level of Consciousness that you require?" asked Raya.

"Mankind has been a warring race. It has hatred in its heart and, as a result, has faced perpetual disease, poverty, conflict, and will lie, cheat and steal to get what it wants."

Raya backed up a step. "You talk as if you're not one of us."

The old man looked at her but didn't answer.

"Of *you* I speak," said the man, his eyes narrowing, the glint of something strange and foreign shining through. "What I am saying is that your kind has not grown to the point where its survival is assured. It may yet grow out of a millennia of brutality--brutality it has inflicted on others, but I cannot attest to it. Such narcissism and self-absorption have prevented your species from evolving to that higher level of Consciousness. While the contents of the white jug might save millions now, it will not necessarily save your species."

"But we have a white jug," said Will. "We just don't have enough for the entire globe."

"Did your great grandmother say that she got two jugs in Ingapirca or one?"

"She said an old woman gave them a black jug—only one," said Raya.

"But not a white one."

"No. I don't know where that one came from."

"Yes, I'm sure you don't. It's something you cannot understand. However, it was all done for a purpose. Perhaps it is the right time, and you are here now to solve a great problem in the world."

"Why yes," answered Will.

Again, the strange look from the man was captivating yet unnerving at the same time.

"Go," he urged. "Go to Ingapirca. It is something that may be destined. I cannot say that you will find what you are looking for, but you should try." Then the man added, looking at Will, "And you, young man, you will go far. You will make a difference in the world and for mankind. I sense you already have."

The old man's remark struck Raya. *My son? Yes. He's right. Will already has made a difference in the world.*

"My son …" Raya began, but she was interrupted by the old man.

"Your son must continue his mission. He has accomplished much in his short life, and he is destined to accomplish much more—if you let him. You and he must go to Ingapirca. There you must look for the old woman. There is no certainty that she will find you, but you must try."

The old man turned and began walking away.

"Excuse me?" shouted Raya. "Where can we reach you later? You seem to be very knowledgeable about the things we are looking for?"

The man turned. "There is no need for you to look for me. I will find you if it is needed."

He walked away, down the street, passing beneath the eerie light of the streetlamps above. Each time he came under a light, his form glowed until he reached the corner.

"Where did he go?" asked Will.

"I ... I have no idea," Raya answered.

Indeed, the man had vanished in the dark shadows between the last two lights. Will and Raya looked at each other in disbelief.

"Will," said his mother, "as the man said, we've seen enough and heard enough to know the answers without even having to ask the questions. We need to go to Ingapirca."

*****

CH 56 – News Update

"Good evening. We have updated information on the pandemic. It began in the city of Chengdu which is very near the western border of China near Mongolia. How the virus started there is still a mystery as the CCP has refused to share information with the rest of the world. Official numbers from China purport only 203,000 infected and 1,856 deaths; however, most officials in the US and Europe believe the numbers are likely fifty to one hundred times higher.

"In the US, we currently have over five million infections and 723,000 deaths. People in the nation are hunkered down in their homes, and all business and commerce have stopped. Governors in all states have imposed restrictions on travel and gatherings. As one woman said, 'this is 2020 Ground Hog Day all over again.'

"As for the cure, the YAF IUV continues to be the one of choice. The president said more will be purchased within the next month and Washington will continue to do so until the plague is no longer a threat. Some have criticized the company's lack of much published test results and that what has been published suggests the involvement of very few test subjects. However, the CDC has reassured the president and the nation that these jabs are safe. The FDA has yet to certify any treatment but its refusal to come out against it has been taken as tacit approval. The IUV continues to be used under an EUA-- Emergency Use Authorization."

*****

CH 57 - Best Laid Plans

"What's going on in Africa?" asked Mr. Big, reading over a report he'd just been given. "These countries aren't buying into the mosquito program?"

The Chairman was livid. He had assumed that the despots of many of the African countries would be the first ones to sign up for the sterile mosquito program. After all, as proposed it would rid their countries of the mosquito-borne disease, and they would be personally paid millions in US dollars—more than enough in their countries to make them very rich.

But word had leaked to those despots that the Family was paying much bigger bribes to leaders of the developed countries in Europe, Asia and the United States than those in Africa. As a result, they all refused to allow the treatments until more money was offered.

"They're demanding more," said Ernst Rholm, a senior official of the GEF.

Rholm was a close confidant of the Chairman's and had been very loyal through the years, ensuring that the directives of the Family were properly executed. He stood next to the massive, black ebony desk, hand-made for the Chairman in the dense rainforest of Mozambique. Such trees were protected by local and national laws, but at a million dollars per tree, it wasn't hard to bribe local officials to allow him to take the wood and have a desk made from it.

"How much more do they want?" asked Mr. Big.

"We're looking at billions, sir."

Mr. Big laughed. "Ha! Hell no. They need to understand that if they don't accept our generous offer, they will not only be without their country—they may also be missing vital organs."

"What do you mean?" asked Rholm.

"You know exactly what I mean. Just remind them of the presidents that suddenly and mysteriously died in 2020 after they rejected our offers."

"Yes, sir. I will convey the message."

But leaders across the globe were not just concerned with the meager bribes. They also worried about the potential of their own people rising up and revolting against them. Less than a full generation had passed since the last pandemic scare, and there were plenty who remembered that time and the tactics used to force them to comply to the mandates of the authorities.

Too many had suffered or died because of the "mistakes" made then, and they were not about to go as quietly this time. Rholm knew that too, but it was his boss, Mr. Big, who refused to either acknowledge it or fully understand it.

During all of 2035, it was reported that only five percent of those living within the nations of Nigeria, Ethiopia, DRC Congo, Tanzania, Kenya, Uganda, Algeria, Somalia and Sudan had been infected with the mosquito-borne illness. It just wasn't enough to trigger demand for the shots in their communities. Although the Families were hoping for Ebola-like death rates of between 55 and 65 percent—ones large enough to ensure world-wide compliance—they still weren't getting that out of the New Malaria. Like in 2020, the mortality rate did not reach those levels. In 2020, they were less than 2 percent. Thus far in 2038, they were higher—almost 12 percent—but still not high enough.

"What if they reject our new offer?" asked Rholm.

"The program is not going as planned. We're way behind on the death quotas. I can't go to the Families and ask for more money for media promotion unless we get those higher. I'll be missing more than my right arm if I do that."

Rholm left to make arrangements to fly to Cairo where the Pan-Continental Conference was about to begin. He knew he would get a chilly reception, but he understood his responsibilities and pressed on. However, by the end of the week, he had made little progress. The developing nations of Africa, Southeast Asia, and now South America had all banded together in a quasi-cartel to stand up to the Cabal. Rholm had the unfortunate duty of calling Mr. Big with the news. The call hadn't gone well.

"You know what needs to be done," said the Chairman. "Pick one or two for termination. The rest will fall in line. I want this done within the next thirty days. Take care of it."

*****

CH 58 - Mosquitos

Bhatti had just come back from a lunch meeting. She had been spending a lot of time with high-level government officials assuring them that her company was more than capable of creating the billions of doses of the new IUV boosters designed to counter the effects of the regression many were experiencing after taking the initial dose of the black serum.

Meeting with the Indian Minister of Health, she told him that the drop-off in effectiveness of the first doses was common with such drugs.

"Look at the COV 19 pandemic," she said. "It was known early on that the initial shots were not going to last more than a few months. Additional boosters were needed for that one too. In fact, they were still giving boosters to people through 2025."

When Bhatti returned to the office, she found a long list of messages on her monitor—each requiring "immediate" action. Many people were directing her to the results of a recent study showing that the original IUV shots were only a temporary anodyne and that when the effects wore off, the aging process returned with a vengeance. People were ageing ten to one hundred times faster than normal. Many queries came from the political community, as well as the media, which was demanding answers so they could spin the story for their constituents.

"Dr. Bhatti, please kindly return our request for an interview," read one message from a prominent news agency in Delhi. "We are being bombarded with concerns about the course of the IUV treatment and its aftereffects. We need something to tell the public to placate their concerns and disarm those trying to attack us for promoting your product. There are many right-wing conspiracy wackos out there, as you know. We need to get ahead of this."

Another read:

"Dr. Bhatti, there was an article in the *New York Daily*—a staunch defender of the Administration here in the States. It says that the stories about problems with the IUV shot are misleading and exaggerated. We need facts to support that claim, so we can continue to defend Carpenter and her presidency. She's getting a lot of heat on this."

Bhatti scrolled through them and hit the delete key before reading anymore. She was tired of having to defend her products even though she knew better than anyone that the allegations were largely correct. Time, she thought, was on her side. She would make her money and get out before the house of cards collapsed. Already, the Family was discussing with her their option of a complete buyout of YAF and rolling both it and Labac into the same group. The companies would be bought by a holding company registered in the Isle of Man, near England—a favorite place for suspect companies to be licensed.

"Dr. Bhatti?" It was Dr. Malok who was standing in her office doorway.

"Yes, what is it? I'm really busy."

"I need to speak to you about a matter of importance."

"*Every* matter is one of importance these days. What is it specifically, Malok?"

"We have a problem in the lab. You should come down."

Bhatti hung up the phone and put on her white lab coat. As she was leaving her office, she felt a tickle on the back of her neck. Swatting at it with the palm of her hand, she pulled her hand away. Embedded in the grooves of her skin, she saw a bloody red smear and a smashed body of an insect. It was a black mosquito.

"*Crap*," she mumbled. She knew instantly what it meant.

She hurried to the elevator and took it down to B6 where Malok was waiting for her.

"What's the problem?" she demanded. "I was just bitten by a black mosquito."

"That's what I wanted to tell you," said Malok. "Some have gotten loose into the air shaft. I don't know how it happened, but we need to evacuate the building."

"No. We can't do that," said Bhatti. "We have billions of doses to get manufactured. We can't afford to do that."

"But people will be bitten. They'll become infected!"

"I asked you to work on an ante-dote, didn't I?" she answered. "You and your team aren't leaving here until you find one."

Malok looked at her in disbelief. He shook his head. "I don't think so," he answered. "I quit."

"You can't quit!"

"Yes, I can." Malok took off his lab coat and threw it on the chair.

Bhatti glared at him, but then ran to the door of the conference room, slamming it behind her and locking him alone inside.

"What are you doing? Let me out!" he cried, banging on the glass.

Bhatti left while Malok continued to yell for help. She then walked into the lab and made an announcement. "Anyone who opens the door to that conference room is fired. Do you understand me!"

Bhatti got on the elevator and waited for the doors to close. It was more than fifteen minutes later when she re-emerged. Walking briskly to the conference room where Malok was being held captive, she opened the solid glass door a crack and said, "All right, Dr. Malok. I will let you out of here, but there's just one thing I need to do before then."

Bhatti took a flask from inside her lab coat and threw it into the middle of the conference room, letting it crash to the floor. From it burst thousands of black specks—all scattering quickly before refocusing their attention on the one red-blooded animal huddled inside the cramped, glass-enclosed space.

"No!" shouted Malok. "You can't do this!"

Bhatti laughed. "I already did. Now you and I are in the same boat doctor. When they've finished biting you, I suggest you begin working on that antedote, don't you think?"

As the other scientists in the lab looked on in horror, they saw what was happening to their CEO and chief.

"I think she's gone mad," said one technician to another.

"She's been mad," said the second one. "I guess you just haven't been paying attention." Then, he wrote a note on his company memo pad and handed it to his colleague. It read: "YAF" and was circled. "What does this spell?" he asked.

His colleague just shook his head.

He scribbled on the page again and pushed it back across the table.

This time, it read: *You're All F**ked.*

*****

CH 59 – The Reader

1965

The birth of their third child and second son, Alexei, was a joyous gift to both Tulia and Luka who had not planned on another child. However, the baby was another sparkle to the home. As if their journeys and adventures hadn't been enough, parenthood had been a much more interesting and captivating turn in their lives—and one they would never regret.

Leonid and Alexei were growing up fast. Natalia, who was already beginning to learn the English alphabet, was an exceptional child as well. All the children were very bright, and it was all Tulia could do to keep up with them.

Meanwhile, Luka had been working on their stone disc problem. He was disappointed in not being able to operate the little box that was supposed to extract information from their special prize, and over time, this disappointment became an obsession. He had tried various ways to coax out whatever lay within the Dropa's grooves, but all had ended in failure and frustration.

"Luka, maybe you should go back and try to figure out the rusty box? Can you figure out how to make that work?" Tulia had asked.

Luka picked up the aged, nearly fossilized relic and turned it over in his hands. "I don't know anymore. I haven't been able to figure out what this is either," he said. "I think it's just a hunk of useless iron. Perhaps they used it as a boat anchor."

"In the middle of China? I don't think so. It must mean something. It must be the key to this whole thing," stressed Tulia.

Luka retrieved the stone and looked closely at the shiny surface he had exposed after Tulia had accidentally scratched off some of the encrusted sediment. Then, he took a chisel from his toolbox and started to run it over the top integument.

"Wait!" shouted Tulia. "Are you sure you want to use that? What if it ruins whatever is on the disc? Just think of what that would do to a vinyl record. You'd ruin it!"

Luka put the chisel down. "Then what am I supposed to use to get the rest of this crusty layer off?"

"I don't know, Luka. I don't know what to tell you."

Luka tried several other ways to remove the rocky laminate without digging too far into the shiny surface beneath it. But the layer was stubborn and didn't want to let go so easily. Eventually, he gave up.

"I'm spending too much time on this stupid thing," he said, tossing the disc and the rusty box back into the trunk with the rest of their worldly relics. "This will drive me mad if keep at it much longer."

"Then by all means, let it go," Luka. "It's not worth sending you to a sanitarium over it. We'll be just fine if it can't be deciphered. Maybe our children or grandchildren will be able to figure it out. If not, we only paid seven dollars for it."

"It was over twenty, once you throw in the decoder machine and the commission for Zhau."

"That's fine. We won't go hungry. We've done well with the others we've collected. Let's not fret about one that went awry."

But like the others, this one would also figure into a future that would change the world.

*****

CH 60 – Men in Black Suits

2018

It wasn't unusual for Raya to go days or even weeks without hearing from her husband, Ben. But when two men in dark suits came to her doorstep one Sunday morning, she knew something was wrong.

"Mrs. Curtis?" asked the taller and older of the two. He took off his gray sunglasses, but his face showed no signs of emotion.

"Yes. What is it?"

"Ma'am, we're here to inform you that your husband, Ben Curtis, was killed overseas yesterday. It was a hit-and-run accident. He stepped off the curb and was struck by a passing vehicle at an intersection. I'm sorry."

Raya felt weak in the knees, and she started to collapse. However, neither man offered to help and only watched as she buckled and fell to the floor.

"Wh … what? How did that happen?" she groaned.

"Ma'am, that's the information we are authorized to give you."

"How? Why?" she continued murmuring, almost incoherently.

"Ma'am, we've told you all that we know. The assistant to the regional director will be reaching out to give you further information. So, have a nice day."

Their job completed, they left.

Once she was able to stand, Raya immediately tried to reach the Agency and find out more, but she was stonewalled. Again, she was told someone would be getting back to her. Three days went by, and finally, the regional director's assistant called her.

"Mrs. Curtis, we're sorry for your loss," he began.

"I want answers!" Raya shouted at him over the phone. "How did this happen?"

"Your husband made a mistake, that's all. He wasn't watching the traffic."

"I don't believe you. That's not Ben."

"Well, that's the truth, Mrs. Curtis."

"What about the body?"

"We will have it returned next week."

"Next week!"

"It takes time to get the paperwork completed. I believe, however, that the body was already cremated, so it won't be difficult to arrange ..."

"What? How could that be? We never approved ..."

"Agency policy," said the assistant.

"I'm going to file a formal complaint to the ..."

"Go ahead. You'll get nowhere, and if I were you, I'd let this go. Your husband is dead. There's nothing you can do to change that."

"I want answers!" shouted Raya.

However, the line went dead.

A few days, she received a call from Daniel's school.

"Ms. Curtis, this is Principal Albright from Monroe Middle School."

"Is everything all right?" she asked, worried.

"I think so, but Daniel said he was followed all the way to school this morning by a dark, four-door sedan. The windows were tinted so he couldn't see inside. And right now, that same sedan is parked across the street from the school."

"Why don't you call the police?"

"We did."

"And?"

"We were told the sheriff would be by to investigate, but that was two hours ago. We've tried several more times, but no one from the department will come out. I think you should come and pick Daniel up right away. It may not be safe for him to walk home."

Raya understood the message. It was loud and clear: Drop any thoughts about pursuing your husband's death or we will hurt your family.

Life after that was never the same. Raya made do caring for her two young boys. Daniel was constantly badgering her with questions about what had happened to his father while Willie was still too young to fully grasp it all. Still, Raya's mom, Natalie, had come to stay with them. She cared for the children while Raya was at the university. But while having her mother close was comforting, it still didn't relieve the pain of losing Ben. That would always remain with her.

*****

CH 61 – The Colonel

After their first meeting, Jack accessed the secure server at the State Department to look into the files on Ben Curtis and his mission to Ukraine in 2018. What surprised him was how similar his mission had been to his. In Ben's case, it was tracking down a colonel named Williams—AK Williams. But Kierney had already told him that. Furthermore, everything Kierney had told him about himself--where he had gone to school, his military career and his ultimate stationing in Ukraine at that time—had all checked out. On the other hand, when he searched for the same information on Kierney, he found no history—only more recent files submitted beginning in 2025, after he had left the Army and Ukraine. There was no other background other than a man showing up in India a few years after Williams's story ended.

It didn't take rocket science to put the puzzle together. Colonel Alan Kierney Williams was telling him the truth.

After Jack finished dialing the number, he tapped his index finger nervously on the desk beside him.

"Mr. K. It's Roger Mankoviz. Where and when?"

Having been lured into the hinterlands of Delhi by Uri, Jack didn't want a repeat performance. Even though he felt comfortable working with Kierney, he had felt the same with Uri but with nearly devastating consequences. However, both men wanted a very public place in town, just as they had for their first meeting. This time, the tryst would take place outside the walls of the Indian Parliament Building near Connaught Place. There was a restaurant that was frequented by many MPs, and it was bustling with the noontime crowd when he arrived.

Sitting at a table wearing a hat and dark sunglasses was Kierney. Wearing vanilla cream slacks, a white starched shirt, and dress brown loafers without socks, he looked comfortable and unruffled by the chaotic world around him. Although seemingly engrossed in reading a newspaper, he was watchful, carefully monitoring the comings and goings of people in and out of the restaurant.

As Jack pulled up a seat, Kierney didn't even raise an eyebrow—continuing to flip the pages of his paper as his cigarette dangled precariously from his lips.

"Do you know Uri Biendar?" asked Jack, signaling for a waiter.

"Yes. Why?" asked Kierney.

"He's been killed."

At that, the man lowered his paper and his shades. "That's a shame—a real shame. I liked Uri."

"So, he was on your side?" asked Jack.

"That is an interesting question, and it's one I've been asking myself for years."

"I don't understand."

The waiter came by and placed an empty cup and saucer in front of Jack, along with a porcelain pitcher of hot water. After selecting a tea bag from the dark wooden case that was offered to him, he secured it inside the cup and began pouring the steaming water.

"Uri has been around a long time," said Kierney. "As long as I have or longer."

"Yes, colonel. I guess you have," said Jack pointedly.

Kierney didn't flinch, but merely smiled. "Uri and I go way back—to the Ukraine, in fact. He began his clandestine career in Kiev where he aided both sides of the Russo-Ukrainian war in obtaining armaments. At the same time, he was an asset for your CIA as well as for the FSB in Russia. He became quite wealthy in the process. I guess things just caught up with him."

"Whoever shot him also tried to kill me."

"Mr. Morris, we work in dangerous times and in a dangerous occupation. Uri was aware of this as well. He paid for it with his life. It is good that you were more fortunate."

Jack leaned forward to engage this man more directly.

"All right Colonel Williams. What is going on? What is it that you need from me? I already know what I need from you."

"Then let's start with what you need from me, shall we?" said the colonel.

"I need evidence that links YAF with Labac. I need facts that show that Labac created mosquitos with the New Malaria pathogen that is infecting everyone across the planet, and I need proof that YAF was manufacturing a cure well before the mosquitos were released. I need evidence of criminal behavior and the knowledge of that by those high-up in Washington. Can you get that for me?"

"Yes," said Kierney. "When I met with Mr. Curtis almost twenty years ago in Kiev, he and I had similar conversations. He was warned about his pursuit of information on the bio-labs, but like you, he chose to ignore it." Kierney stopped, also moving forward in his chair to engage his contact. "What will you do with the information, the proof, I give you? Will you take it to your superiors at State? Do you understand that they are not on your side?"

"I don't know," he answered the colonel.

"Well, until you know, I wouldn't go down this path. Your plan needs to be well thought out and executed quickly. Otherwise, you will be dead before the words of this matter can leave your lips. If I give you the information you seek, it will be your death warrant."

"Why are *you* still alive?" asked Jack.

"Good question. I really don't know why they continue to be unable to kill me. It's not for a lack of trying. I am careful—very careful. Yet, I understand that if they want me dead, they will find a way. Perhaps it's only a matter of time before the inevitable comes. In the meantime, I will continue to get information on what is going on and, perhaps, be able to pass it along to someone who is able to get it to someone in Washington who isn't already compromised. Otherwise, I'll have to wait until the time is right when I might be able to muster the right forces to act on my own. Those are a lot of uncertainties Mr. Morris."

"Yes."

"So, then you also know what I want from you or someone else brave enough to try …" began Kierney, "… if you are able and willing to reach someone in Washington with power, authority and honesty—indeed something quite rare—then I can give you what you seek."

"Now?"

"Are you the person I've been looking for, Mr. Morris?"

"I think so."

"You must know so."

"Then yes," Jack answered.

"Then you can pass along this." Kierney again handed Jack his folded paper. "This is everything you need to …"

At that moment, a car squealed around the corner and a passenger inside threw a heavy pipe through the front window of the restaurant, shattering it and spraying people nearby with sharp glass. The object landed on the floor inside, and seconds later, a tremendous explosion ripped through the place, filling it with smoke and debris.

From behind the counter, one of the employees picked up a phone and, coughing and wheezing, frantically called for emergency help. The scene was one of terrible carnage as people fled the café, in shock and bleeding. There was no doubt about the attackers' motives.

*****

CH 62 – Brett Major

"We have good news to report," said Brett Major of Channel Seven News as he sat comfortably behind his anchor's desk. "The cure that was released to prevent New Malaria is having a dramatic effect in reducing the spread of the outbreak. Even countries in Africa are reporting a significant drop in cases and deaths due to the disease. In addition, many African leaders are reporting promising signs for other diseases, such as Hepatitis and Meningitis since the cure's roll-out. It is widely believed that the change in health policies in Uganda, The Congo, and Botswana to accept the jabs following the sudden deaths of their presidents has been the turning point for the overall improvement in mortality rates there."

However, on the Channel Seven website this was posted:

"There is optimism, but also skepticism. The last time the CDC recommended a vaccine or cure—in 2021—the world saw significant, long-term death rates due to blood clots, myocarditis and the body's over production of antibodies, a reaction known as a cytokine storm. The government and CDC have remained adamant that these increased deaths were caused by mutations in the original virus from unvaccinated people where the virus infected them and then, suddenly, mutated. No evidence has ever been produced to back this up. There have been numerous studies to the contrary, in fact, that those who were vaccinated were the ones where the virus mutated most aggressively. Most of these studies have been labeled "misinformation" and banned, as I'm sure this post will be. Still, the data has been archived by many of us still willing to carry on the fight."

Another post read:

"It is scientifically proven, although not to one hundred percent, that natural immunity for those not immuno-compromised and without multiple co-morbidities is the body's best way to fight off infection from these diseases."

Both posts were taken down by the news website.

*****

CH 63 - To Ingapirca

The trip from Quito to Ingapirca was no easier for Raya and Will than it had been for Luka and Tulia years earlier. It still took hours by bus, and by the time they arrived it was the middle of the afternoon.

Hot and humid, the jungle-like surroundings were both beautiful and intimidating. In the center of the lush, verdant greenery was a cleared space where Inca ruins soared into the cloud-dotted sky. Built with huge stone slabs—most weighing many tons—the pyramid-like temples and buildings were part of a vast complex that made up one of many cities within the expansive Incan territory.

The Incan Empire was not the first great dynasty of the Andes region. It was preceded by two other large-scale empires: the Tiwanaku (c. 300–1100 AD) near Lake Titicaca and the Wari or Huari (c. 600–1100 AD) which was centered around Ayacucho.

However, the Incas were the last of the great empires that rose to such heights prior to the arrival of Francisco Pizarro and the Spaniards in 1532. Before that, from 1438 to 1533, the Incan Empire dominated the region, conquering other tribes of the Andean Mountains and absorbing them under their governance and span of control. At its largest, the empire joined Peru, western Ecuador, western and south-central Bolivia, northwest Argentina, a large portion of Chile, and the tip of Colombia. It was, by far, the most significant civilization in South America at that time, and perhaps in all of that continent's history. The Empire's last remaining strongholds surrendered to Spanish forces in 1572, bringing an end to the rich society that had once created extraordinary cities, united cultures, and a connection of remote states governed by a uniform system of rules and laws.

After arriving at the ruins, Will was struck by what he saw. It was exactly what had been in his dream all those months earlier—all before any of the current crisis had surfaced. He thought about mentioning it to his mother but felt it would only add to her overall skepticism about their journey there.

Raya and Will spent the afternoon wandering through the overgrown grounds and climbing up the thousands of steps leading to the apexes of temples and those leading down into the belly of the king's dungeons. However, with all the incredible sites, their focus was on one thing and one thing alone: finding the old woman.

Even though they understood how irrational it was to expect her to appear—someone who was likely in her seventies in 1964 and, therefore, impossibly over one hundred and fifty then—they still pressed onward in the hopes that perhaps a granddaughter had taken up the cause.

But by five in the afternoon, there had been no sign of a native old lady—or any old lady. There wasn't even a tourist who looked old enough to qualify as a potential candidate. Thus, as the park was readying to close, the two dejected travelers boarded the last bus for the trip back to Quito.

"I guess it wasn't the right time," said Raya glancing over at her son who was sitting next to her near the back of the bus.

"I don't understand," Will answered sadly. "I thought for sure we'd find her. The old man said we would."

"No. He said we *might*. He didn't say we *would*."

The bus was old and pockmarked with many dents and black scratches along the sides. Not only was one front headlight broken, but the single door only worked when the short but stout bus driver forced it open manually. When the time came to leave, he closed the door, yanking on it with both hands before pulling it the rest of the way to close. There were thirty other tourists on board, representing a variety of countries. What they had most in common was that they were all tired and ready to return to the comfort of their hotel rooms.

The driver threw the bus into gear, and as it engaged, it began bucking violently before settling down and easing forward. It picked up speed as it left the park, exiting through a set of wide, but ramshackle, gates.

Will looked out the side window which was streaked with mud and marred by symbols and letters carved into it by miscreant tourists using their rings as chisels. It was just as well that he had no view. Only minutes into the ride, he quickly fell asleep against his mother's soft shoulder.

Hours into the drive, clouds began to thicken and darken overhead, and soon the pitter-patter of rain began to fall, dancing on the bus's hood and windshield and forcing the driver to switch on his wipers. Soon, the road became muddy and slippery as the few drops turned into torrents causing a small river of rain and silt to flow down the middle of the roadway as they chugged up one windy, hilly passage after another.

But fitted with old and nearly bald tires, the bus hit a slick patch and began skidding sideways. The driver fought to keep it on the narrow road, but when a small red truck came from the other direction, he veered sharply to miss it. As the bus headed toward the sheer cliff, the driver panicked and whipped the wheel sharply to the other side. Fishtailing, the bus slid completely off the road, narrowly missing the cliff but bouncing harshly before flying into a shallow ditch.

The incident jarred the tourists on board, leaving them stunned and sore, rubbing their heads and necks. But now they were all stuck in a craggy gully; their bus unable to move.

The driver tried to back the bus out of the ditch, but the bald tires only spun helplessly, unable to gain any traction.

"*¡Mierda! ¡Estamos atascados!* (Crap! We're stuck!)" shouted the driver, throwing the bus into neutral before launching his arms into the air.

He forced open the door and went out to look at how badly he was stuck. He was outside for several minutes before returning, shaking his head. In the meantime, some local villagers had noticed the accident and run to the ditch to help. Others from the village also ran to the scene; however, they only saw an opportunity to sell their wood carvings, pottery, jewelry, and weavings.

"*Tengo muchas cosas buenas. Mira. Ver. ¿Lo que quieras?* (I have many good things. Look. See. Anything you like?)"

"*¿Ves algo que te guste? Dame un precio.* (See anything you like? Give me a price.)"

The bus was quickly enveloped by the vendors—young and middle-aged— all hoping to make a sale that would help their families through another day, another week.

Raya was sympathetic to their plight, and she pulled down her window to look at some of the things being thrust her way. Most was of little value, and she shook her head kindly. However, she did buy a few things that were nice, and paid what the villagers were asking, not engaging in barter which was the custom.

Then, Raya saw someone else pushing through the crowd toward the bus. This person stood out from the rest, as her movement caused others to respectfully clear a path for her. It was obvious that she was someone of stature within the community.

"Mom! Look!" said Will, pointing.

It was an old woman.

Her head was covered with a pristine white scarf juxtaposed against her dark complexion. Her face was filled with wrinkles, deeply etched by life's experiences. It was as if a complex maze had been drawn on her visage—one that would be impossible for anyone to solve. She appeared suddenly in front of Raya, and without a smile, she stared at her to ensure she got her attention.

"Do you think …" Will began.

"I don't know," said Raya, sitting up.

After capturing Raya's gaze, the old woman stepped back, disappearing once again into the crowd as mysteriously as she had appeared.

Raya jumped up and moved along the aisle to the front to get off the bus; however, at the door she was met by the bus driver who was talking on his cell phone. Seeing her, he pulled the phone away from his ear and put his hand out to stop her.

"*No se puede bajar del autobús aquí.* (You can't get off the bus here.)," he said, shaking his head vigorously.

Raya looked at the driver and then turned around. Will was right behind her.

"We have to get off, Mom. We have to!" said Will.

Raya pushed her way past the driver, and the two hopped from the bus. The driver shook his head again and continued his conversation, likely trying to get help.

But as they left the bus, several big, strong men from the village came and began pushing on the front bumper. The driver rocked the bus using his gear box to spin the tires front and back—all working together to free it from the thick mud. Within a few minutes, the bus was back on the road and ready to resume its journey.

"Good," said Will. "Let's ask the driver to wait a few minutes while we find that woman. It shouldn't take long."

However, as soon as the bus was back on the road, the driver re-engaged the clutch, and it sped off down the road, rapidly disappearing around the bend. The only trace it left behind was a plume of purple smoke that had belched out the back exhaust as the driver had shifted into second gear.

"Well, I guess we're not sleeping in a comfy hotel room tonight, are we?" asked Will.

"I guess not," his mother answered, worriedly.

Raya pushed her way through the remnants of the crowd that was now dissipating, and as she walked into the village, she spotted the old woman. She was standing beside a crumbling shanty holding a baby in her arms and with a small delicate young girl standing next to her, half clothed and covered in mud.

The old woman again did not smile as they approached, but there was a look of understanding in her face. When they reached her, she handed the baby to the young girl and held out her hands without saying a word. In them were three necklaces made of different colored beads.

Raya's heart sank. They had gotten off the bus to follow this woman, hoping she was the one who would help them with the white serum, the cure they were seeking. Will shook his head and began to sulk away, devastated by how their trip was ending. They had come so far to find something and were leaving only with three beaded necklaces and a few other trinkets.

They turned and began walking back to the road, hoping another bus might pass by which would take them to the heart of Quito and their hotel.

"You seem disappointed. Are you looking for something? Something special?" asked the old lady coming up from behind them. What was odd was that she spoke in perfect English.

Raya and Will were startled. Even though nothing had changed in the woman's appearance or demeanor, they sensed something else had. She seemed energized, and Will believed he saw an aura emanating from her body—a corona of golden light which spun off her in waves, as if she had been set on fire and was emitting heat.

"Yes," said Raya walking back to her. "Do you know what we're looking for?"

Without changing expression, the old woman motioned for the child to run back into the shanty with the baby.

"Are you worthy?" the woman asked.

"Worthy?" Raya answered.

"Yes. Do you think your kind is worthy of receiving this important gift? It is unique. It is powerful. It is something that will allay many illnesses but at the same time, it may cause more hardship and misery if not held in righteous hands."

"How is that? Isn't it the cure we seek?" asked Will.

"Whenever there exists something that can impact so many—whether for good or for bad—it also draws evil around it. That evil will seek to take advantage of it—to exploit it—for its sole benefit and to the detriment of all others. Whatever evil can do to take advantage of those most vulnerable, it will try to. Wherever there is a chance for evil to gain a foothold, it will seek to. Whenever there is an opportunity to make money and usurp power from others' misery, it will attempt to. That has been the history of your kind—to allow evil to have its way—has it not?"

"Our kind? That's what the old man in Quito said to us too," said Will.

"But it is a truth, young man."

"Perhaps, but there are plenty of cases where mankind has done the right thing," said Raya.

"Like when Lincoln freed the slaves or when Catholic missionaries covered the globe to convert the masses," said Will.

"Those were hardly altruistic endeavors," answered the woman. "Your president was attempting to hold the Union together, and the forced drive of the missionaries was also about bringing in more contributors to the churches' bursars. Is that not true?"

"I don't think that's fair," Will responded.

"But we are improving," Raya chose to answer.

"Are you? For a long time, you were. This is true. But recently, your course has reversed. Dark elements have been allowed to seep into your culture and society. These have taken over, extinguishing the flickering light that had begun to grow and flourish—a light sparked over two thousand years ago."

Raya and Will grew silent, as if the schoolmarm had caught them cheating on a math quiz.

"However, I recognize that there are some who are willing to fight back against the shadows," she said. "They are willing to use good to defeat the bad. The Creator made all—both good and evil; however, He expects each of us to travel the more difficult road toward good and resist the easier Siren's song of evil. Humility is more powerful than arrogance. Generosity more potent than selfishness. Love much greater than hate. In the end, good will triumph over evil, but only when people—humanity—unite in a single cause and reject the worldly power and materialism that is dangled as a shiny trinket to distract them and lead them away from Him.

"You are fighting on the right side," she continued, looking compassionately at Will and his mother. "Your great grandparents did too. It is those like you who must lead the fight against the evil. You must rally those around you to defeat it. With the support and help of the Almighty, I trust you will succeed—not just in this battle, but the greater war." Then, she added, "Do you believe you can do this?" She looked directly at Will.

"All I can do is try," he answered.

"That is the answer I was looking for. You have humility, not arrogance. Had you said *yes absolutely* and without hesitation, then I would not help you. Had you said *no*, I would have known that you did not have the fortitude to withstand the coming storm of challenges."

At that moment, the little girl ran back from the shanty. She was holding two things in her hands. One was an ancient, white jug. The other, an old, worn book. On the cover were the words: *Book of Jeh.*

"What is this?" Raya asked, taking the book.

"This is the book that contains the recipe to make the white elixir. It is buried within its pages. It should be a familiar book to you."

Raya looked at the book and shook her head. "No, I don't know this book."

The old woman took her thumb and ran it across the cover and over the words and beyond. Revealing themselves in gold were four more letters: *ovah*. It was now clear—the *Book of Jehovah*, the Creator. It was the Bible. The woman then opened the cover. Inside was a folded sheet, and when unfolded contained a full sheet of ingredients and amounts.

"The recipe," said Raya. "These are the compounds that constitute the white elixir—the cure. This is the cure, right?"

"This is what you seek," the old woman answered. "But one cannot be without the other," she added, pointing to both the jug and the book.

"We need to produce enough of this white serum to save all the people of the world who are getting sick," said Will. "How do we do that?"

"This sheet of paper will not help you," said the old woman.

"But I thought you said ..." Will began.

However, the old lady gently interrupted.

"Having the recipe will only attract the most evil of your kind. They will seek it too. They will do terrible things to have it and keep others from getting it. No, the remedy must be made available a different way."

"How?" asked Will.

At that moment, the ancient, white jug held by the little girl started to tremble in her hand. Then, it began to glow, as if there were a brilliant lightbulb inside and someone had just plugged it in. The color was so intense that it took Raya's breath away, and she turned to shield her eyes. Will looked away too, unable to look upon it. The power within it was beyond imagination.

The old woman looked at the jug and smiled. Although her teeth were slightly yellowed and imperfect, they conveyed a sense of joy and satisfaction that was deep and earnest.

"You may take this," said the woman, holding out the jug, "but it will cost you."

Raya was stunned. After all that the old woman had said, after all the scolding and berating, after all the admonishments, and it all came to this?

"How much?" asked Raya, hesitantly.

"One peso," said the woman.

"But that is less than a nickel in U.S. money," said Will.

"Yes. But you understand that there is a cost to everything that is worth having. The cost of happiness is forgoing temptation. The cost of family is accepting each other's talents and foibles. The cost of love is faith and belief. The cost of getting this jug has been great already. Your Gramma has put you through that test before. Life is not easy, but if you fight back and struggle for what is right, you and mankind will be rewarded. Only then can you find joy and peace."

Raya reached into her wallet and took out some Ecuadoran bills. She handed all of them to the old woman. "There's extra here for the people of the village," she said.

The old woman smiled and nodded, taking the money. She handed the bills to the child next to her who ran down the muddy road to another shanty, screeching with joy.

"Thank you," said the woman. "The people here are in need and will use the money wisely; I can assure you. Your generosity is greatly appreciated. But there is one other thing."

"Oh, what's that?"

"As you say, this little jug will not be enough to save the world," said the woman.

"You're right," said Raya, dejectedly. "And you said the recipe you gave us will not help either. So, what are we to do?"

"Have faith."

"Faith?" Raya asked.

"He will provide. Have faith in Him."

Will took the white jug and shook it mildly, letting the thick liquid slosh around inside. "Then what is this for?" he asked.

"Are you familiar with Matthew?"

"Matthew who?"

"Matthew 15:34," she answered.

Realizing she was referring to the Gospel of Matthew, Raya answered, slightly embarrassed, "I know it's a Gospel, but I don't know what passage you're referring to."

"You will," said the woman, pointing to the book.

Raya watched as the old woman walked away, disappearing with the young girl into the dilapidated shanty. Raya felt a warmth in her heart she hadn't felt in some time. It was a peace and tranquility she had rarely known during the previous many years, especially since Ben had died.

As they left the village and approached the road, a sound arose not far away, and Raya and Will turned to look. There, coming up the rutted, pot-holed path, was another rickety bus, chugging and belching away. No other buses were scheduled after the one that had left them stranded, and they were surprised to find one at such a late hour. This bus lurched up the hill, sliding and skidding from side to side just as the previous one had. But this one slowed before it spun out of control. Raya raised her arms and waved wildly at the driver hoping he would stop, and stop he did.

The man inside the bus opened the door and called out. "Do you need any help?" he asked in English but with a Spanish accent. He smiled knowingly.

"Yes," said Raya, "We missed our bus. Can you take us back to town?"

"*Sí.* Climb aboard. I'm taking this bus back to the city for maintenance anyway. I have no other passengers. I'm happy to help."

"Thank you," said Raya before getting on the bus.

When they reached their seats, they sat and looked at each other, wondering whether they fully understood what had just happened. Will held the white jug while Raya held the book.

The bus started up, and Will sank down into his seat. Raya opened the Bible and turned to the New Testament. Matthew was the first book and she flipped pages until she reached Matthew 15:34. She smiled.

"What is it?" Will asked.

"It's the passage the old woman gave us."

"What does it say?"

"And Jesus said to them, 'How many loaves do you have?' They said, 'Seven, and a few small fish.' He told the crowd to sit down on the ground. Then He took the seven loaves and the fish, and when He had given thanks, He broke them and gave them to the disciples, and they in turn to the people. They all ate and were satisfied. Afterward the disciples picked up seven basketfuls of broken pieces that were left over. The number of those who ate was four thousand men, besides women and children." Raya looked up from the reading. "I guess that answers our question about how this little jug will cure so many, then."

"I'm still not sure, but as she said, we must have faith," Will said. Then, he added, "And ya' know what?"

"What's that?"

"If today had happened any other way, I would have worried," said Will.

"Yeah, you're right about that."

Then, Raya looked to the front of the bus and smiled.

"What is it?" asked Will.

His mother only nodded toward where the driver was seated. Above his seat was a placard that read: *Mi nombre es: Jesus.*

*****

CH 64 –Mumbai Airport

In the background Jack could hear the sirens wailing as he picked himself up off the floor of the restaurant. He had blacked out when the bomb had gone off. Now completely destroyed from within, the café was littered with fragments of glass, furniture, and, unfortunately, bodies. Where only moments earlier people were sitting having an enjoyable and relaxing lunch, now they were lying hurt or dead, many crying out for help.

Across from Jack, where Kierney had sat, he saw only an empty chair. Kierney was gone, and there was no trace that he had been injured, let alone killed, by the incident. Lying next to Jack was a packet of cigarettes--Goldflakes— the brand that Kierney was smoking. It was a full pack, completely unopened and having an intact sealed wrapper around it.

Jack stuffed it and the envelope that had been buried inside Kierney's paper into his coat pocket and walked briskly out of the restaurant. The last thing he wanted was to be caught in a cordoned-off police web that would soon encircle the block. Hailing the first cab he could find, he headed directly to the Indira Gandhi International Airport to get out of India while he still could.

But when he arrived at the airport, he noticed an extreme level of security— much more than what he'd found when arriving a few weeks earlier. Suspicious, he canvassed the departure areas; they were being patrolled by heavily armed military units. Unsure whether there was something else going down or whether it was a result of the bombing, he didn't want to take any chances. Kierney had warned him, and now that he carried with him information that could get him killed, he knew utmost caution was his best chance of survival. He understood there were powers in the world that would stop at nothing to ensure that what he had in his pocket would never see the light of day, and most certainly would never make it out of the country and into the hands of someone in Washington who could do something about it.

Seeing the danger, Jack hailed another cab and left the airport property, abandoning his hopes of a quick escape. Instead, he headed for another transport hub—one that offered another means out of the country. It wouldn't get him to America, but it would get him out of New Delhi and ultimately out of the country.

The bus was packed with locals, and it made several stops along the three-day trip to Dhaka, Bangladesh—a grueling ride with no amenities and no reasonable places to stop for a night's rest. It was, without doubt, the most tortuous trip of his life.

The only tense moment had been at the India-Bangladesh border, where Indian officials studied Jack's passport, issued under a U.K. sponsor and reading as for one Roger Mankoviz.

"You British?" asked the Indian border guard.

"Yes. Can't you tell by my accent?" Jack replied, tired and a bit cranky.

"We don't see many foreigners on buses at this check point. Why are you leaving India and going to Bangladesh?"

"Business," Jack said, keeping his answers brief.

"Why the bus? Why not fly?"

"Well, you see, I was just in the neighboring city of Calcutta, and I thought I would just take the bus. I didn't realize how far it was."

"You mean Kolkata," corrected the officer.

"Oh, yes. We still call it Calcutta in England."

The border agent looked at him suspiciously, but then waved him through. The agent in Bangladesh had no problems stamping his passport. It was just something he was paid to do—not create more work for himself by challenging someone trying to enter his country.

From Dhaka, Jack was able to catch a flight to Amsterdam and then on to Washington. Exhausted, he sent a message to Raya telling her he would be landing at Dulles Airport within the next day, but she didn't receive the message until much later. She was already in Quito and having quite an adventure of her own.

*****

CH 65 - Bhatti and Malok

Now that both Drs. Bhatti and Malok had been bitten by the rogue mosquitoes, the race was on to find a real cure for them. The disease spread quickly, causing both to deteriorate and sink deeper into the virulent symptoms of the New Malaria strain. Although initially revealing itself with a fever, the chills, achiness, a racing heartbeat and vomiting, the pathogen soon progressed well beyond these discomforts. Not risking the likelihood of death, the two doctors began daily injections of the black serum to stave off the effects until a more permanent solution could be found. Using larger-than-normal doses, they hoped to give themselves more time. Initially, it had worked, but like the millions of others who had taken the jab, they soon regressed.

"Why haven't you found a permanent cure yet?" shouted Bhatti, showing signs of severe regression after only two weeks. She was only in her early forties but now looked closer to seventy. The black elixir was now failing in its attempt to halt the shadow of death from coming any closer. Their time was running out.

"We're still working on it," said Malok, who looked no better than she. "I have this prototype, but we haven't tested it."

Malok held up a test tube containing a deep yellow liquid that looked almost like liquid gold. His hand shook from tremens as he showed her what he had.

Bhatti rolled up her sleeve. "I want it. I want it now!" she demanded. "Stick me!"

"No. Like I said, we haven't done any testing on it. It could ..."

"I said, stick me!" she shouted again.

Malok grabbed a syringe and withdrew a small amount of the liquid from the tube.

"More. Put more in there. I want to make sure I'm cured!"

Malok complied, adding more to the syringe.

"I don't know what side effects you might have from this," he said as he injected it into her arm.

As the gold serum drained from the syringe, she closed her eyes and smiled.

"I feel better already," she said. She sat down in a chair nearby and lay back, letting a peaceful smile come across her face.

"Dr. Bhatti, are you alright? How do you feel?"

"I'm good," she answered, as if floating in some blissful, hallucinogenic state. "I'm *real* good."

Malok couldn't see any dramatic changes in her body—either good or bad. However, these compounds generally took days, if not weeks, to see any result. His concern was more immediate; yet, when nothing negative materialized, he was cautiously optimistic. Bhatti wasn't returning to her normal age, but then again, she wasn't aging any more either.

"I'll check on you later today," said Malok. "If you feel bad or notice any unusual symptoms, call me right away."

"I don't think that will be necessary," said Bhatti. "I'm feeling better than I have in a long time."

Bhatti left the room and went back upstairs to her office. There was a spring in her step rather than the slow, plodding pace of someone needing a walker. Meanwhile, Malok looked down at the syringe and the gold liquid still left inside. Seeing his own wrinkled arm which had wasted away to almost nothing, he rolled up his own sleeve and refilled the syringe. Then, he plunged the needle into his own vein, emptying the entire plastic tube.

Almost instantly, he felt the same euphoria—just like the one described by Dr. Bhatti. He felt good, youthful, invigorated, alive. There was optimism there too. *Perhaps this will work*, he thought.

Joyful, he finished working on some final testing of the new drug and went to the elevator to go upstairs to check on his boss. Getting off the elevator, he approached the desk of Bhatti's assistant who was talking on the phone and didn't want to be disturbed. She continued talking as he stood at her desk and motioned for him to go into her office.

"She's free. You can go in," she said, momentarily pausing her conversation.

Malok carried his computer tablet in one hand while he used the other to open the door.

"Dr. Bhatti, I have …"

Across the room, he saw Bhatti sitting at her desk. She was upright in her chair but stiff and rigid. She was unrecognizable—completely desiccated, if not mummified. It looked as though she'd been dead for two thousand years. Her eyes were frozen open, and her face had the expression of utter terror, as if the last thing she saw was her body quickly withering away.

Malok dropped his handheld computer, letting it crash to the floor. He then looked at the needle mark in his arm. It would only be a matter of hours, if not minutes, for him too. He could only stare upon the body of Bhatti and the fate that awaited him.

*****

CH 66 – Home Again

It had been a tough assignment, and even though it had been only three months, it had seemed like three years. Jack wrote his report and submitted it, understanding he would be called in to explain it.

"Jack, there are some irregularities in your report," said Katz. "You need to explain them. First, why didn't you finish the job we asked of you? I told you before you left that it was a critical mission and that if you failed there would be consequences."

"Yes, I understand," said Jack stoically.

"Then why didn't you finish the job?"

"I never had the opportunity—just didn't have the opening."

"Really? Outside sources tell us that Kierney was seen at a restaurant near the Parliament building in New Delhi. They also describe another with him—someone matching your description, Jack."

"I wasn't able to get close to him. The location was too public. Too many people were at risk. Then, when Uri was killed, all my other leads dried up. I decided to come home."

"So, you weren't there—at the restaurant?"

"Yes, ma'am. I was, and I was armed. But the window to take out Kierney never materialized. Too many people could have died."

"But my sources tell me a bomb went off in the restaurant anyway, and people did die."

"Yes, and I was lucky I wasn't killed. After the mayhem, Kierney vanished. I couldn't get a shot off."

"Then why did you travel to Dhaka, Bangladesh to fly back to Washington? Our contacts in India state that someone with your profile was being sought in connection with the bombing that occurred at that restaurant. Five people were killed there."

"I don't know why they would suspect me or even know I was there," Jack answered. "I had nothing to do with it. The car came out of nowhere."

"Then what did you accomplish for us?" asked Katz, bluntly. "It seems like nothing. Kierney is still on the loose and threatening our … I mean … the labs in New Delhi."

"Not as much as I would have liked, ma'am. It's all in my report."

"And you were looking into operations at the YAF biolab—of course against my direct orders. What did you find out about it?"

"It's a biolab," Jack answered with intentional vagueness. "I wasn't able to find out much more than they worked on the cure that was given out after the New Malaria outbreak."

"They were," said Katz. "However, we have learned that the CEO and COO tragically died in a terrible lab explosion. The company has been taken over by several of its majority shareholders. I believe the interim CEO is named Alias Birnbaum. His nickname within the CIA is Mr. Big. Have you heard of him?"

"No, can't say that I have."

Katz tossed the folder back across her desk at Jack, as if disgusted.

"I see. Well, is that all you have to say, then? After everything you've seen these last few months?"

"Yep, I believe so."

Katz shook her head. "You're a disappointment, Jack. We were expecting so much more from you. Now, we'll have to send someone else to look into this matter and take care of the loose ends you left. This is not going to look good on your record."

"Well, I did what I could. I told you that I wasn't the best one for the mission."

"If that was your intent, then you achieved it. You failed miserably."

"Thank you, director. Is that all?"

"Yeah. Get out of my office and out of my sight. I don't want you near another mission," said Katz, huffing.

Jack left the meeting and the building unsure what would happen next. He was sure Katz didn't believe him, but she had nothing to prove him wrong or dispute his report. She was stuck, and Jack knew it.

However, his next move was very unexpected. He pulled out a prepaid cell phone and punched in a number.

"Yes, this is Jack Morris. Can I schedule an appointment to see her?"

"What's this about?" asked the woman on the other end of the line.

"It's about national security," said Jack.

"Yeah, right. I hear that all the time."

"No, seriously. Tell her I'm Raya Curtis's husband, and I work for the State Department. I have information she needs to know. It's urgent."

There was silence on the line for a few minutes before the woman came back on the phone.

"She asked if you could come by tomorrow morning at 7:30? She starts early. Do you know where her office is?"

"Yes. Put me down. I'll see her then."

*****

CH 67 - Touchdown

Their plane touched down at Dulles Airport outside of Washington, D.C. It was six hours late, but that was due to bad weather in Quito before they left.

"Jack, we're back," said Raya, holding her cell phone to her ear. "We just landed."

"I didn't know you were getting back so early. I'm tied up right now or I'd come out to pick you up," said Jack.

"Don't worry about it. We'll just take a URide back to the house."

"How was the trip? Did you find what you were looking for?"

"I'm not sure," Raya answered. "I'll fill you in when I get home."

When Raya got to the house, she saw a gray sedan parked across the street. In front of it was a white repair van with the logo "Ted's Appliance Repair" on the sides. Jack hadn't mentioned needing any repairs at the house, and she had never heard of "Ted's Appliance Repair" in all the years she'd lived in D.C.

It was only an hour later that Jack came home. After opening the door, he put the car keys on the table and gave Raya a big hug. But then he put his finger to his lips and motioned for her to step outside.

"What is it?" Raya asked after closing the back door.

"I've missed you," he answered, while taking her hand and kissing her. "You're a sight for sore eyes."

"Jack, what are that sedan and van doing in front of our house?" she asked.

"Raya, they're CIA. They've bugged the house and possibly our cars," he said, "We should also assume we're being video-taped. It's pretty hard to track down where all the devices are, so we'll have to do everything we can not to say anything that may incriminate us."

"Incriminate us for what?" she asked.

"I'll tell you later. Just know that the FBI and CIA have switched sides in this war. They're now fighting against us—their own citizens rather than against our real enemies. I never thought I would see the day."

"You mean like it was before President Ross came into office."

"Yes, I'm afraid so. It didn't take long for the swamp creatures to come out from under their rocks and latch onto the Carpenter Administration. They are part and parcel of the same beast."

"What happened in India, then?" she asked.

Jack told her as much as he thought he could but was careful not to mention Ben and what he knew about his murder. When he finished, he asked, "So, more importantly, tell me about Ingapirca and why you went there in the first place."

Raya filled him in on Shannon, Max, and their trip to Ecuador, showing him the white jug and the book they had gotten from the old woman.

"How is this going to work?" Jack asked. "We can't just startup a lab and create this stuff? We need billions of doses, and even if we knew of someone who could make it, how would we be able to trust them?"

"You're right," Raya answered. "All I can say is the old woman told us to 'believe.' That's what she said. There is no way we can produce everything needed. I don't see how."

Jack sighed. "I guess I'm not as religious as I should be, Raya. I just don't think believing something will happen will actually make it happen. It's not that I don't believe in God; it's just that I don't see how all this is just going to materialize. Is it magically going to appear?"

"Maybe a miracle or two," said Raya, thinking about Matthew 15:34.

"Let's just say I don't think He answers every prayer. I'll put it that way. I think He expects us to do something too."

"So, what are we going to do?"

"I made a call today. Let's see what happens from that."

"To whom?"

"I'll tell you after my meeting tomorrow," Jack answered.

"Well, unless it's the Pope, I'm not sure it will work."

"I think the Pope was busy, so I had to go with the next best thing."

*****

CH 68 – Georgian White House

Jack arrived in Atlanta late that evening and stayed downtown in a hotel in advance of his early morning meeting.

Her compound was heavily secured with Secret Service as she had experienced constant death threats against her ever since she left 1600 Pennsylvania Avenue following the last election. It hadn't helped that the current president, Carpenter, continued to berate her and blame her for all the nation's woes. It had been an embarrassment to many that a sitting president had so disrespected a former president, but it was an unfortunate sign of the times. Aside from trying to pull Secret Service protection from Ross, Carpenter had spearheaded every effort to find misdeeds of the former president and bring charges against her after she left office. Besides instructing the FBI to raid her home in search of government documents, bugging her home, her car, and hotel rooms where she stayed, arresting many former assistants and Cabinet members and charging them with bogus offenses, accusing the former president of being a traitor and threatening to arrest and imprison her at the Guantanamo Bay, Cuba military base, the current president had become unhinged. Already beginning to panic over the massive number of deaths increasingly linked to the mosquitoes and the IUV cure—both of which she wholeheartedly endorsed—Carpenter was acting increasingly irrational on other issues too. Domestic and international policies were in shambles, leaving the nation and the economy in turmoil.

Yet, Ross had risen above it all. She was still wildly popular throughout the country and held great influence over matters both at home and abroad. Allegations of election fraud and ballot stuffing during the last election were gaining steam as more evidence was being produced and finding its way through the judicial roadblocks being erected as quickly as the opposition could muster them. Now, it had all come to a head, as the man-made pandemic and the fake cure was in the process of causing the Great Die-Off, rapidly becoming known as the GDO.

Meanwhile, the GEF was having its way with the world, and the Families seemed very satisfied. Their game plan was finally being realized after nearly two centuries of careful planning and strategic execution.

"She will see you now," said Margo Statler, President Ross's Chief of Staff.

The Ross estate had been passed down from generation to generation within the family. It had been a plantation for hundreds of slaves prior to the Civil

War, but afterward, all the slaves and indentured servants were freed. The Ross family had partitioned off some of their land and given it to many of the slave families to farm and make a living. These actions had still not been enough to placate many who called for the seizure of all lands owned by her and other such families.

The Ross manor house was stately and dignified with a curved portico supported by ionic columns in front and a broad, sweeping porch on the back. Inside, the rear Palladian windows, which were covered by thick, rich wool and silk draperies, were pulled back to reveal a magnificent view of the five-acre yard, ten-acre peach grove, and many more acres of woodlands and streams beyond. The drive up to the house was made of red brick which had been fired in the furnaces in Atlanta just before the Civil War. The original manor was built in 1728 by Virginia Ross's paternal ancestor, Cornelius Ross, before a series of additions were built and other dwellings included on the property.

Ross's chief of staff took Jack into a private part of the home where Ross had her office. Going through a set of white French doors, Jack saw the former president reading from her desk monitor—her red split, reading glasses dangling near the tip of her nose.

President Ross looked up from her monitor and rose to greet her guest. She smiled and extended her hand.

"Mr. Morris, it's good to finally meet you. As you know, your wife and stepson are very special to me. Once I heard your name, I knew I had to take the meeting. Please, have a seat. What can I do for you?"

Jack took the next ten minutes to brief the former president. Not once did she interrupt him but instead sat quietly, fixated on his every word. When he had finished, he waited, studying her reaction, but to his surprise the only one she gave was a nod of understanding.

At first, he thought he had either bored her or said something that had offended her. But soon, she sat up, took off her glasses and began asking him a series of questions. More than casually interested, Ross peppered Jack for the next hour and a half, and after the questions stopped, Jack asked, "Well? What do you think we should do?"

"*Wow,*" she said finally, sitting back in her chair. "I'm speechless. I know what they've tried to do to me during the past year and a half—to destroy my reputation and my legacy. Now, they're trying to do the same to this country of ours. As you know, I've fought back, and I will continue to fight back. I want to save this country—again. The only thing these people understand is power and tenacity. They will yield to nothing less, and they will return again if they think we've lost our focus or our nerve. They are a cancer that isn't easily killed. We cannot be too vigilant, Mr. Morris."

"Yes. I've learned that too. But what can we do now, Madam President? How can we stop this madness from continuing?"

"What are your suggestions?" she asked. "I'm sure you came with some, or you wouldn't be here now."

"I have some, but they require two things: one, influence ..."

"... and two?"

"... courage, Madam President. I came because I think you are the only one with both."

Ross smiled. "Go on."

"How close are you to the second level leadership in the Pentagon?"

"You mean those below the Joint Chiefs and most of the Pentagon and generals who have all been compromised?"

"Yes. The Colonels, Lieutenant Colonels, other officers and the rank and file."

"I have some very close friends in the military at those levels," she answered. "I'm told the rank-and-file support me over the current president by a factor of four to one."

"Good. We're going to need their help."

*****

CH 69 – Not Enough

Raya looked at the white jug on the mantel trying to think of some way to magically increase the amount in it by a factor of a million. The fire was crackling in the fireplace, and the flames pranced whimsically on top of the logs, signaling the seasonal descent into fall and winter. Yet, as she listened to the television broadcast and watched the pyrotechnic show next to her couch, her mind drifted back to what the old woman had told them.

"That little jug will not be enough to save the world," the woman had said. "But you must have faith."

Then her mind went to Matthew 15:34. *Seven loaves and four fish. That was all they had to feed four or five thousand people; yet, somehow, it was enough*, she thought. Those words stuck in her head, but they also terrified her. *What if it wasn't enough?* she thought. *What if …*

Will lay in bed upstairs, listening to the ferocious tempest brewing outside as the winds howled as he'd never heard them before. He rolled over expecting the majestic, old oak tree outside his window to blow over or get struck by lightning. *Then, would the fires from the ignited tree reach the house and engulf his bedroom—turning it into a flaming hell?* he thought. He felt like the Apocalypse of the Bible was headed their way. Indeed, about an hour later, he was awakened by the sound of thunder ripping through the black skies of the night. The rain pounded the house with fury, and he thought, at times, that the winds would blow the roof off above him. However, the storm passed quickly, and he fell back asleep.

The next morning, he rose and got ready to catch the city bus to school. The skies had cleared, and the weather forecast predicted a clear, but crisp day. Next on the broadcast was the morning anchor, Lisa Solemni, who was replaying scenes from the prior evening's news.

"We now have an update on the story we aired last night," said Solemni, "and we will go to Todd Lancaster who is still on the scene. Todd …"

"Thanks, Lisa. Yes, we have learned of an unexpected discovery within the city limits of D.C. and officials are already scurrying to claim it." The picture shifted to the outside of an old naval complex on the city's southeast side. "The discovery was made in a former military warehouse here in D.C." continued Lancaster. "In the area formerly known as the Old Navy Yard, workers last week found thousands of abandoned crates of ancient ceramic thought to have been made in the Andes Mountains in South America during the fourteenth century or perhaps earlier. How they got into the warehouse and why they weren't removed by the military when the warehouse was turned over to the Smithsonian Institute a few years ago is a mystery. It is unclear what, if anything, is in the jugs found, but D.C. officials are already fighting with federal authorities over who owns them. We will stay on top of this story as it develops."

"*Ah ha!*" Will exclaimed aloud. "That's it! That's what the old woman was talking about."

Will called for his mom. "Mom! You have to come and see this!"

Raya listened and was amazed. "Well, I'll be …" she muttered, smiling. "I'll make sure Jack sees this when he gets up."

As soon as Jack rose, Raya told him the news.

"Isn't that great!" she exclaimed. "That's how the old woman is going to get the serum to the rest of the world. It's a miracle, Jack!"

But talking to Jack, Raya found he was skeptical.

"Yes, that's great, but apparently there's a question about who controls that warehouse," he said. "It sounds like the District and the feds are fighting over it. This could get tied up in the courts for months—years until it's resolved, and during that time the serum can't be distributed, if it ever is!"

"I think you're just paranoid at this point," said Raya. "Come on! This is good news!"

Later that morning, Jack stepped outside the State Department and put a call into the former president.

"Jack," answered Margo Statler, "I'm afraid President Ross has been locked out of the D.C. warehouse issue."

"What do you mean?"

"The White House told us those jugs were seized by the military. The Pentagon is now in control of them."

"Why?"

"We weren't given an answer. It just happened yesterday after we inquired."

"Did you say anything about them being a possible cure for the pandemic?"

"Yes, of course. Why?"

Jack sighed. Based on everything else he knew about the corrupt Administration, he didn't have to think too hard about what had happened. Now, all their hard work was in jeopardy. What would happen to the precious white serum was anyone's guess.

***

Two days passed, and the story about the jugs went silent—likely killed in the press by the White House. None of the media outlets would discuss it— it was as if it had never happened. Yet, Jack was able to tap some of his sources to stay on top of what was going on.

"Well, what's happening, Jack?" Raya asked.

"All I can find out is that a few of the jugs have been taken as samples to see what the liquid is made of. Those were sent to Fort Detrick for analysis. The rest, I don't know. Either people don't know either or won't say."

"Do they know how many bottles are in there?"

"I heard close to twenty thousand."

"But even that many bottles won't be enough for the global population. And even if we had a hundred times that many, how would we get them distributed everywhere in time? It's a logistical nightmare."

"We have to start someplace, Raya, and right now that would be the U.S. I asked President Ross to contact people she knows at the Pentagon who are sympathetic to our cause. If anyone could distribute that stuff, it would be our military."

Just then Jack received a call. They were outside on the back porch when he answered the phone. It was a short conversation, but one no less impactful. When he put down his phone, his face was gray and ashen like he'd been run over by an eighteen-wheeler.

"What's wrong?" Raya asked.

"I … I'm speechless," Jack answered. "You won't believe what they're doing to those jugs."

*****

CH 70 – Unconscionable

"Have we verified it?" asked President Carpenter, sitting nervously behind the Resolute Desk in the Oval Office.

"No, not yet," said the Chief of Staff, Fanny Lightner. "Our labs at Ft. Detrick and the NIH are analyzing the contents now. We've administered the liquid to mice and some other test animals to see if there is any change."

"And?"

"It's promising. It appears that many, if not most, of the mice are regenerating their bodies. The aging process looks to have abated or even reversed. They're returning to their previous conditions before they were infected."

Carpenter sat quietly, as if deep in thought.

"Madam President?"

"Yes. I want all the jugs destroyed," the president answered.

"I'm sorry. I'm not sure I heard what you said," noted Lightner.

"I said *destroy* the jugs! All of them!"

"But they could save tens of millions of lives!"

"I don't have to give you a reason! I'm the president. When I tell you to do something, I expect it to be done. Is that clear?"

Lightner had not worked for Carpenter very long—having been recommended by a close mutual friend. Since starting with the new administration, Lightner had done everything she'd been asked—even when she felt things crossed the line ethically, if not legally. Like others at the White House, she had pushed on, believing in the "bigger picture," the "greater good," and the "worthy cause." Now, she knew better. Those were all slogans—shibboleths—that were only meant to brainwash those who couldn't ponder more deeply than what they would have for breakfast in the morning. For her, the line had now been crossed—no, it had been obliterated.

"Hello, I need to speak to her. Is she in? It's really important," said Lightner, immediately getting on her personal cell.

"Who may I ask is calling?"

"This is Fanny Lightner. I believe she knows who I am."

*****

Jack turned to Raya, still shocked by what he had heard.

"Well, what is it?" she asked him.

"Carpenter is having it all destroyed. She ordered that all the jugs to be crushed and their contents poured into the sewer."

"What? Why?"

"You know why."

"To ensure her investment in the lab companies continues to make her money and the Families get their six-billion reduction in the global population—the Useless Eaters."

"Yes, or at least most of them."

"What about Virginia? Can she help us?" Raya asked, referring to the former president.

"She has to," Jack answered. "People are still dying by the thousands every day."

"By the millions," Will said, coming into the room.

"Then tell me what we can do Jack?" she asked.

Jack hung his head. "Let me call President Ross again. If she can get through to her military friends, then maybe we can stop this."

"And a little prayer wouldn't hurt," said Will.

"No, it most certainly wouldn't," answered Raya.

*****

CH 71 – News Flash

"Good evening. This is Brett Major. Tonight, we begin with news coming out of Hawaii. Dr. Herbert Jankowski is the Director of the Mauna Kea Observatory Complex on the Big Island of Hawaii, and he joins us now to discuss a startling finding. Dr. Jankowski, thanks for being with us."

"Thank you for having me."

Dr. Jankowski was a highly reputable astronomer who had dedicated his life to the study of comets in the Solar System and their origins. Bald, with a well-trimmed, gray goatee, Jankowski was a learned man who received his PhD in Astrophysics from Stanford University as well as a PhD in Mathematics from MIT.

"Dr. Jankowski, you held a little-covered press conference last week which described an object in space that you claim may cause serious damage to the earth. What can you tell us?"

"Yes, we identified a sizeable comet that has a trajectory which is currently on a collision course with the earth. At this time, we do not have precise numbers regarding its size, but it is expected to strike the planet within the next seven days."

"And why do you think your discovery and admonition have so far gone unreported?"

"We were told not to broadcast the discovery as it would only cause panic among the populace."

"Who told you this?" asked Major.

"Those in Washington. We were specifically told not to talk about it."

"Yet, you are. Why?"

"We feel the people have the right to know what's happening and plan accordingly. I know we will get in a lot of trouble doing this interview, but I believe it is my responsibility to tell the public what we know."

"What do we know?"

"The comet is known as P/2038 G2, but we originally thought it was another Haley-class comet with a periodicity of about twenty-five years—P/2013 P1. However, that comet does not have an elliptical orbit that brings it very close to Earth. The path of 2038 G2 was found to come near the orbits of three inner planets—Venus, Earth and Mars. It was only recently that we found it was headed our way."

"Should we be concerned? How big is this comet?" Major asked.

"It's difficult to assess the size of a comet due to the icy nature, but we can use a magnetometer and other tools to estimate it. But let's start with the largest comet discovered to date: the McNaught comet of 2006. It was determined to be 60 miles in diameter—a huge size for a comet. By contrast, the one we discovered, P/2038 G2, is less than one mile in diameter— actually, 1.2 kilometers. Depending on where it hits, it might be anywhere from very damaging to catastrophic. If it were to strike in a sparsely inhabited area like Siberia or the Australian "Outback", it would likely cause very serious damage to everything within about a 300 KM radius, dig a substantial crater, and scatter ejecta over a radius of 400 km or more. If it were to strike a populous area like India, Europe or the Americas, the death toll could be in the hundred-million plus range. A water impact might be worse, causing a tsunami capable of inundating all coastlines on either side of the ocean, destroying cities as far as fifty miles inland."

"Do you think that will happen?"

"It appears so. I just want people to know—to get prepared."

"Well, I hate to leave you on that dire note, but that's all the time we have. Thank you, Dr. Jankowski. And next we turn to John Tribel and his review of the newest movie to hit theaters in the coming weeks, after this message from our sponsor."

*****

CH 72 - Hail Mary

Former President Ross took the call and listened to what Carpenter's Chief of Staff Lightner had to say. Based on what she heard and what she knew from Jack Morris, she moved quickly. Her next stop was an urgent call to Associate Justice Hiram Baldwin on the Supreme Court. He was a good friend, and they shared a common desire for upholding the *Constitution* and keeping the Union together. Not since 2024, and before that 1861, had the nation faced such a threat. After their conversation, Justice Baldwin took immediate action and issued an injunction against the Carpenter Administration to stop any destructive acts with respect to the white jugs in the warehouse. Unfortunately, the White House ignored the injunction, not even responding to it. This forced Baldwin and Ross to contact the DC police to try to have it enforced directly; however, this too failed, as the police chief was in the pocket of Carpenter and the DC mayor, Ezalia Janson.

As the jugs were being destroyed, Ross had no other choice but to go to her Plan B: the military.

Colonel Abram Reynolds, the most highly decorated and respected man in the military was one whom Ross could trust. Others at the Pentagon who had stood up to the illegalities going on in the Administration and the one previous to Ross's had been summarily dismissed or involuntarily "retired." In some cases, they were given a dishonorable discharge after serving the country loyally for as long as forty or more years. It had been a travesty and had greatly hobbled the US military's ability to perform its duty of defending the country. Reynolds had only been lucky, but even he saw his time was running out.

"Colonel, I wouldn't ask this of you, but I feel we have no choice," said Ross after laying out the situation and the pros and cons of alternatives as she saw them. None were attractive, but there seemed to be only one that had a chance of success.

"I understand, Madam President. You realize that we could all be arrested, tried and shot as traitors against our Commander in Chief?"

"Yes, sir. But I would rather die for my country than let the despots ruling us turn it into a Stalinesque dystopia."

Coordinating the independent news media, the white hats of Colonel Reynolds, the National Guard of Virginia, and all other resources available to her, Ross had Reynolds order the military forces still loyal to upholding the

Constitution to raid the warehouse and stop the illegal destruction of the jugs. It was subterfuge in one sense, but just as the patriots of Washington's army risked all to battle their British foes and fight for freedom, Ross saw no other way to save the country, if not the world.

It was after dark, late on a Friday night, when Reynolds's troops stormed the warehouse armed with XM6 rifles and vest pockets filled with extra magazine clips. With only fifty ATF agents supervising the destruction of the thousands of jugs, the rebel force met with little resistance. Over four hundred marines were dropped at the warehouse site by a fleet of CH-47K Chinook army helicopters, all landing in the vast east-side parking lot. There, they disembarked and rushed the perimeter of the facility. Forcing open the doors, they commanded the ATF agents to drop their weapons and get down on the ground. Within an hour, the facility was secured, and the destruction of the jugs was halted.

Carpenter was stunned when she heard the news, and she called on her Chairman of the Jt. Chiefs, General Michael Crist, to send in an Army regiment against them.

"I can't have them stop what I've started," she said. "It's disloyalty and treason! They should all be shot!"

"Yes, ma'am," said the Chairman. "I fully understand. I will mobilize a SEAL group, along with a regiment from Quantico as supplemental force. We'll take care of business for you."

Yet when Crist gave the order to his generals, who then passed theirs down the chain of command, the rank and file did not obey. At the threat of court martial, virtually all to the man refused.

"We will not kill our own men!" they answered their commanders. "You will have to shoot us first. We respectfully stand down, sir."

Shocked by the insubordination, Crist had the men arrested and thrown in jail cells, but it did nothing but embolden them.

"I'm sorry, Madam President," Crist had to admit, unable to lead his men, "but my men refused. They won't go in and fight against their brothers and sisters in arms."

"You have your orders, General!"

Crist took an epaulet off his uniform and placed it on the president's desk.

"I am unable to carry out your orders. Consider this my resignation."

"But the Families expect us to complete the job we started. We can't allow this to happen! We can't let this cure get to the masses in the world. It would save the very people we're trying to kill off. They're a burden to society. They're useless peasants, for god's sake! Don't you understand?"

"Not anymore, ma'am." Crist saluted Carpenter and walked out of the Oval Office.

"This is treason!" shouted Carpenter, watching him leave. "You *must* obey your Commander in Chief!"

Moments later, the president's executive secretary buzzed her boss.

"Madam President, you have a call from NASA Director, Cynthia Ramos. She says it's important."

"Not now. I'm busy."

"But she's says it's really important."

"I just told you no!"

Carpenter took no more calls the rest of the day. But what Ramos was trying to communicate was the news released by Dr. Jankowski regarding the approaching comet. Carpenter didn't hear about it until the next morning when she saw it on a TV news broadcast.

"And as we have been discussing all morning," said the TV host, "there is a massive comet on a collision course with Earth."

Carpenter took a sip of her black coffee and smiled. "Excellent," she said to her Chief of Staff, Lightner.

"Why is that good news?" Lightner shot back, already preparing to submit her resignation within days.

"Because it will divert attention from what's going on in the warehouse. Can't you see that?".

However, later that day, it was leaked to the press that the president had ordered the destruction of the ancient jugs which were thought to be a cure for the disease ravaging the world. Shortly after, a reporter discovered the connection of Carpenter to foreign bank accounts where she was receiving hundreds of millions in payments from YAF and Labac. That information was also leaked. However, all was drowned out by the frenetic uproar over the pending cataclysm about to strike all mankind. It was all working in their favor—Carpenter's, Mr. Big's and the Family's. In fact, the White House did not even respond to the charges, believing it would all blow over by the time the comet story passed. It is more than ironic. It was delusional beyond any measure of normality.

"Is there anything you want me to do?" asked Lightner, grudgingly.

"Get the U.N. Secretary on the phone. I'm bringing in blue helmets."

*****

CH 73 – A Higher Power

The day after the Channel Seven interview with Dr. Jankowski, men in black suits pulled up in front of his home in Paukee, a town just north of Hilo. Minutes later, neighbors saw him handcuffed, dragged to the sedan, shoved into the backseat and driven away. He never returned.

However, the story didn't die. Other astronomers took up the case and quickly verified Jankowski's claims. Indeed, they confirmed that there was a large comet heading toward Earth and that the impact would be catastrophic.

The Internet exploded with the news, and the pressure was on for the major media outlets to cover it. After being given the green light from the White House, the story monopolized every minute of coverage for the next several days.

But according to the predictions, P/2038 G2 was expected to strike Earth within the next two days—most likely hitting an area in the Northern Atlantic Ocean about 800 miles east-southeast of Bermuda. Such a strike would create a tsunami toward both Western Europe and the East Coast of America—one that would rise as the seabed grew shallower with the Continental Shelf. Experts warned of wave heights exceeding 100 meters or 330 feet along the coastlines, wiping out many of the large urban centers there. Tens of millions, if not a hundred million or more, would perish.

Yet, as President Ross focused her attention on securing the white serum to stem the spread of the diseases, she realized that such efforts, in the end, might be moot. Should the comet strike where anticipated, worry over the pandemic would seem petty by comparison.

"Jack," said Ross, contacting him at his home, "I think we have to abandon our fight over the white jugs. It is quite irrelevant now that we have an even larger threat. Besides, all military personnel have been redirected to ensure an orderly evacuation of the major cities along the coastlines. There would be no means to distribute the white serum anyway. I'm not so sure it could have been distributed by the military as widely as would have been needed to become a global cure."

"I understand," he said. "You're right. In light of the latest events, I guess Carpenter and her Administration is going to escape justice once again."

"I wouldn't say that," Ross replied. "Judgement Day is coming whether we like it or not, and now it appears it will be here within the next forty-eight to sixty hours. It's likely she will see it, just as we all will."

"What about the white urns?" Raya asked, also on the line. "What will happen to those?"

"Thank God we were able to save most of them. It looks like only a small portion were destroyed—about twelve percent. That's a lot, but it could have been much worse. I'm working with Colonel Reynolds to find a place where they will be safe."

"What about the current president? Is it true about the UN troops?"

"She's trying to convince Secretary Khalil to acknowledge her request and send the blue helmets into the states to shut things down. However, the comet has also affected those plans. All forces around the globe are in a heightened state of readiness for the landing of the comet. Her attempts at thwarting us in that arena will fall on deaf ears."

"Well, if there is anything I can do, let me know," said Jack.

"You've already done that," said Ross. "We owe you a great deal, Jack."

"No, Madam President. You're the one to whom we owe a great deal. We owe the survival of our country to you."

"Perhaps. We'll see what happens during the next few days. Oh, but there is one thing I need to ask you. I received a telegram today."

"They still send those?"

"That's the thing. It was unsigned, but it came from Ecuador. It consisted of only two sentences. *See the power of faith.*"

"And the other?"

"*Your kind is worthy after all.* Do know what that's about or from whom that might have come?"

"I have no idea," said Jack.

"But I do," answered Raya. "I'm shocked, but without going into the entire story, all I will say is that it is a message from a higher power."

"Why would the president of Ecuador send a former U.S. president an unsigned message?" asked Ross.

"It was a higher power than that," said Raya. "I am hopeful, now."

"About?"

"About the future," said Raya.

"How can you say that when there's a comet that's …"

"Yeah, I know. But I also know, there is a higher power than man," she answered. "It will take that, of course, to save us."

*****

CH 74 – Four to Impact

The world braced for impact. Strategies for firing nuclear missiles or other projectiles at the comet were considered but abandoned by the Russians and Chinese, as their scientists had calculated there would be no chance of success and efforts were better spent handing the mass exodus from the coastlines.

In the United States and Europe, however, the politicians weighed in and demanded something be done. So, NASA launched two craft at the comet, hoping to deflect it. There had been no time to secure nuclear warheads to them, and only that had prevented a greater tragedy as one craft had exploded soon after liftoff and the second had been unable to make contact with the comet which was traveling at a speed of 27 kilometers per second.

Jack, Raya and Will sat in their family room watching the news as it showed live scenes beamed from the TMT at the Mauna Kea Observatory in Hawaii. The roads out of Washington, D.C. and other major cities had ground to a halt with people trying to flee to safer ground farther inland. Sadly, with cars running out of gas or electric charge, virtually every means of passage had been sealed off. Consequently, many decided to stay in their homes and deal with what came their way.

"As you can see in the blurry image," said Brett Major from his anchor desk at the studio, "the comet continues to glow brighter as the heat from the sun burns off more of the icy shell that constitutes its structure. We are told that the nucleus is about one kilometer in diameter and is made up of mostly ice and dust coated with dark organic material. According to NASA, the ice contains mainly frozen water but perhaps other frozen substances as well, such as ammonia, carbon dioxide, carbon monoxide and methane. The nucleus may have a small rocky core. Some scientists believe that life on Earth began from the impact of such a comet striking the planet and infusing its organic material into the ocean. From there, life is thought to have sprung. How ironic that such an event might also end all life here."

"That's not very optimistic," said Will, watching the screen.

"It's a reality we can't dismiss," said Jack. "We have to face things as they are, not as we wish them to be."

In the upper righthand corner of the screen was a timer which showed the countdown until the comet was to strike the earth. At this point, the location of the impact was certain—just where it had been predicted days earlier, in the North Atlantic. Although some people continued efforts to flee the coastline, authorities had largely shut down all escape routes as they had become clogged with miles of abandoned cars.

The clock now read 4:15:43 or 4 hours, fifteen minutes and 43 seconds.

"What do you think we should do with what time there is left?" asked Will.

It was Max who came into the room, joyfully wagging his tail. He was oblivious to what was happening around him, but he was happy. He was with people he loved and people who loved him.

Will looked down at his pet. "Max, buddy. Is everything going to be okay?"

Max barked, his tail continuing to cut through the air.

"Yeah, I thought so. You're always right, aren't you boy?"

Will petted his dog, rubbing his belly and then working his way up to his neck and then his ears. Max was in heaven. He loved it when his owners took the time to pay attention to him—that and feeding him.

"What was that?" asked Jack, watching the screen.

"What?" asked Will before looking up.

"There. Did you see that?"

Indeed, there was a bright flash on the monitor, and then a white glow that encompassed the entire field of view. It was as if the connection had gone to white noise—a white, virtually blank screen of nothing.

"I think we've lost the connection to the TMT," said Major, adjusting his earpiece. "Perhaps we can try to … oh, apparently something has happened. We are being interrupted by our parent in Washington. Standby …"

The broadcast shifted to NASA, showing a huge room filled with computers, monitors and equipment. People were scurrying in and out of view while others remained steadfast in their seats. In front, on a series of screens that covered over eighty or more feet, were various pictures and graphs. In the middle was a screen which mirrored the nearly blank white sheet that had shown on screens worldwide only moments earlier.

"This is Chuck Radley, Director of Communications at NASA. We are interrupting your scheduled programming to cover the latest developments of the comet which has a trajectory to intercept Earth in less than four hours. However, our instruments have detected a change in the mass and path of the comet. Approximately eight minutes ago, an event took place as the comet was nearing our moon. A strong beam of energy from the dark side of the Moon pierced the blackness of space and struck the comet as it approached. We have computed that the object's trajectory was radically changed and is now expected to only graze the earth's atmosphere and not inflict a major event on all of us.

"This does not mean we will be unscathed by the effects of this celestial object. As more data comes in, we will be able to analyze it, but we anticipate that the comet's massive tail will blanket the earth and may cause significant disruptions.

"And now back to your regularly scheduled programming."

Raya looked at Jack and Will.

"Is this what I think it is?" she asked.

"Our salvation?" Jack answered with a look of disbelief.

"I think it's our miracle," said Will.

*****

CH 75 - Aftermath

Chuck Radley had been right. The comet had missed the earth, but the fallout from the debris in its tail wreaked havoc on communication, travel, agriculture and a host of other things society took for granted. However, there had also been something else—something strange and unexpected.

Scientists had discovered that the organic material that fell onto the planet in the wake of the comet's near miss contained unusual compounds unlike what they had ever seen before in such bodies. The earth had been blanketed with it, and it found its way quickly into food sources, water reservoirs and even the air humans and other animals breathed. Yet, it was not found to be harmful. In fact, it was found to be quite beneficial.

Within six months of the event, the U.S. death rate from the black serum jabs and the Labac mosquitoes dropped to almost zero. Globally, similar results were being seen. Whatever had been in the debris tail had killed the pathogen that was killing the world. Indeed, analysis of the dust revealed that it was almost identical to the liquified properties contained in the white jugs.

"I guess we were worth saving as a species after all, weren't we?" Will asked, sitting next to Shannon on the couch in her living room.

"What did your Gramma say to you, Will?" asked Shannon. "Did she tell you a comet would come and save the planet?"

"No, we heard something like that from an old lady in Ecuador."

"You're joking."

"Nope. It's the truth. It really is strange."

"Coming from you, that's saying something," said Shannon.

"And if it weren't for President Ross, it wouldn't have happened at all."

"Do you think the new president will come around?"

"Time will tell. Hopefully, he will see the writing on the wall."

Much had happened since the comet's passing. The evidence against President Carpenter was re-introduced and widely circulated throughout the airwaves. Her flagrant dismissal of the comet emergency and neglect in acting to protect the citizenry was too much even for Congress to ignore. The people wanted her head, but in the end, she resigned to avoid certain impeachment and a Senate trial that would have found her guilty of treason, bribery, and high crimes and misdemeanors in accordance with the *Constitution*.

"I'm just happy it's all over."

"And you're feeling fine?" Will asked.

"Yeah. Pretty much."

Will leaned in and kissed her. "I don't know what I would have done if you would have … you know …"

"Yeah, I'm kinda' glad about that too." She smiled at him. "I just want you to know how special you are to me."

"Shannon, I love you," Will blurted out. It was almost as much of a surprise to him as it was to her.

Shannon stood with her mouth open, her eyes wide and unblinking. "Excuse me?" she answered awkwardly, not sure what she'd just heard.

Will took a deep breath. "Well, there. I said it. It's true. Ever since Russian class in high school I've known that I was in love with you."

Shannon froze.

"I'm sorry," Will said. "I shouldn't have said that. I …"

"No, Will. You just surprised me, that's all."

"Oh."

"Will?"

"Yeah?"

"I love you too," she admitted.

"Really?"

"You're so special in my life, I just can't imagine it without you either."

Will grabbed her and began kissing her. Then, he gently pushed her away, holding her at arms' length.

"What is it? What's wrong?" she asked.

"What about your parents? How will your mother feel about this?"

"Well, she's had her ups and downs with you. That's for sure," Shannon answered. Then, she laughed. "I guess we'll just have to tell her when she's in a good mood." *****

CH 76 – Reassessment

It was another emergency meeting; however, this one was conducted over a secure, private video feed. Each participant was setup in his or her own office, some thousands of miles apart, allowing the face of the chairman to illuminate and dominate all their screens.

"I'm calling this emergency meeting to address our latest setback," said Mr. Big, the chairman. "Again, we have failed in our mission to cull the herd of humanity. How many more of these incidents can we afford to lose before the general populace catches on? I fear we may be at the end of our thousand-year directive."

"You can't possibly blame us for something that hasn't happened during the last thousand years—perhaps the last ten thousand. We could not have anticipated this within all of our Monte Carlo simulations. It wasn't rational."

"But it happened. We should have considered *everything*."

"It doesn't matter," said another member of the secret group. "You as well as we know that the memory of the masses is short. It only takes a few years for them to forget what has happened, and with the help of the media and those we've paid handsomely in high government positions, we can rewrite history, so it bears no resemblance to what actually happened. We've been successful at this in the past."

"Charles is right," said another. "We already had the major publishers of public-school History books rewrite them for the disastrous rollout of our pandemic during the 2020s. All evidence of the intentional release of the bioweapon COV-19 into society and our concocted vaccine remedy… from which we made billions I might add … has been expunged. You can't find it anywhere—not even Online now. It's all been glossed over and those millions of unfortunate souls we targeted as scapegoats are all now six feet under. No, we redirected blame to others then just as we will now. In fact, several of us already have projects well underway to cover this unfortunate event; so, there is nothing to worry about."

"What are they?" asked Mr. Big.

"Quite simply, that the organic material from the comet was the cause of the entire pandemic and the deaths of millions. It was one big calamitous event that will never occur again."

"People won't believe that," said another member. "The comet's arrival was well after the start of the pandemic."

"Was it? I don't recall it that way," the former gentleman said with a grin, "and I don't believe the Big Tech companies who censor the Internet or the big media companies will remember it that way either."

"I agree," said yet another member. "People in general are stupid—another thing we've succeeded at these past several decades. Destroying the education system and placing professors throughout the university system who only agree with our narrative have sealed their fate. Hell, most young people today don't even know who George Washington or Winston Churchill were!" He chuckled at his own musing.

"Perhaps you're right," said Mr. Big. "We do have the next program ready for rollout, and 2045 is only a few years away. Perhaps we should wait. Heck, we can also test our latest genetic alteration therapy that induces and exacerbates Alzheimer's. We're working on it at YAF as we speak. If it's successful, then, no one will remember anything anyway!"

Many attending virtually laughed heartily at the thought.

"Quite right!" exclaimed another. "Remember this, though, that 'They will own nothing and be happy!' I recall that phrase as if it were yesterday. They heard it then too but were too stupid to understand it or believe it."

"I don't think there is anything to worry about," another member said, agreeing. "We have too much money, too much power, too many people in our back pockets to be defeated. It can't happen. We have the howitzer; they have a fly swatter. Who's going win that fight?"

"What if there's another comet?" asked Mr. Big.

"Let it come. By then, we'll have that howitzer ready to fire right at it!"

The meeting continued, all discussing ways they could plan better for the next assault. In the end, they came to an agreement. There would be another attack—a final assault—and the timing of it would be sooner rather than later.

Mr. Big pounded the gavel. "This has been a productive meeting," he said, concluding the session. "I will discuss our plans with our Sponsor to get his approval. I hope he will agree. His powers are far greater than ours, after all."

*****

CH 77 – Voice from Beyond

Will tossed and turned, but he couldn't sleep. He had been so elated that Shannon loved him as much as he did her that he couldn't think of anything else. He had wanted to race home and announce it to his mother—as if he were already engaged to be married—but had controlled himself, waiting for the right time and place. *I think I'll wait until it's official and we're engaged*, thought Will.

"Will …"

It was a voice he knew and one that, at first, always sounded as though he were hearing it from the bottom of a swimming pool. He opened his eyes and glanced around the room. There was no one there, but he didn't expect to find anyone either. He kept his eyes open, waiting for the inevitable. But when nothing else happened within the next few minutes, he said aloud, "Gramma? Are you here?"

"Will!"

This time he was sure of the voice, but the sound was more muffled and distant.

"Hello?" he called out.

"W …"

"What is it? Who is it?" Will asked again.

"Will …"

This time the voice was clearer, but it was a different voice—not that of his Gramma.

"Who are you, and what do you want?" Will asked apprehensively.

The image that took shape was that of a man, but Will didn't recognize it and couldn't tell if it were young or old.

"I have an important message for you," said the apparition. "You once sought to open an ancient, stone trunk that you and your brother rescued from an old safe house that burned down. Do you remember?"

"Yeah, of course."

"But you weren't able to open it. Were you?"

"How did you know that?" asked Will.

At that moment, the image cleared, and the voice became more distinct. It was British.

"I'm Brandon Morris, the grandfather of your stepfather, Jack. I tried to open it for months in Moscow many years ago, and I finally discovered the answer. I will tell you how to open it, but it will take practice. You must be patient."

Although Will didn't know the man, he saw the resemblance of the ghostly figure to his mother's husband. "Okay, then what do I have to do?"

"I will help you, but you must be able to speak the words according to the symbols *exactly* as they were originally spoken. It is a lost language—not spoken to this day."

"Then how will I know how to speak them?"

"I will speak them to you now," said the spirit.

Almost immediately, the foreign, nearly incomprehensible, words began flowing.

Will grabbed his cell phone from his nightstand and flipped it to the recording app, so he could turn it on while the spirit was making the sounds. But shortly after, the spirit stopped.

"Tell me again," said Will. "I didn't catch the first part of that."

But the image of Brandon Morris vanished.

"*Crap!*" said Will, rewinding what he had recorded. He pressed Replay but what he heard started several seconds into the monolog.

"Crap, crap, crap!" Will said, tossing his phone on the bed in frustration. *Now what am I supposed to do?* he thought.

But his thoughts quickly turned to the stone trunk that he had buried somewhere in the landfill years earlier. It had been some time since he had thought about it, and he could only hope it was still there. *Why am I getting this message now?* he wondered. *What is inside that trunk that is so important?*

Will laughed. *Whatever it was would most likely be critical to saving the planet once again. He'd just escaped from being extinguished by a massive comet that was poised to destroy the world and mankind with it. What else could possibly happen?*

It would be something—of that, he was certain. And even after everything he'd been through, he could hardly wait.

*****

APPENDIX

Charles Marie de la Condamine (Jan. 28, 1701-Feb. 4, 1774) was a French mathematician, physicist, explorer, and geographer. La Condamine was sent to Ecuador in 1735 to measure the Earth at the equator. He also scientifically explored and mapped the Amazon region as he rafted to the mouth of that river. Earlier in his life, La Condamine took exploratory trips to Algiers, Alexandria, Palestine, Cyprus, and Constantinople.

At the time, there was a debate as to whether the Earth was wider around the equator or around the poles. The King of France and the French Royal Academy of Sciences sent two expeditions to determine the answer; one was sent to Lapland (this expedition included the Swedish physicist Anders Celsius) and another to Ecuador. La Condamine was in the Ecuadorian group, which included Louis Godin and the mathematician Pierre Bouguer.

The Ecuadorian expedition left France in May 1735 and landed in Colombia before traveling overland to Panama and then on to Ecuador. La Condamine hiked through the rainforests with Pedro Vincente Maldonado, a local governor and scientist-mathematician. They sailed up the Esmeraldas River and then climbed the Andes Mountains. Finally, they arrived in Quito, Ecuador, on June 4, 1736. By 1739, they finished their work, measuring the length of an arc of one degree at the equator, but they got word that the Lapland expedition had already finished their work and had proven that the Earth is flattened at the poles.

La Condamine remained in South America for four more years, doing scientific work and mapping some of the Andes and much of the Amazon River. He returned to Paris in 1745, 10 years after he had left France.

La Condamine's journal of his 10-year adventure, "Journal du Voyage fait par l'ordre du Roi á l'equateur," was published in 1751. La Condamine is also said to have thought of the idea of introducing vaccinations for smallpox in Europe since he had suffered from smallpox as a child (Edward Jenner later developed the actual vaccine).

*****

About the Author

Alex Ross Carol is a pen name used by the author. He lives with his family near Chicago and began writing for enjoyment at the age of fifty.

The author wrote *The Strange Books of Gramma Zulov* as a series with previous books including: *The Sibylline Books (Book 1), The Map of Ptah (Book 2), The Wheel of the Han (Book 3),* and *The Elixir of St. Germaine (Book 4).*

The next book, Book 5, is about a strange stone from Nepal.

There may be others that come later, but that depends on how much time the Fates allow. In any event, he hopes you enjoyed this book and will continue with others to come in the series.

*****